Spellbinding praise for THE LEGEND OF MENEKA

'Rao's writing is utterly compelling, and I believe she will continue to be a powerful figure in speculative fiction'
Hannah Kaner, No.1 *Sunday Times* bestselling author of *Godkiller*

'With sumptuous language and sultry, high-stakes romance, this is a glittering gem of a book'
Hannah Whitten, No.1 *Sunday Times* bestselling author of *The Foxglove King*

'A heartstopping, magical adventure as tantalising and complex as its eponymous heroine. Filled with electrifying twists, radiant passion, and seductive tension that will keep you at the edge of your seat, this book is bound to enchant'
Ehigbor Okosun, No.1 *Sunday Times* bestselling author of *Forged by Blood*

'Rao's writing is a feast for the senses, elegantly whisking you off to a dreamlike world where every corner glitters with magic, and the sensual and the sacred collide'
Thea Guanzon, *Sunday Times* bestselling author of *The Hurricane Wars*

'Ecstatically epic . . . Rao's prose hums with starlight. As befits a retelling of one of the most celebrated celestial nymphs in Hindu myth, this book is nothing short of resplendent'
Roshani Chokshi, No.1 *Sunday Times* bestselling author of *The Last Tale of the Flower Bride*

'*The Legend of Meneka* is a lustrously beautiful mythic romance, both empowering and seductive'
Tasha Suri, *Sunday Times* bestselling author of *The Isle in the Silver Sea*

'Effervescent, passionate, and romantic, *The Legend of Meneka* is a brightly burning flame of a tale set in a world gleaming with magic and helmed by a woman on a journey to self-discovery . . . Sure to set fire to the fantasy landscape'
Amélie Wen Zhao, No.1 *Sunday Times* bestselling author of *The Scorpion and the Night Blossom*

'Spellbinding . . . A sweeping romantic tale re-examining the role of the temptress'
R.R. Virdi, *USA Today* bestselling author of *The First Binding*

'Seductive and sensual, an utter delight, with the yearning turned up to eleven . . . This is a downright feast of a book, and its heat will linger on your tongue'
Andrea Stewart, *Sunday Times* bestselling author of *The Gods Below*

THE
RISE
OF THE
CELESTIALS

ALSO BY KRITIKA H. RAO

THE RAGES TRILOGY
The Surviving Sky
The Unrelenting Earth
The Enduring Universe

THE DIVINE DANCERS DUOLOGY
The Legend of Meneka

CHILDREN'S BOOKS
Shivi's Big Leap

THE RISE OF THE CELESTIALS

KRITIKA H. RAO

HARPER
Voyager

Harper*Voyager*
An imprint of HarperCollins*Publishers* Ltd
1 London Bridge Street
London SE1 9GF

www.harpercollins.co.uk

HarperCollins*Publishers*
Macken House,
39/40 Mayor Street Upper,
Dublin 1, D01 C9W8
Ireland

First published by HarperCollins*Publishers* Ltd 2026

1

Copyright © Kritika H. Rao 2026
Designed by Jennifer Chung
Map copyright © Virginia Allyn 2026
Interior illustrations copyright © Hoan Phan/IllustrationX 2026

Kritika H. Rao asserts the moral right to
be identified as the author of this work.

A catalogue record for this book is available from the British Library.

ISBN: 978-0-00-865051-3 (HB)
ISBN: 978-0-00-865052-0 (TPB)

This novel is entirely a work of fiction.
The names, characters and incidents portrayed in it are
the work of the author's imagination. Any resemblance to
actual persons, living or dead, events or localities is
entirely coincidental.

Printed and bound in the UK using 100% Renewable Electricity by CPI Group (UK) Ltd

All rights reserved. No part of this publication may be
reproduced, stored in a retrieval system, or transmitted,
in any form or by any means, electronic, mechanical,
photocopying, recording or otherwise, without the prior
written permission of the publishers.

Without limiting the exclusive rights of any author, contributor or the publisher of this publication, any unauthorized use of this publication to train generative artificial intelligence (AI) technologies is expressly prohibited. HarperCollins also exercise their rights under Article 4(3) of the Digital Single Market Directive 2019/790 and expressly reserve this publication from the text and data mining exception.

*For Mom and Dad,
who grew me up on stories*

NARAKA – THE HELLISH REALM

- BRIDGE OF FLOATING STONES
- SERPENT'S CAVE
- YAMA'S PALACE
- WARREN OF CATACOMBS
- THE HELL OF PINCERS
- TORTURE CHAMBERS
- HOUND STABLES
- DUNGEONS
- THE WARPED FOREST
- THE HELL OF CHIMERAS AND BEASTS
- TOWARD THE BLACK MIST
- DEN OF ILLUSIONS

PATALA - THE UNDERWORLD

CHAPTER 1

Loving him changed my life.
I expected heartbreak. I expected betrayal.
I never expected this.

KAUSHIKA'S FINGERS SKIM OVER MY ARM. "TELL ME, Meneka," he says quietly. "Are you content?"

His voice is casual, but I startle. We are both naked on the cot within our hut. A single golden flame burns on the floor in the corner, flickering and throwing shadows on the walls. The candle is down to a stub, and soon it will die out. The hut is cast in dimness, and we are only an hour away from dawn. In minutes, blue daylight will creep into the cottage, bringing with it the scent of fresh dew.

I do not look out the window in morning's anticipation. I keep my gaze on Kaushika. We have been resting in companionable silence, waking slowly and giving each other languorous smiles. He has said nothing beyond his morning murmurs, and I have been relaxed in his silence, but at his question my heart races in nervousness.

A month has passed since the battle in the skies. Last night I dreamed of Amaravati again, of its fragrant night gardens and its glorious, curved arches. In my dream, the city was resplendent, but something dark approached it, unbeknownst to its citizens. The darkness covered the city in seconds, even as devas and their devotees sang and danced in gaiety. Amaravati's magic burned away into nothingness, while I screamed and screamed from the mortal realm for the devas to stir.

I awoke from the nightmare covered in a cold sweat, babbling to Kaushika about the Vajrayudh, sick with longing for my city. He held me close, rocking me back to sleep. He did not question me then, but I remember the things I said to him in the terror of the night, the very same things I said at the end of the battle. *Amaravati still needs protection . . . The city is my home. I will do whatever I can to safeguard it, even if I must do so from you.* Surely his words now are a cautious start toward a conversation we should have had long ago. This is an invitation, and there is still so much unspoken between us.

I should answer him sincerely. His question is one I have been contemplating. Yet if I do, we will become strangers again, enemies condemned to be on opposite sides because of our differing loyalties. I am not ready to relinquish what I have here with him. Is he? I turn to him, searching his face.

He lies next to me, his long legs stretched out against mine, his one arm supporting his head as he looks down at me. His other hand continues to skim over the bare skin of my arm. Warmth shoots through me at the heat of his touch. I shiver under the watchfulness in his gaze, aware of our nudity, our closeness. His stiffness is hard against my thigh, and I nudge my leg forward, testing. He twitches in response.

Hunger replaces the question in his eyes. I bite my lip, suppressing a grin. Slowly, I brush my thumb over his lip. His eyes darken, and he almost opens his mouth to bite my finger but that would be too quick. He has more resistance than that.

He raises an eyebrow instead. "Not in a mood for conversation, then?" he asks dryly. "I've learned ways to make you talk, apsara."

Sure enough, his fingers hover up from my arm, dipping down to the swell of one of my breasts. I freeze, as Kaushika cups it gently, feeling its weight. His fingers wrap around my back, and his thumb poises itself just over my nipple. The heat of arousal floods me, with this simple action. It is all I can do not to arch my back and give in to his touch. I exhale softly, waiting, as his eyes gleam, reflecting the candlelight.

"Is this what you want from me?" he asks. "The payment you would seek before gifting me your words?"

"Payment?" I answer innocently, raising my brows. "I've asked for nothing. Perhaps I want to lie here a bit longer, enjoying the stolen moments before dawn. I don't seek to make you do anything you don't desire yourself."

I manage to shrug a bare shoulder. The movement rubs my nipple against his poised thumb, and his eyes glint. The muscles in his arms ripple in the candlelight, as if embers are alight within him, but still he does not brush the bud. He watches me, amused. We both know what we're doing. I have set the pieces of our game in motion. Despite his questions, he has indicated he is willing to play. Both of us are in silent agreement. We will forget the nightmares of the dark. We will steer ourselves into playful matters. We will allow ourselves to be distracted. The anticipation makes me squirm.

"My desire?" he drawls. "I thought we were talking about your contentedness, but if you want to address *my* desire . . ."

His words trail off. I lick my bottom lip, dampening it. Kaushika tracks the movement, and his gaze turns molten. A sweet ache is starting to rush through me, growing fast into a torrent. He grins, and his fingers tap against my back, raising goose pimples on my flesh. His thumb begins to make lazy circles across my nipple. The bud stiffens in an instant, and he looks at it contemplatively while my breath quickens.

He dips his head to my breast. I am already damp from need, the slickness slippery and sliding down my thighs. A sound escapes me, urging him wordlessly to continue, to take my nipple in his mouth, tease it with his tongue, graze it between his teeth, bring me to the edge of climax—but at the last instant, Kaushika looks up, suppressed mirth in his gaze.

"My desire is to know," he says, the laughter in his eyes merged with the heat of need. "*Is* it enough? To lie here, enjoying the moments before dawn together?"

I blink. I have lost track of the conversation, and it is a point in his favor, to be so utterly in control while I writhe under him. I thought I had distracted him, but Kaushika has never been an easy quarry, to be so easily seduced away from what he wants merely because of our positions. He is too intent, yet

I—I am already losing this contest of seduction, even though I was the one to invite him to it.

I utter a growl of frustration that he should turn the tables on me this easily. Kaushika laughs and sits up, pulling my arms over my head. He angles his body over mine, looming over me. His nails flutter from my breasts, his touch tracing the delicate skin on my wrists, before his fingers interlock with mine.

His weight settles on top of me, and he twitches over my hips again, positioned exactly where I need him. Kaushika moves his hips slowly, watching me, meeting my gaze, then dips his mouth to my neck, sucking softly, laving a path along my throat. The scent and feel of him unleashes a wild fire in me. I arch my body, seeking more, trying to free my legs to wrap them around his waist, but he holds me down with his body, his movement excruciatingly slow, torturing me.

I twist under him again, but he shakes his head, uttering a *tsk*ing sound. "Come now," he murmurs, chastising. "Why the haste? You said you wanted to enjoy such stolen moments. Am I not being obedient?"

A slow pressure builds inside me. My core grows tight, and my breathing strained. Hot spirals of need coil within my stomach, leaping from one glorious sensation into another. Pleasure is turning into rapture, and there is an exquisite ache in this waiting, but lust rises heavy in me, making my body sweat.

He is turning me inside out, his questions and his actions like shifting currents of the sea, one moment making me doubt one thing, the next moment easing me. I know enough to understand the rules. If I beg him for release, I will have to answer his questions in return. Payment, he called it, and perhaps that is true. It will be one filled with gratitude and satisfaction, but he will have won. Kaushika is more practiced at seduction than I have given him credit for.

"Malicious," I whisper. "You are obedient but malicious."

I begin to roll my hips, tempting him, showing him how our act of pleasure together would make us even, without any need for explanations. His eyes widen in surprise, and a sharp gasp falls from his mouth. A sizzle cracks the air. Magic sparks from us, and flames ignite his fingertips even as dewdrops form on my body like the tiniest jewels.

Warm steam rises where his bare skin touches mine. It does not hurt, but there is an implicit danger in the melding of our powers. We breathe in an ocean of push and pull, our desires swelling, our fears receding, and teetering danger ready to swallow us whole.

"Never malicious," he whispers. "But I like to hear you speak your mind. Clarity is a gift we can give to each other, is it not?"

He dips his head down again, licking at my collarbones. A sharp tingle rushes through me, radiating from where his tongue touched. I swallow a gasp, and the sound is smothered by his own rush of exhalation.

Yearning shoots through my body, and my thighs tremble, so wet that I can hear it in our movements. If I wasn't already on the cot, I don't know if I'd be able to hold myself up. If I weren't a creature of lust, I would be shocked to be aroused so quickly.

Kaushika's head lifts. His eyes are full of promise. "Is this what you want?"

My breath is coming out too fast to pay attention to his words. A carnal need is taking me over, and the steam and heat of the room are heady, making my mind swim in delicious intoxication. Kaushika grins, and bends to lick the dewdrops off my skin. I shudder as his hair grazes my cheek.

"Just say the words," he says, his mouth over my ear. His breath is warm, sending tingles down my spine. "And I will give you the pleasure you seek."

Yes, this is enough, I think. *No, it is not*, I add on the heels of it. Kaushika is torturing my mind, seeking clarity when we are submerged in the haze of our desire. His questions will unravel the moment. I cannot have him triumph.

I free one of my hands from his grasp and reach between my legs, slipping my fingers between our bodies. Kaushika quirks an eyebrow, but he knows what this means.

The very fact that I am resorting to this, instead of simply answering him, tells the both of us how much I want him. Will he take me now, submitting to my need? Or will he make me submit to him and force me to speak? I smile a slow smile, letting him see that I am no easy prey.

I dance my fingers against my entrance. Pleasure shoots through me, and it is magnified by the heat in his eyes as he watches me. Kaushika shakes his head ruefully.

"You should not do this when I am here to serve you," he says in gentle reproach.

"What makes you think I need you to give me my pleasure?"

I ask. This time, I am the one who teases him, even as I tease myself. My actions are a challenge. *Take me or watch me*, I tell him silently. *One move will satisfy you, and the other will vex you.* I insert one finger inside myself, then another. The relief is instant, and my body bucks as I ride my own hand, the wet sounds shocking and succulent. I am panting, my eyes hooded, and I find the nub of pleasure within me, stroking and flicking, pressing to the point just shy of pain.

Desire blazes in his eyes. "Oh, I know you can take care of yourself. But isn't it better this way?"

He pulls my hand back, and his own thumb begins to circle my entrance. Kaushika places his stiffness against me, the tip of him touching me, mocking me. The friction is too much, and my body reacts involuntarily, pressing into him. I take him in my hand, stroking him root to tip, feeling the sheer hardness of him.

Kaushika growls in appreciation, and it is the first sound of pleasure he has made. The need in his voice almost makes me weep. No matter how much he tortures me, I know he is moments from giving in too. The realization is exhilarating, consuming my mind, that I have driven him to this. It is my power and body and beauty that have brought him here.

My fingers tighten in his hair. My body cannot stop bucking, asking for him, the relief I need. His tongue traces a path from my mouth down to my collarbones and over my breasts. I utter a frustrated sound, remembering his agonizing teasing, but the sound turns into a gasp as Kaushika takes one nipple in his mouth, grazing it lightly between his teeth. My body jerks, a near sob falling from my lips. A soft laugh escapes him—he moves slightly. A thick finger probes inside me, *curling*. Magic sizzles in me, but my legs tighten around his hand. I move faster, eyes closed. His finger circles my swollen bud, and my hips rise off the bed, one leg wrapping around him.

"Kaushika," I breathe, rocking my hips.

I can hear the smile in his voice. "Isn't this better?" he asks again, and his mouth hovers over mine.

He hardly needs an answer. It is clear that I crave not my own touch but his. We are suspended in this moment, both of us waiting for the other to acquiesce to each other and ourselves.

I cannot hold back anymore. "Yes," I gasp. "Yes, this is better. It is always better with you."

Satisfaction flares in Kaushika's eyes. He takes my mouth in his, and I ravage it, opening my lips for the sweet taste of him. The kiss is reckless on my part, careful on his, but behind his watchfulness, his desire rears its head—and in an instant, Kaushika switches, pressing me down hard, flicking his tongue into my mouth, biting my lips softly, drinking me until I cannot breathe.

He pulls his mouth away from mine, and before I have a chance to protest, he dips his head and sucks deeply off my breast, his tongue flashing and teasing, before he turns his attention to the other one. I twist, in ecstasy and agony, wishing to savor this sensation but needing more. I want all of him. I want his hands and his tongue and his teeth and his fingers, and I want him *now*.

Faster, I think again, chasing his kisses with mine, nipping him when he raises his head.

Kaushika senses my impatience and positions himself over me. His hands grip my hips tightly. He hesitates just a second, perhaps to prepare himself or to prepare me. I clutch his shoulders, arching, and with a groan that tells me, sage or not, he is well past his control, Kaushika thrusts into me hard.

A cry escapes me. The suddenness of it is almost shocking, almost painful, with how he fills me, but it is a pain I yearned for. A loneliness I wasn't aware of melts as he takes me, as he completes me. The last terror of the night withers away, as magic flares around us, steam rising with the fire of his body and the liquid of mine. We are ensconced in soft vapor, his leg moving against mine, his hand pushing my hips down. I close my eyes, feeling the spaces of emptiness within me fill with his power. All I feel is him, him, *him*. The sensation inside me after being teased is too much. I almost break, my rapture ascending over me. He fills every inch of me, and the pleasure is so exquisite, my vision blanks behind my closed lids.

A tide rushes over me, deafening, and my back arcs. I take Kaushika's mouth with mine, and our tongues crash into each other with a force, licking and soothing. He smells of rosewood and morning, and his body is slick with sweat against mine. Desire pools in my belly, and he thrusts inside me hard and fast, bruising my lips with his own, his fingers playing with my nipples, then stroking my bud down there, driving me insensate with the assault. His breathing is harsh, his teeth graze my lips, biting, nipping, and his body is trembling. Suddenly I do not know which one of us has won this game. And isn't that the point of it?

Our lives are a learning of each other, an unlearning of ourselves. His soul is a mirror to mine, our intimacy so linked that it surpasses anything I can explain. It is not merely our lust that threads through this lovemaking. It is the summer days of looking into each other free from the demands that enslave us. It is peace unencumbered by the hold of our identities. We know we have secrets between us, but neither of us keeps them to deceive the other. We keep them because we treasure what we have, before the world attempts to change our hearts. I have made love to several others in my life, but with him, it is merely about our love, with no other agenda attached to it.

I laugh, a rich sound, and Kaushika smiles against my lips.

My hips buck, and he thrusts into me over and over again, fast, sharp bursts. The pressure builds into the power of a volcano, and I am liquid, sliding against him. My thighs shiver uncontrollably—and then, ecstasy erupts through me, bliss soaking me.

We come together, both of us riding the cascading waves of pleasure, while Kaushika's mouth utters praises of my beauty and strength that I am too pleased to decipher. I clutch him hard, and I taste the half shock, half joy of his abandon. Kaushika cries out, slumping against me as he finally releases himself.

My pleasure shoots through me, oblivion behind my ears and eyes, in the rhythms of a familiar song. My whole body relaxes violently, the spaces of darkness pouring out of me in blurred astonishment.

For a long minute, neither of us move. I close my eyes and

breathe him in. The scent of camphor swirls within me, coiling around my heart. Kaushika's weight over my body is as recognizable as my most precious jewelry, pieces that I discarded to be with him in such a way. He shifts a little, his arm draped on my breasts like a heavy necklace. I take comfort from him, focusing on the sensation of his skin on mine, Kaushika pulls me closer and nudges my temple with his nose. A sigh of satisfaction escapes him, making strands of my hair flutter.

I steal a sideways glance to see his eyes are closed. His lips are curled in the softest smile. My heartbeat quickens to find him so vulnerable, so relaxed. I want to excite him again, to repeat what we have just done, and do it in another way, over and over again, until we are both senseless. I want to play this game again, a variant of it, this time making *him* admit that the pleasure he gets from me is a hundredfold what he can give himself. Idly, I conjure up images of all the ways we have yet to discover each other's body. There is so much yet to teach him. So many toys to use. So many ways to *shock* him. I draw lazy circles on his arm with my finger, tracing out a pattern of dance, and look outside the window to the breaking dawn.

Streaks of pink paint the horizon, chasing the last stars away. Warmth washes over my naked body as more light floods across the sky, creating a corona around gray clouds. A slight mist lingers in the air, and I can taste it like the freshest nectar. The blessed hour before Surya fully awakens the world rouses my senses, and though I am not ready for the bliss of this moment to end, the rising dawn tells me holding time is impossible.

Without my permission, the golden tether connecting me to

the City of Immortals tightens behind my navel. I have been away for too long from Amaravati. This time I have delayed in the mortal world of my own volition instead of a mission I've been commanded to accomplish. Homesickness curls through me with suddenness. Can I even return home?

My parting words to Lord Indra after the battle were a promise of my arrival, and I recall Indra's curt nod to me. Still, I am unsure if his nod meant permission. I have not succeeded in eliminating Kaushika's threat to the lord yet. For all I know, if I attempted to return, the lord would simply exile me—far from Kaushika, and away from the city too. It is why I have not called Amaravati's wind, but that the lord has not summoned me either tells me that he is biding his time too.

And what of Shachi, who came to me in the dead of night only two weeks ago? The queen has commanded me to turn Kaushika's favor toward her in order for her to take the throne from Indra. Shachi could just as easily visit me again, this time demanding answers. What will I tell her? I am caught between the lord and the queen, unable to know whom I must please.

Kaushika would have clarity from me, but I have remained silent on our circumstances, *hoping* to gain such clarity. Living here with him in stillness has been a quiet rebellion, a slow warfare, radical in its self-preservation, sacred in its gentleness, deliberate in its nourishment. The hut Kaushika and I live in shines with the domestic bliss we have been enjoying since we made up with each other. I know I have not been wrong in embracing this peace. I clutch him, trying to relax and return to the satisfaction of our lovemaking. I turn away from the dawn, hoping to silence the rising nervousness within me. *This is enough*, I tell myself. *For now, this is enough.*

But try as I might to stop it, the anxiety that had startled me with Kaushika's initial question returns. The pleasure from our lovemaking subsides. The dancing motes of sunshine filtering into the hut and the glow of magic I feel inside cage me. An ache takes over my chest, making it hard to breathe, as the darkness of my dream returns, the City of Immortals melting and decaying due to the Vajrayudh.

Kaushika stirs, reading the change in my mood. He arches a brow in a silent question, but I shake my head, offering him a smile. He does not push me to speak. Instead, he lifts his head up from the pillow, and glances beyond me to the window. Then he sighs, knowing that dawn means duties. His eyes linger over my body in appreciation and reverence and the slightest bit of frustration.

"Every morning you make it harder to leave you, apsara," he says.

"Do not blame me for your choices, sage," I tease back.

He laughs at that and stretches, dislodging us both from our comfortable positions. Kaushika stands up. I ought to be used to it, with every night of intimacy with this man, yet I cannot help but marvel at the sheer poetry of his body.

His skin is a rich brown, and underneath it the glow of tapasvin magic radiates like a river of fire. Muscles cord his arms and legs in the remembered heritage of his kshatriya upbringing. Kaushika collects his shoulder-length hair into a deft topknot, then gathers a fresh pair of linen pajamas from the shelf next to the bed. He pulls an accompanying kurta over his chest, and the light from his chakras dims slightly, the sapphire blue of the throat softening, the emerald green over his heart shading.

I rise as well, not bothering to dress. Instead, I glide over to him, emphasizing my curves with my movements. He looks every bit a rishi now, with his hair tied up and the unassuming attire hiding his strength, but nothing can obscure the aura of magic around him, which shines as though he is a deva. Still his eyes flare as I stand opposite him. Perhaps he is thinking the same thing I am. How much we appear like the people we are. Ever the apsara. Ever the sage.

Yet I have never been one thing and one thing alone.

I have come through pain and fire to learn who I am over the last many months. I have learned what I am capable of.

Raw tapasvin power rushes through me, mingling with my own celestial magic. Heat enters my throat, and I concentrate, humming a chant. A braiding of luminosity flickers in the air in front of us. Mist forms in the shape of a portal. It is not much, but I hold on to it, willing it to strengthen.

"You amaze me," Kaushika murmurs. "The kind of power you can wield . . . I have never encountered it before."

My lips curve in a smile. His praise warms me, but I am frustrated, too, at my failure. He has been teaching me mortal magic for the last two weeks. I have already learned more runes than I did at the hermitage, along with mantras that even the devas of swarga would envy. This spell, though, I am unable to master. Kaushika has demonstrated many times how to open and close a portal to travel—an enchantment I have only managed once before, when I released Nanda from her curse. Even though I mimic my method from then, using the magic of raw prana woven with the familiar one of Amaravati, the spell takes too much out of me. I grow short of breath. Kaushika steadies me as I sway, but my body cannot contain this much raw force. The tether of Amaravati feeds me celestial power, but I have never been the strongest in capturing wild prana through tapasya. I tremble and let the magic collapse. Mortal and celestial power swirl in me, subsiding slowly.

Kaushika's fingers curl around my arm, pulling me to him. He reaches his other hand to smooth the wrinkle at my brow. "Do not be disappointed," he whispers into my hair. "This spell is one of the most difficult ones I have created. No one from the hermitage is capable of it. That you can conjure even this much is incredible. Slow is not failure—it is caution."

I nod. If I learned how to open a portal at whim, I would not need Indra's permission to return to Amaravati. I could live my life with Kaushika and replenish my magic at Amaravati without the deva king to stop me. I have not confided my reasons to Kaushika; it is one step away from a discussion of our loyalties I still feel too raw to have, but I know I can't delay any longer. During our lovemaking, I skirted his questions, not wishing to break the moment of peace, but now that we are ready to face the day, my silence will become tantamount to deception, no matter what I fear. I brace myself.

"You asked me a question before," I begin. Kaushika brushes my hair, tangling his fingers in it. He cocks his head, studying me, and I am encouraged by his open curiosity. "You asked me if I was content. Before I make up my mind, I must know. Are *you* content? Do you have what you want?"

Kaushika's mouth twitches. He strokes my cheek. "You have looked into my lust with your celestial magic, Meneka. You know what I want. We play this game together, do we not? I am not always the victor. You are not always the vanquished. Or have you forgotten what you made me admit only yesterday?"

The memory rises within me, Kaushika sprawled on the cot last afternoon, his arms tied with bands of my magic, his eyes gleaming while I straddled him. I made him spill truths to me then, of his fantasies, of his desires. Of every hidden lust, while I tracked a slow path from his waist down to his legs, taking him in my mouth, but stopping each time he paused speaking. He grins at me now, and I cannot help but flush.

I shake my head, not wanting to be distracted again, even though the temptation is acute.

"That's not what I mean," I say. "Our lives here are an extension of our own hearts, in understanding we are better together, that we are powerful and complete in our union. But . . ."

I trail off, unsure of how to frame my question.

In bringing this matter up I will be breaching an unsaid line between us. Kaushika and I have deliberately not spoken about the war between him and Indra. I have not asked him about his whereabouts when he leaves the hut, and he has not asked me about mine.

We have been cautious, speaking of academic, philosophical matters instead of anything substantial. I have told him of Indra and Amaravati, but it has been in the form of childhood stories, my grudging reverence for the lord clear. He has listened silently and thoughtfully, making no pronouncements of his own ire with the lord.

In our own way we have tried to build a bridge between our differences, hoping to learn of each other while we live together. Perhaps, like me, he fears a misunderstanding born of haste. Perhaps, like me, he does not wish to lie. But he still broached it this morning. Kaushika has shown me he is ready. I cannot be a coward.

I inhale, trying to find the right words. "I know you leave to perform your tapasya every morning. But it is not simply to restore your magic, is it?"

"It is not," Kaushika answers slowly. "I am unmaking the meadow too."

My eyes widen at that, and I can't help but smile. Kaushika created his meadow to threaten Amaravati. If he is destroying it, it is a step in the right direction for him to keep his promise to me. That he will not harm my city or my kin. That he will not harm my sisters. Could it be that I have convinced him to forgo battle with Indra, with my stories and reverence for the lord? I have been delaying this conversation for nothing.

I close the distance between us, energized. "Then your vow to find salvation for King Satyavrat's soul," I say. "Have you given that up?"

Kaushika's gaze grows wary, but he touches my cheek. "You know I cannot give that up, Meneka. I am simply looking for a different way to fulfill it. I think I might have found it."

I want to ask him what that way is, but already we have spoken about this more than we have so far. His eyes drift to the lightning-bolt blade that I threatened him with not two weeks ago. It is encased in cloth now, sitting upon one of the shelves, but nothing can mask its glow. Kaushika did not ask me where I got it, no doubt thinking it a spoil of war, but his vow to save the king's soul and have it enter swarga despite Lord Indra's refusal led to our first alienation. It led to the creation of an alternate heaven, one that was deemed an abomination even by other sages. It caused a catastrophic battle in the same forest where we reside now. His vow was the reason I threatened him with the blade, extracting a vow of my own, that he would not hurt my kin anymore.

I see the hesitation on Kaushika's face, the resignation, as though he is steeling himself for an argument and then an inevitable final goodbye. Whatever prompted his earlier question, it is clear he is as nervous about breaking our peace as I am. It scares me, despite the progress we have already made by speaking. I do not wish to rush into this indelicately, so I back off. I navigate us to safer waters.

"Once you have achieved this vow," I ask, "what then?"

He looks taken aback. Then his face relaxes.

"After I achieve it, I will seek enlightenment like those of my kind. I will continue being a rishi."

"But what kind of a rishi?" I insist. It is a fine distinction, but I attended the Mahasabha with him. I saw the different cadres of sages, those who chose to live an ascetic life and those who participated in the world to benefit their own agendas. I expect

Kaushika to give me another nonchalant answer—but instead his mouth grows serious and he steps back from me.

He gazes outside the window, but I can tell he is really staring into himself. Sunlight gleams into the cottage, and the first flush of sweltering heat sweeps in, making me sweat.

When Kaushika finally speaks, his voice is slow. "I have contemplated this question a long time. I thought I knew the answer in all those years of arduous meditation. It is why I sought the path I did. Why I built my hermitage around the principles of Shiva. But then . . ." He looks toward me, and in his eyes, I see humility and a buried surprise. "Then," Kaushika says, "I met you."

A fluttering takes over my chest. "What do you mean?"

He pulls me closer, his thumbs whispering over my bare shoulders. "Rishis are meant to acquire the knowledge of the cosmos. That is what I intended to find—and still do through my enlightenment. But I used to be guided by power. Now I want to be guided by love. By knowing what is *just*. I'm not sure how to do it, and if my actions now will help with this. But all I can do is try. That is what I attempt with my tapasya now, seeking to understand more, even as I feel the pull of my karmic vow to Satyavrat."

These last phrases invite more questions. I know I should inquire about them. Yet there will be time enough later. It is a victory that we have begun to speak of it; there is no need to dive headlong into a rift like we did once already.

I fold myself within his embrace, then rise on my tiptoes to brush my lips against his. Kaushika whispers to me that he will be back as soon as he can. I follow him to the threshold and watch him go, soaked in sunshine.

Only when he is out of sight do I turn around.

The hut is a few spans wide, with the cot Kaushika and I share and a few shelves lining the wall adjacent to the window. Pots, pans, and instruments of everyday use sit alongside several neat pairs of clothing. Nearly all of them are from the hermitage or from Kaushika's own stores, and all are simple and unpretentious as befits a yogi, but I approach the package tucked among my clothes that contains apsara raiment.

I bring the slim package to the cot, opening it for the first time in days. The smoothest silk whispers between my fingers, its texture like running water. The sari is gossamer thin and made of dreams, its color iridescent, one moment a startling green, another a fiery gold. Jewels accompany the sari, drenched in Amaravati's magic. My tether flares inside me, responding to the power. The garments and jewels are so beautiful, they shine in the cottage in their own light, making everything around them look dim.

Almost guiltily, I inhale the perfume they exude. Flowers and incense, lightning and kumkum. These are presents from home, a gift—no, an *instruction*—from Queen Shachi. I have not dared to let Kaushika know of them. So far, these have been hidden among my things, covered by illusion, yet with the nightmare still echoing in my mind, I long to feel their familiarity. Bands of longing and homesickness wrap around my chest as I let the jewels trickle through my fingers.

Admiring these ornaments feels like a betrayal of everything

Kaushika and I have built here. I am not the same apsara who knelt before Lord Indra, begging to live in Amaravati, and choosing to go on a final mission to seduce a sage out of desperation. I fought to be here, to live in peace, to choose my love. I danced in front of the gods and stopped a battle between the mortal and immortal realms. I was blessed by Shiva, the Destroyer. I found completion.

Why do I fear telling Kaushika the truth then? It is true that he has proven himself reckless and dangerous in the past; it is a reason why I am approaching this carefully. Yet is that not a disservice to how far we have come? If I am not the same woman who set out on a mission to seduce a sage, then Kaushika is not the same man, intent on destroying heaven. His unmaking of the meadow is sign enough; it is one I have unconsciously been waiting for. I tuck the jewels back, resolving to speak openly with Kaushika when he returns. I will tell him about Shachi, and how she sent halahala to his hermitage. I will tell him about Indra hoarding celestial magic, and how I took back Amaravati's power even after he cut me away from them. These are secrets I have not dared utter to anyone, but with Kaushika I must make an exception.

"It is better with him," I whisper, the same words I admitted during our lovemaking. "It is always better with him."

I spin the illusion back. After all this care so far, it would not do to have Kaushika stumble on it without my explanation. I am just putting the finishing touches on the illusion when a vision sparks through me. A familiar clifftop beckons, the vision lasting only for an instant, but my breath hitches in fear. It is a summons. One I have been expecting. One I have been dreading.

Only another celestial would call me this way; only someone wishing for a report. I come to myself, staring around the hut. My hand drifts to the heavenly clothes I have just hidden, but I retract it. If I am being called for a meeting, then there will be an expectation to dress in a particular way, but I cannot let any agent think that I am dissatisfied with my life here. I have a rare and precious thing with Kaushika, not merely the peace we share, but an ability to be free for a time from future missions, from Indra's retribution and Shachi's machinations. I cannot let any celestial forget what I have gained.

I hurry to dress, but eschew the clothing that would brand me Shachi's plaything. I reach for the simplest pajamas and kurta, akin to a yogi.

I only make one concession to my attire. Unlike Kaushika, I do not tie my hair into a topknot. Instead, I let my raven locks run free, stopping only to tuck the crescent wooden comb in my hair, a gift from Kaushika that once belonged to him.

The instant I wear it, prana courses through me like a fresh breeze.

The comb is no ordinary ornament. It is an amulet Kaushika himself made that is as powerful as any jewel from swarga. Once I thought the comb contained mortal magic, but I have learned since then that the comb is an amplifier, just like the jewels from Amaravati that allow an apsara to pull more magic from heaven.

The amulet takes one's own wild prana and helps to guide it. The use and direction of it depends on the practitioner.

I think back to the times the amulet responded to me—when I first made a true rune, and when I lit a lake up on that fateful night I meant to seduce Kaushika. Each of those times, my magic bloomed because of my love for him. I wear the comb now, warm and secure in knowing that he has given me a part of himself to keep forever.

Fully dressed, I finally leave the cottage to make my way toward the same clifftop where I once made my reports to Rambha. The day is clear, Surya spreading his warmth across the mortal realm, reminding me that he sees it all and—if he wishes to—could inform Indra of my actions. I spin a ward around myself, uttering a chant from the hermitage, so I cannot be spied upon. I trek through the woods, climbing up the small hill, wending my way along a path that is familiar.

I expect to see an agent waiting, but I am the first to arrive. I settle down on a rock, staring at the glistening river flowing underneath. Memory washes over me of all that has occurred at this very clifftop, within these woods. My encounter with Shiva, the battle that decided Kaushika's fate and Indra's direction, even the clarity of Rambha. This place has witnessed too much.

How different my life has become in such a short time. I have come to a deep understanding of my own power, but there is still so much to learn about the magic I wield. No immortal has done tapasvin magic before, just as no mortal can do celestial magic. I alone am capable of combining the two into a braiding of unified power, and though Kaushika has tried to help me understand it, he has simply explained it as power being power. He is amazed by my ability, but he does not question it, merely acknowledges it as my due.

I shake my head, vexed with his adoration of me, yet charmed by it. Kaushika accepts me as I am, but this combined power I use separates me not just from my kin, but from him too. I must know—how is it that I can do such a magic? Is this why I was able to snatch back Amaravati's power despite Indra cutting me from it? Will the agent from Indra come now, demanding to know about this ability? Or will the agent be Shachi's? Indra is a known threat, but Shachi lurks in the shadows, dangerous beyond reckoning. I have disobeyed them both by living my life in peace in the last few weeks.

My fingers worry the hem of my kurta, and noticing the movement, I still myself.

I have agonized over Shachi's instruction. The queen commanded me to turn Kaushika toward war with Indra again. To seduce him so he would join her in overthrowing the lord from his heaven, so she may sit on the throne. She is the most powerful devi there is, and though her instructions worried me, I feel compelled by her too. I recall growing up in her gardens, tugging on her sari for the sweetmeats she'd bring apsara girls. Shachi is the only mother I have ever known, a part of my own divinity. She has told me of her anger toward Indra, and it is an anger I share. She protected Sundari and Magadhi, two other apsaras that were sent to seduce Kaushika. If not for her, they would have suffered Nanda's fate, cursed to be frozen as rock for a thousand years. Indra forsook the apsaras, but Shachi sheltered them. Why do I feel so conflicted between her and Indra, then? Does she not deserve my loyalty? The choice between them should be so easy.

Still, I cannot forget the method of her warfare. Halahala that nearly killed Kaushika, me, and so many other mortals. The underlying threat that I would suffer if I failed her. Her words reducing me to *her* weapon.

I drum my fingers on my knee. Kaushika searches for a way to fulfill his vow without needing war. He told me he wanted to be guided by love. What do *I* want?

Magic awakens in me, and a familiar breeze prickles my skin. I stand up and straighten my shoulders, trying to banish my doubts. I smooth my face, wishing not to give anything away. Yet I find my doubts melting when I see who it is. A smile breaks through me. She is here, my sister and friend, arrived from heaven.

CHAPTER 2

Nanda looks glorious.

Her sari is a luminous yellow, reflecting the dawn. Her blouse is an amber shield, with patterns of roaring animals that seem to leap from her chest like powerful illusions. Jewels cover her from head to toe. The sparkling maang-tikka trailing down her forehead. The long jhumkas dangling from her ears. Pearl necklaces, and chiming bangles, and gleaming anklets that blink in the sunshine. Even her makeup is jewel-encrusted. Her large eyes are limned with gold, and her lips are coated with a dusting of crushed diamonds. She has always been lovely, wielding her beauty craftily; it is what made her one of swarga's elite apsaras. Now she looks like she is on a mission.

She envelops me in her arms, her hug tight enough to make me gasp. Magic swirls from her jewels, and envy startles me. Each of her adornments can channel swarga's power. The jewels are so potent, I could use Amaravati's magic from them myself if I tried. How much would I be able to do if *I* were the one wearing them? I try to dismiss the uncharitable thought. Relinquishing my jewels in the mortal realm was my own choice. Nanda's last foray here caused her great pain, and I know she is dressed this way as a defense against any unseen threat. I squeeze her tight, letting relief flood me that it is Nanda who is here, and not someone else. We are united by our experiences—both of us sent to seduce Kaushika, both of us once forsaken by Indra, both of us on the wrong side of heaven's war. With her, I can be myself.

She draws back and pinches my cheek. "Such simplicity you've embraced in the mortal realm, sister," she teases, her eyes twinkling as she studies my attire. "Don't tell me that your love has turned you this modest? Though I expect an ascetic sage would be too much of a prude for anything else . . ."

Nanda does not speak only of my clothes. She has guessed at the sexual pleasures Kaushika and I give each other. For someone like Nanda, the game Kaushika and I play is likely too simple. I blush, but I meet her gaze. I cannot let her—or anyone else—define my intimacy with Kaushika. The two of us will come to discovering each other on our own terms. So what if we're starting slow? I know Nanda does not mean to criticize, but still I feel the pinch. I no longer rely simply on celestial power, and that has made me an aberration as much as my role in the war has. I am a deviant apsara. A rebel apsara. I am different from my sisters in so many ways. Her words only heighten my sense of loneliness.

"Maybe *he* is not the prude," I say lightly, shrugging one shoulder. "Maybe it is me, this time."

Nanda laughs at that, the sound raucous. "Oh dear," she says. "If the mortal realm has changed you this much, then it might be time to return. You can't tell me you don't miss it, Meneka!

Surely life with one man forever, no matter how powerful, cannot be enough for an apsara's desires!"

A huff of laughter escapes me this time, though her words cast a shadow in my heart. Domestic bliss notwithstanding, for the last two weeks, a restlessness has lived within me. I have longed for the familiarity of home again, for *Indra's* heaven. I have felt guilty that I should want it after everything that has happened. Perhaps that is another reason why I haven't allowed myself to speak with Kaushika about everything we must confront, attempting to balance my desire to stay with him with my desire to return home. I have not wanted to appear dissatisfied with what we have. After all, he has been making sacrifices for me. He has not yet returned to the hermitage.

Nanda watches me closely, and I smile again, this time with more sincerity. I remind myself that I should not take offense at her words. This is Nanda through and through, irreverent and rowdy and titillating all at once. There is a reason *she* was sent to seduce Kaushika in the first instance, with her easy smiles and her enviable ability to be instantly likable.

Yet I see the way her fingers move ceaselessly, ready to unleash illusions. I see her restless actions, the constant swinging of her braided hair, the tapping of her feet, the way she nervously arranges and rearranges the pallu of her sari. Where once she taught me the importance of stillness for a dancer, to have control over our limbs, it is as though she suddenly needs to remind herself that she can move.

A quiet sadness wrenches through me to see the horror

lurking under her callous salacity. Only a few months ago, Nanda was cursed by Kaushika to become an inanimate object for a thousand years. It was my magic that released her from such a terrible fate, allowing her to return to heaven. We had once been student and teacher, but after everything we endured together, I feel much closer, sisters in every meaning of the word. I understand the distress she tries to hide.

I pull her down next to me. "Are you well?" I ask carefully.

Nanda simply tilts her head. "Well enough," she says. "I should ask you the same. Your life here . . . Are you content?"

I am amazed to hear her ask the same question Kaushika did. Then I understand it for the gentle rebuff it is.

Nanda cares about me, but she does not wish to speak to me about her healing from Kaushika's curse. She knows I love him. She knows I have chosen him. It is *her* love for me that stays her tongue, resorting only to these innuendos and hints, and I am grateful for it. I don't wish to hear open recriminations regarding my lover—not when our love is so young. She is telling me with her questions that her pain is hers alone, locked underneath the memory of the curse.

I sigh inwardly.

"Well enough," I say echoing her, but then my brows crinkle in worry. "Tell me the city is safe, Nanda. I dreamed of Amaravati decaying, and I know it is because of the Vajrayudh." The celestial event that occurs every thousand years is nearly at swarga's doorstep, merely three months away. When it falls, all beings of heaven will grow weaker. "Tell me that the city is preparing for it," I urge. "Tell me my dreams are merely dreams."

"Would that I could," Nanda replies, a frown marring her face. "Amaravati is more fragile than ever. Mortals do not pray to Indra like they once did, and there have been asura incursions in the city of late too, though none near the palace, thank the lord."

I bite my lip in unease. That mortals feel ill will toward Indra is not surprising; Indra has done little in recent times to earn their love. But asura incursions . . . Asuras are demons of the hellish realm, natural enemies of the celestials. Perhaps it should not be surprising that they sensed weakness in the city and are striking now, but Indra should still be able to protect the realm. He is the father of heaven. How weak has he become since I last saw him?

"Is that why you're here now. Did Indra ask you to meet me?" I study her clothes more intently and frown. "He did not send you for another mission this soon, did he?"

Nanda shakes her head, and I exhale, relieved. "The lord ignores me," she says, bitterness twisting her mouth. "I dance in his court, I perform the most pious prayers, I visit his temples within Amaravati regularly. But he does not care. It is as if *I* was in the mortal realm, living with his enemy."

After the battle, Lord Indra and I parted in near hostility, though I protected him with my actions as much as I did Kaushika. I have not had to endure living near the lord after such resentment, but I know it cannot be easy for Nanda. The lord's presence is embedded within the dust of Amaravati. If he has been neglecting her so badly, then the very air is likely difficult to breathe.

"The lord is callous as a matter of habit," I say. "But what of your other sisters, those in your cohort? Titollama and Urvashi and Dhriti. They were close to you when I was still in training. Surely they are happy to see you safe."

Nanda's face falls. She shakes her head. "They are angry with me," she whispers. Her fists clench in her sari, and it takes her a moment to master herself.

I do not pursue further. I understand. She has been shunned by her sisters, those apsaras taking their cue from the lord—all of it done not because she failed her mission but because she chose a side against him during the battle. Because she chose to be loyal to *me*. I squeeze her hand bracingly.

"Well, I am glad for you," I say. "Seeing you now is a balm to my soul." I cock my head curiously. "How *do* you come to be here if he has not allowed you?"

No apsara is permitted out of Amaravati unless sent for missions. Before Kaushika, I never thought about how terrible this edict is; after all, we are Indra's most prized weapons, and heaven is well, *heaven*—who wouldn't want to live there forever? I have been hoping to learn the spell to open portals to escape heaven's gilded cage, but for the first time, I realize this thought mirrors that of the yogis, those who do not even aspire to swarga but seek to break through all illusions of maya into enlightenment. I am startled at myself. The hermitage and my sojourn in the mortal realm have affected me beyond what I know.

"Has Indra changed his mind about our freedom?" I ask.

"Do you really think that likely?" Nanda scoffs. "I am here because my last mission remains unfinished. I am able to travel as I wish—and Indra in his neglect has forgotten it. So long as the lord does not look in my direction, I can go where I want."

Her voice is full of resentment, but I cannot help but rejoice. "Then you are free," I say, nudging her shoulder with mine. "You can visit me here more often. I would visit you too if I was certain of such a gift, but I don't think the lord will forget me easily after all the trouble I have caused him. If I show myself in heaven now, who knows how he will react?"

I smile to lighten the envy that tinges my words, but Nanda does not return it.

"I did not come here merely for your company, as welcome as it is." Nanda's face becomes uncharacteristically serious. "Beware, Meneka. You joke about Indra, but I am here to warn you about him. No immortal can grasp the city's magic like we once did. Even if your lover has ceased his hatemongering, mortals still spurn the lord. With the Vajrayudh approaching, the lord is looking to place blame somewhere. I suspect he will move against Kaushika soon to gain a victory and remind the mortal realm of his power. You are in danger."

The Vajrayudh edges closer with every passing day, raising tempers and sowing disharmony within swarga. I was sent to seduce Kaushika before its arrival, and I stopped Indra and Kaushika from destroying each other, but it is as I've feared—not an end but only a pause. Will I have to stop another battle—this one instigated by Indra? Or—as Shachi has commanded me—am I to encourage one so Indra is vanquished and the way is clear for the queen to take the throne?

"The lord is too focused on Kaushika," I say, frowning. "He should look to his own house to see who threatens him there."

"Do you mean Queen Shachi?" Nanda asks shrewdly, tilting her head. "Who do you think guided me to come here, Meneka? You have the wrong measure of the queen. Indra rages and raves about Kaushika in his court, but it is Shachi who calms him, telling the lord he must not attack the sage again. That Kaushika means no more harm to him, and upsetting the sage any more will only end in ruin. She fears the devastation it would unleash on the mortal realm and on you."

I am surprised to hear this. I open my mouth to refute the queen's sincerity; whatever she has told Indra is surely some kind of ploy—but Nanda's wrists curl into mudras before I can speak. An illusion forms from the tips of her fingers. I see her in a jewel-encrusted antechamber, rainbow light dancing off the walls. Queen Shachi reclines on the cushions, and Nanda sits in front of her, part supplicant, part friend, pouring out golden soma in two delicate cups. It is an honor to be asked to dine with any of the devis, let alone she who rules them all, but this image is more intimate than that. I watch as Nanda weeps mid-sip. Shachi rises from her cushions and crushes her to her chest, stroking her hair. I cannot hear the words being said, but whatever is occurring is comforting my friend. How can I take this away from her by uttering suspicion about the queen? That Shachi cares about Nanda, I have no doubt. The queen is complex, but she has always loved the apsaras as her daughters. She would have saved Nanda from Kaushika's curse if she could.

The illusion wavers, then dissolves.

Nanda's voice grows softer. "Only the queen has stood by my side through the last few weeks, sheltering me from the censure of others. If it were not for her, my life in swarga would be unbearable." She takes a deep, tremulous breath, then visibly bolsters herself. "The queen wishes to protect you too—and because of you, Kaushika as well. She asked me about what happened after the war. The way you and Kaushika live with each other in the hut. The way he came to us, helping to repair the forest after the battle. How it was that *you* freed me from my curse. She asked me of the mortals and the hermitage, and those that taught you the use of wild prana."

"The queen flatters me with such attention," I say wryly, though inside, I am alarmed. No one knows that Indra cut me off from Amaravati, but my use of wild prana is no secret. Long before I understood it was my own ability that allowed me to use prana magic, I wondered if it was Indra's blessing. That is what Rambha convinced me of once. But Shachi must suspect it is my own talent. What does she intend to do with such information?

Nanda reads my expression and answers gently. "She sees there is power in your love with that man. No matter what he has done to me, I know he loves you too. She sent me here to tell you to trust her."

My eyebrows rise. "Do *you* trust her?"

"Should I not?" Nanda counters. "She is a goddess. We have

trusted Indra all along, and look where that has brought the two of us. In Shachi, there is kinship, at least. There is the grace of femininity, the promise of friendship."

It is too simple an explanation, and wariness sparks through me, making my hackles rise. Indra and Shachi are not very different. They have been married for millennia; they are a part of each other, their souls intertwined, neither of them knowing where one begins and the other ends. They are like Shiva and Shakti, coiled around one another, giving purpose and identity to each other. One of them likely thinks a thought, and the other performs an action without their knowledge. Indra might have forgotten how closely he is tied to Shachi, but *she* has not. She reminded me of her name not two weeks ago—Indrani, she who belongs with Indra. It is this bond with the lord that allowed her to access the halahala.

Nanda would have me align myself to Shachi instead of Indra, but in performing my mission with Kaushika, I have encountered the lord's power and cruelty. I shudder to think of the goddess's.

"Indra and Shachi are power made flesh," I say. "I have begun distrusting the devas and devis altogether."

"You do the bonds of sisterhood a disservice, then," Nanda replies fiercely. Suddenly she looks more like herself, her eyes glinting, her mouth angry. "Shachi is not merely a devi, she is our mother, a sister, a woman. I know you are in love with Kaushika, but have you considered how dangerous he is? You are asking me to abandon you to the mortal realm—asking our queen to abandon you—when you do not accept our invitation of trust. Yet you are all alone here, Meneka. What if something should occur? What if Kaushika harms you? Who will help you? You are forgetting your home."

I make a sound of protest. I want to explain to her that I am not in any danger from Kaushika, but before I can form the words, the wind changes.

Both Nanda and I jump to our feet.

The breeze smells like lightning and storm, fire and brine. It is tinged with honey and star-anise, neither sweet nor spicy but something in between, seeping into my very core, calling to me. The star-anise sparks a fondness, a pain. Almost I think it is Rambha calling me—but no. Someone who owns Rambha. Someone who owns me too, despite this brief stint of freedom. Someone who *makes* swarga heaven.

Indra.

The tether connecting me to Amaravati tightens, and I exchange a wild look with Nanda, knowing she must feel it too.

This is a call directly from the lord, one I have never experienced before, but imbued with deep familiarity, like Amaravati's soul is singing to me. I cannot refuse it. I reach out my hand, and Nanda grasps it tightly, slightly panicked. The plans Nanda was sent to warn me about are coming to fruition. We are too late. We are not prepared.

The wind ruffles around me, swirling my loose hair, making me breathless. I try to resist its hold on me, but I am too entranced. Though my thoughts remain lucid, my body itself feels too relaxed to make a rune with my mortal magic to clear my head. It is as though I am a thrall, incapable of following my mind.

Regret fills me. In some part of my heart, I've known I must return to Amaravati. I have even longed for it, but now I am being taken against my will, same as Nanda. What will happen when I do not return to the hut today? Kaushika and I have barely sorted through all that has happened. I hoped to tackle our next challenge together, side by side. I wanted to tell Kaushika everything *today*, as soon as he returned from his meditation. But now I must face Indra and Shachi without a solution of how Kaushika and I will be reconciled. Without sharing my heart with him, or knowing any of his secrets. We were so close to it this morning. I should never have distracted us with sensual play.

Panic swirls through my body, unable to be released past Indra's enchantment. Amaravati's wind wraps around me, light yet firm, as though the lord is picking me up in a hand.

I am whisked away, the mortal realm disappearing from my sight in edges of amber.

CHAPTER 3

I arrive in the City of Immortals, my body unsteady.

Familiar relief rushes through me as I smell the cinnamon-scented air, but the relief only lasts an instant. As soon as my feet touch the ground, I stagger. Underneath me, the pavement is brittle. Tiny cracks feather across the road, radiating from where I stand. Blackness gapes within the cracks, glittering with stars. Nanda's grip on my hand tightens.

We are within the city's crescent gates. My magical tether coils inside me like an alert snake, wary. Mornings in Amaravati are tinged with dew and warmth, the city dancing to a silent song, yet now an unnatural gloom surrounds us. Shadows whisper in hidden corners, and the air feels heavy and thick like sludge. At the edges of my vision, I discern a yawning darkness like the maw of a ravenous creature. Before I can cry out, the visage rights itself, the dust blinking brightly, the gloom fading. Even the cracks under my feet disappear. It is as if nothing untoward is occurring.

I blink, glancing at Nanda, and from her wide eyes I know she has noticed the aberration within Amaravati, no matter how much the city tries to disguise it. This is what she meant when she said the realm was weakening. It is worse than I feared; I have never seen Amaravati so. Images rush me, but instead of memories of Indra reigning strong, I see him defeated and on his knees, his adversaries circling him like hawks, mortal kings and sages, ferocious asuras and rakshasas. It is not Indra's majesty that coats me anymore, but his guilt, his fear. Nanda and I stand together, shivering, watching as shapes emerge from beneath the crescent gates.

I expect to be accosted by the city's guards, but it is familiar faces that find us. Sarala, Urvashi, Titollama, and Dhriti are some of the most elite apsaras, belonging to the same cohort as Nanda and Rambha. Their names come to me as if from a distance. I see myself being trained by Sarala. I watch myself mesmerized by Urvashi's great beauty. Dhriti and Titollama are even grander in my memory, sparkling full of silver stars, their dance movements exquisite. My younger self would never have dared to raise my eyes to theirs. Even now my gaze falls, unable to hold theirs. I detect anger in them, brimming just underneath the surface of their smooth skin.

Each of these apsaras is lovelier and more lethal than the next. Urvashi with her full, luscious curves, her rounded bottom, her moonlike face. Titollama, who declared herself an apsara, disdaining her birth-body of a man. Sarala and Dhriti, who look nearly alike, born as sisters bound by blood. All their braids are filled with fragrant perfume. All of them wear the sheerest saris, the most delicate jewels. Magic pours from their gold bangles and ruby nose pins, their sapphire necklaces and jade earrings. They surround Nanda and me, and I feel lightheaded in their presence.

"Nanda," Urvashi intones. "The queen has called you to her. You are to go at once."

Nanda's face floods with relief. "Come," she begins, tugging me, but Urvashi blocks my way.

"Not her. She is to be presented to Indra. The lord has personally asked for you, Meneka."

Nanda frowns, opening her mouth, but no words emerge. Events are outpacing us. These apsaras are loyal to Indra. They fought for the lord during the war, casting illusions to entice and seduce Kaushika's army. They have been waiting here for me and Nanda at his command. We dare not speak freely in front of them. That the devi has called Nanda is a good sign; she will be protected. But if Indra has asked for me . . .

"Trust the queen," Nanda whispers to me, an order and a plea. She squeezes my hand, and lets Dhriti and Titollama lead her away.

Urvashi begins walking in the other direction, and Sarala nudges me forward. I have no choice but to follow. I exchange one last desperate look with Nanda and begin down the path to the palace. The apsaras are more tense than I have ever seen. To be so fully armored in their jewelry and magic, as though preparing for unseen marks . . . Once again, I am reminded that I know little of what goes on in swarga. I have been gone too long.

"What does the lord want with me?" I ask. "What does he plan?"

Urvashi studies me coldly. "You have forgotten yourself," she says, and her tone is bitter. "You appear like a common mortal, not a heavenly beauty. Are these truly your choices?"

I know she is refusing to answer my question, but her words pinch me. So much resentment is laced through her tone that I am taken aback. Urvashi's castigation is not for my clothes alone. Her disapproval is because of my actions in the war. I recall what Nanda said, about Urvashi and the others forsaking her, and anger cords through me. How dare she lecture me on my choices? She and the others are the ones who abandoned me, leaving me to deal with the terror of the mortal realm during my last mission. They could have given me consideration for my choices, yet all they give me is judgment. I raise my chin and meet her gaze unflinchingly.

"It is too late to do anything about that," Sarala says. Her voice sounds like honey poured over rocks, but now it is jagged with tension. "She must be presented to the lord at once. She does not have time for more appropriate attire." Her gray-eyed gaze transfers to me. "Be careful of what you say, girl. Remember he is the king of devas. Give him the respect he deserves. Try and remember who you are. An apsara of Indra's court."

I frown at her words. There is more to this warning than a simple order for devotion. That it is apsaras who greeted Nanda and me, that Urvashi and Sarala are so concerned with how I appear, even their own beauty . . . Whatever is occurring is not merely about me. My actions have impacted all the apsaras of swarga, including the ones who were on the other side of the battle. Perhaps after my rebellious actions, Indra has tightened his hold on these women, refusing to let them out of his sight, denying them his blessings of power. What else could account for such condemnation toward me? Sarala is reminding me that apsaras are Indra's weapons. Yet the apsara who is his favorite I do not see anywhere.

"Where is Rambha?" I ask. "Why is she not with you?"

Urvashi scowls. She exchanges a cryptic glance with Sarala, but does not respond. Instead, both glide faster, and it is all I can do to keep up with them. We wind our way through the city, past mansions and orchards and festival grounds lined with colorful pennants. It is astonishing not to see any citizens promenading the tree-lined boulevards, to see no celestial children, the playgrounds empty, the swings so still. Out of the corner of my eyes, I detect a darkness to the golden arches, a withering to the flowers. The constant hymnlike rhythm to the city distorts, sounding shrill and off-key to my ears. I blink, and the city rights itself again.

We march in silence until we reach Indra's palace. We enter the crescent-shaped gates that mimic the gates of Amaravati, and I expect to take the path I usually do, leading into the alcove where I report to my handler about my missions. But Urvashi leads us away from the corridor toward the main doors. It is an area I have never been in before, and my mouth drops open as we emerge into a wide hallway.

Magic slams into me with the force of a thousand winds. Jewels encrust every wall, and it is as if I am in a hallway full of rainbows. The roof is open, and the sky is a kaleidoscope of different moods. Each step reveals a different view, one filled with a billion fat, glittering stars, another with terrible storms that crackle with lightning, and still another where the sun is captured within white clouds in a crimson dawn.

I glance at the other two apsaras, but they are too intent on keeping their step to notice my discomfiture. It strikes me suddenly that this is the route that most citizens and supplicants take when visiting Indra. The ceiling has been designed by Indra himself to show all the many skies of which he is lord.

My throat feels parched, and my head swims. I know it is his magic that is influencing me so, but there is nothing I can do about it. Held hostage by his immense power, I cannot even remember my tapasvin magic. We arrive at the threshold to the throne room. Urvashi nods at a guard, who lets us in.

It is unlike the last time. Though the room's aura rushes me, making me stagger, the throne room looks different. No longer can I see the murals and artifacts that line the walls. Except for a path that tracks to the front, every inch is full of chatting citizens. Their auras mingle with one another, noisy and colorful, coated with the chamber's own magic. Jewels glitter everywhere, and Amaravati's power surges through me, making my golden tether thrash, yet subduing me at the same time.

Last time, the throne room smelled like ghee and camphor, like prayer and song. This time, a brininess sharpens the air. Perfume, soma, and smoke assault me, and my head spins, unable to discern any clarity. Above, the sky is a murky gray, the ceiling shrouded in mist, telling me nothing of the lord's thoughts.

The apsaras leave me, melting into the crowd. I feel naked without my raiment, and I cannot believe that I have been so foolish as to not wear the clothes I was given. Queen Shachi did tell me that the clothes were for the next time I came to the city. Even if I could not have guessed when that would be, I should have been prepared. Perhaps in her own way, she was trying to help me even then.

I hear the whispers of the court as heads turn to study me. I hear them speak Kaushika's name and talk of the battle in the skies. I defied Indra, they say. My life in the mortal realm is an insubordination, they whisper.

They make way for me, and I raise my eyes to the dais at the other end, expecting to see the most important devas of Indra's council seated in their customary places—Agni of tempestuous fire, Vayu of the ceaseless winds, Surya of the fierce sun. Yet only two figures grace the dais—Lord Indra and Queen Shachi. I swallow and begin my long trek to them.

The lord of heaven glowers as I approach. Indra is as handsome as ever, his chiseled face pinpointed like a shard of lightning. Dressed in a glimmering purple kurta and indigo dhoti, the lord is resplendent, his presence making everything else hazy by comparison. Garlands weave around his neck, some made of flowers, some simple silver and gold, all of them gifts from the assembled devotees. I realize I have come here without any offering to the king of devas.

My nervousness heightens as I notice the crown on his forehead. It is no longer the golden one of dawn he wears during peacetime. This one is thinner, more ominous, each blade spearing from it a weapon in itself.

Golden dust dances around him, but even as I watch, it turns to black, before winking gold again. His aura flickers too, dimming, then blazing into a sudden white, blinding me. Storm lord as he is, Indra has always been turbulent, but now chaos consumes him. The vajra spins in and out of existence in his hand, as though he cannot decide if he wants his battle blade or not. I recall the time the lord pointed that very blade at me, threatening to end me for my betrayal of him. Rambha's enchantment saved me then. Who will save me now?

The warnings of the other apsaras ring in my head. I had been hoping to work with Indra, to make him see that my devotion to him still exists despite my actions in the war—but he has brought me here to be punished for my audacity. The lord means to clarify his dominance in one stroke of his blade.

I look from him to the figure sitting on his lap, searching for help. Next to Indra, it is easy to miss her, but Queen Shachi smiles at me. She does not appear as electrified as I have come to expect of her, and that troubles me more. Has Indra subdued her so much with his fury? If so, what does it mean for the plans she hatches? I have decided to trust in her now when I have no choice, but in doing so, I could be trading the lord's blade for a serpent's bite. The way she sits now, calm and calculated, tells me I still do not know her agenda.

Her sari is a demure pink, and her aura does not whiplash. It pulses steadily, scented with fresh lotus, and she settles

Indra's free hand around her waist, as though to remind everyone watching that she is his queen. That no matter his favorites and concubines, it is she who belongs on the throne with him. Nanda told me she has been advising Indra. Shachi wants me to trust her, but I am a rogue apsara with unclear allegiances, privy to both the lord's secrets and hers.

A blaze of rebellion bursts through me at being played for a fool. I have been brought here with such suddenness in order to frighten and manipulate me. Yet if I am to represent the other apsaras, I will not dishonor my kind.

My fingers curl, and illusions pour out of me, coating me head to toe. A luscious braid, lined with starlike emeralds, replaces my loose locks. The kurta and pajama from the hermitage disappear. Instead, a fiery orange sari, the shade of righteous tapasvin flames, ripples from me, hugging my curves. I wear no jewels, but I feel the weight of them on my skin, so powerful is my illusion. Crystal bangles tinkle on my wrists, making delicate music. My jhumkas are light as air, but they reflect the golden dust of the throne room. I settle a maang-tikka on my forehead, and it flares in the brilliant hues of the rainbow.

I do not need blessed amulets to sustain this illusion. I use the magic from the many people assembled. My eyes meet Indra's, and I see his fury grow.

Alert and graceful, I sink to my feet, my illusory sari pooling around me like petals. "My lord," I say, bowing my head. "My queen."

For a sharp moment, the courtroom holds its breath.

Then Indra leans forward. "Welcome home, daughter," he says softly, "from your mission in the mortal realm."

My head jerks up. I stare at him.

The lord's eyes move from me to the rest of the assembly. "Behold, citizens of Amaravati," he intones. "Heaven's greatest devotee has returned a hero. Honor her as you would a devi, for she has done the impossible." Indra's laughter rings out like rumbles of thunder. "Not only did she successfully seduce the great Sage Kaushika, she stopped his act of war, lured him into abandoning his hermitage, and entranced him into forgetting his vows of asceticism. He now lives as her thrall in the mortal realm, a puppet on her leash." The lord's arm flings out, gesturing to me, and his eyes glint. "Behold, the apsara Meneka, who made a fool of a mortal sage. She will tell you what fate awaits those who threaten me."

I am stunned. Indra's words confuse and immobilize me.

Cheers and applause fill the chamber. People shout the lord's name, Shachi's name, even *my* name. I want to refute him, but what will I say? The lord speaks truly, even if he does not speak the truth.

The courtroom might believe his declaration, but it is clear to me that he despises me, and it is amazing that he has not killed me. Even if he is trying to save face, to put to rest rumors of my insubordination, would it not be easier to behead me now and reassert his power? Or is it because of Shachi? Is the goddess protecting me? Does she really care for me? My mind spins as I try to see all the hidden snares I have walked into.

Shachi rises, and Indra takes her hand. The two of them descend from the throne.

Against my will, my body trembles. It is fear, not piety, that makes me shudder. I bow my head, too overwrought by their magnificent power. Their shadows hover over me, and I inhale deeply, hearing my shallow breath resound in my ears. I have spoken to the lord and the queen before and held my own. Yet here in Amaravati, when all the jewels of heaven augment their power, when the air glitters with their majesty, when they are seemingly *united* . . . I see how small I am. How they could crush me in an instant if they so desired. I am a celestial. But they are divine.

"Daughter of heaven," the two of them intone formally. Their voices echo in the throne room. "Rise and let the others see how devoted you are."

There is something amazingly magical in the way they speak. It reminds me of the chants learned at the hermitage.

I rise, my mind slow and blurry, and turn to the crowd. The citizens cheer, several shouting benedictions and blessings, all of them singing Indra's name. The lord rests a hand on my shoulder, for all the world as though I am his most favored apsara. I feel the weight of his power, and it crushes me.

Shame, humiliation, and confusion pound inside me. Under the watching eyes of the citizens, my old uncertainties return. I attempt to hold on to the wisdom I gained through the last few months, yet being back here, in this manner, all my confidence evaporates. I am once again an unlearned apsara, clutching

Rambha's pallu, wishing to be like her. An apsara who was never devoted enough. An apsara who always needed to try harder.

I cannot hold anyone's gaze anymore.

My eyes drop, and Indra makes a gesture. I find myself being led out of the throne room, away from the king and queen and their courtiers.

CHAPTER 4

It takes a moment for my head to clear. I have been brought to an adjoining antechamber. It is not the familiar room where apsaras wait to report to their handlers. This one looks like a small armory.

Weapons of every kind embellish the walls. A golden chakra, bright as Surya, rotates slightly, its edges lost in a blur. A massive hammer, its head several times larger than my own, is misted in soft clouds. Crossbows made of wood, their lotus fragrance telling me they have been consecrated with great prayer, are veined with blood. These are weapons of legend, each one of them used by Indra against asuras and ambitious mortals through many millennia.

I don't have to wonder why I have been brought here. I fit here, too. I am Indra's weapon, even if I have forgotten it in the bliss of the last few weeks. I call on Amaravati's wind to return me to the mortal realm back to Kaushika, where I have always been more than a blade, but of course, it does not listen to me. Indra blocks my leaving. He is reminding me of my powerlessness here as much as he did with his speech. *Remember who you are*, Sarala told me. *An apsara of Indra's court.* Resentment pricks my tongue like bitterleaf. I do not even bother attempting to make a gateway with my mortal magic. It would sorely deplete me, and after this morning, I know I am not capable of creating one yet.

My mind churns with everything that has occurred. Am I forgiven? Surely not—I am certain I did not imagine Indra's rage. Then what is the point of such pageantry? The lord delights in spectacle and ceremony, but he never does so without a reason. I drop the illusion of my apsara raiment now that I am alone, hoping that a reminder of being a yogi will help me think.

Sly laughter echoes in the antechamber as my illusion falls. "Why stop there, Meneka?" a male voice drawls. "I would see your entire body, if you would grace me so."

I spin around at once, fingers sparking with magic.

I did not notice before, hidden as he was in the shadows of the chamber, but my eyes widen when I see who it is.

From head to toe, Matali is beautiful.

Thick black hair falls in ringlets to his shoulders, framing a high-cheeked androgynous face. His lips are full and luscious, and they part in a tiny grin as I approach. He sits on a small cushion on the floor, his gaze on the stringed sarangi, and I receive a complete view of how generous his eyelashes are. Brown eyes glint in mischief, and though he is not looking at me, he knows I am studying him. He is enjoying it.

A wave of nostalgia washes over me. In my early days of training, Matali and I spent most of our free time together. He played the music to which I molded my dance. At nights, he loved me, learned me. His casual strumming of the sarangi now, the aura of constant joy around him, even the way he hums under his breath, all of it takes me back to the years before. Dance and song, laughter and music, lust and heat fill my senses. Even the scents return—of myrrh and musk, and the swirling tendrils of incense smoke.

In those days of training, Matali and Rambha were my closest companions, loyal as they were to Indra, each of their devotion matching the other's. Perhaps that is why I was drawn to them, hoping unconsciously they would show me how to be devoted too. With Kaushika, I found my balance. But Matali sparks a fondness in me I'd thought long dead.

I approach him, my steps soft. The defensive magic on my fingertips vanishes. Even as I walk, I match the rhythms of his music with my own footsteps. Mellowness swishes in me like honey wine.

Matali stands up, still plucking at his instrument. "Beautiful as ever," he hums, studying me. "Ah, Meneka, I have missed you, dearest."

I chuckle, not recognizing the sound that comes out of my throat.

Like all celestials, Matali has not aged at all. His skin is a brown so deep it is reminiscent of fertile watered earth. It glows with Amaravati's magic, a dusting of gold that makes my breath hitch. A yellow dhoti covers him from waist to ankle, and on his feet are bejeweled shoes, undoubtedly filled with more magic. He is bare-chested, but I can hardly tell that. A dozen flower garlands loop around his neck, and sweet sugar perfume wafts from him.

As he circles me, the instrument begins to sound breathy. I feel a flush grow under my neck to be serenaded so. Like in a dream, I see the times I have been intimate with Matali. Our lovemaking was joyous and carefree, in the way of all celestials. No profound feelings were attached to the sex we had; it was for pleasure alone, and is that not the best way? Not like Kaushika . . . everything so *serious* with Kaushika. I grow warm—and Matali curls one of my stray locks of hair around his finger. He leans in, his lips inches from mine, hovering.

I watch it happen as if from a distance.

You should not allow this, a voice whispers in my head. *Beware, Meneka*, Nanda whispers from this morning.

I step back from him, suddenly realizing what is occurring. His charm is doing more than reminding me of our good times.

Matali is trying to *hypnotize* me.

Just as apsaras create illusions with dance to seduce their marks, gandharvas use music. The celestial singers are natural opposites and partners to apsaras, music to our dance, song to our movements. We are a deadly combination of heaven together, but we are each other's weaknesses too. Not only do gandharvas regularly create songs for apsaras to dance to, they create specific melodies to lure apsaras into a precise form as well. And Matali—with intimate knowledge—is crafting a song specifically to soften me.

I snap out of his charm. My fingers draw the rune of clarity. It sparks, and the last echoes of his spell leave my mind.

Anger roils in me to be treated this way. I carve more runes in the air, and the shapes orbit me head to toe. The rune of force. The rune of persuasion. The rune of terror. Battle shapes, all of these.

Matali retreats, knowing I have awoken from his enchantment, but I advance upon him like he is my prey. I hold on to my wild prana, not yet unleashing any of my magic but ready. "What is going on?" I demand. "Why did you try to glamour me?"

Matali glances at me, then shrugs, uncaring of the danger. He plucks a string on his instrument, tuning it. "I heard you'd taken up with a mortal lover. You've been lowering your standards. I thought I would simply remind you of true pleasure."

My prana sizzles within me, furious. *He* would remind me of true pleasure? He is nothing compared to Kaushika. My lovemaking with him was meaningless, but with Kaushika it is real and passionate, uncoiling the depths of me. Kaushika could destroy Matali with a simple chant. *I* could ruin him, with so much yogic magic within me. I could force him to answer my questions. I could unravel his intent.

I am on the verge of releasing my runes toward the singer, when the chamber doors open, and my prana locks in me, strangled, before I can do any damage. The runes around me vanish without my permission, leaving me gasping.

I turn my neck, painfully.

Lord Indra enters the chamber, his face like a thunderhead.

"You dare?" Indra hisses, stalking toward me. "You dare threaten my most prized singer, my ever-loyal devotee?"

My limbs release. I hurry away from the lord, nearly tripping over myself. My gaze moves to Matali, but the gandharva remains unperturbed. He returns to his cushion on the floor, and begins to play a mischievous melody.

The storm lord is incandescent with rage. Gone is the restraint of the throne room. Lightning cracks at his fingertips, and his aura is the color of rainclouds. It surrounds Indra, nearly exploding out of his body, attacking my senses with its sharp, briny scent. The vajra on his back appears in his hand, before returning to its brace.

A childish protest rises to my lips to say that Matali started it, but I hold my ground. I study Queen Shachi, who has followed the lord. The queen does not meet my eye. Instead, she walks over to a small enamel-inlaid cupboard to pour out some wine, for all the world as though that is more interesting than anything occurring in the chamber.

I try to breathe evenly. I even attempt to make another rune to help me, but my wild prana does not respond. Indra dissolved my magic with his anger, and I do not have to wonder how. He is the lord of heaven, the king of all devas, and this is his palace and home. He fought Kaushika, one of the greatest sages there is, in the mortal realm where the lord's power was weaker. I am but a beginner. All magic is prana, including my tapasvin magic, but Indra *commands* pure prana without the need for meditation like tapasya. He is divinity, breathing and living such magic all the time. Of course I cannot challenge him.

Still, I raise my chin. "My lord," I say, surprised at how smooth my voice sounds. "I thought *I* was your ever-loyal devotee. After all, am I not the hero of the war?"

Indra's eyes flash like shards of lightning. "Foolish girl. Did you really think you were forgiven so easily after what you did? You forced my hand, leaving me no choice but to utter those words. Did you think people in Amaravati did not talk after your rebellion during the battle? If one unknown apsara can defy me in this manner, what is to stop the others doing so as well? What is to prevent me from being overthrown from heaven?"

I inhale sharply. My eyes dart to Shachi. "There are plans to overthrow you?"

"There are always plans," Indra snarls, and electricity sizzles off the vajra on his back. "Incursions occur from the demonic realm. Asuras attack the city walls in the dead of night, and Amaravati's shield weakens. Citizens have already been removed from the outskirts, from their homes around the walls." His scowl grows deeper. "Do you have any idea what would happen if I did not rule Amaravati? I built the city with my bare hands. I am the architect, the rightful ruler of swarga, and my very essence flows like blood through this realm. If I am not on the throne, the three lokas themselves would suffer beyond reckoning. Mortals would die like insects. Already with the advent of the Vajrayudh, I am weakened, and so is the city."

I am taken aback by this frank admission.

That he would say this to *me*, an apsara he clearly cannot trust, shows how distraught he is. I find myself seeing beyond his anger. The manner in which the weapons appear and disappear. His briny aura of burning clouds. The sullenness of his mouth, the crease in his forehead, the naked emotion in his eyes.

Lord Indra is *scared*. More than he has ever been.

In the background, Matali's music changes, growing calmer,

more peaceful, as though to give the lord some solace. Nothing Indra has said is untrue. Every living creature knows Indra must rule heaven. Even Kaushika acknowledged that Indra and swarga are inseparable. It was why he attempted to build an alternate heaven.

Indra's fear for all the realms mirrors my own. Despite his excesses, the lord has loved his devotees, whether they be mortal or celestial. I have thought so through the worst of my missions, believing him to only have lost his way. I reminded him of his love for his devotees during the last battle. It was why he relented at all. No matter what he thinks, I have been devoted to him. I cannot bear to see him like this.

"My lord," I say gently. "No one wishes to see you weakened. I have only ever wanted you to stay true to yourself."

My words are an echo of what Kaushika said to me once, but Indra's gaze narrows. "You would say that?" he sneers. "*You*, who have harmed me already? Your lover's actions have spread impiety against me across the mortal realm. Look what your prince delivers with King Satyavrat now. He is as much to blame for the state of Amaravati as any demon."

Indra waves a hand, and the air in front of us solidifies, becoming glass-like. Among a thousand stars, I see a golden sphere rising from the mortal realm toward Amaravati. Without being told, I know what I am looking at. This is the soul of King Satyavrat, to whom Kaushika owes a vow, one that will fulfill Kaushika's own karma.

"He continues to defy me," Indra says furiously, beginning to stalk again. "This is *my* heaven. *My* home. How dare he presume to dictate who must enter? He threatens the very order of the cosmic planes even now."

Despite my sympathy, my ire rises. Kaushika vowed to me on Shiva's own name that he would not hurt my city or my kin. Just as I believe the lord still loves his devotees, I believe Kaushika's word. I *must* believe it—anything else would be a betrayal.

Besides, Kaushika told me only this morning that he was finding a different way to fulfill his vow, one that would not harm the city. He has already dissolved his army. He no longer meets with royals to foment hatred toward Indra. He is even unmaking the meadow. The lord is quick to blame the sage for the mortal realm's irreverence toward him, but he has taken no responsibility for his own negligence. I have not forgotten the village of Thumri.

"You make an enemy of him for no reason," I say coldly. "All Kaushika wants is for King Satyavrat's soul to find peace. If you will only allow this, he will become your ally. He might even reverse his teachings in the mortal realm, helping others believe in your grace. I have not been idle there; I have been teaching Kaushika about Amaravati's wonders. I have been relating tales of your greatness. We could all ride out the Vajrayudh in peace, yet you must play your part in this too."

I am amazed at my own audacity to speak so brazenly, and Indra stops pacing to loom in front of me. From her corner, Shachi looks up, giving me a swift, searching glance.

"Do not presume to advise me, apsara," Indra hisses, and I feel my body chill.

Goose bumps erupt on my skin. The lord exerts the tiniest bit of his presence, and my head begins to spin. Storm, sunshine, honeyed amrit, and a soul-deep grief circle me, reacting to his divinity.

I feel blind, the boundaries of my awareness shifting and receding. I inhale deeply, trying to remember the scents of Kaushika, of camphor and rosewood and the lucidity of the hermitage. I wonder if this finally will cause Indra to smite me. Surely he cannot bear such irreverence from a mere apsara? I notice the lord's fingers curl into fists, and weapons disappear from the wall and appear in his hand, before returning to their place. He stares down at me, and his lips purse.

My bravado leaves me. "My lord," I say, bowing my head. "I meant no offense. I only meant to say there is a way to find peace."

Indra throws me a disgusted look. "It is not about peace anymore, dull child. The king's soul wandered the three realms searching for a home when I denied him entry into swarga before. The only home it remembers is the one it occupied in its body in its mortal form. If this foul thing touches the city, Amaravati will burn." Indra waves a hand toward the glassy air.

I look closer, my eyes widening.

This is no immortal soul like I'd thought before.

The orb contains a corpse encased within the magic of prana.

Horror and revulsion course through me, making me take several steps back. I am seeing an abomination.

Corpses have no place in heaven. Amaravati is a place of souls, of gods and immortals. Corpses belong back within the soils of earth, to be returned to it, assimilated within it, according to all laws of prakriti. Kaushika told me the king's last rites occurred according to his kingdom's customs, and mortal customs change from land to land. Perhaps the king's body never burned on a funeral pyre.

Or perhaps Kaushika did this deliberately, a treacherous voice whispers in my mind. *He was wary when I questioned him about his tapasya, this morning. He looked resigned, as if readying for a fight. Perhaps that was guilt on his face, knowing I would dissent from his methods.*

"He has not told me about this," I blurt out, trying to silence my inner voice. "He does not know the risks. If I could only tell him the dangers, he will realize this is the wrong path. He understands the laws of prakriti, and if I can explain the consequences to him, he will relent."

Yet even as I speak those words, a terrible realization comes to me. Kaushika has flouted the laws of prakriti before. This was why he built the other heaven within the meadow, ignoring the warnings of the sages of the Mahasabha. He even forced Indra in the lord's natural essence to acquiesce to his demands. I have forgotten how brutal he can be, lost in my domestic love and our unremarkable lifestyle. But Kaushika already killed celestials in the previous battle. What else is he capable of?

I try to shake these thoughts. This is a betrayal of our feelings for each other, our vows, and how much we have changed. "My lord," I begin. "Allow me to return and speak with Kaushika. I can convince him of his error. I am certain."

"What will speaking achieve?" the lord returns caustically. "You have had an opportunity to find out more, but you have not asked, and he did this right under your nose. How true is your love if you do not even know each other?"

I blink at the bitterness in his voice, but he is not looking at me. His eyes study Queen Shachi, who demurely sips her wine. A new despairing thought fills me. I did not tell Kaushika about the secrets I was holding, because I sought a solution to both our differing loyalties. Could it be that Kaushika did not tell me of his secrets because he was choosing his vow to Satyavrat over his vow to me? Will his love for me be always overshadowed by his hatred for Indra? And what of my own devotion to the lord and my city? In my heart, I try to weigh it against my love for Kaushika, but all I see is the unending tilt of scales, unable to come to a decision.

Indra reads my mind. "I am told you never believed it was I who sent the halahala," he says.

I nod. My words are a croak. "I have been devoted, my lord. This is the truth."

Indra narrows his eyes. "It is a truth I must believe for now, for I have little choice. I am being magnanimous to you, child, in sparing your life and declaring you a hero. Kaushika is not raising this corpse alone. There is asura magic at play, one that is coming from patala directly. Asuras would greatly benefit in fomenting discord in swarga before the Vajrayudh, and there are vestiges of their magic around the secret vaults. It seems the sage and I have a common enemy. They have sent halahala to his hermitage, blaming me for it, and if I find out who and turn them over to the prince, he and I could vanquish a common foe together." Indra smiles, a cold smile. "As you said, my devotees need to be reminded of my greatness, and Kaushika could become an ally, setting it aright. Before the Vajrayudh comes, I will have the sage's allegiance."

My lips are dry, and I stare at Shachi. I hear her whispers in my head, urging me to trust her. Nanda murmurs in memory about Indra's plan to work against Kaushika, but the lord has stated he wishes to join forces with the sage. Which is the truth? I must be cautious.

"How would asuras have been able to access your secret vaults, my lord?" I ask daringly.

Indra's scowl deepens. "Amaravati declines with each passing day, becoming easy prey to them, and they are capable of the kinds of evil magic that devas would never use. It must have occurred during one of the incursions." The lord throws a look of frustration toward Shachi. "Perhaps you see now, Queen, why I do not allow you to leave Indralok or allow your people in. What damage would they do if I were to open my gates to them, this close to the Vajrayudh?"

In her corner, Shachi merely nods as though contrite.

I stare from her to Indra.

Could the lord be so blind? Has he forgotten how powerful Shachi is? He remembers her asura ancestry, then how could he be so dismissive about her involvement? I have no evidence of Shachi's agenda, and if I speak now, Shachi will simply deny it. Though Indra is clearly displeased with the queen, and seems to be listening to me, he will believe his own wife and consort, a *devi*, over a rebel apsara. He will not think Shachi capable of it—he never has. If I speak now, it will achieve nothing except make an enemy of Shachi. When I cannot see where the chips fall, I dare not play my hand.

"Why are you telling me this, my lord?" I ask quietly. "Why have you summoned me?"

Indra regards me. "You claim devotion, child. Then prove it once and for all. Travel to patala, to the realm of the asuras. Go to the kingdom of Puloma, from where Queen Shachi hails. You will find its residents more amenable than any other kingdom's, easy prey to your charms. The asuras are always well informed of one another's business, gossips that they are. Matali will guide you in the realm, helping your cover, but you must learn what the asuras know about this corpse. Someone is manipulating Sage Kaushika's vow, in which case uncovering them will show him I can be an ally. Or Kaushika himself is associating with asuras, and I will brand him for an imposter sage, dallying with demons."

I blanch. Stories and songs I've heard about asuras return to me. The dragon-demon Vritra, who once created great drought in the mortal realm, killing thousands of people until Indra intervened. Andhaka, with a thousand arms and a thousand heads, who lured his prey into mind-numbing darkness for eternity. Tataka, who was a flesh-eater, known to kill yogis and sages for sport. Asuras can bend the forces of cosmic prana in ways celestials cannot fathom.

I cannot believe it; Kaushika working with demons to infiltrate Amaravati. But he has already broken so many laws of nature. If Indra found even a hint, it would ruin Kaushika. The other sages would descend on Kaushika in fury and damnation, duty-bound to kill him, worried about the power he could unleash with the demons. I would not be able to protect him.

"Why me?" I ask, trying not to despair. "Surely there must be someone else more worthy? The queen hails from Puloma, and you have ambassadors there. You do not need me."

"You are tied to the sage. Kaushika will not believe any of my other agents should I send them for this task, but he *will* believe you when you present the culprit. Besides, my agents will be watched, but you are a mistress of illusion."

It should be reason enough, but my gaze darts to Shachi again. Indra is arrogant, but he is no fool. He does not trust Shachi fully; it is why he is not simply sending her to patala to uncover the conspiracy. Perhaps he even suspects her of treason but needs to find the evidence. That is why I am being sent there, pulled into this conflict between them. Yet again a pawn.

The thought straightens my spine. "No," I say vehemently, looking from one to another. "I will not do this. Find someone else to go on this mission."

"Do not refuse me, apsara," Indra says. "I will not force you, but if you choose not to go, it will be as you asked when you volunteered for Kaushika's mission. You will never leave the city. Is that what you want?"

I see myself from that first mission, on my knees, begging to remain in Amaravati. The lord promised me in front of his deva councilors he would grant me this on the success of my mission. After declaring me a hero, he can hardly retract it, but even though I have longed for my home, how can I live without ever seeing Kaushika again?

I remember Kaushika's wary look from this morning when I questioned him about his vow. Despair fills me; without me to counsel otherwise, he will storm the city during the Vajrayudh on a dangerous rescue mission, driven by his hate of Indra.

"He will come searching for me if you imprison me here," I warn. "I don't think either of us wants that, my lord."

"We do not," Indra agrees, and his smile is cutting, full of teeth. "It is why I have sent word to him already. You will not be missed. So I ask you again. Do you take this mission? All I want is the balance of the realms restored."

What choice do I have? The lord has thought of everything. My tongue is too caught within my throat to make any coherent reply. I nod silently.

Indra gestures to Matali and whispers in his ear, embracing the singer tightly. The gandharva bows to him, and then to Shachi. I watch them, reeling from everything that has occurred in one morning. Matali's aching music leads me out of the chamber, and I follow.

CHAPTER 5

This time my departure from Amaravati is different. No longer do I leave from the antechamber alone in the middle of the night. I am not even sent to the kalpavriksh, the wish-fulfilling tree, nor do I make my way to the front gates, from where I'd usually leave for missions. No one prepares me, no handler, no friend, not even jewels given to me to power my illusions. My mind twists with what I saw, the corpse rising toward Amaravati, and the asura magic assisting it. I think of the secrets Kaushika is hiding from me, and the ones I have hidden from him. Regret tightens my body, at my lost chance to clear matters.

I follow Matali, who still flirts with his sarangi, and we march through the palace, through chambers and hallways, until we are outside again. Now that court attendance is finished, citizens mill on the streets, heading toward the puja grounds and houses of pleasure. Weaving through them are guards with gleaming weapons. The farther away from the palace we walk, the more evidence I see of asura incursions. Gashes score the pavements and houses, unable to be healed despite the city's magic. Branches dangle from trees, limp and rotting, affected by sickening spells. There is a stench underneath the incense that lingers like smoke and poison, and I cough as a whiff comes to me. I do not wish to go on this mission, but seeing Amaravati deteriorate this way frightens me more than the thought of patala.

I hasten to match Matali's pace. "What did the lord whisper to you?" I ask.

The singer gives me a sidelong glance, his lips twitching. "He told me not to get eaten by the demons."

I give him a narrowed look. He is lying; worse, he is *laughing* at me. "He would send you to the underworld even though you are so precious to him?"

Matali merely shrugs. "The lord does not inhibit my freedom. He knows a singer must travel to tell his tales."

"And what stories do you seek?" I ask, raising an eyebrow.

This time Matali does crack a grin. "Perhaps we will meet Ilvala, who once turned a sage into a goat, cooked his flesh, and ate it. Or we will meet Jara, who with one look can turn even immortals into decrepit, wrinkled creatures. Maybe I might have a word with Maricha, who desecrates sacrificial altars and lives in filth. There might be a cautionary song or two to compose about the cruel Prahasta, who burned the mortal realm with unyielding fires." Matali's smile becomes wider. "There might even be a demon who ravishes apsaras, sweet Meneka. Gandharvas are messengers and keepers of lore. We must learn *all* the stories, and maybe your presence will find me a new one for the ages."

I know he is trying to scare me, and I should not give him the satisfaction, but a vein of cold terror throbs inside me. Indra must be desperate if he is sending *me* on this mission, if he is sending Matali, a most favored devotee, to act on his behalf in these dangerous times.

The singer has surely been ordered to keep his eye on me. I am to seek a conspiracy within patala, perhaps questioning and enticing the locals, but Matali is dressed in all his finery, carrying nothing but his potli full of instruments. The bag disappears as we walk, hidden on his person. He will present himself at court as a traveling musician, and he is meant to guide me, but I speak no more, knowing the singer will not give me straight answers.

We come upon the edge of the city, and I gaze at the towering walls. The back gates to Amaravati are enchanted, hidden within these walls, and I have only ever heard stories of them. They appear not to be gates at all, covered with illusion due to Indra's strong magic. Only true faith in him opens the desired pathway to different realms. Even Indra must pray to his own divine self to use these gates. Nervously, I wonder if the lord can use these portals anymore. If he remembers himself at all.

Nanda waits for us under a large frangipani tree. She hurries forward as she sees me. No longer in her beautiful apsara sari, Nanda wears clothes as plain as mine, a gray kurta and pajamas that look like they belong to one of the palace's attendants. No jewelry adorns her, and though her hair is still tied in the thick braid favored by the apsaras, simple metal pins hold it together instead of gems and gold. A bag prepared for travel rests by her feet. I realize she is going to accompany me. I feel relief to have a friend, but I am fearful too. Nanda is in no shape to go on such a dangerous mission.

"Are you all right?" I ask as I rush to embrace her.

"I'm fine," she says, returning my hug. "The queen spoke to me before she left for the throne room. She told me about your new mission—"

"And you volunteered to come?" I ask. When Nanda nods, I shake my head in despair. "Oh, sister, did she not tell you where we are going?"

"She told me," Nanda answers. "But I would not leave you to go alone." Her words are brave, but I see the signs of fear on her face, the slight twitching of her hands, the dilated pupils, the nervous pinch of her aura that smells like burned rose petals. I want to argue with her, tell her to change her mind, but I know she will not listen, and it will only undermine Shachi when we are being observed by Indra's agent.

Nanda makes a face and gestures at her simple clothes. "The queen said we would not be able to take our jewels with us. We would have to hide that we are apsaras on this covert mission, for patala is not safe for celestials. But surely there are limits to it." She runs a critical eye over me and shakes her head. "Secret or not, you cannot travel to a mission with your hair undone."

She pulls me closer, carefully removing pins from her own braid. She turns me around, and I feel her clever hands brush over my scalp.

A gasp escapes me as the metal pins weave through my locks. Amaravati's magic sizzles, tugging at my tether, powering it. These pins appear lifeless, so much so that even I was deceived, but they have been covered with a deep illusion. I do not know what gems they conceal, but they are swarga's amulets, and my magic sharpens in me, readying. I am astonished at their power, but of course, Nanda is an elite apsara. Those superior maidens have always had their own secrets and weapons. I ought not to be surprised. I am grateful for her, yet suddenly I can see how little I was sent with on my mission to seduce Kaushika. Anger courses through me toward the lord. He sent me on an impossible mission before, expecting me to die. Perhaps he means to do the same thing again.

Nanda leans forward, and I feel her breath on my ear. "I've learned more, sister. Shachi told me Indra sent Rambha on a mission to the mortal realm. She implied Rambha is meant to seduce the sage's allies for the lord."

I stir, trying to give her a sidelong glance. I remember only too well the royals Kaushika once gathered to his cause. Their impiety remains a threat, but I'm surprised.

"Indra did not want to part with Rambha before, not this close to the Vajrayudh," I whisper. "He wouldn't even send her to challenge Kaushika, though she asked. I would not think he would take such a risk now."

"The queen said Rambha insisted. Shachi says Rambha told the lord he could not stop her. She has freedom to move between realms as she wants, after all, a boon given by Indra himself."

Indra and Rambha are closer than mere lord and devotee. They are lovers, and the lord has always allowed her liberties he would never extend to any other apsara. Though Rambha came to the mortal realm to fight against Indra, she was forgiven immediately. If she insisted, using all her charms and allure, Indra would not be able to deny her. Rambha must think the lord in deep danger from the mortals if she asked for this—she who once claimed a boon to stay in Amaravati to be close to him. Did it pain the lord to send her away? I recall the summons he sent to me this morning that reminded me of Rambha. She was infused in his call, perhaps an indication of how much he misses her.

"Shachi has told you so much," I think aloud. "Perhaps she truly means to protect the apsaras."

"Do you finally believe me?" Nanda inserts another pin into my braid. "The queen tried to dissuade the lord from sending you on this mission, but when she could not, she summoned me so I could give you this." She turns me around as though to examine her handiwork, but I see where her eyes point. I had not noticed it before, hidden as it was under her kurta, but discreetly she removes a bangle from her wrist, pushing it into my hand. "A token of her love for you. She wishes for you to keep it on your person throughout the mission, to remember that you have friends in swarga who wish you well. It is meant to protect you."

The bangle is made of gold, but with a dullness to it that tells me it is old, very old. I itch to examine it closely, but I can feel Matali's eyes on us. The cadence of his music grows curious.

I slip the ornament onto my wrist. I remember another such bangle that Shachi poisoned with halahala. A token of love, she calls it, but is that true? Shachi did not give it to me herself when she could have, likely fearing what Indra would think of her action, but by sending this to me, she is reminding me of her power. I do not sense any poison within this piece of jewelry, yet the queen is silently telling me I am to be loyal to her. Indra has sent me on a mission to find asura enemies, when one sleeps in his bed.

In the city beyond, the songs and prayers begin, customary for this hour of the day. I feel bereft of home, of Kaushika, of any kind of certainty. Lightning cracks in the sky as if to remind me I must remain devoted to Indra. *You belong to me now*, Shachi whispers from my memory. Red nails and the approach of a storm merge in my mind. I begin to breathe faster in panic.

Indra and Shachi. One is the lord who owns my soul, another is the devi who is a part of the Goddess Divine. Two equals, both fearsome, both entwined. I must choose one of them soon enough. Nanda is an elite apsara, more practiced in intrigue than I. She came to me in the mortal realm, forgave Kaushika, endured Indra's wrath all for me. Shachi gave me the lightning-bolt blade to defend myself from Kaushika should I need to. If Nanda and Shachi trust each other, should I not do the same? What has Indra ever given me in return for my devotion but grief? My wrist circles the bangle, before I notice the motion and stop.

Matali pushes himself away from the tree. "If you are quite done adorning yourself," he drawls.

Nanda and I turn to him. Behind him, a part of the wall shimmers in the shape of an arch. Matali has unlocked the back gate, opening a path to the underworld. Silver glitters on the arch, but within there is nothing but terrible darkness.

All three of us gaze into the portal. My mind brims with

everything I've learned. I am as unprepared for this new mission as I was for the one before. At least then I was familiar with the mortal realm. My magic will not protect me against asura and rakshasa demons now. They are as powerful as any celestial. It is all I can do not to shake.

Matali extends a gallant hand. "After you, my dear," he says, winking at me.

Gritting my teeth, I enter the darkness.

CHAPTER 6

I am surrounded by black clouds. I am twisted within a nightmare.

Instinctively, my wrists try to form mudras, but I am immobilized. A heavy wind traps me, its clutches sharp even as it carries me farther away from home. A terrible stench climbs up my nose, reminiscent of corpses and sickness. My stomach roils, and I am unable to breathe. When I crack open my eyes, I catch glimpses of horrible flesh-eating creatures, blood dripping down their fangs. Chimerical beasts rip in and out of my vision, grabbing at me. I scream until my breath is snatched away and I come to a stop on hard stone. My knees knock together, but somehow, I manage to keep myself from falling.

Nanda clutches my arm, her breath coming out in short, panicked gasps. Her eyes are wide, and she stares around us, her mouth soundlessly moving in prayer. I turn to gaze at Matali. The singer knows more than either of us about this place. I expect to see him laugh at our distress again, but to my surprise, his mouth hangs open and his fingers on the sarangi are limp. All his earlier bravado is gone.

"We are not supposed to be here," he breathes out.

We are shrouded in complete darkness, the only light coming from our own heavenly auras. Sharp though my eyesight is,

I cannot pierce the echoing black. "It's exactly how you said it would be," I say, confused, but he shakes his head.

"I was tormenting you, and you knew it. You ignorant apsaras have only understood the immortal realm as heaven and hell. But you have never known the subtleties of lore like the gandharvas do."

The sarangi he is holding disappears, and in its place comes a mridangam, a battle drum belonging to Shiva. If he has managed to replace his instruments, his magic still works here, and I feel for my tether inside me. It lies limp but alive, and I know I am in a natural realm unlike Kaushika's meadow.

Matali makes no sense, however, so I look to Nanda. "Indra plays a subtle game, sending us here in such darkness. If he means to scare us into submission, he does not understand the bravery of apsaras."

The gandharva hears me though my voice is pitched low. He answers before Nanda can. "This is not the king's doing," he says, scowling. "The lord has no control here."

"If you are trying to blame Shachi, you will have to try harder," Nanda says. She has regained some of her composure, and her grip on my arm lightens, though she does not let go.

Matali shakes his head again. "Shachi hails from patala, which lies just below the mortal realm. The underworld is as beautiful and lush as swarga, if not more so. It is filled with the most enchanting asura maidens, the most beautiful and virile demons. It is rich with music and dance, and the gardens that flower there are luscious enough to make even a citizen of Amaravati weep. *That* is Shachi's kingdom and realm."

Something about that raises a thought in me, but I push it away for a more immediate one. "If we are not in patala, where are we?"

"Naraka," Matali says, his tone clipped. "Or Yamalok, as many stories call it. This is hell in every meaning of the word."

I stop breathing.

Yamalok.

The abode of Lord Yama, the god of death.

I have heard the stories. Who hasn't? I have mistaken naraka for patala—a sign of my own privilege in heaven—but now that Matali mentions it, all the stories come rushing back to me.

Yamalok is a place of dark evil, a bottomless pit infested with the worst, most depraved creatures in all the three realms. There is no food here, no water. No rest, no salvation, no peace. Souls wander within this accursed place in eternal damnation, tortured by methods that fail my imagination. Yama himself is no friend to the celestials. Indra's archenemy, king and god of all dark, evil things, Yama despises creatures of swarga—we who cannot die except in rare circumstance. Our very existence is a frustration to he who rules death. Suddenly I am grateful not to be wearing any jewels from heaven that would announce who we are. I hurry forward to Matali, intending to snatch at his ornaments and rip them from him should he attract any attention, but a bloodcurdling scream pierces the darkness. All of us jump, and my teeth start to chatter.

Matali spins around, his face pinched. The mridangam in his hands sounds a low beat, and with each strike the darkness shivers a little, but that is the extent of his magic. Though he is chanting mantras and prayers, the path he seeks does not reveal itself.

A hiss sounds close to me, and something slithers, dragging on the rock floor.

"W-we must call Amaravati's wind," I say, touching Matali's arm, feeling the bangles warm with magic. His mridangam echoes inside my heart, and though I know we are in danger, my feet want to join its rhythm with my own dance, churning a dual magic.

"I have already tried," Matali says, and his gaze in the dim light of his aura is terrified. "It is the city itself that has brought us here. Amaravati's magic grows wild. The wall opened a path to naraka when it should have—"

He cuts himself off, and his mouth trembles. Nanda clutches me again, and my own heart shudders in fear, for we have all heard the same sounds.

Howls and snarls echo from all sides, and the baying of feral wolves. For a hysterical moment, I am reminded of the time I first entered Kaushika's forest in the mortal realm. Then too, I thought I was being attacked by terrible creatures—yet this time it is no deception. The darkness shifts, waves and undulations forming on it, a glimpse of fangs, the scent of bloodied saliva, the hot breath of a beast. I feel the eyes of a dozen unseen creatures watching us.

Nanda cries out in panic, and so does Matali. The gandharva begins to run, and Nanda snatches my arm. We tumble together in the darkness, following the light of Matali's aura. Behind, I hear the snap of teeth, though when I glance back, I see nothing. I attempt to paint a rune of wind in the air to deter the creatures, but my prana is severely depleted. I have not had any opportunity to perform tapasya to replenish it.

Nanda pulls at me, curling an illusion with her wrist at the same time. It merges with the drumbeat of Matali's mridangam. A sharp bright light emerges from my friend, and unleashes in the direction of the following hounds. Barks and howls echo in the darkness, seeming to come from all directions. My heart climbs into my mouth.

"This way!" Matali pants, and neither Nanda nor I look to see if her illusion has completed itself.

We skid on the rocky terrain toward the massive cave mouth where Matali waits. A glimmer of dim green light emerges from the cave, and I pause, uncertain, but only for an instant. The baying sounds closer, and I hear a male voice shout a hunting command. Nanda steps next to me, her face focused. Her hands come together in a complicated mudra, Garuda's Wings. She thrusts the illusion out. A giant eagle forms in the air, rushing toward the hounds and the hunters. She yanks me into the cave, not waiting to see if it works to distract the riders.

The three of us find ourselves in a massive warren of pillars with lethal bladelike protuberances growing from them. A terrible heat pours into the cave, and I immediately start sweating. I see the color shift on Matali's glorious clothes, even Nanda's simple kurta, telling me their clothes will keep them cool and comfortable. Those are made from celestial threads, yet my mortal attire is drenched in seconds.

Light reflects from giant honeycombs in the ceiling. At first glance, they appear like glowing stars, but I shiver, for the honeycombs are moving. Worms, perhaps, or luminescent snakes stretch down from them, slithering one on top of the other. They are far above us, and I look away, revolted. Nanda and I follow Matali as he puts more distance between us and the cave mouth. None of us can hear the hounds anymore, but it only makes sense to get as far away from them as we can. At least it is silent in this cave, the danger clearly visible.

Matali stops, rounding a particularly vicious-looking pillar, then collapses on the floor, his courage abruptly leaving him. Nanda and I huddle close together. She buries her head in her hands, and a soft sob emerges from her.

Despite the heat, I cannot stop shivering. "Those hounds," I say. "There was a rider. I heard him."

"A yamadut," Matali answers. His face looks sickly and pale in the dim light. Here, in literal hell, his gorgeous clothes from Amaravati emanate their own glow, providing me comfort. "They are messengers of death," he continues, seeing my perplexed expression. "The ones who torture souls for a time until those souls are churned out into birth again. Minions of Yama, who perform their duties with relish on the orders of their master. They will burn your flesh off, skin you with dull blades, whip you and cook you—"

"Stop," I say, cringing. "Stop, Matali, enough." I place an arm over Nanda, who shudders, and Matali falls silent too. The silence echoes with unheard terrors.

I attempt to clear my throat. Nanda does not need to speak;

I can tell from her diminishing aura that her courage is fading. We cannot afford to lose our nerve. We must think of a way out, but Nanda is in no temperament to perform more magic. I look to Matali again. "Sing of beauty, Matali. Remind us of heaven. Indra knows we need it."

I expect him to deny me, claiming caustically that all beauty is forgotten here. Yet Matali must need this reminder as much as Nanda and I. An instrument appears in his hands, a golden harp no bigger than his palm.

His fingers pluck at the strings, and a soft delicate sound emerges in a whisper of hope. With that alone, my heart skips a beat, and tears rush to my eyes. I am suddenly grateful that he is here with me.

Matali begins a song. A tremor shakes his voice, but the melody wraps around the three of us, crooning. It is a love song to Lord Indra and Amaravati. He sings of golden sunrises and the gush of waterfalls. He sings of consecrated temples and gleaming gardens, and flower-lined pathways that turn iridescent in the moonlight. He sings of the lord's beauty, and the jewels on his body, and the power of prana radiating from him into all of Amaravati, inseparable from his life force. Nanda looks up, and her fingers flicker in a gentle mudra. Tiny stars float from her fingertips, encasing us in a cocoon of swirling magic. I think of home and soma, of lotus ponds and temple bells. I think of lightfalls and morning hymns, and indigo colors streaking through a dusky sky.

Matali's song comes to an end, but the magic has worked its

charm. We are ensconced in a surreal peace, a quiet moment that pushes the gloom of the cave away. My breath evens, and Nanda no longer looks as terrified.

I see in this moment how much Amaravati means to me. Here, when we are separated from everything we love, it is the memory of home and our city that gives us hope. The yogis in the hermitage live an ascetic lifestyle, and with Kaushika I have come to embrace it too. He has not understood my love for Amaravati, though he has accepted it. How can I explain this peace to him? It is mine alone.

I study Matali, whose curly head is bent over the harp. The singer hums quietly to himself, and there is no tremor in his voice anymore, though from his posture I can tell he is as aware as I am that we have only kept the fear at bay temporarily. It will return any second.

"You knew about the rising corpse," I say to him. "When Indra showed it to me, you did not seem surprised."

Matali glances up, and his expression shifts, a ripple of anger on it. "You and your mortal lover have done so much damage. Corpses do not belong in swarga, they belong here—" He cuts himself off, his eyes drifting to the dimness around us, and shudders. He speaks faster as though to move away from discussing naraka. "Such a thing is against prakriti. King Satyavrat's corpse will destroy swarga if it touches the gates of Amaravati. The city will burn and decay, becoming colorless. This is what your love has wreaked."

I want to defend Kaushika, tell Matali of his vow and how Kaushika has already begun to unmake his meadow. I want to say that Kaushika would not do this deliberately, and that something is amiss. But my nightmare in the hut returns to me. What if the reason Kaushika asked me about my contentedness was to judge whether I would approve of him raising the corpse? Whether I would be amenable to agreeing with him? Suddenly, our innocent game of sensual pleasure becomes much darker. I huddle into myself, trying to hold on to the love I feel for him, but in this terrible place, it is hard to remember anything good.

Nanda looks from Matali to me. She must wonder what we are speaking of, but before I can explain, she speaks. "How did we come to be here? We were headed for patala."

"I do not know," Matali answers. His face grows sullen, and the melody on his instrument becomes annoyed. "I chanted the mantra I was supposed to. I have been trying ceaselessly to return. I have tried calling Amaravati's wind, but it does not listen." He looks at us balefully. "The lord cannot hear us from here. We will have to think of another way or pray until our combined voice reaches him. Can you two apsaras say your devotion to Indra is so unconditional that he can hear you from naraka?"

Nanda and I do not answer. All of us know the answer to Matali's question. Besides, would prayer help us now? It could be as Matali said, a decay of Amaravati that ruined his chant. Heaven knows I saw the deterioration occur with my own eyes.

Yet I cannot believe it could be this simple. From Matali's tone, I know he does not believe that he chanted the wrong mantra either. Shachi told Nanda and me that Indra was planning something terrible—it must be this. But then why send me here, especially with Matali, who is so beloved to the lord? Why not simply dispose of me in swarga?

"You said patala was beautiful," I say. "Does this mean asuras are not dangerous?"

It is a thought that came to me earlier, and all the stories tell us of asuras and their hideous ways, but I've learned since Thumri how song and legend distort the truth. Matali is a gandharva, and he will know what's real.

"Asuras *are* beautiful, but they are dangerous too, far more than any weapons of swarga. Once, during the Churning of the Oceans, there was terrible war between the asuras and devas. Battle after battle occurred, devas and asuras dying, and all three realms shook with the hate and magic. The war would have destroyed it all, but good counsel prevailed with the intervention of Lord Vishnu, He Who Preserves. Indra and Shachi wed each other to end the war between their realms. Obeying the treaty of peace, devas no longer attacked patala, but asuras still strike swarga when they can get away with it. It is in their nature to do so. They are cunning and devious, their beauty like barbed poison."

"Yet you pursue them," Nanda observes dryly. "You wish to dally with them."

"They are a better challenge than you apsaras," Matali retorts. "And their beauty and imagination surpass yours. The things they can do to give pleasure, the toys they can use . . ." He sighs. "I've heard the stories. If we ever get out of here, I will write the songs."

Nanda utters a soft snort. I lean forward, more interested in what Matali has let slip than his ideas on lovemaking. "If asuras attack as a matter of course, why is Indra so bothered by them now? The lord ought to be used to it."

Matali gives me a dirty look. "You really do not know?"

When I shake my head, he utters a grunt. "Typical apsara behavior, to be lost in your own illusion. It is because of your mortal sage, Meneka. He has fomented deep hatred for Indra, and Amaravati is too weak now, with the advent of the Vajrayudh to withstand even the attacks that should pose no worry. It is Kaushika that is the problem. Not the asuras."

I fall silent at that, and the two of them don't break it either.

Eventually, Nanda leaves my side and moves closer to Matali, asking him softly about the methods that asura lovers use. Soon enough, the two of them are chuckling and murmuring, touching each other.

Nanda grins at me, and spins an illusion of privacy. Her smile is mildly apologetic, but she knows better than to invite me to their play. I shrug at her and offer an easy smile back. I cannot begrudge the both of them whatever comfort they find in this terrible place. Already, the darkness moves closer, diminishing the glow of comfort from Matali's song. If I let myself, I can hear distant screams in the background, the sounds of metal scraping somewhere, the mutters and crackling of some strange beast.

The two disappear behind Nanda's illusion.

I draw my body in close. I feel the intricacies of my braid, then carefully extract Kaushika's crescent comb from it. It glistens in my hand, the unearthly light from the ceiling reflecting on it. Within me, I search for the rushing torrent of my prana. It is only a small trickle compared to what it could be, and though I do not have enough tapasvin fire to attempt strong magic, the comb is an amplifier. I hold it, and braid my wild prana with my celestial magic, murmuring the chant to create a portal. We need to find a way out of here, and Indra will not hear us, not with our questionable devotion.

The comb vibrates in my hand. Hope sparks in me, but while beams of golden light flicker and sputter on it, and the air in front of me grows mist-like, nothing else occurs. My focus falters. I am filled with regret and fear, for letting my city and kin down. For not sharing my secrets with Kaushika when I had the time. For naïve innocence, and unspoken suspicions, and the darkness within myself I thought to erase. The incantation I murmur fades away. I can do no more than I did in the hut.

The comb falls limp between my fingers. I stare at it, silent tears tracking down my cheeks, and imagine myself safe in Kaushika's arms.

CHAPTER 7

I must have fallen asleep, for I awake suddenly, unsure of where I am.

I am unmoored for an instant. There is deep magic in the air, like I am within an enchantment. My early days of training as an apsara rush back to me, when I was taught to know another apsara's illusion. No apsara can enchant another; we are initiated into a sisterhood to understand the shared power we all wield. Though this enchantment reminds me of apsara magic, it has a different potency too. It pricks my tongue, tasting earthy and rich. I feel no sense of doom, just a delicate ripple over my body. Familiarity flavors it, as if it is tinged with my own perfume. I *am doing this,* I think in slow wonder. I don't know how, but this is the same magic I am trying to learn, arcane and mysterious and with an intent of its own.

With that realization, my mind becomes clearer.

I find myself on a misty landscape, tendrils of morning whisking away in the cool breeze of a forest. In my hand is the crescent comb, shining with a warm light, tingling on my fingers. Power seems to be springing from it, but it is just an amplifier. My own magic ensconces me.

The mists drift away, and I see that I am within the forest by my hut in the mortal realm. Relief and elation chase away the last shadows of my despair. Vaguely, I know I am still in naraka, but I can sense the thrum of meditative magic, and my footsteps grow hurried, climbing down to the hut I see in the distance. A silhouette rises in the morning—Kaushika, body erect as he sits, eyes closed, in front of the statue of the celestial dancer. I call out to him, but he does not hear me. I hurry forward, nearly tripping down the hill in my haste.

It is a terrible thing to disturb a sage from his tapasya. Apsaras have been incinerated for less. Yet I feel an urgency within me, a fear that this strange enchantment I manifest could come to an end any instant. I must stop Kaushika from raising King Satyavrat's corpse to swarga. I must tell him of what has happened to me.

I open my mouth to call out to him again, but someone emerges from the hut next to Kaushika, and I arrest my words. She sways forward, a look on her face that is part fury, part hatred. Rambha is a terrifying vision to behold, so beautiful and wild that I come to a standstill. I stare at her, the gray shimmers of her sari, like silky folds of water turned into cloth, the diamond jewels over her body like tiny pieces of moonshine. She is lethal and stunning, and a searing pain goes through me at how much I have missed her.

Then I spy the lightning bolt Shachi gave me clutched in one of her hands.

I am unable to tear my gaze away, unable to move, caught by the horror. Rambha is wreathed in strands of silver light, inverted and inverted again like she is wearing a cloak of the night. It is an illusion of invisibility, a magic only elite apsaras know, but long ago she taught it to me too. There is no way to pierce it. She is completely hidden.

Rambha advances toward Kaushika, stroking the lightning blade lightly. There is something in the way she touches the blade, in reverence and pain that I know she views it as a part of Lord Indra. Hatred flashes in her eyes again as she positions herself behind Kaushika, caressing the blade.

No, I think slowly.

I watch, unable to move.

Rambha pulls her arm back, the blade poised toward Kaushika's neck.

The movement unlocks me. "No!" I scream, running toward them. "Rambha, stop! Please stop!"

She does not look toward me. I know then that she cannot hear or see me, neither of them can. This enchantment I am in does not allow it.

I clutch the crescent comb to my heart. *Help me, Shiva,* I pray in desperation. *Help me, Shakti,* I ask of the Great Divine Goddess.

"Kaushika," I cry out in despair.

He opens his eyes. Hope, relief, then confusion fly across his features as he jumps to his feet, looking around, barely avoiding the blade an invisible Rambha plunges at him. His eyes search for me, and though I call out his name several times more, he does not hear me again. I watch, distressed, as Kaushika utters one chant after another, but nothing he does matters. Rambha retreats, a watchful expression on her face, as he wanders back and forth across the courtyard calling my name.

Finally, Kaushika stops. His chest heaves up and down, and his hands, which had been curled into fists, slowly open. I recognize this action. He is forcing calm back into himself, trying to steady his mind like a yogi.

"I will find you," he says, and though his voice is soft, I can still hear him through this dream-enchantment. "I will find you, my love." His gaze transfers to the star-filled sky. "If you hurt her," he says, and I know he is speaking to Indra. He does not complete his thought, but it is clear for me to see—and to Rambha.

Her eyes narrow. A calculated expression flashes across her face, and the beginnings of a smile. She lowers the lightning blade and tucks it into her sari belt. I should feel relief that she is staying her attack, but I know that smile of hers. She is hatching a plan. She is more dangerous now than she was before. My blood chills.

I think of how she touched Indra's blade. She came willingly to the mortal realm to perform this mission, despite the boon she received so long ago to stay close to the lord. In her mind, *Kaushika* is the cause of Indra's suffering. The one who began it all with threatening the lord with his power. She stayed her hand before because of me, but now the lord's desperation has made her desperate too.

I stumble forward, calling out Kaushika's name again. If he heard me once, he could again—

But something pulls me back, an invisible force. I blink, and—

The mists fade. I am back in the dimness of the cavern within naraka. My chest is inches away from being impaled on one of the sharp-bladed pillars. I stagger into Nanda's arms, and a wretched sob escapes me. Nanda wrenches me to her, her heartbeat thudding against me. Behind her, Matali stares at us wide-eyed, for once at a loss for words.

"What were you doing?" Nanda demands, alarm in her voice. "Meneka, you almost killed yourself. What were you *thinking*? If I hadn't looked for you, if you had been lost—"

"I saw Rambha," I say, voice cracking. "I saw her, Nanda, and she is not in the mortal realm to seduce a noble. She is there to hurt *Kaushika*. Indra told me he sent word to Kaushika about my absence. This is what he meant."

A look of shock and pity crosses Nanda's face. I wipe my eyes and take a deep breath.

"We must press on, or pray to Indra," I begin, trying to gain control of myself. "Please—if you have loved me at all, you will help me find a way—"

An echoing howl silences me from speaking further. The three of us exchange wild, terrified looks, because we can all tell the hounds are back, and this time they are close, within the cave.

It is too late to escape. Too late to hide.

Sudden light shines into our faces, blinding us. I throw an arm over my eyes in defense, but I catch a glimpse of the creatures that already surround us, creeping between the pillars. Hounds as large as horses, their scent as fetid as something lying dead in a still pond. Their eyes glint white, and fearsome though they are, it is the riders atop them that frighten me more. Nearly twenty of them tower over us, and each appears to be a fearsome warrior. Several wear garlands of skulls and shrunken heads, while others are masked, holding cruel, curved whips. Their auras are dark, and I discern no scent to them. They begin to circle us, weaving between the pillars, yowling and calling out threats.

Matali starts to alternately swear and pray, instruments flashing in his hand one after another. Nanda's wrists are curling into mudras that will likely be useless against the yamaduts. I search for my wild prana, trusting it more than any illusions I can make with Amaravati's power, and though I know no rune will work against so many foes, my fingers begin to sketch out a shape.

A sharp movement from one of the riders arrests me. He inhales deeply, and though he is masked, I sense a somber watchfulness from him. His eyes are on my wrist, where Shachi's bangle glints. Something spins lazily between his fingers. It looks like a blade, but as my eyes adjust to the blazing light, I realize it is a quill edged with ink. Surprise eases some of my terror.

Matali notices where my gaze points. His own face becomes even more frightened. He averts his eyes and bows low. In a blink, all his instruments disappear, and though he cannot cast an illusion like an apsara, his own garments lose their sheen as though to make him smaller, more forgettable.

"Forgive us for our intrusion, lord," he says breathlessly. "We did not wish to disturb your . . . ah . . . your hunt. We will just be on our way."

He attempts to edge back, but one of the hounds pushes closer from the other side, and he yelps, knocking into me. The riders laugh raucously. I shake where I stand.

"Our hunt?" the leader asks, amused. "We have been seeking you since you arrived here. Surely you did not think we wouldn't find you. You are in our realm, strangers, and we have ways to know who enters. Besides, you leach out a strong scent like the freshest meat."

I gulp. I cannot tell his face, but his voice is too cultured to utter such threatening words. Once again, I am reminded of my own naïveté. What am I to expect? This is *hell*.

"Do you know who I am?" the rider asks.

Nanda and I shake our heads, exchanging a confused look, but Matali grows pale. "Chitragupt," he mumbles.

"And who *is* Chitragupt?" the man asks idly.

I glance at Matali, and I see the battle on his face. He wishes to respond to the rider, but also seems to know that any answer is only going to give up our identity in some way. Yet it is too late for subterfuge. The gandharva glances at the saliva dripping from the hounds and their terrible eyes, and he shivers. Matali comes to a decision.

"You are an advisor to Lord Yama," he says, his eyes downcast. "You are his greatest counselor and a messenger. The quill you wield is no ordinary instrument. It records the good and evil actions of every life, and with your account, Yama decides his judgment of each immortal soul."

"Yet you lot are not immortal souls, are you?" Chitragupt says softly. "You are *immortals*. Celestials. Very curious."

Matali jerks up, and starts to speak, tripping over his own words, describing in great detail how our arrival here is a mistake, but Chitragupt's hound snarls and the gandharva falls silent.

"This is beyond me," he says to the other riders. "We must present these interlopers to Yama."

I feel faint hearing this. Yama is fierce and unyielding, a monster that the citizens of Amaravati fear even more than asuras from patala. He is the lord who weighs each soul's karma upon death to decide whether it must go to swarga, or remain in hell. Celestials with our immortality confound his judgment; he hates us.

Matali sways, and Nanda utters a whimper. We begin to babble, but our protests mean little. Pushed and prodded by the riders, we are bound by thick rope and thrown over a hound each. I choke, inhaling the creature's terrible stench. I utter Indra's name in my mind, praying for the wind of Amaravati to rescue us, but there is no answer. We are far from heaven, abandoned, and each one of us knows it.

CHAPTER 8

The first few minutes, all I can do is try to catch my breath. The riders begin down a path, winding their way past the thorny pillars and out of the cave. The light that nearly blinded me and my companions mutes to a dull glow, circling the entire party. I feel my heart pound in my chest, and though I try to pay attention to the quiet conversation of the riders, the grunts and occasional howl from the hounds make it impossible to understand what the riders are saying.

My rising terror threatens to unhinge me. I cannot shake the memory of Kaushika outside our hut, his face desperate, and a dangerous conviction in his eyes, close to madness. He is furious, and echoes of his words circle me. *If you hurt her . . .* Rambha saw something in those words that she will use. She nearly killed him, and it was only my half-heard warning that saved his life. Fear clutches my heart, both for me now and for Kaushika. I want to rely on my training from the hermitage, but I cannot find the calm to attempt any of the yogic exercises that can help me. My mind gravitates constantly toward what will become of us and how we have come to be here.

We pass caverns and canyons, going deeper into the bowels of the earth. Glistening stalactites made of writhing worms rise like massive anthills. Chasms break open on our path abruptly, and I swallow my cries. Though the riders navigate the terrain expertly, seeming to know where the next abyss will open, I am completely disoriented. Every now and then, a bloodcurdling scream of terror echoes from the surrounding caverns, pain and torture coiled through it.

Sweat drips down my temples and back. My friends and I must find a way to escape, not merely to accomplish our mission and all that it entails, but because we will not survive here. We are weapons of swarga, we are not soft creatures, but this place is the antithesis of everything we are. If we linger here, our magic will fade, like a flower kept too long in the dark, losing its beauty and potency.

The hunt arrives at the palace, and it is only because I know where we're headed that I realize what this place is. I have been within Indra's bastion, which is resplendent like the lord. Mortal palaces have ranged from luxurious to bare. The one in naraka is different from them all.

We enter through a cave mouth, dripping with dank water. The minute we are within it, an eerie silence rebounds in my ears. I can no longer hear the screams from the rest of this godforsaken realm, but I almost wish for those sounds because the silence is too heavy, swirling with terrible magic. In my mind, I see the eyes of my marks, the glazed features, their thrall-like movements. They seem more dead than alive, and I have to blink several times to remind myself that they are not really here. It is the silence and the dark magic of this place creating this vision in my mind.

The cave leads us into a stark, gray hallway. Firelight flickers in wall sconces, and my heart leaps on seeing it—Lord Agni is here; he can help us. Yet even before I can utter a silent prayer begging him to intervene, I know that he will not hear us. This firelight is Agni in his elemental form, controlled by the hellish creatures against his will. The real lord rests in Amaravati, protected behind the city's gates. If Indra cannot hear us, neither can Agni.

Nanda, Matali, and I are forced to dismount. We are marched through a cold hallway that twists and turns like a labyrinth, until we arrive at what can only be a throne room, yet this chamber, this realm—they are the exact opposite of Indra's swarga and my home. A shadowy power echoes in the air, a keening sound that sets the hairs on my neck standing.

The thick magic plays havoc with my eyes. Rock walls engorge and diminish, filling my vision as though about to smother me. An unearthly light flows in the air, waving like smoky fumes, and the scent here is cold, like that of a mildewed grave. I shrink further into myself, clutching the tether from Amaravati for some comfort, yet everything here reeks of death. I catch a glimpse of my companions. Nanda's face is full of terror, her eyes wide like two moons. Matali is faring no better, his mouth opening and closing soundlessly as he looks around us. His eyes meet mine, and he shakes his head once. I want to ask him what he means but of course, I cannot; I simply try to contain my own dread.

We are pushed and hustled along the cavernous hall toward the twisted throne. Lord Yama sits there, his fierce countenance turned into a frown. Next to him is a mortal, dressed in simple clothes, hair in a topknot. If I did not know any better, I would think Yama is in conference with a sage. Indeed, I overhear part of their conversation as we approach.

". . . but is that a good act?" Yama muses, "if it is done with the wrong intention? Or perhaps it is the intent that matters, for the consequences of most acts are beyond mortal and divine control, thus—"

He abruptly stops as he notices the hunt, and raises a brow.

Yama is ferocious. His skin is dark leather, and his mouth is fanged, two golden hooks at the end of each fang ringed with bone jewelry. His eyes are dark silvery slits, which watch us shrewdly. Unlike Indra he wears no crown, declaring who he is. Yet there is no need to. Even seated, he is a giant, towering over all of us, nearly ten feet tall, his body muscled and hairy like a beast. He wears a black dhoti and is bare-chested, and around his neck burns a garland made of blue embers. It lights into orange fire, singeing the air, scenting it with funereal smoke.

Yama's one hand, ringed with more bone jewels, rests on his knee. In his other is a noose, corded with cruel blades. It is the whip with which he drags immortal souls to naraka to serve their term if their actions warrant it. He is to naraka what Indra is to swarga; I can discern similarities, in the insouciant and self-assured way Yama holds himself, a part of prakriti. His aura is a magnificent halo, surrounding his entire frame, casting a dark light around him. Scented with a sheer otherness, like stagnant water and withering diseases, his power makes me nauseous.

I shake where I stand, my mind crowding. I feel judged in Yama's very presence, my mind jumping to every terrible thing of my past, every perverted thought. I am a failed apsara. I have never been as devoted to Indra as I should have been. I am a coward—too spineless to speak honestly to Kaushika when given a chance, too naïve to see his seduction. I have failed over and over again, and now Nanda is in danger once more because of me; my whole city and realm are in danger. Tears clog my throat.

Yama nods to the mortal next to him, who rises and disappears in a swirl of smoke. Alone on the dais again, the lord of death beckons all of us closer. My guards prod me, and I'm pushed along with the other two celestials, while Yama's creatures fill his throne room to watch the spectacle. Matali bows low. Following his example, Nanda and I do so as well. Chitragupt alone of the hunt climbs the short stairs to the dais. He murmurs something to the lord, then takes his place by Yama's side. The lord flicks his whip once in intrigue.

"Two apsaras and one gandharva," Yama says softly. "Some of Indra's most prized possessions. Here?"

His choice of words sends a chill through me. That is how he would see us, neither as celestials nor as fellow immortals, but as something to be used, perhaps discarded. I've fought with Lord Indra, but he has never treated us in such a demeaning manner. Yama, lord of death, would kill our dignity too.

I keep my eyes lowered. Next to me, I feel the other two quake.

"They say it's a mistake," Chitragupt says, laughing.

"No mistake," Yama replies. "Not with their kind. Sent here as punishment, perhaps? And yet they are not dead. A cruel jape by their lord, if this is the case, but then again, Indra is crueler than people think. He sends them to a place he would fear."

Chitragupt lets out an amused huff. "You have always wanted this, lord. A unique challenge to judge the karma of Amaravati's people. They have always considered themselves above your judgment before. You've been presented with a gift."

"Or a test," Yama says. "It is convenient, wouldn't you say? Indra presenting a gift to me?"

Chitragupt hums, then falls silent. I wonder what silent communication is passing between them, and risk glancing up. Chitragupt is observing the three of us silently, his stance impassive, but Yama leans forward, his gaze abstracted, as though he is seeing beyond what any of us can see. A smile of relish plays on his fanged mouth, making me anxious. *Reveal your lust,* I think, before I can stop myself, and a horrifying image comes to me—Lord Yama standing over a weakened, wasted Indra, his foot on Indra's chest and the noose tightening over the deva's throat. Behind them is the smoke of battle, the scent of corpses, and even as I watch, Indra seems to fade, diminishing into golden dust.

I gasp against my will. Hastily, I drop my eyes again, but Yama hears me and turns in my direction. He rises to his feet, and next to me, Matali utters a soft moan. Yama's footsteps echo in the cavernous hall as he climbs down the dais, and then he pauses before me. Something glints at the edge of my vision, a dark glitter, hell's magic, and I feel a slithering over my skin. I tremble.

"Look at me, child," the lord says.

Nervously, I raise my eyes to him.

"You are unique," Yama says quietly. "You have been touched by Shiva."

Images bloom and fade behind my eyes, of my life within Kaushika's hermitage. I see myself speaking with Anirudh and Kalyani about the nature of devotion. I remember that time within Shiva's temple when Kaushika and I bared our souls to each other, not knowing that was what we were doing. I feel Kaushika's skin whisper over mine. I feel him leaning forward, his fingers interlacing with my own. The thought of him now, in danger from Rambha, sends a spiral of pain through me, and I hear his voice from my memory. *Converse with yourself, Meneka.* I jerk back to where I am, eyes widening.

Yama watches me quizzically. My memories of Shiva are intertwined with my feelings for Kaushika, yet it has been little more than a month since I sat around the tapasvin fire, speaking with the Lord of Destruction. It was the most profound experience of my life, yet Shiva never terrified me the way Yama does. The Destroyer is far more powerful than the lord in front of me, burning illusions and capable of breaking the very cycle of birth and death that nourishes prakriti.

But Yama *owns* death. For the brief period between birth and rebirth, souls must obey his dictates. Not even Shiva can change or challenge that—it is wrought into the fabric of the three realms, as surely as Indra's own presence in swarga. Yama's magic does not show him everything, only pieces of my past, allowing him to sift through them as though flipping through a book whose language he cannot quite read. What does he make of what he saw?

Yama's gaze travels from me to my companions. "These two are bound to you. I can see the strands weaving your lives together."

I receive an image behind my eyes, the very same one that Yama is seeing. Golden tendrils of light dance between Matali, Nanda, and me. At first I think it is simply Amaravati's magic, swirling around us, coating us. Then the image grows clearer, and I notice that each tendril is a luminous bond, crafted like a chain link. These are the bonds of karma, of cosmic cause and effect, the very same element that Yama uses to judge souls.

I startle, staring at my companions. Nanda is bound to me because I rescued her from Kaushika's curse. But Matali . . .

Oh. *Matali* was one of the gandharva ambassadors sent to treat with Kaushika. I know this beyond doubt. When Matali failed to stop Kaushika's vengeful plan against Indra, it was necessary to send other apsaras, including myself. That I was the one to finally tame Kaushika . . . It has created an unseen link between us. I realize that Matali is here on this mission not only to report my actions to Indra, but to redeem himself.

Yama's eyes glint in triumph, and I shrink back. He has shared this vision with me for a reason, allowing me to see from his own eyes. The lord of death has been watching my reactions, and it has given him crucial information about me. I do not know what he will do with it, but my own apsara magic allows me to see into people's lust. I have destroyed lives with it. Yama could do so much worse. A thread of fear coils around my heart. Yama nods thoughtfully, and moves from me to Matali.

The gandharva keeps his eyes downcast, but Yama utters a small chant and a streak of rebellion goes through Matali's body, straightening his spine. Just for an instant, the singer is surrounded by a hundred instruments, each of them minuscule, each exploding within his aura like magnificent weapons, the sitar, the tabla, the flute, creating a symphony that dazzles me.

Then the image is gone, and Matali gasps as though this response has been forced out of him. Lord Yama grins. "Your secrets intrigue me, singer," he says, before moving on toward Nanda.

A soft cry gurgles from Nanda's throat. The sound catches my heart, and I attempt to move, but I am frozen in terror, only able to watch as the death lord descends upon her.

Nanda is shaking so hard, her aura wobbles around her, saccharine honey and burned rose petals. Yama regards her for a long second, then his brows knit together.

"Oh, child," he murmurs. "You are familiar with hell already, are you not?"

I am shocked to see a sunken sympathy on his beast-like features, but it must be a trick of the dim light, for the next moment, avarice and intrigue grow in his voice. Yama sweeps away from Nanda and returns to the dais. Chitragupt whispers something in his ear, and the lord nods, eyeing each of us in turn. His aura bristles, and he crosses his legs, leaning back.

"Why are you here?" he says shortly. "The truth now, children."

Nanda and I both look at Matali. He is our guide, the leader of this mission, but Matali simply turns a sickly color. "We got lost," he says. "We were headed for patala, my lord, and I must have sung the wrong chant, uttered the wrong directions. Most humbly, my lord, we beg your forgiveness for this intrusion."

The words sound deceitful even to my ears. Matali is too self-possessed about his talent for this to ring sincere. Chitragupt grins, and Yama merely sighs and says to him conversationally, "See how easily these creatures lie. Yet mortals fear *us* in hell, glamoured by their pretty faces. Tell me, who is the real danger of these realms?"

Matali sputters, trying to protest, but Yama forestalls him.

"You attempt to protect your lord," he says. "That is a noble endeavor, but arriving here is no mistake. He controls the winds of Amaravati, does he not? He wishes you to suffer. All I wish to know is why."

Still, none of us speak. I suspected Indra of sending us here too, but does the lord hate me and Kaushika so much? He sent Rambha to kill Kaushika, while getting rid of me in naraka, pretending to extend a hand of friendship. It feels so convoluted, and I do not believe that he faked his fear of the asuras and the deterioration of Amaravati. I cannot believe he would risk Matali in such a way. Until I am sure, there is no benefit to speaking. Yama hunts Indra—I saw into his lust. The lord of death would only use Indra's fragility against Amaravati. Different though our allegiances are, my companions and I are united by purpose: We do not wish harm on our city. So all of us keep silent, despite Yama's expectant glare.

He shakes his head as if disappointed. "Very well, let's play this through. What is occurring in swarga that you're sent to patala, three of you together, no less? Does the Vajrayudh not approach?" A slow smile of delight spreads on Yama's leathery face. "Is Indra *scared* this time? Does he send you on a mission of aid?"

I do not have to look at my companions. I can sense their alarm, like a ripple in the air. Our devotion to Indra ranges from pure obedience to considered defiance, but we all have loved him. The sly delight in Yama's voice raises my hackles. We all shake our heads furiously, tripping over our words, like children caught stealing honey.

"Oh no, no," Matali breathes, smiling a weak smile. "We are sent as, ah, as entertainers. To sing and dance, as an, ah, an indication of swarga's beauty."

It is so unbelievable, dressed as Nanda and I are, that Yama laughs and his demons stamp their feet, shaking the cavern. Yama cracks his noose and gestures to a rakshasa guard, a creature with a wolf's mouth and the body of a man. "Search them."

I cringe as the beast approaches us roughly, its long-nailed paws scratching at our clothes. Matali secretes several packages of gold and silver, gifts presumably for his conquests in patala. Nanda's ordeal is swift and futile, revealing nothing of importance, even within the bag she carries. But to my chagrin, the wolf-beast snatches at my wrist with its sharp nail and holds up the bracelet from Shachi. I yelp, trying to grab it, but at a gesture from the lord, the beast takes it up to the dais.

Yama accepts it wordlessly, picking it up with a lazy finger.

The moment Yama touches it, the bracelet opens in a flood of light. I cry out a warning, reminded of the halahala at the hermitage—there is a terrible, ominous shade to the light, freezing the instant, similar to that time. Yet instead of poison, something else pours out of the bracelet. A song that sinks its notes into my heart, tugging at me. I exchange a wild, puzzled look with the other two celestials, but they look just as confused as I feel.

Yama's expression changes.

He grows alert, sitting up straight, all his levity and callous laziness forgotten, staring at the bracelet.

"My lord?" Chitragupt asks.

"They dare?" Yama growls, and his hands curl into fists. "They dare judge *me*?" His visage becomes terrifying, a roar erupting from him, shaking the hall. "Who sent this message?" he demands, turning to me. "Who coded it? What do they want from me?"

I recoil, and Nanda utters a half sob. Matali begins to chant a mantra, instruments spinning around him, the sarangi, and dhol, and the bamboo bansuri, in a vain attempt to charm and pacify the lord of death with music.

It makes no difference. Yama's magic is too strong. It sweeps over us, locking our limbs before we can scatter or perform. His gaze livid, he rises from his throne, gesturing to his guards. "Take them to the questioning chamber. Let us see if that won't extract truths from their lips."

CHAPTER 9

The questioning chamber is a long, dark hall, swimming in gloom.

A sickly green light pours into the chamber from somewhere below. It is so disorienting when compared to Amaravati, where light pours in from stars above, that I am momentarily confused. I blink to clear my head, and the chamber spins in my vision, but in moments, my eyes adjust. I see that the chamber is actually a hallway filled with grotesque sculptures of mortals in pain, their limbs rearranged. Paintings of chimerical creatures writhe in unbelievable shapes, and murals showing divine creatures impaled on blades wreak havoc on my mind.

I press my body close to the other two celestials as we're thrust inside. I hear my own terrified breathing echoed in them. Nanda is trembling so hard that her body is vibrating, her aura sharp and brittle. Matali gives me a wide-eyed look. The guards push us in and leave. It seems a bad sign, and I attempt to go after them, explain our innocence, but the door shuts before I can move.

Something moves at the edge of my vision—a coiling creature of smoke, talons, and teeth. Around it, other creatures form like a pack of wolves, hunting us, even as the three of us press our backs together to keep the hellish beasts in sight. I spin out an illusion of golden dust at the same time as Nanda does. Matali is singing under his breath, a fierce, fiery chant, meant to emphasize the celestial magic of apsaras. Our magic combines and takes form, becoming Indra's lightning. It pierces the gloom toward the creature, but the beasts disappear in a snarl of smoke—only to reappear on another side of the chamber, continuing to hunt.

"Heavenly creatures," Yama says, his voice tight. "You do like to see matters only as you wish, not as they are."

I turn to see where he is. I did not know he followed us in here, but he moves through the chamber in a rush of magic, one second looming behind us, the next far away. I glimpse his face, full of terrible retribution, even as more creatures break away from the marble sculptures, coming alive, prowling and slithering toward us. I shoot out illusory lightning from my fingertips, trying to keep them at bay. It is ineffectual. They simply re-form, nightmares made solid.

"We do not know what that message was," I say. "The bangle is a mere trinket, meant as a reminder of home."

I do not know why I am protecting Shachi, but the thought of giving Yama information on anyone in swarga terrifies me. If Shachi thought to protect me, I cannot give her away. I can only hope that whatever was in the bangle informed her of our dire situation. Perhaps it was a charm, unleashed if I was in danger. If so, she might be attempting to send aid already.

Yama's roar cracks the floor. Snakes and worms ripple from the abyss toward us.

His form becomes clearer, and smoke curls around him,

growing into a thousand arms, reaching for us. I feel the other two tense next to me, our backs touching as we spin out illusion and song to deter and distract his magic. Nothing we do makes any difference.

Yama spins Shachi's bracelet in his hand, scowling. I try to watch the dark magic he has unleashed, even as I shoot another dusting of gold at the creatures snapping at me. I must think of a way out by using what I have learned. Yama became furious after the bracelet opened. He said the bracelet questioned him, a king. What could Shachi have embedded in it to anger this god, one who is removed from patala? If the charm inside was for my protection, why has it only landed us in more danger?

It is as though the lord hears my thought. His fierce animal-like head snaps toward me, and he advances, cleaving his way through the hellish pack of creatures.

I quail, readying my magic to slow him down somehow, but before I can think of how, his power spins toward me, and I cannot breathe. Bands of black fumes coil around my body, viselike. I gasp, thrashing, and Nanda utters a cry, reaching for me, but both she and Matali are trapped in similar bands, all of us lifted clean off our feet.

"You continue to lie and deceive," Yama says, angrily. "That is what creatures from heaven do, is it not?"

The words are an echo of what Kaushika once accused me of. Despite the black rope of smoke nearly smothering me, I am taken aback. Uncannily, all of this reminds me of Kaushika— the use of the wild creatures, the anger, the righteous power. Yama turns toward me, and knowing that he can see pieces of my past, I try to dismiss any thought of Kaushika, but it is too late. I have already shown Yama my weakness; I have shown him the shape of my heart.

"The answers lie within you," Yama intones. "You *will* tell me."

Yama curls his claws. Magic eddies around him, dark and dense. I receive a glimpse of Matali and Nanda, raised up in bands of smoke, their heads thrown back, each under an enchantment. I focus on my power from Amaravati, on my tapasvin fire, and Kaushika's crescent comb in my hair burns, responding to my desperation.

Then—

Something immense, something sacred and powerful, reflects my own soul in an endless pool of silvery water.

The pool surrounds me, braided with an arcane magic, and for an instant I swim within it, a nymph of heaven, and my heart sings in recognition.

Everything changes around me.

I am no longer in naraka.

The scent in the breeze, the sunlight warming my skin, the sweet melody of the birds, all flood my senses. I am back in the mortal realm. Back in the forest where I lived with Kaushika. This is another enchantment, like the one I found myself in earlier. Terrible danger has unlocked this magic from within me. As before, I have no control over it; I do not even understand it. I am not prepared for it now any more than I was before, but I part the leaves in front of me. My heart is racing. Cold sweat beads my skin in the remembered terror of what I witnessed here before. My head spins, and in a corner of my mind, I see remnants of darkness and terror, and hate-filled monsters stalking me. My body shivers, as if I am about to take sick.

Beyond the trees, I see the hut where Kaushika waits for me. I take a deep breath, feeling the golden sunlight on my skin. My steps quicken as I approach the hut. I open the door and step inside—and freeze.

Kaushika is within, but he is not alone. His arms are loose by his side, and his eyes are hooded. A small frown mars his handsome face, but he does not resist as another woman—an apsara—twirls around him, golden dust flickering from her fingers, released by a mudra.

At first, what I see makes no sense. I am looking at my own body. The way this apsara lifts her chin, the tilt of her head, the soft sashaying. It is unnerving to see myself this way, but then I realize I am looking at Rambha. She looks like me, yet there are parts of her in this image too. It is as though I am seeing a melding of her and me, distorted. I appear a thousand times more beautiful, a million times more devoted.

Everything is edged with mesmerizing blurriness. Her clothes, her stance, even her mudras are all ones I have used, yet there is a sharpness in her magic that is entirely her own, a potency and danger like that of a cobra, twining around her and Kaushika. The tilt of her cunning smile cuts me. The flash of victory in her eyes haunts me. Rambha rakes her teeth slowly over her lower lip, luscious and kissable, contemplating her prey. I watch this occur in frozen alarm. This is Rambha through and through, but it is me too. I am looking at what I would have been had I followed in her footsteps.

I shut the door behind me with a bang. This time I am close enough to *make* Kaushika hear me. I stride forward and grab his arm. I feel the tension of his muscles. I smell the camphor and rosewood of his skin, and the pulsating strength of his magic beating beneath his veins in a rhythmic song. He is so familiar that tears spring to my eyes.

He doesn't look toward me. Gently, I tug, denying the horrible realization that is curling through my mind. "Kaushika," I whisper, unable to speak any louder, through the choking of my throat. "It's me. Meneka. I'm here."

He does not respond. His eyes remain on Rambha. She does not look toward me either. A sound of frustration escapes me. Like before, they cannot see or hear me. Though I am here, witnessing this, *feeling* the solidity of my love, I am not in the forest or in the hut, but in some terrible middle space between the mortal and immortal realms. I am a wraith, condemned.

A sob of despair rises to my throat. I tug Kaushika again, more forcefully. "Snap out of it," I say. "Kaushika, listen to me."

He frowns more deeply. Rambha—my sister, my mirror, this sharp reflection of my own soul—smiles as she swans closer to him, all poison and charm.

"We are devoted to each other, are we not?" she says softly, running a crimson-painted finger down his cheek.

"You know I would tear the three realms apart for you, Meneka," he says.

His voice is his own, yet dull. He speaks words of heat and passion, and I have heard of those who aspire to hear such things from the ones they love, yet tears rush to my eyes. Memories come to me of marks who have whispered such things to *me*. Queen Tara, who destroyed her kingdom because of me. Nirjar, who flayed himself, and Ranjani, who committed great crimes toward her own people. Thralls, all of them. Why is Kaushika saying this?

I step forward in panic, trying to place myself between him and Rambha, but though I have been able to touch him, whatever magic is at play here prevents me from coming between them. This is no dream. This is truly happening, and I am here, forced to watch it, the worst version of hell that I could ever conceive.

Rambha smiles and twists her body alluringly, her wrists turning from one mudra to another. The golden dust of Amaravati pours from her jewels—from *my* jewels, the ones that Queen Shachi gave *me* to seduce Kaushika. Dressed as she is in my clothes and my skin, she is my nightmare realized.

Because in that space between wakefulness and sleep, while I have been ensconced in Kaushika's arms, I have idly wondered. Wondered if I could have ever seduced him the way Indra once sent me to, the way Shachi charged me to, if I did not love him. Wondered if Kaushika would ever have been able to resist me, had I unleashed my magic. He is powerful, but I have learned of myself too, and the games we have played with each other have always been tinged with the undercurrent of my unfulfilled mission. Rambha is showing me what I could have been, what I *should* have been, and terrible shame cords through me.

Kaushika's fingers are pressed into tight fists, tight enough to draw blood despite his blunt nails. I touch his arm, and attempt to prize open his fingers. "I love you," I whisper. "I *know* you. This is not the shape of our devotion, Kaushika. Listen to me. *Hear* me. We—*you*—are better than this." My last words are a choked sob.

Kaushika looks up at Rambha. "You have always been my moral guide."

"I am," Rambha says, smiling.

I am, I think, wretched.

"And you think I should turn my magic inward?" Kaushika asks, brows furrowed.

"Shiva does so, does he not?" Rambha says, cocking her head. "Tapasya is the yogi's way, and it is because Shiva turns his power inward that he retains it."

"It is," Kaushika murmurs, still frowning. "Yet I have never claimed to be as powerful as the Destroyer."

"Do you not wish to be the best of all yogis anymore?" Rambha challenges, speaking in my voice. "My love, you once made a meadow in another realm, creating another heaven. You protected Kalyani and the hermitage from halahala. You even defeated Indra, or would have, had events allowed you to." Rambha smiles, and her teeth are sharp, edged in glorious venom. "You can do anything," she whispers, leaning close to him, her breath lingering in his ear. "Anything at all."

Her fingers spin, manifesting visions only she and Kaushika can see.

How does Rambha know anything of tapasya, the sages' method of magic? How does she know anything of Kaushika's reverence to Shiva? What is she encouraging him to do and why?

As fire races across Kaushika's skin, the answers dawn on me.

I once reported on Kaushika's doings at the hermitage to Rambha, who acted as heaven's emissary. She delighted in the way I sowed confusion in the minds of the yogis back in the hermitage, when I was still intent on my mission to seduce Kaushika for Indra. My words set me on a path of self-learning—but Rambha has remembered all that I have told her, and is using the knowledge.

Of course, she did not come here to seduce Kaushika without preparing for it in every way. She has taken everything I told her, and now is spurring Kaushika to become like Shiva himself. She knows that powerful though he is, this is beyond him. Shiva is the Lord of the Universe, that is why he can turn the magic of the cosmos within himself, breaking the cycle of karma to view the universe in its entirety. Attempting to do anything similar will destroy Kaushika. Instead of killing him herself, she is letting him do the deed on his own.

I watch, horrified, as golden flames lick across Kaushika's dark skin. His face is awash with light, but his eyes are turned inward, pushing his magic deeper inside. My hands rise, trying to touch him—but his heat is too strong, it engulfs me, forcing me back.

"Kaushika," I cry, tears running down my face. I cannot believe this is happening. This must be untrue. "Kaushika, please. Don't do this. You know this isn't the way."

Flames course over his body. His magic does not burn him yet, but Rambha twists her wrists and dances in front of him, her eyes ablaze, reflecting his light, and I know it is only a matter of time before he destroys himself.

In desperation, I seize Amaravati's magic, yanking at the tether behind my navel. My wrists curl, and I create a counterillusion, one that reflects to Kaushika the true bliss he and I have shared.

My illusion does not lock. Instead, in this middle space, I catch a glimpse of the illusion Rambha is carving. I see Kaushika standing over Indra, the lord's vajra in his hand. The lightning bolt is poised at Indra's throat, and Kaushika's eyes gleam in vengeance and retribution and fury, to finally bring this hated deva down to his knees. The illusion shimmers, then disappears, taking my own carving with it.

I stare at Kaushika aflame, and see in his eyes the torment of being made to choose between his vow to King Satyavrat and the one he made to me. I see his hatred for Indra and his disregard for swarga. I see his love for me, holding him back from doing something regrettable. This same love has made him vulnerable, and flames lick his fingers and shoulders, rushing green and golden over his throat and face. Even Rambha steps back, and I think, *This is it. He will immolate himself, in thrall to her.* She has charmed him in the deadliest way possible, perverting his desire and wisdom, spurring his weakest self on, turning his own knowledge of the cosmos against him.

I have always dreaded it, and Rambha is showing me.

That the power of her illusion is greater than the power of my love.

A sob rips through my chest.

"No!" I cry, and yank at the cord connecting me to Amaravati. My rage, my helplessness, my despair, pour into it. I hear Kaushika say from a lifetime ago, *Feed who you truly are into your devotion*, and I do. My failure as an apsara, my anger with Indra, my suspicion of Shachi, and all of my loneliness. Tapasvin magic bursts within me, my prana braiding with the golden power of Amaravati. The crescent comb in my hair feels like it is on fire. Something flashes behind my eyes, an enormous force resembling a silvery pool of water. I grasp this strange magic unthinkingly, uttering the first chant that comes to my mind in an attempt to take Kaushika away from this place.

Kaushika jerks back, clear-eyed. The flames subside from his body. He turns to me, finally seeing me, and it is as though I am watching myself from his eyes. I appear a phantom to him, a specter in the mist, a being of water and vapor.

"Meneka?" he says.

"It's not possible," Rambha breathes, able to see me as well.

Kaushika turns toward her, and understanding floods his features. His eyes grow furious, and a whip of fire rises from him, coiling around Rambha's throat. He reaches for me in the same moment, but the chant I am uttering finally locks.

A portal opens across the worlds, like a window with three sides.

Kaushika and Rambha in front of me in the mortal realm. And behind naraka and Yama's surprised, calculating gaze.

Another realm beckons, one with sweet air, and my power surges in me. It is too much to hold this three-sided portal open. I cry out, and Matali and Nanda tear through their smoke chains to run, sobbing, toward me. I reach out and grab Matali's hand. With my other hand, I attempt to snatch Nanda, but she trips and falls, even as the hounds surround her.

The gateway shivers, beginning to close. I tug hard, and Matali and I fall through one side, sucked by the portal's power. Nanda, Kaushika, and Rambha diminish behind us, left to their own nightmares.

CHAPTER 10

I do not know where we arrive.

The world spins in my eyes, and nausea rises through me. I clutch Matali's hand in mine, disoriented. He weeps next to me, and the both of us land on soft grass, dropping to our knees, huddling. Scents drift to me, lotus and petrichor, threaded with a fresh morning frost. We are on a small hill, and the grass below our feet sways, curling around our ankles lovingly. Marigolds undulate in a soft breeze, but they are not the kind I am accustomed to. These flowers are ringed with white, their petals twice the size of any flowers I have seen in the mortal realm. Sweet music whispers in the air, as though the landscape is singing and greeting us. I stare, unable to comprehend this sudden beauty, and Matali recovers from his weeping swiftly, humming in surprised appreciation.

Below us is a forest, dark green and misty. Tendrils of fog rise from the trees, blue and purple, and fireflies twinkle in the air. Cascades of light form and die in the distance like starlight is captured in this realm and made to shine in pleasing ways. Everywhere I look, I see glistening ponds and lakes, silver gleams that dissolve into shadow the more I try to arrest them with my eyes. I glance above, and the sky is a riot of shifting blues and purples—no true sky, but a glittering illusion of one. In truth, the entire realm is edged with a strange enchantment. I try to capture details but they buzz away from my mind, for though this place is beautiful, it is unfamiliar too, and I do not belong here. Still, we are no longer in naraka. There is no foulness in the air, and all through the landscape, a silvery light shines as though moonbeams have been netted and jeweled within rock and grass and soil.

I clutch Amaravati's tether to me, and it flares with power. Beguiled as I am by the sudden beauty, it takes me a moment to gather myself, to understand what has happened. I was in the mortal realm. I saw Rambha seduce Kaushika. He was in thrall. Was it a vision of hell, meant to torture me, a punishment by Lord Yama? Did I break him out of his enslavement, or does he still suffer? The chant I uttered was one that Kaushika taught me, but though I have escaped naraka, I have left someone behind.

Nanda! "We have to go back," I say.

"How did you do that?" Matali asks at the same time. The gandharva has gathered himself too, and his expression is avid like he cannot believe where we are. "This is patala. You have brought us to the underworld. What magic did you do? That chant—*teach* me."

His gaze is avaricious, and a slow, curious smile is climbing his face, but I brush him aside. I breathe deeply, trying to feel my prana in the dewdrops of my heart.

"Nanda," I say. "She is—she is—"

"Still in naraka," Matali replies, sobering. His mouth draws into a frown, and bells appear in his hand, ringing like a funeral dirge. I know him enough to see his sorrow in the melody. No matter his agenda for Lord Indra, he is aghast at leaving our sister behind too.

I search for my magic. Amaravati's tether pulses with golden power, but my prana from my fledgling tapasya is completely spent. Even without trying, I know I am not capable again of the kind of magic that I just did. I do not know for certain *what* I did. It happened on its own, similar to the other times. I have been learning of this braided magic, but my training has been slow, my aptitude too limited. Tears shimmer in my eyes, and I stare at Matali.

"We must do something," I say, my voice trembling.

"We must rest," Matali replies flatly. "Then we must be on our way to the palace where we were bound before we detoured to naraka."

"You would leave her behind? You lay with her last night, and you would abandon her?"

Matali takes my hand, patting it softly. "If you want Nanda back, getting help from our allies here is the only way. Look, there, in the distance. That is where we must go."

I see where he points. Far beyond the forest and hills rise golden sun-bathed mountains. I blink, for if this is patala, then surely that is not sunshine I see on the mountaintops. Surya would not shine in the underworld.

Then I realize that the mountains are made of gold, *true* gold, even more than I have seen in swarga. Nestled within them is a glimmer of silver. My sight tries to seize it, but the vista defies entrapment. It blurs and shimmers, and all I can see are glimmering patches of silver-wrought windows, spires that curl like glass, and the occasional flock of startled birds wheeling around the mountains. I stare, trying to make out the shape of a structure, but it disappears, merged with the landscape. It is as though whatever secrets and beauty the mountains are hiding are too much for my eyes to behold, celestial though I am.

"Queen Shachi's palace," Matali confirms. "You have brought us to Puloma, her kingdom. Have you ever seen anything as magical?"

His voice is a wistful sigh, and a small harp appears in his hands. He plucks at the strings, and the melody is so full of longing and ache that my heart swells in unrestrained emotion, despite the circumstances of our arrival.

Matali begins to walk down the hill toward the forest. Slowly, I follow, the questions within me circling again.

How is it that we are here? If I opened the portal, why did it not take me to Amaravati? It must be because my mind was on Shachi's bangle, instead of Indra. Does that mean I can return us to Amaravati if I only replenish my tapasvin magic and focus on Indra? Matali and I have arrived at our original destination by accident, but we do not have our belongings anymore, nor the bracelet that was supposed to keep me safe in patala. Without any of these, we are interlopers; our welcome here is likely to be as hostile as the one we received in naraka. I shudder, wanting to voice this, but Matali has already reached a clearing, humming to himself. He beckons me, beginning to gather sticks for firewood.

I am too entrenched in grief and confusion to find more words.

We make camp.

OUR PROGRESS IS SLOW. EACH DAY, WE WALK A LITTLE farther, and I let Matali lead the way. Time moves in strange ways here. The palace looms at times, close enough to touch and distinguish the shapes of the guards. At other times, it broods far away, cold as ice and ineffable. The path we take meanders like a river. I rip my clothes on a thorny bush, leaving behind a patch of white cotton, waving like a pennant. Though we walk for hours on the road, we come upon it again, like the path has circled back. This occurs twice, until Matali advises me to take the ripped cloth with me. I obey, and it is only then that the road moves toward the palace. I am being told not to *litter*. The realm is watching me.

We come across woods and meadows, hills and fields, and crossroads that lead away into the dim horizon. Once, we come across a still pond where a mysterious singing calls to us, but though Matali, intrigued, wants to explore it, I force him to press on. We travel through mists and dusk, and in my blurred vision I see dancers—sisters—attempting to show me different mudras. Devis flash in my eyes, whispering to me, Shachi, and Parvati, and Durga, and Kali—all the forms of the Goddess. I know it to be a mirage, for we see no one, not even asuras, a fact that only disquiets me.

"It is because this realm recognizes we are not of here,"

Matali says. "It is trying to confuse us, keeping its people away from us while it decides whether we are friend or foe." Far from feeling my uneasiness, the gandharva smiles as though this is a grand adventure.

"You are not scared?" I ask.

Matali flings out an arm. "What is there to fear? We escaped naraka. Patala is dangerous, but here we have allies. We have not been plagued by demons yet, and as long as we are able to find our way to the palace unmolested, we will be safe. You are an apsara, and I am a gandharva—we will not be attacked easily here. Spin us an illusion, and I will craft an enchanting melody, and we will arrive at the golden gates soon enough."

"You expect our welcome at the palace to be warm," I observe, frowning. "Nanda and I were told to be discreet, to find conspirators in patala against Indra. I cannot simply announce myself there."

Matali simply shrugs, unconcerned. "You are with me. You were told to be discreet by Indra, but he sent me to guide you, and after our experience in hell, we can do away with the secrecy and gain some comfort. It will be dangerous if we are caught by a rogue asura in this realm—they do not bear heavenly creatures any more love than we do them. This is why you were given no jewels. Those would only announce who you are. But we must alter our plans now. I will declare us as Indra's envoys, and we will be treated with respect. Your mission to find conspirators will become harder when they know who you are, but at least you will be safe. Shachi lives in swarga, and the palace cannot harm us, not when they know she is Indra's hostage. They will not want to cause a diplomatic incident or have Shachi be harmed in any way. It is thanks to her marriage with the lord that the old wars before the Churning of the Oceans came to an end, after all."

I am intrigued to hear Shachi be called a hostage. I remember her by Indra's side, seated on his lap, smiling her mysterious smiles. She did not appear like a prisoner, nor has she behaved like one, demanding and threatening the lord, even insisting he turn over the apsaras to her. She is the queen of devis, yet Matali—who is Indra's favored devotee—calls her a captive.

Could it be that Shachi simply found a way over the years to make the best of a bad situation? If so, I have been deeply unfair to her. Shachi gave me the lightning blade to protect me. She gave me celestial clothes to assist me. She even sent Nanda to warn me, and all her actions have shown how she wishes me well. I recall what Nanda said to me. *In Shachi, there is kinship . . . There is the grace of femininity, the promise of friendship.* I have indeed forgotten the bonds of sisterhood by viewing her as an enemy. Indra has always pitted apsara against apsara, wanting us to prove our devotion to him. He has done the same thing with Shachi. A rage takes me over that he could make me forget my own kin so easily.

I open my mouth to ask Matali more about Shachi's imprisonment, but the singer has already wandered away from the subject.

"Remember not to gawk when we come to the palace," he says to me, as if I am an uncultured deviant. "There are stories about its beauty that will surprise you. You will see, Meneka, there are beauties here that will make you forget even your mortal lover, and if you partake—and I advise you do—remember that asuras are known to enjoy—"

"What did the lord of death show you?" I ask, interrupting him. Each time I have rested my eyes, I have been troubled with the memory of Kaushika with Rambha. The first time I saw Kaushika, I used the crescent comb, but this time . . . Did I only see my worst fears, or was that vision in the hut a true event, made visible to me by Yama's strange magic? I recall the flash of heat from the comb. I recall the braiding of magic.

"Tell me what he showed you first," Matali answers, watching me shrewdly. I do not reply, and he laughs, his voice a huff. "You have forgotten yourself," he says, strumming his lute.

It is so close to my own thought regarding Shachi that I balk. "I have only forgotten myself because Indra has made me," I snap.

"Indra?" Matali's laugh grows richer. "Did Indra ask you to betray your kin? You fought against your sisters, Meneka. You have been rebellious, betraying not just the lord, but the entire cadre of apsaras. Your love has been selfish, wreaking havoc on your world, and the worst is that you do not seem to care."

His words are venomous, and I cast my mind back to Urvashi, Sarala, Dhriti, and Titollama waiting for me in Amaravati. I think of apsaras fighting one another in the battle. I recall watching my sisters' remains floating into ashes. Matali claims it is devotion to Indra that binds me to my sisters, then what of Shachi and everything the goddess has done for me? What of the battle between Indra and Shachi for the throne? Neither the lord nor the devi made a secret of wanting to rule the apsaras, and I think of Magadhi and Sundari, whom Shachi rescued from seducing Kaushika, my apsara sisters who now are loyal to the queen. The goddess's voice echoes in my mind: *You belong to me.*

There is something hidden within the heart of this that I am not seeing, but I feel pulled by its forces as though I am at the center of it all. Confusion makes me weak, and I stand, swaying.

Matali grabs my hand and pulls me close to him, rising as well. "You worry unnecessarily," he says smoothly. "I know of ways that can soothe you, lovely dancer."

A soft melody radiates around us, like he is making the air sing, in the whispers of leaves, the call of silver birds, the chiming of bells. With each passing day, Matali has left the nightmare of naraka behind, his own gandharva magic becoming stronger, full of vitality and strength. I am reminded that he chose to come on this mission, seeking fame and glory and the joy of conquest. Indra needed someone to watch over me, but Matali volunteered, much like Nanda did.

He pulls me toward him, stroking my hair gently. His thumb grazes my lips, tracing the outline of my mouth. He bends his head to me, beginning to nuzzle my neck, and I stare at the landscape beyond, the beauty that is so different, the allure that is poisonous. Never have I felt so removed from Amaravati as I do now in his presence. That his power has returned to him while my own suffers shows me exactly how confused my devotion is. I pull away and turn my back to him, walking toward a small pool of water glistening through the trees.

"You're no fun anymore!" Matali calls out, but I walk until I can no longer hear his music.

For a while, I do not notice the beauty that surrounds me. I simply close my eyes, and try to breathe in the ways I've been trained to at the hermitage.

Peace eludes me. My mind buzzes with our journey. I see visions of patala behind my closed eyes, the strange twilit magic, and Shachi's palace calling to me. I see Nanda's horrified face, and the demons of hell. I press my hands to my ears, shaking my head, but I can still hear the snarls of the hounds, and Yama's roars. How is my sister faring? What has become of Kaushika? Is he on his way to Amaravati to avenge me? I imagine the destruction of my city by his hands, the fields burning, the mansions decaying. I hear the screams of Amaravati's citizens and the grim chants Kaushika utters, hatred and fury in his voice, all because he seeks vengeance. I see him breaking his oath to me in a mistaken desire to protect me. Worse, I see that I am at fault. Before me, he was suspicious of celestials, but in my desire to lead him to love, I have only made him susceptible to Rambha's seduction.

It is too awful a thought. I wrench my eyes open and force myself to notice the details of the clearing I am in. The pool is ensconced within a patch of radiant silvery stalks that shimmer in the evenlight of this realm. A chirruping sound comes to me, perhaps a squirrel or a small mouse, and it is almost comforting to know that such creatures exist in the underworld, alongside asuras I have yet to see; that they live and are unconcerned with the politics of heaven and earth, and that in the end, we are all small compared to the vastness of the cosmos. When I peer into the pool, I expect to see the moon, for there is a silvery brightness in the air. But of course, Lord Chandra is in heaven, preparing for rest as the Vajrayudh comes. I can almost forget that this is not swarga. If not for the way my tether snags within me, I would not know.

Slowly, I begin to loosen my braid. I unweave the pins Nanda gave me, and let the peace of this place wash over me. The crescent comb falls into my hand, and I stare at it.

Kaushika called it an amplifier, but it did more than simply radiate my power to me. It helped me gain access to pure prana, a feat no other immortal except Indra and his devas can do. The comb allowed me to braid the power of Amaravati with my life force; it helped return my celestial power to me after Indra cut me off from it. There is magic in it, and I have never been able to perform the braided fusion of celestial power and tapasya without it.

It allowed me to open a portal from naraka. Surely if I did it once, I can do so again?

I focus, clutching my tether from swarga within me tightly. With each breath I take, I try to replicate what I did earlier, a careful interweaving of my golden thread with the river of prana—but I have tried this throughout the journey, and the weaving falls apart, dissolving into dust.

I utter a sound of despair and frustration. It is not the braiding alone that I cannot grasp. There is another magic behind the portals opening, one I received a glimpse of before. I viewed it as silvery waters, but when I fully submerged, it resembled a thousand other things: fire and storm, gold and earth, and a luminous radiance that was like looking into the reflection of the cosmos. In some ways, it reminded me of my conversation with Lord Shiva. The Destroyer touched me between my brows; he showed me infinite worlds. *That* is the power I briefly used. How can I access it now?

I stare at the comb, and I imagine Kaushika again. This is his amulet. It connects me to him. And I am an apsara. I can twist reality.

I curl my wrists into a mudra. I begin to carve an illusion—for once, for myself. I see them, two lovers on a frozen pond, a memory from so long ago. Kaushika did not know I was an apsara then. I was charged to seduce him, once and for all. Yet it was on that night that the magic I used to open a portal appeared out of me, without my volition. I watch the illusion, yearning not just for the knowledge of the magic but for Kaushika. I see him come up to me. I watch him remove my jewels one by one, dropping them onto the ice like they are worthless stones. *Powerful though these amulets are*, he says, *you do not need them.* His fingers curl the edge of my sari, and he tugs, unraveling it, removing my clothes. He runs his thumbs over the rising peaks of my nipples, then takes one of them in his mouth. He kneels in reverence, his hands on my hips, and drinks deeply of my sex, tongue flicking between my legs.

I shiver, watching this.

I shiver within the illusion too.

Desire, lust, and despair twine within my heart, locking my throat. I clutch the crescent comb to me, watching as Kaushika continues to pleasure me, his head bowed as though in prayer. We are exquisite and powerful, a sage and an apsara bound to each other. We are hungry and alive, and we have always belonged together. I have always believed our love made us stronger. The illusion confirms this.

Within the illusion, magic explodes out of me.

As though my mind is simply a mirror, sparks cover my fingers that create the mudra. The illusion dissipates, but silvery magic floods me and half hopeful, half scared, I sing the chant to open the portal.

Air ripples, and a light breeze comes to me, scented with camphor and rosewood. The crescent comb trembles in my hand, but I do not drop it. I lean forward, past the glistening, rippling air, and I see him. Not in an illusion, but there, just past the shimmers, close enough to touch. His hair is bound in a sage's topknot, and his eyes are closed, palms resting loose and open on his folded knees. He is meditating, deep within tapasya, and my concentration shivers. A sob climbs my chest, and carefully I reach out a hand, but I do not touch the strange mirror, afraid of dissipating it. I do not know if I have summoned this or if it is simply a dream, a vision of my making.

"Kaushika," I whisper.

His eyes fly open.

There is confusion in them, a strange dullness, and beyond it, the heated will of combat. I recognize it. The same expression a mark makes when deep in thrall, and fighting it. How many marks did I break, those who had the same fight? There is nothing quite like an apsara's magic.

I try to speak, but tears spill from my eyes. All that has happened since I was with him last rushes through me. The abduction from the mortal realm, the resentment and hostility from my apsara sisters, Indra's mission and Shachi's machinations, Yama's test and Rambha's betrayal, Amaravati's decay and naraka's terrors, Matali's flirtations and Nanda's loss—all of it cascades over me, making me shudder helplessly. Kaushika's condition is the worst of it. My magic wobbles, and I stifle a desolate cry. I try to regain control over my emotion. I attempt to remember the yogi's way.

It is too late. The window starts to close.

The air distorts Kaushika's face, but I still see his fear, his panic, his anger. All of it pointed like hatred. Toward me.

Then he is gone, leaving a whisper of camphor in the air.

I bury my head in my hands and weep.

CHAPTER II

Time passes in fitful bursts. Each day I attempt to open the portal again, but the magic does not reveal itself. Each day, we tread more of Shachi's realm, seeing strange wonders in the distance. Giant constructions rise out of the earth, but though we near them, they disappear in a blink, hidden behind magic. I see windmills and watermills, and I am reminded that patala is a realm just below the mortal one. Asuras have taken the workings of mortals for their own, using them in tandem with the magic they possess. Though this realm is immortal, it relies on industry, on machines and human knowledge. It is an outlandish concept compared to heaven where we use the power of the devas and prakriti. Despite its beauty, this place is nothing like Amaravati.

"Would it not be better to return home?" I ask Matali. "Tell Indra what has occurred and ask him to help Nanda? We can restart our mission."

But the gandharva merely shakes his head. "I have tried, and the wind from the city has not heard my call." Matali throws out a hand, and the rings on his finger glint. "Patala has its own protections from swarga, just as swarga has from the underworld. If we are to return to Amaravati, it will have to be from the palace. There are pathways built into the palace to the city's gates."

"And naraka?" I ask. Nightmares of Nanda being tortured infest my sleep. I know I must save my tapasvin magic, but that choice is a betrayal, and my heart grows heavy at the thought of my lost sister.

"Any help we receive will be from Shachi's kin," Matali says relentlessly. "We must be steadfast. Enjoy this beauty, Meneka, and be grateful you are not trapped in hell anymore. We will find aid soon enough."

I do not argue. Matali is rarely serious, but when he is, I would be a fool not to listen. Gandharvas are more than singers and storytellers. They are warriors too, weapons just like apsaras. Indra sent Matali as my guide, and though our slow pace builds an itch under my neck, I obey him, following the path he chooses.

We begin to see asuras dot the landscape, turning over the soil with their strange magic, mining rubies and emeralds, singing in a musical tongue. They are not so different from mortals or celestials, except for their sheer size and changed features. Each appears to be at least ten feet tall, no matter their gender. With my celestial vision, I see their skin of different hues, dark like Shachi's on some, olive and green on others, and pale as the moon on many. All of them have great rounded ears that end in pointed lobes, and nearly all wear jewelry of gold and silver, pierced into their skin over dark eyebrows and along the jaw. An aura of great strength surrounds them, and even from far away, I can tell their beauty.

There is something in their laughter that sinks its teeth into my heart, making me wish to please them. Each of them glimmers like an incandescent sun, so alluring to behold that I find it hard to look away. It is prana, radiating inside their body and sheathing them in a soft armor of light. Each time they move, it appears as though the land is rejoicing in their existence, and I cannot help but think that celestials in swarga have never belonged to their home in the way the asuras do here.

Their beauty is no obvious thing like that of celestials or apsaras. Instead, it lurks within them, aiding their strength, speed, and mannerisms, their every movement an instrument giving voice to the symphony that is patala. I am enchanted, and wish to observe them closer, but it is Matali who helps me exercise caution. He points to their teeth ending in sharp points and their elongated nails, which could easily carve into our delicate skins. Weapons are sheathed on their backs, swords and knives and scythes that end in cruel hooks.

"Not all stories about asuras are wrong," Matali says soberly. "Prone to violence and rage, their magic fueled by the strongest emotions, they can turn on us in an instant. Once they were kin to the celestials in the sky, but it was their harshness and brutality toward their own kind that led them to be divided from us, forcing them to build a home in this realm."

How much brutality against one's own kin can exile one from heaven, I wonder. My judgment of Shachi, my abandonment of Nanda, even my anger against my sisters—are those not a kind of brutality too? I keep my thoughts to myself, and shortly after, we see a fight break out amidst a seemingly gentle trio in a field.

One moment, there is laughter and song, and the next, the song changes to a scream as two asuras attack the third, impaling him with their swords. They carry the still-writhing body between them on their blades, their laughter resumed, disappearing into the near woods. I shudder as I watch, and tighten my hold on my own power, telling myself I would never be as callous toward my sisters, no matter the accusations Matali leveled at me. Disguised under the illusions I carve, Matali and I steer clear of the asuras.

My tether from Amaravati blooms and fades from time to time, though with the hairpins Nanda gave me, I am able to pull enough golden power to protect us. When we stop, I ensconce myself in tapasya, but my focus was never perfect to begin with, and only trickles of the power enter me. After a few failed tries, I do not try to open portals again. I know I must rebuild my magic in order for it to work.

Soon, patala's pastoral lands give way to asura villages and towns. The mountains loom closer, and I realize that they are made of earth and metal, the gold a beautiful gilding, reflecting the majesty of the realm. The palace, now that we're closer, is more like a mortal fortress than the celestial abode of Indra. Built within the mountains, it is a labyrinth, half castle half city. Stone archways rise, circling the foothills, and we come across drawbridges over giant lakes, temples to Shiva and Shakti, and stables housing massive steeds and bulls.

Asuras mill everywhere, in markets and town centers, and

it is bewitching to be in their heady presence, but the danger keeps my mind clear. A drunken fight occurs in front of us, a few male asuras seizing a maiden by her hair and dragging her away. One of them turns to me and Matali, saying something in their strange tongue. I shrink back, not understanding, but Matali laughs and replies, though I hear the strain in his voice. He shakes his head, and I finesse my illusions, and the two of us hasten away before we are asked to partake in the brutality. We wind our way past market stalls gleaming with spices and gemstones until Matali leads us to two guards standing languidly by a diamond-encrusted door.

"Drop your illusion, apsara," he whispers to me.

I obey nervously, but though the guards leap in alertness on seeing our celestial forms, Matali is quick to engage them, speaking in their tongue. The asuras exchange a glance and let us through the door. One of them accompanies us past a fragrant rose garden into a stone hallway covered with embroidered tapestries. I glance at Matali uncertainly, but on entering the palace, his nonchalance returns. He smiles at me, and a playful drum appears in his hands. He taps at it, chatting to the guard, and I have no opportunity to speak with him.

We are led from one hallway into another until we arrive in a narrow open corridor lined with pools of lotuses. Beautiful asura maidens sit at the pools laughing and chatting, and I am reminded of the apsara groves in swarga. The same lotus ponds, the same quiet chatter, the same song of sisterhood—all thrum through these women. I used to once belong to such company, but my sisters in heaven forsook me because of my love of Kaushika. I watch the easy laughter, feeling wretched with homesickness.

My guard beckons to a beautiful demoness, an olive-skinned woman, her ears pierced with several gold earrings. She turns to me, bowing and pressing her palms together in respect.

"My name is Holika," she says, and her voice rumbles like honey and thunder. "Rishi Meneka, I am relieved to see you. We have been waiting for you, desperate to hear news. I would offer you refreshment and rest first, but with respect, I must ask you to accompany me immediately."

I am taken aback by her words. Even Matali looks surprised. Our arrival here was meant to be a secret under Indra's instruction, so how is it that they have been waiting for me? Why does Holika refer to me as a sage? I am instantly suspicious. *Reveal your lust*, I think, but I come upon a shield in the maiden's mind. If I had not seen such a thing in Kaushika in the mortal realm, I would be more frightened. Despite her respect, Holika has been warned of me and my power. My disguise is already unveiled. I will not be able to fulfill Indra's mission successfully.

Dread makes my belly squirm. I nod to Holika, and Matali makes to follow us, but she turns to him and flashes him a smile, glinting and lovely.

"Singer of Indra's court," she says, and suddenly Matali is surrounded by other asura maidens. "A celestial being of your beauty and stature will surely be curious about the beauty here? Allow my sisters to show you this realm's true charms."

The women around Matali giggle, and he breaks into a smile. He spreads his hands, and I hear him say something raucous as

Holika leads me away. I want to protest, knowing Matali and I are being separated, but it is happening too fast. With a despairing look at the gaggle of women around Matali, I follow Holika.

We enter through an archway, and I am brought to a small sitting chamber filled with music. The asura woman gestures me inside, and I stare at the people dancing within, their movements warrior-like. I look to a quiet corner by a window, where a lady of the underworld sits, and my feet falter.

It is not an asura queen I see. It is the queen of *heaven*.

Shachi.

She sits on a heavily carved wooden chair, reaching for a strange fruit. She wears no sari, but her body is sheathed in diaphanous ribbons banded over her chest and arms. The ribbons loop through her wrists and fingers, swirling before and around her in a fiery skirt so she looks half a poisonous blossom of the wild and half some magnificent creature of legend that would entice you into its lair. The bands of clothing are of every color imaginable, shifting in my view as I come closer. They beckon me one instant and make me wary in the next. I cannot look too closely at them, for they shiver with a strange magic; if I perceive them from the corner of my vision, they resemble many arms, an extension of Shachi's power. Surrounded though I am by maidens and demons, each more striking and handsome than the next, Shachi outshines them all. I have only ever seen her as a devi of swarga, dressed in clothes from heaven, but here she is a force of nature, taking my breath away.

Shachi looks up, and her face breaks into a warm, surprised smile.

A hundred questions pour into me, but I do not know if I can ask them. I search her expression that appears free from artifice, simply watching me in concern as I approach. Her hair is unbound, and long black tresses flow to her waist in gentle waves. I have always seen Shachi as a queen, but now she seems like a woman, relaxed and powerful and content in the realm of her kin. Memories come to me of when I was a child, playing in her groves. Tripping and falling on my run to greet her when she brought sweetmeats. Congregating around her with my young sisters, boasting about the latest mudra I learned. I see the Shachi of then, and she merges with the one I have come to know since—and for an instant I do not know which one she is.

Shachi beckons me forward. The asura maiden next to me makes sounds of encouragement. I move slowly, in a daze, noticing the lion resting at Shachi's feet, presumably asleep, its massive head resting on its paws. I eye it warily, for it is large enough to be ridden. What is Shachi doing here? When did she arrive? What has become of Indra? I try to corral my thoughts, still bedazzled by her beauty, and my eyes slip from her, unable to behold her for too long. My gaze lands on the man sitting next to her, watching me impassively.

Impossible.

Kaushika.

It is him. It is really him.

I cannot believe that I did not notice him, but of course, next to Shachi, I would probably not notice even Shiva. Kaushika stares intently at me, his gaze magnetic and aloof at the same time, as though waiting for something. He is still dressed in his simple pajama and kurta, every bit a sage, yet his aura shines a thousandfold stronger than I've seen in the mortal realm. It explodes out of him, bathing him in radiance like he is a deva. A hundred rainbow hues glint in his chakras, at his throat, his forehead, and behind his head, resting like a halo. Under the cotton of his kurta, I see the slash of his holy thread, but it is a weapon, pulsing with tapasvin energy. He is every bit as glorious as Shachi. Her power is raw, immediate. His is contained, waiting.

I sway where I stand, and do not resist when Holika leads me to a small jeweled stool to sit with them. I am being given a place of honor, to be seated so intimately with the queen, as if we are equals, as if we are sisters, or fast friends. I should feel exalted. Yet a sharp agony clutches my throat, and I cannot take my eyes off Kaushika.

How has he come to be here? What has happened that he looks at me so polite and cool, as though he does not know me? His power shines bright because he is replenished with tapasya, but surely he does not believe that I was a part of Rambha's deception? Surely he understands I was a victim too? My gaze does not leave him, and he does not look away either. I feel his coldness like an arrow within my heart. Where is the man who wants to be led by love? I remember his expression from the half portal I opened during my journey through patala. He appeared then as if he were still fighting off Rambha's illusion. Has he killed her? Will he kill me now?

Holika pours glasses of honeyed milk for the three of us, then retreats to the shadows. I take a sip, and it hurts to swallow.

Shachi leans forward. "My brave apsara," she says, and her brow is furrowed in concern. "The kingdom has been expecting you, but you arrive here under strange circumstances. Tell me, what has become of your sister? Catch your breath, and speak words that will calm me."

The milk is fermented and thick, leaving a pleasing aftertaste of cinnamon and cardamom. I take another sip, this one slower, trying to buy time.

There is a secret warning in her words. What will calm her? Is she wary of me? Perhaps she knows that I have been wary of her. She has been a woman trapped; perhaps she saw no other way to the throne than to threaten me. I do not want to judge her the way my sisters have judged me, but I still don't know everything about her, much less about Kaushika's arrival here.

From below my lashes, I try to read him, to force him to *see* me, my gaze burning at him. I take my cue from Shachi's words. "We lost our way, my queen," I say slowly. "We arrived in naraka instead of patala."

In a few words, I tell them of our misadventure within hell and our encounter with Yama and Chitragupt. I do not mention the chamber Yama questioned us in, nor the visions I saw of Kaushika and Rambha. I do not share how I performed strange, arcane magic that opened a portal and brought me to patala. I merely lean forward, and make my voice urgent, focusing on the most pressing matter. While I sit here, drinking honeyed milk, my sister is likely caught in an endless cycle of torture.

"Devi," I say. "Nanda is trapped there. We must rescue her. I did not mean to abandon her. Help her, I beg you. She will be destroyed in naraka."

"Be at ease, Meneka," Shachi says softly, making a quieting gesture with her hands. "I will find a way to release her. Yama cannot hold her. She is an immortal and a part of the living world. I must discuss the matter with my counselors to decide the best way to free her."

"It must be done immediately," I insist, daring impudence for Nanda's sake. "The lord of death is furious. I saw retribution in his eyes towards the celestials. We must inform Indra. We must ask him to send Amaravati's wind to her. Surely there must be ways you know to reach him."

"Indra cannot be contacted so easily," Shachi replies. "He has closed the gates of Amaravati. The Vajrayudh is only two months away, and the city is fortified, with no one allowed in or out without Indra's express permission. He unleashes Amaravati's wind now only as he sees fit, and he will not stir himself for Nanda. I myself have never been able to come and go as I please. When the gandharva on your journey sent no missive informing Indra of your arrival here, I begged permission from the lord, and he sent me in his stead." Her face falls in pity. "I am sorry you went through such an ordeal. You are here now. You are safe. Soon your sister will be too. Remember, Meneka. I do not like apsaras harmed."

I blink at this. Matali told me that the queen was Indra's captive, but I am still surprised to hear she needed permission to leave Indralok. If so, how did she arrive in the hut to give me weapons and swarga's magical clothes? She came with Magadhi and Sundari, the apsaras she saved from suffering Nanda's fate, and it is true she does not like us harmed, but I look to Kaushika, wondering what he makes of this. Though he doesn't move, his gaze intensifies, heating me. I try to think clearly, of what Shachi is trying to tell me and what Kaushika is thinking, but I cannot discern the message in these twisted games.

Shachi catches my look. "You must wonder how the sage comes to be here," she says quietly. "He arrived only a few hours ago, claiming he saw you open a gateway to patala." She bends a head toward Kaushika in respect. "We were discussing how to find you and where you could have vanished when news came from the palace guards that you were here. Your love is surely to be celebrated, Meneka. The sage was ready to war with Amaravati, thinking your absence to be a part of Indra's schemes."

Her voice is guarded. My head swims, and I close my eyes. Shachi praises my love with Kaushika, but I want to laugh at the irony. Kaushika's arrival occurred a few hours ago, but though each of us has experienced the passage of time differently, he did not come to me immediately. From the magic burning in him, I can tell he stopped to return to his full strength first. Only so he might be prepared before coming to the underworld? Or perhaps he did not trust whether I was his enemy or his lover. I feel far from Kaushika while being so close to him. My worst fears are come true that he would think to so easily break his vow to me to never hurt Amaravati.

Perhaps Rambha *did* seduce him, forcing such ideas into his head. Under her thrall, he *would* attack Amaravati, then be defeated. Indra would parade him around the city, a sage who obeyed the lord like a pet, and regain his honor among people who murmured about the lord's impotency. Or maybe Kaushika wishes to attack Amaravati not because he is in thrall, but because of my deception, thinking me disloyal, capable of such terrible betrayal. Perhaps he has forgotten his vow, or that I would never ask such a thing of him. Whatever the reason, he is not *my* Kaushika. I want to speak clearly, but the danger of a misstep stays my tongue. He should not be here. I have led him to his doom by simply being a part of his life. By simply allowing him, and myself, to fall in love.

Kaushika sets his cup down and stands.

He approaches me, and I lower my cup of sweetened milk too and rise to meet him. There is something in his expression, but it has taken him very long to come to me, and a part of me is too angry to attempt to understand what is going on in his mind.

Kaushika closes the distance between us and bends low. His hands come up to rest lightly on my shoulders. He leans down and places a dry, chaste kiss on my cheek, a kiss that could mean anything. His breath is like a cool, comforting breeze, but I feel terrified. Who is this man now?

"Meneka," he whispers. "I am glad to see you safe."

His words strike me like blades. We had a chance to speak honestly, but my cowardice prevented it. It caused all this—the separation from him, Rambha's seduction, his frigidity now. I step back from him, choking on my words.

"Forgive me, devi," I say, looking at Shachi who has been

watching us. "I feel faint. Perhaps I can rest before we continue our conversation."

Shachi nods, her gaze darting between me and Kaushika. Kaushika does not move, but his eyes flash with anger. At Shachi's indication, Holika steps forward from the dim shadows. Murmuring to me, she leads the way outside. I flee the chamber, leaving Kaushika behind.

CHAPTER 12

I am shown to my chambers, a private suite worthy of a visiting royal. Jewels hide within the latticed windows, creating prisms of colors, and candles made of everlasting light glow in wall sconces. A subtle scent of sugar wafts in the air, and though I cannot see where it is coming from, I hear a soft susurrating melody within the room, a repetitive rhythmic chiming as if emerging from a hidden music box. A massive four-poster bed covered with a dozen pillows stands on clawed feet, and in a recessed level awaits a basin with a large selection of bath oils and perfumes. Silk shawls and dove-feather cushions are everywhere, in a rich display of wealth and abundance.

I stare at the opulence, surprised. Shachi is treating me like a distinguished guest. From asking me to sit with her to these luxurious apartments, she is giving me more admiration than I deserve as a mere apsara. Though I have not forgotten the way in which she came to me in the hut, claiming me for herself, reminding me I am *her* weapon, her actions now show nothing but care. Maybe there is a secret intention behind such treatment; perhaps she is trying to sweeten me. I want to relax and enjoy the beauty, but I feel wretched instead. I don't know what to believe anymore. Shachi is overtly extending a hand of friendship, but Kaushika seems lost to me already. He was as clear-eyed as I have known him, yet neither of us trusts what is occurring. More than anything I want to speak with him, to tell him my mind, yet even if I have the opportunity, how can I rely on his understanding?

I do not know if he is the Kaushika I left so abruptly in the mortal realm. Too much has happened to the both of us. I am out of my depth, sinking in a stormy ocean, and I cannot rely on the memories he and I share. Our love is fragile, a few hard cracks away from being shattered. What Rambha has done, whatever plans Indra has hatched, even Shachi's secrets, those are sure to have a consequence. The thought of it is so heavy that I stop for an instant, clutching a bedpost, my head spinning. I want to fight for him, but the odds seem insurmountable.

Holika, who has accompanied me, hovers in concern. She leads me to the recessed oval basin made of pure gold and helps me undress. She brings stone-heated water, her immense strength allowing her to carry the heavy buckets single-handed with ease. In a few short trips, the basin is full.

I allow the asura woman to massage oils scented with patchouli and hibiscus into my hair and over my skin. She pours a few perfumes of my selection into the water, lilies and rosehip and moon-mint. When I step into the basin, I see that it is deep enough that my feet do not touch the bottom. Holika produces a horsehair brush to scrub me, but I dismiss her with a kind word. I do not know what I will divulge to her in my overwrought state, and likely she has been sent to eke secrets out of me. I have decided to trust Shachi for now, but I must be careful to keep my own counsel.

When I hear the door close behind Holika, I take a deep breath and submerge myself into the water. The events of the last few days swim inside me, one image darting after another, like schools of fish too fast to catch. A nagging feeling burrows in my mind. The bed calls to me, and I know I must rest, but my body is too agitated to sleep.

I have not been around this much luxury since I left Queen Tara's palace; I have only drifted from one mission to another. I think humorlessly of how Shachi's care is affecting me. I thought myself above such luxuries after embracing a yogi's lifestyle, but unbeknownst to her, Shachi is seducing me back with what I have denied myself. These beauties are not just indulgences; they are a homecoming, an indication of safety. Within them, I sense Shachi's maternal embrace.

I rise from my bath and don the simplest nightrobe I can find. Nearly all are heavily embroidered, each an ornate sari or lehenga, but I find a simple sheath made of soft pale silk within one of the cupboards. I wrap it around my chest like a band, and trail it around my waist and legs in the form of a dhoti. Satisfied, I step outside my quarters into a small garden. Tall fruit-bearing trees ensconce the garden in privacy, and balmy air ruffles my damp hair as I begin to take a turn along the paved path.

It must be nighttime now, though night and day are difficult to tell here in patala with no Surya to guide anything. Still, there is a quiet in the breeze I associate with evenfall. The lights that glimmer from occasional lamps have a hazy quality to them, like dusk is trapped within them. Vaguely, I wonder if this is what asura magic does. Takes memories and materiality from the mortal and celestial realms, and turns those into stunningly original displays. If so, Indra has grossly misunderstood asuras. This is not theft. This is . . . beauty.

My walk brings me to a small pool. Its surface glints like ice, unmoving, and all along are more jewels, encrusted within the surrounding rocks. I sit on the grass, watching the display of light like so many silent firecrackers. This is the first measure of peace I have felt in days, and my breath evens. It takes me a while to realize it, but I have begun breathing in the patterns I was taught at the hermitage. My tether from Amaravati whips within me, filling with power, and my prana sizzles in a torrent.

I did not wear the crescent comb in my hair after my bath, but I carry it with me, gripped in my hand. I feel its smooth wooden texture now. I close my eyes, and hear Kaushika's voice, *Give yourself the permission you need.* I smell his skin, the camphor and rosewood lingering in the air, and I hear the soft sigh that precedes the culmination of his passion. Heat stirs in my belly, and I can almost feel him if I only—

My eyes fly open.

It is as if I have summoned him with my yogic practices. Kaushika steps onto the grass, soundless like a panther. My gaze meets his, and he smiles ruefully as if to say, *Well, you caught me.*

My heart thuds in fear and anticipation. I do not move, and I do not speak either. I simply watch as he pads over to me, then takes a seat, careful not to touch me. Incongruously, I am reminded of that time he and I spoke after visiting Thumri, nearly a year ago. Then, too, I was wary of him, unable to know his mind. How is it that after all this time we have returned to the same place, unable to trust each other, despite the love we share?

He senses my reticence. His face clears of any amusement, and grows serious. "I have warded the garden," he says, his voice soft. "None may overhear us. We can speak freely, Meneka."

Can we? I raise an eyebrow at that, for it is not merely the thought of being overheard that silences me. What does Kaushika want? Who is he now, ever since our separation? Did I even know him back then, when we were making love in our cottage? He is raising the corpse to Amaravati, despite his vow. So much of what I have seen has left a bitter taste in my mouth, and I feel all my old doubts about him resurfacing. He is not at fault, for he has come to speak with me, but neither is he innocent. The recurring nightmares about Amaravati's decay have only increased the turbulence of my tide-swept mind.

"If we can speak freely, then I ask you to begin," I say. "Tell me your truth. Tell me what has happened to you."

Kaushika tilts his head, studying me for a long instant. "When you did not return that morning, I knew something terrible had occurred. I waited for you for a time, then wondered if you had returned to swarga. I attempted to call Amaravati's wind, but it did not respond to me, though I used prayers and chants that should twist prakriti to my bidding."

"Indra would never allow it. You heard the queen. With the Vajrayudh so close, the lord cannot take any risks, and seeing you at the gates would only alarm him. He would have strengthened Amaravati against you, for you are still his greatest threat."

"Indeed," Kaushika murmurs. "Perhaps it was my action that

forced him to shut the gates of the city for everyone. Perhaps this is why he could not hear your prayers from naraka, or why he will not send Amaravati's wind to search for Nanda now."

I say nothing to this. What good will my agreement do? Nanda is still trapped, no matter who was at fault. Rescuing her is what matters now. I shiver, remembering the horrors of naraka. Suddenly, this luxury feels like blood price.

"What did you do then?" I ask, trying to escape these dark thoughts. "When swarga did not allow you in?"

"I sought you in other places," Kaushika says simply. "Whatever little you have told me of your adventures in the mortal realm, I began there. First the hermitage. Then at Athira's kingdom, and Reva, and Queen Tara. None of them yielded anything."

I lift my eyes to him. Kaushika searching these kingdoms for me, an apsara—the image is unexpected. Did he ask them about strange, celestial magic? Did he see the effect my seduction had on these rulers and recognize it as one he endured eventually? I still remember them all, Tara most keenly, my mark before Kaushika and one who set me down the path of meeting him. My romance with him is so new, so short-lived. I have come to know of his past, but in interviewing Tara and the rest, he has learned about mine too. She was his ally in the war. What must he think of me now?

"I returned to our hut soon enough," Kaushika continues, and his voice grows quiet. "Several times, I thought I heard your voice in the breeze. I thought I was going mad, or there was some terrible arcane magic at play, one that even I am unfamiliar with. Imagine my relief when you did return to the hut, dressed in all your finery from swarga. All I felt was gratitude. That you had come back. I didn't think to question you, just to love you."

Tears burn the back of my eyes. "It was not me," I say, and my voice comes out broken.

"I know," he replies. "I think I must have known instantly, though she was very good." A grim, ironic smile tilts his lips. He gestures at the crescent comb I clutch in my hands. "She wasn't wearing this, for one thing."

I cannot meet his gaze. My body trembles, and I tighten my hold over the comb. I was there, watching Kaushika's seduction by Rambha, but how long was he under her enchantment? He said he wished to love me, then did Rambha use that need?

"What did she do?" I rasp. "What did she make you do?"

A darkness falls on his face, and he does not speak for a long time.

I don't know if I want the answer. I see Queen Tara's face in my mind, the slack-jawed look, the ashy skin, the heavy-eyed languor of her movements. All my marks became my thralls, but I had rules, those I created after my first and only intimacy with Ranjani. Rambha would have no reservations. Horrific images crowd into me: Kaushika made to defile himself performing sexual acts for her. Kaushika flaying his skin while Rambha watches in relish. Kaushika writhing under her body, while she conquers his will and agency. Rambha wore my face, trying to enchant him. What has he endured under her spell? What does he see now when he sees me?

"Please," I ask, tears tumbling from my eyes. "Did she violate you? Did she—did she—" I cannot complete it, but Kaushika shudders and ends my agony.

"She violated, but not in the way you're thinking. She did not touch me physically, nor make me do things that would haunt me."

"Then what?" I ask, wiping my face.

"Were you not friends, once upon a time?" he asks in return. "Were you not sisters?"

I nod silently. The question is a twist of the knife, but another bitter smile tilts his lips.

"Perhaps it was that which stayed her hand, then," he says. "Or perhaps the command from Indra was different. Perhaps she knew that if she truly dishonored me, she would have you to answer to. Whatever it is, it is a small blessing. She did not do anything, except reveal to me my own ambition. I saw you—*her*—and I found myself in a blurry illusion, yet the illusion went past my lust for you into something deeper, something I've always hungered after."

"And what's that?" I ask, my voice trembling.

"Power," Kaushika says, meeting my eyes. "She showed me what I could be, a brahmarishi, the greatest seer and sage ever to be. She showed me the control I seek over the universe. She showed me unending cosmic power at my fingertips, to do with as I want—and she turned it against me. If I hadn't broken out of it, it would have been my end, burning my own soul. I would never have awoken . . . if it weren't for you."

The silence grows heavy between us. He does not blame me; no, he is grateful that my magic assisted him, yet he has experienced the true seduction of an apsara. Even if he forgives me for what I have done, he will not forget it—not now, not when Rambha's deception has shown him his own vulnerability. In her seduction, he has seen my poison. All the things he has done for power, from making his meadow to going to war, even the speed with which he has become a sage, must twist within him.

Romasha and Anirudh came to me in the previous war, though they were Kaushika's most devoted friends. They saw he was fueled by rage, not the dispassion of a yogi. The other rishis of the Mahasabha warned us all of Kaushika's ambitions. He once wished to churn a soul into rebirth within his meadow, an act no being, divine or mortal, is capable of. I know all this, but I have never thrown it in his face. Power has always been his weakness, his deepest lust, and he has tried to rise above it—in seeking to be guided by love. I have encouraged and strengthened the brighter side of him.

But Rambha . . . she lowered him into the murkiest caverns of his mind, showing him his worst ambitions, his cruelest dispositions.

Reducing him to it.

What must he have seen of himself when trapped by her illusion? What failures must entrap his mind now?

"You must despise my kind," I whisper.

"I don't despise you," he says quietly.

"You should," I return. "If I had not made you weaker, if I had not been weak and had chosen to speak with you about our secrets when you offered me a chance, none of this would have happened."

I am unable to say more, my throat feeling thick. I knew about Kaushika's ambitions and power-hungry ways. If I had chosen to confront him and guide him through it, would Rambha ever have been able to manipulate him? He is forgiving of me, his face open, free of judgment and accusation, but his judgment means little. It is my own I must contend with, and I am sick to the stomach, thinking of all the missions I once did. I am ashamed of being an apsara, when it is apsaras who have hurt him most.

My fingers fiddle with the crescent comb, and light ripples on it. Kaushika gestures with his head. "You have been using it," he says. "It is attuning to you, becoming yours completely. You used it to awaken me from her spell, did you not?"

"Yes. It brought me here. It has only ever worked in times of great turmoil, with magic I still do not understand."

Kaushika raises a hand and slowly, waiting to see if I pull away, he runs a thumb down the comb, moving it back and forth. I watch, mesmerized, knowing what kind of response the same touch can elicit in me. My core clenches, and I squeeze my thighs together to stop from trembling. I want him to touch me, seize me, pull me onto his lap. I want to push him down, demand answers from him, love him and punish him and free him. I don't move.

"Did you kill her?" I ask. It is a question that has haunted me. I recall Rambha's face distorting, the mirage slipping from her body, and Kaushika's magic lacing her, raising her in a storm of righteous tapasvin fire. I recall the hate on his face. Immortals cannot die easily, but he is a sage of untold power. Even Shachi seems wary of him, treating him with care, and Rambha has erred grievously.

"Would it have been better if I had?" Kaushika answers. He shakes his head, reading my despairing expression. "I have not forgotten Nanda, Meneka. I make mistakes all the time, but I try to make new ones instead of repeating those of the past. Neither you, nor Nanda, nor Rambha had a choice when you were sent to seduce me. She is safe at the hermitage, watched by Anirudh and Romasha, and likely put to work. It is nothing she won't survive, but Indra cannot whisk her away with his magic like he did you. Tapasvin wards surround her, and she is our prisoner. I promise she will not be harmed."

"She will hate the hermitage," I observe. The simplicity of the place, the endless chores, the arduous prayers . . . Rambha will see it only as a barrenness. The ascetic lifestyle of the sages is not meant for one like her. For her, it will be akin to being frozen, much like Nanda was within stone.

"I cannot have her return to swarga yet," Kaushika replies. "She will warn Indra that his ploy has not worked. It is what I was trying to tell you silently—that you must keep your secrets from Shachi, for I did not wish Shachi to warn Indra about Rambha either. After you opened the portal to come to patala, I regained my tapasvin magic and followed you here, for I recognized where you were going. That is how I came to be in

Shachi's palace, but it does not mean I trust her. She could still turn you or me over to Indra."

"Shachi has no love for Indra," I say. "Indra held her as hostage in Amaravati, and ever there has been intrigue between the two. It is affecting the throne and all of Amaravati's citizens. Now you and I are caught in it too."

A dark look enters Kaushika's features. "They play games, these immortals. They do not understand whom they are trifling with. To treat a sage this way, to cast obstacles in our meditation and power, it will only end badly."

"I am an immortal too," I point out. "Do you believe this of me as well?"

Kaushika rakes a hand over his face. "I don't know what to believe anymore."

We grow silent again. I want to ask him about his vow, and King Satyavrat's corpse. I want to tell him where I stand, but I do not even know it myself. Answers lurk just beyond seeing, and he and I have both endured so much. We only have each other in this strange realm, which is unknown to the both of us. We are surrounded by cunning enemies who would come between us, who would turn us against each other. I cannot alienate him, and perhaps sensing this, Kaushika presses closer to me, and takes my fingers in his hand wordlessly. He begins to trace circles on my palm, lost in thought. I have seen the turmoil within his heart, and how both his vow to Satyavrat and the one he made to me yank him in different directions. Which will he choose?

I don't pull away, but things have changed between us since

that morning in the hut. He chose to replenish his power before coming to seek me. What if such a delay had destroyed me? Against my will, I stiffen in the memory of the way he spoke to me in the visiting chamber.

Kaushika reads my consternation. "I am sorry," he says. "For not welcoming you with more warmth earlier. I did not dare reveal my feelings in front of the queen, not when I could not know of her allyship. Not when I was unsure how my words and actions would affect your own well-being. Will you forgive me?"

The words stagger me, and I am instantly ashamed of my selfishness. That he should ask for my forgiveness after his own experience with Rambha shakes me. I feel humility, pride, and relief burst through me, and a fire that sparks like the comfort of home after a long journey. It is astonishing that he can turn me away from the worst interpretations of my mind with just a fleeting touch, with a soft word. He says he is guided by me, but in truth, *he* guides me. In his eyes, I see nothing but love. This is how he sees me. His muse, his light, his goddess, and despite what he has suffered, he gives me consideration instead of hate.

A fierce, territorial growl escapes me. I lean in, straddling him without warning, and I capture his mouth with mine. I kiss him deeply, savage in my need, and under my lips, I feel his shock. My impulsive action is unexpected, and he is too traumatized by Rambha. It returns me back to myself, and though it costs me everything, I shudder away, my chest heaving. My legs are wrapped around his hips, and his hands have fluttered to my waist, an action born of memory, but I stare at him in pain.

Suddenly, the games we played with each other in our cottage take on a new meaning. The last time he told me that words were important to him, to ask and gain permission. Yet here I am, taking his choice away, no better than Rambha. A wretched feeling constricts my chest, and I draw back, horrified.

"I—I'm sorry," I stutter. "Oh, Kaushika—I shouldn't have—" My voice trails away, full of heartbreak. "I should have asked. Is it still all right for us to do this? Do you still want this?"

In response, Kaushika draws me closer. He takes my face between his hands, and bends down to kiss me, my cheeks, my nose, my forehead. I feel his hardness beneath my curves, and relief pours into me like a river. I am thirsty for more, unable to be quenched. I grow breathless with the scent of his skin, the feel of his mouth. "Always," he whispers. "I always want this with you. I always want *you*."

He sounds as if he is convincing himself as much as he is convincing me. I laugh, though it sounds like a sob. It was so simple between us a month ago. That time in the hut seems like a dream remembered in the haze of a half-awake morning. Can we ever capture it again? Our games were innocent and simple, and we kept our different loyalties at arm's length, wanting only to be with each other. We allowed ourselves a moment of peace, but that moment was enough for Indra to come between us again. Can Kaushika and I ever be together without interference? I am reminded that he was once my enemy. That even now, through his meditation, a corpse ascends to ruin my city.

He leans his head against mine. "I was so afraid. Of what could have happened to you."

"Indra said he would never let me see you again. I was scared too."

"They cannot keep us apart," Kaushika murmurs fiercely. "We belong together."

He snakes his hand through my hair, pulling me roughly. His eyes are closed in pain. I think of all that he has witnessed since the time I came into his life. Our first meeting in the forest, that ride from Shiva's temple, the time we saved each other after the halahala poisoning. Each of them marked with a revelation, each leading to several more.

His mouth meets mine, and this time I allow our kiss to be sweet. *Be slow*, I tell myself. *This is a relearning.*

It is more than that. In my mouth, there is a question, and I pour it into him, seeking discovery, and his mouth opens, allowing my tongue to dance within it. A soft groan escapes him, and I can feel my resistance breaking. I want to savor this. I want to mimic what we had in the hut, but there can be no easing, no simplicity. This is a punishment, of our secrets and betrayal, and Kaushika's hands grip my hair tightly, pulling. He tastes of heat and tantalizing morning fruit, and there is desperation in his gesture like he wants us *now* in all our clarity and betrayals, even as I want to return us to the innocence of what we once had. Despite what he says, he is angry with me, and I feel it in his kiss.

"Meneka," he says. "Give this to me. Let this heal me."

"We should take our time," I say, though I chase his kiss with my own. "We should slow down."

"I need this," he replies. "I need *you*. I need to know us again."

I cannot fight this any longer. I kiss him with deep ferocity, licking his lips, then drawing back to press my mouth against his eyes, his cheeks, his jaw. Kaushika smiles, and I flick my tongue out to taste his dimple. I graze my teeth along his neck, and my hands reach for the fabric of his kurta. Blind passion overtakes me, and the sounds from my throat are hungry and hot and seeking.

"Let me see you, then," I say, tugging. "Let me show you my love, Kaushika."

He shivers against me, and reaches down to whip his kurta off. His trousers follow suit, and I am quick to remove the bands of my garment too. Kaushika helps me, impatience and roughness in his gesture, snatching at the pale white cloth, unwrapping it by fistfuls, flinging the whole thing away until I am as bare as he is.

His muscled chest is a wall covered with slight beads of sweat, and sprinkling of dark hair. Within his body, the chakras of prana radiate with life and color. He is all I can see, all I can think about, and I stare at him, astonished again by his grace.

His eyes drink me up. I follow their direction, and feel my flesh tighten and pucker where his gaze lands, as he devours me without even touching me. The night breeze ruffles my loose hair so it falls over my nipples, and I shiver. We kneel, and I see the hunger and lust gleam in him.

Kaushika reaches a hand and brushes my hair away, grazing my breasts with his fingers. "Do not hide yourself from me, Meneka," he murmurs. Heat shoots into my stomach, pleasure making me warm and liquid. Kaushika's exhale is a ragged sound, and he turns me around, my back melding into his chest. I am on his lap, his stiffness right below my entrance, and my back arcs, gasps hurtling through me.

We fit perfectly, and Kaushika maneuvers a finger, then another inside me. I shudder at the suddenness of it, at the slick sounds, and the wetness that slips down my thigh onto him. He holds my hips firm with one hand, spreading me wide, thrusting inside me faster. His fingers tease and pinch my delicate bud, and a cry builds in me, swelling. This is not lovemaking; this is hard and fast sex, and I relish it as he pulls my hair back, sucking on my throat, biting with his teeth just to the point of pain but not beyond. My hands scrabble at his hips, wanting to anchor, and stars shimmer in my eyes, though I know we are in patala and there are no true stars here. His skin, his breath, his scent are all I can feel, and Kaushika's tongue laves and soothes the path up and down my neck. His fingers curl, and I cry out an animal sound, pleasure shooting in me.

I do not ask—I don't need to. Kaushika raises my hips slightly, pushing me down on all fours. He towers behind me, and a wretched sob escapes me as he plants himself in me in one deep thrust. His fingers still torture my bud, thrusting in, but his other hand teases and pinches first one nipple, then the other. The sensation of these mixed assaults drives me into paradise, and my gasps resound in my ears.

We are two halves, joined where we need each other the most. I am filled with him, in every gap, every crevice, and it is exquisite torture. Kaushika is not slow; he is not gentle. He thrusts himself in again punishingly, his hands painful on my waist. He is chanting my name, and in his mouth, the word seems like a curse, a plea, a song. My hips crash into his lap, then lift, crashing again, and the walls of my sex shiver and shudder, trembling hard. He leans forward, his breath tickling my ear, and wrenches my hair back so I see the dark hunger in his eyes.

"Give yourself to me," he growls.

"And you to me," I return feverishly.

A glitter of satisfaction and anger and desire shines in Kaushika's eyes. He grips me to him, pounding hard, taking his pleasure with a fury. I feel his greed, his intoxication, and the untrammeled desire between us is a reckoning, for all that we have been made to see and do while apart. This is a pent-up scream. This is a homecoming. This is healing.

"Meneka," he says, and that is all I need.

I let myself go.

A sob escapes me, my entire body shivering, lights overtaking my vision. I swim in a sea of star-filled radiance. I fly in a storm of incandescence. He thrusts into me in deep and unquenchable ferocity, over and over again, intoxicating and mad. His pleasure shoots out of him, rough and fast. I ride the waves of his climax entwined with mine, and around us the night is aglow with unheard whispers and the sighs of leaves. Blankness takes me, and I explode out in shards. I am aware that Kaushika has turned me around again. That he is kissing my collarbone, licking my neck, stroking my face. That he is soothing all the exquisite pain he delivered. His teeth graze over my skin, and he is speaking softly, slowly as he comes down from his climax. I am too replete with lush joy to make sense of it. I grow limp against him, and he pulls me closer to his body. We drift next to each other, entangled like two hands folded in devotion.

CHAPTER 13

We are silent for a long time.

I am drowsy from the relief of our joining and the nearness of his presence. Kaushika nestles me close to him, and I breathe him in. It is tempting to forget we are in patala, that our home in the mortal realm is far from us. I can almost believe that the gleams of the jewels dancing off the rocks are stars caught in swarga's skies. That Kaushika and I have made peace, and all is well.

The respite loosens something in me, and slowly I begin to speak. I tell Kaushika of everything since my return to Amaravati. I tell him of my homesickness while I lived in the hut with him, and of Amaravati's decay. I speak of the hostility of my sisters, and my welcome by Indra in his throne room. I come to telling him about what transpired in the antechamber with Indra and Shachi, but it is here where my voice falters. Kaushika has not spoken, letting me pour my worries into him, but now I need to hear his voice, denying an awful possibility that my trust in him is mistaken.

"You vowed you would not hurt my kin or Amaravati," I say.

Kaushika turns slightly toward me. "I did."

"Yet the tapasya that you did every morning, attempting to find a way to fulfill your vow with Satyavrat . . ." I take a deep breath and gaze at him, perplexed. "That is his corpse rising to heaven, Kaushika, not his soul. Do you not know the dangers of such a thing?"

"The corpse, yes," Kaushika says, and his face turns into a frown. He pushes himself up, his fingers interlacing mine as he pulls me up to a seat. "My tapasya was never to raise the corpse. I was praying to Lord Yama, for him to grant me an audience so I may discuss my vow with him, but the intensity of my meditation began to raise the king's corpse. Once I saw that, I did not attempt to stop it. Yama was ignoring my call to him, but he would not be able to ignore a corpse rising towards heaven. Sooner or later, he would have to grant me an audience. The corpse was merely a means to get his attention."

I search his face. It is too cavalier, the manner in which he says he allowed this to happen. "You endangered my city in baiting Yama," I say, and an edge enters my voice.

"I meant to stop the corpse before it could reach Amaravati, Meneka. But I knew you would not like my method. I should have told you of it, but—" He shakes his head. "For days there has been interference. The corpse is ascending too quickly to swarga, beyond my control. I am unable to stop it."

Asuras, I think. This is the mission I was sent on, to find the conspiracy. I tell Kaushika as much, and he nods. "It is well we are here in patala, then. We can uncover this together. Combined, we will end this threat quickly."

"This threat would never have happened if you kept to your promise," I point out.

"I did try and speak with you about it," he reminds me gently.

I refuse to get sidetracked by guilt. "Tell me now. Why do you need to speak with Yama? What concern does he have with your vow? He is the lord of death."

"He is also the lord of dharma," Kaushika says. "Of justice and righteousness. Mortals and immortals both forget that there is a reason it is Yama who decides whether a soul must ascend to swarga or be punished within naraka before it is churned out into rebirth. Indra might be the lord of the higher realm, but it is Yama—despite his fierce countenance—who has always been the more righteous of the two. He is a true scholar and teacher, the bearer of the divine law of right and wrong, of ethics and morality, of truth that surpasses the passage of time. He is the arbiter of cosmic justice. I sought an audience with him for I sought to learn from him."

It is clear Kaushika admires the lord of death. He has not betrayed his vow to me, but nor has he found it in his heart to drop his vengeance against Indra. I think of the circumstances in which I extracted his vow, at blade point and on his knees. Does he regret his promise now?

"Swarga is Indra's home," I say. "He was incensed that you sought to raise King Satyavrat without his say-so."

"It doesn't matter what Indra thinks," Kaushika replies, and a tone of hardness enters his voice. "If Indra will not allow him into swarga, then I must seek Yama's help. I have always thought that Satyavrat deserved to be in heaven, not merely because of what he did for me and my kingdom, but for the pious life he lived. Yama as the righteous lord must tell me who is right—Indra or me."

"The lord of death is not as righteous as you believe him to be," I retort, and it is difficult to contain the undertone of heat in my voice. "Yama made my companions and me suffer. He used his magic on us to question us about our intent in naraka, and the visions I saw . . ." I shudder. I don't want to think about Rambha dancing for Kaushika, twisting his lust. "He bears no love for Indra. He would not give you unbiased advice, even should you find a way to speak with him."

"He *is* the ruler of naraka," Kaushika says. "Was it he who showed you the visions?"

Yes, I almost say, but it would be a lie. Nanda, Matali, and I were taken to the questioning chambers, and we were caught in bindings of dark smoke, but if my own vision was anything to judge by, Yama did not inflict it. It was my fear, carved into reality.

"What will become of Nanda?" I ask instead, miserable.

Kaushika shrugs, unperturbed. "Lord Yama is the deity of righteousness. He will not mistreat her. She will be safe enough."

I recoil, anger lashing through me again. "You would not say this if you endured what she did."

He looks at me, surprised, but I stand up, away from him, fidgety. Kaushika has never truly cared for celestials, believing us spoiled and flighty. It was only a vow to me that stayed his hand in attacking my home; before me, he hated all celestials for the damage our king wrought on him.

"Nanda has suffered terribly," I continue, heat flaming my cheeks. "Lord Yama's *righteousness* forced me to see things that will haunt me for the rest of my immortal life. He might not have used his magic to show me false visions, but he showed me the worst reality I could imagine. Nanda will become trapped in her own mind the longer she has to endure something similar. This unwarranted punishment—she has suffered in this way already. At your hands, Kaushika."

My last words are a whip, and I turn to face him. I expect astonishment, even anger on his face. Instead, Kaushika's countenance becomes resigned. He stands up and approaches me with his palms raised, as though coming toward a wild creature.

Slowly, he takes me in his arms, and his body is warm against the cool breeze of the night. We are both still naked, and a hot desire rushes through me, but I force myself not to relent. I stand with my arms crossed over my breasts, even as Kaushika encircles me, his fingers wrapping around my waist, pulling me closer.

"I am not trying to be callous," he says. "It is only that I understand Lord Yama—he is a yogi at heart and, like Indra, an ancient being. He has been charged with keeping order in the realms too, to be a guardian of it similar to your storm lord. It will be against his ethics to truly hurt Nanda."

Kaushika tips my chin up, and when I gaze at him mutinously, unmoved, he sighs, and nuzzles my nose with his.

"Don't give up on me, apsara," he says softly. "I need you by my side. You have become my counterweight, humbling my pride, and at the forefront of my mind as I try to be guided by love. You once asked me what I want, and what kind of sage I wish to be. Then hear me when I say I wish to be the kind who can do right by all creatures of the mortal and immortal realms." His fingers dance over my waist, tracing patterns into my skin that make me tingle. "I will go personally to Yama to find your sister. She won't come to any harm. I promise you."

With his mouth hovering close to mine, and his naked body melding to my curves, it takes me a moment to understand him.

When I do, I draw back and stare at him, alarmed. "I castigated you for your callousness, but I do not mean that you should go to hell yourself to get her. You do not have to do this for me."

Kaushika shakes his head. "I am not doing it for you alone, my dear, as much as I love you. I owe a debt to Nanda, for what I once did to *her*. Besides, I require an audience with Yama, do I not? This way, I will achieve what I need, and fulfill my karma towards Nanda, while rescuing her."

I refuse to be comforted. "What if Yama decides to punish you for daring to break into his kingdom? He has already ignored your call—he will not be pleased you came to him without permission."

The thought seems to amuse Kaushika. His lips lift. "I am a rishi," he says simply. "And I am a devotee of Shiva. There is only one being who terrifies Yama, and that is Shiva. Yama may be the god of death, but Shiva is the Lord of the Universe, the Lord of Destruction. Yama dare not touch his devotee, at least not one who is a sage. I do not come to Yama to steal anything. I come to confer and consult. While I was in the mortal realm, he could pretend not to hear me, but when I present myself, he will have no choice."

I recall the ephemeral figure I found Yama conferring with

during my arrival to him. Everything Kaushika says aligns with it. Yet I cannot still the anxiety in my heart.

"Shachi will not let you go." I protest. "She will not give you permission. You need it, do you not—to find the path from patala to naraka?"

"The lower realms have their own pathways to each other, yes, but she will not deny me. She has treated me with all the respect of my station. I have only to make the request, and if she denies it, I will simply open a portal." He tilts his head and studies me. "What troubles you about my plan to see Yama? It can't be that you fear my welfare in naraka. You know I can take care of myself."

I bite my lip. He knows me too well. A shard of apprehension burrows under my skin. Even though the two could not be more different, Lord Yama reminded me of Kaushika. Their desire to heel and tame Indra. The use of wild creatures for defense. Even their abhorrence of celestials—no matter that Kaushika is trying to change his path to love. Yama might have been ignoring Kaushika thus far, but upon meeting him, he might find in the sage a unique opportunity. I recall what I saw when I looked into Yama's lust. His desire to crush Indra makes me shudder.

Kaushika strokes my hair, waiting.

I gather my courage. "What if Yama asks you to destroy Amaravati to fulfill your vow? What will you do then?"

"Two opposing vows," he murmurs, his brow crinkling. "Two desires pulling my soul in different directions. It is not a new conundrum, Meneka. Such a thing has happened before. If destroying your city is truly Yama's counsel, then I will have to decide—either to give up one vow to fulfill the other, or to find a compromise between the two. It is not an ethical dilemma a sage is unused to."

At the hermitage, I was a part of several lessons where disciples discussed law and ethics, morality and dharma—but my city's welfare cannot be reduced to a philosophical quandary. Kaushika's vow to me is the foundation of our trust with each other; he cannot think to simply abandon it. My panic must show on my face, for Kaushika cups my cheek.

"I don't make vows lightly, my dear," he says. "When I vowed to bring no harm to your city or kin, or to your sisters, I meant it. Just as I meant my promise to King Satyavrat. I intend to find the best solution I can. Will you trust me to do it?"

"Yes," I whisper, for what else is there to say? I trust him. I *must*. Panic and distress for my city still eddy within me, in half formed images of Yama poisoning Kaushika further with visions of hate for the celestials. The lord of dharma would wrap his reasons within logic, using the jnani's way to reach Kaushika's heart, but after everything that has happened, Kaushika is here, willing to move forward. He is trying—and if he is, I must too.

"Do you trust *me*?" I ask.

"Yes," he says unblinkingly.

Still, I hesitate. "This compromise you seek between your vows . . . I think there is a solution to it, but I do not know if it is the right way, and if it will align with Yama's advice."

"Your advice matters too," Kaushika replies, smiling a little, but I don't return his smile.

I remember how he brought me to the Mahasabha, knowing I would differ from him in my opinion. He has claimed more than once he needs a counselor to oppose him. Yet this is a secret I have held too long.

It is difficult to speak, but in halting words I finally tell Kaushika of Queen Shachi. Of what she said when she came to me in our hut. How she enchanted him into sleep, and how she threatened that she would have him rule swarga by her side, deposing Indra. I even tell him that it was the queen who sent halahala to the hermitage.

I expect Kaushika to grow angry, both with Shachi for performing such magic on him, and with me for my silence and complicity. I expect this to simply confirm his hate and prejudice against the celestials. But instead his eyes grow sad.

He takes my hand in his. "I am sorry you lived with such pain and turmoil for so long," he says. "You were right, I have no need to rule swarga. And I have no wish to be a consort to the queen." He hesitates, and his gaze meets mine. "You protected Shachi for so long in keeping this from me. You are clearly afraid of my anger towards her. Do you not think her a danger, despite what she has done? What if she is the one raising the corpse?"

"I have wondered that too, but it is not so simple as that with the queen. She is akin to my mother, beloved now by my sisters. She has protected me from Indra, and she sent Nanda to warn me about the lord's plans. Yes, she resorted to desperate means, but she has suffered. I will not judge her for her worst actions, not when she has tried to keep faith with me ever since. She is not so different from Rambha or Nanda—and you forgave them. Can you find it in your heart to forgive her too?"

"Have *you* forgiven her?" Kaushika asks. "You suggest that Amaravati need not be hurt, that Shachi will be the compromise between my two vows. You seem to side with the queen, while still being loyal to Indra. Which do you choose?"

"I don't know," I say, wretched. "The more I learn of Indra and all his excesses, the less faith I have in him—but it is not Indra who has my loyalty. It is my home, it is swarga. Harming Indra will harm Amaravati, and that I cannot abide. I only offer all of this to you so you can think about it too. So you can find a way—so *we* can, together."

Kaushika is quiet for a long moment. Several emotions pass on his face, consideration, confusion, curiosity, like dark clouds racing over a bright sun, too fast to catch. He has never understood my love for Amaravati. He is a yogi, with a yogi's detachment; it is his lot to give up worldly possessions like home. But Amaravati is my soul, my heart. I have protected the city with every mission. Indra is an integral part of it, and though I am furious at the lord for all that he has done, I don't know how to explain my need to protect him any better than I have.

I am already pushing my luck in asking Kaushika to forgive Shachi. Will he be able to ever extend such mercy to Indra, the lord he has spent so much time hating? And what of my own loyalty when I suggest Shachi as Amaravati's ruler? The queen once suggested to me that she would rule, keeping Indra as her concubine. The lord would not relinquish his power easily; then would Shachi have Indra as her thrall—leashed and alive and under her control? Could I be party to such a thing—could *Kaushika*—when both of us have seen the pain of forced enthrallment? Without Indra, Amaravati would die, and though I have suggested a solution, the path to it is too twisted. There is so much that remains murky, with the queen's and the lord's intentions hidden from me and Kaushika, the conspiracy we have been dragged into pulling us like quicksand. It is hard to believe that only a month ago we were ensconced in the peace of our hut.

Kaushika takes a deep breath. "I will keep what you said in mind. If Shachi is the way forward, I will consider her. Do you wish to return to Amaravati, to help keep the city safe until I have decided?"

My heart feels lighter, and I nudge closer to him. "Is it even possible for me to go home? I don't want us to be parted again."

"Neither do I, but if I go to naraka, you needn't stay here." Kaushika closes his eyes and utters a soft mantra, but while the air ripples around us, nothing else happens. He opens his eyes, shaking his head. "The wind of Amaravati will not take you from here, as we have learned, and I cannot open a portal to the city either, not with Indra fortifying it. But you are an immortal, a citizen of Amaravati. The golden blood of swarga runs through your veins. You once used a braiding of great power, merging mortal prana with your own celestial magic, to open portals before. You have its knowledge within you. That will be the way of your return."

"It is not the braiding alone that opens portals," I say, my shoulder lowering. "Kaushika, there is something greater beyond the braiding—a magic that is a stranger to me, yet familiar like my own breath. It is a magic I experienced when Shiva showed me a glimpse of the cosmos, but I have tried over and over again to make it work, and it has never come to me when I have wished for it. It comes only when I have needed it, driven by desperation."

"The infinite power of all reality," Kaushika breathes, and his eyes shine. "Meneka, you have been gifted with something beyond imagining. Not just a manipulation of prana, through tapasya or your bond to Amaravati, but prana in its purest form—the way that Shiva himself sees it. This is the power in its purest source that sages seek—that I have wanted to touch, through my own journey to become a brahmarishi."

I recall my encounter with Shiva. The subtle incandescent strength of him, burning through the illusion of maya. The spontaneous, self-contained presence that saw into the essence of the universe. The power I experienced on opening the portals resembled a pool of silvery waters—but it resembled fire and rain too, soil and metal, light and song, as if it could mold into any shape because of its infinity. I am astounded that this is the magic I use, and I am unable to speak.

"You must practice it," Kaushika urges. "Meditate, and find out how to control it. There are trainers here who can help you."

I make a sound of objection in my throat, that the asuras will not know of this power, and Kaushika understands me even though I don't say it.

"Power is power, is it not?" he says. "All our magic, whether mortal or immortal, is a manipulation of prana, and what you have tapped into is prana in its uncontaminated source form. Yogis use tapasya to access it, and celestials use their bond to

Amaravati, but learning of asura magic will only help you find another path into this source. The queen will know of something. We will ask her together. If you trust her as much as you do, then she will help."

I nod silently. I once connected to pure prana through tapasvin magic, an impossibility for celestial beings. After Indra cut me off, my own apsara magic returned to me, responding to the prana residing within me. Why should asura magic be any different? If all prana is the same, then all different magics are merely rivers emanating from the same glacier.

Kaushika pulls me closer, grazing his teeth against my neck. "Come daybreak, we will find a way to make our requests of Shachi," he says. "But for now . . ."

He kisses my fingers one by one.

I lean into him, softening. For now, I allow myself to quiet my worries.

CHAPTER 14

In the morning, Kaushika and I make our way toward the queen together. Holika comes to wake me up and does not seem surprised to see him in my chambers. Bowing to both of us, she leads us through a warren of gardens and corridors, through golden tunnels with skylights and jewel-encrusted fountains, toward a wild pathway leading into quiet woods.

Soft chatter comes to us as soon as we are within the trees. Someone seems to be calling out instructions, and I hear a chorus of responses. The path winds past low-hanging branches and raised stone. We enter a large clearing where several asura women stand in combat formation, magic spinning around them like dark smoke. I swallow a gasp as one young girl spins a web over her adversary, lifting the other asura nearly twenty feet into the air. The asura flails, attempting to block with her own magic, but panic grows in her eyes as the younger one utters a mantra. Smoke becomes barbed, riddled with needles. I clutch Kaushika's hand, but he does not react, watching with narrowed eyes. We cannot hear the asura scream, gagged as she is by magic, but it is obvious she is in pain. Her head swings side to side, but her aggressor does not relent.

Holika gestures to us to keep moving, and I tighten my fingers in Kaushika's. He leads us on, and I keep my gaze in front of me, not wanting to see any more of this violence. We pass a few others in training to see Queen Shachi resting on a cushioned swing beneath a vine-covered pergola. Her lion paces back and forth in front of her, and attendants bring her nectar to drink, but she waves them away, eyes tracking every movement of magic like she is a lioness herself. Shachi sees us arrive, and beckons us to sit by her.

"The parijata," she says, gesturing to the canopy as we settle ourselves. "Is it not magnificent? Like the kalpavriksh, this blessing came from the Churning of the Oceans too. Our magic—*asura* magic grows tenfold under it, helping us hone it for when we might need it."

I glance over and around me to the woods. Now that Shachi has mentioned it, I notice the resemblance between the parijata and the kalpavriksh. What I had initially assumed were several trees is in fact a single one, with massive gnarled roots coiling and writhing through the soil, upturning even the stone pathway. The tree breathes, rustling softly, creating a rhythmic melody. If I allow myself to look past the violence of combat, I can feel my heartbeat slow down enough to respond to the hushed peace, the sense of age, the quiet gravity.

I recall my last time at the kalpavriksh, when I bowed and made a wish to find true devotion. I could not have imagined it would bring me here, to this twin. Is the tree similar enough that I can pray for its wisdom to affect me now too?

A deep homesickness for Amaravati wrenches through me. In all the schemes I am embroiled in now, the city is held hostage. One misstep, and I will hurl Amaravati into chaos. The thought is so terrible, I take my hand from Kaushika and hold myself, shivering. Kaushika glances at me, confusion in his eyes, but does not speak.

It is Shachi who understands. She offers me a faint smile.

"This tree will fulfill wishes too," she says. "Yet it only fulfills the wishes of asura-born. Our magic is old, more ancient than the devas and mortals believe. My mother taught me how to wield it, and she is lost even to my memory. I cannot remember her face or her voice, but sometimes I grasp a scent that reminds me of her, the curl of vapor when whipped just so—" Shachi slices her fingers, and damp air snakes around us for an instant. "Or the slash of water scented with asura poison—" She spins her wrist into a mudra-like shape, and water appears out of nowhere, cording into a rope.

Shachi drops her hand, and her voice grows sad. I wonder if the same melancholy of homesickness that lives inside me has found a path into her heart too.

"Danu, she was called," she says. "My mother was a primordial goddess, one of the first ones to appear in the cosmos. Free to roam, discovering the ends of the universe and her own form, she ruled over ancient waters, passing the magic down to her daughters. Once it was the same magic as what swarga uses, merely a different flavor of it, like a fruit fallen from the same tree, but different in its own unique manner. I forgot so much of it, embracing swarga's tastes. Prana churns for me there in a different way, the celestial way, but I have known this fruit too. I remember it now the more I taste it."

I am mesmerized by this confession. I can see it clearly,

Shachi a glorious young princess millennia ago, within this very grove learning how to use her magic like these asura girls. Time changes much, but beneath the parijata I sink in a sense of stillness. The ageless queen, now with her hair down and her clothes deceptively simple, looks almost as young as I am.

"Goddess born of water. Wed to the lord of storm," I murmur. "Is this why you and the lord are bound to each other?"

"Yes," Shachi says, looking at me. "But I am bound not just to Indra. I am bound to apsaras too. You are creatures of water, and water shapes all around it. That is what gives you your magic to carve illusions." She moves her fingers, and a vision forms in front of us, a sun peeking out from clouds. "My mother taught me the power of mirages too," she says.

I try to see how she is carving her illusion. The shape of what she conjures is unlike any an apsara would make. Our illusions look into lusts, they take form and inspiration from our marks, and each mudra unleashes a different silhouette.

Shachi's do not seem to require either mudras or insight into lusts.

The sun she creates is heavy, like I have stepped into a painting. It electrifies me, but a cold sweat gathers on my skin. Unusual and profound, this magic is imbued with the casual violence that is different from my charms. Where apsaras guide prana into the silky rivers of illusion, Shachi's mirage is turbulent and all-consuming. I have felt nervous in front of her, and now I know it is because of the pull of her magic, amplified by her divine nature.

I look away from the false sun, and Shachi lets it dissolve.

Her pet lion pads up to her, and she scratches it behind the ears as though it is a tame house cat. Kaushika takes my hand again, and I let him.

Shachi watches this, and her expression grows soft. "I wish to be open with you," she says to us, though her eyes capture mine. "Indra sent you to find the asuras who are helping King Satyavrat's corpse rise to Amaravati. It was I who did this."

Kaushika and I share a look. His fingers tighten on my hand. I know he is angry that she meddled in his cause, that her actions nearly wedged a thorn between him and me. I smooth out his fingers, telling him silently to hear her out.

I turn to the goddess. "You would put Amaravati in danger like this?"

"I would have Indra be scared," she responds, and her eyes flash for an instant. "He sits on his throne, thinking himself above any other deity or devi. I can stop the corpse in an instant, but the closer it approaches the city, the more easily Indra will be to depose. I do not wish harm on Amaravati, but a scared Indra is a foolish Indra, and now is not the time to stop the attack. If it helps the sage in his own quest, is it not to everyone's benefit?"

Kaushika's eyes glitter, and I feel his cold anger. "You call it help, yet some would call your action interference. Some would call such games deceitful. You sent halahala to my hermitage—to *me*, so that it would poison at my touch. You specifically wished to harm me. Speak your mind clearly now, Queen. Are you trying to manipulate me? It is not right to try a sage's patience."

A mix of emotions passes over Shachi's face, anger, pride,

then finally humility. A part of me is ashamed to witness this, and I grow irritated with Kaushika for threatening her like this, but another part of me is curious. Nothing he has claimed is a lie. Shachi must explain.

The queen drops her gaze.

"I could not be more open with my intents before," she says. "Not with Indra watching. When Meneka reported on her mission to seduce you, we learned about your vow to Satyavrat in swarga. Your demand only seemed fair to me, and I tried to convince Indra to allow the king's soul in, but nothing I said made a difference. He refused to relent. I took it upon myself to help you. I sent halahala to you hoping to incite the other sages of the Mahasabha in helping you against Indra. When I saw the corpse rising to the skies, I aided it, encasing it in asura magic and hurtling it towards the City of Immortals. All of it not to harm you, but to assist you."

Her words are soft, and her tone nothing but sincere. I find myself captivated, believing her, but I remember her quiet anger too when she visited me in the hut, hidden behind gleaming eyes and frightening words. She is a goddess, an asura queen, and though she is being submissive now to Kaushika, I can sense her pride, her fury at Indra, for being made to do things in such a way.

This strange magic swirling in the air, the lion that bares its fangs watching me unblinkingly, the queen, regal and magnificent, and all the asura warriors training in dark magic . . . They tell me how much Shachi gave up for Indra. How difficult it must have been for her, to be forgotten for millennia in swarga, while Indra flaunted his carelessness and concubines in her face. I see Shachi as a woman, a mother and a sister opening her arms to me. Impulsively, I reach out and squeeze her hand. She blinks in surprise, but squeezes back.

"I love Amaravati," she says to me. "It gives me no joy to threaten it, for the city is my home too. Yet Indra is shortsighted and stoking the fire towards his own downfall. Did you know, Meneka, that Indra summoned you with the intention of punishing you? It was I who convinced him to treat you like the hero you are. He has never fully understood the power of goddesses, of devis, and of apsaras. It was no easy task to change his mind."

"The corpse incited the lord to send me here," I say. "Why did you want me in patala?"

"I wished for you to be in a place of safety," Shachi says gently. "Once Indra took it upon himself to summon you, I knew swarga would be dangerous for you, especially after your role in the war. A rogue devotee, hoping to curry favor with the lord, or a warrior's family hoping to exact revenge—how long until you were harmed by a citizen of the city? I fed Indra the words he spoke, and for a time that would have protected you. But he could just as easily take it away, and his devotees who fought in the war, who lost kith and kin, would find it easy to blame you. I made sure that Indra would send *you* to patala for the mission. It was why I gave you a token of my protection and love. None would hurt you in this realm with that bracelet upon your wrist. It contains a deep enchantment, a song of my love and friendship, a reminder of who I am."

"I lost the bracelet in naraka," I say. "Yama has it now, and in it he saw something. A message." I recount to both her and Kaushika how incensed Yama grew at the message. How he began to torture me and my companions because of the message. Kaushika frowns, his hand gripping mine as I narrate this, and I wonder if he finally understands Yama's danger. I want to ask him, but it would be impolitic to do so before Shachi, so I simply turn to the queen and say, "What did you encode in it that would infuriate the lord of death in such a way?"

Shachi's brow creases. "Only that you should not be harmed. The bangle was a token, one that belonged to my mother once. It would work in any of the lower realms, but is meant for patala. If Yama was incensed because of my instruction to keep you safe . . ." She shudders, and for an instant, her shoulders hunch. "I put you in harm's way with it, and I am deeply sorry for that, sister."

First to be called a rishi, then to be called a sister. These are both unearned, and I am neither of those things. I grow silent, remembering Yama's fury. The bangle Shachi gave me unleashed a magic that reminded me of the braided magic I use to open portals. When Yama released the message, I was submerged briefly in a pool of infinite waters, my eyes opened to a deep cosmic power. Was that asura magic? I feel a longing for it racing through my heart. I try to recollect events from then. Yama grew infuriated that someone should presume to instruct him. Like Indra, he would not take it kindly that Shachi attempted to dictate terms to him in his own realm. I wonder what he is making Nanda suffer, and I shiver.

"It is not safe for you to be without a token such as the one you lost. Here," Shachi says, and removes another bangle from around her wrist. She takes my hand and slips it on before I can protest.

I feel the cool silver, and a sharp tingle runs up my arm. It is another enchantment of protection, and I glance at the asura girls around us. The bracelet could contain another unknown spell, but Shachi is my only protection here and I cannot afford to refuse this gift. I bow my head in acknowledgment, and tuck my hand away.

The queen catches my look at the asura warriors and shakes her head. "Asuras are not so different from celestials. We are a misunderstood race, and we are not looked upon well." She glances at Kaushika. "Perhaps I should have tried to speak with you before interfering with your vow. But I did not know how you would receive me. I am sorry for my harmful actions."

I do not know what to make of her comparison of asuras to celestials. The tales of asura violence are many, but I have seen Indra's own violence firsthand. Who is to say what stories have been repressed in swarga? I search Kaushika's face, wondering if he will only be angered further by her admission; he hates celestials, but he could be condemned by other sages for his dalliance with asuras too.

Yet to my surprise, he simply nods. "I have no enmity with the asuras, no more than I have any love for devas. I am a rishi, and it is part of my order to be equanimous. A sage after all must do right by all beings, and I want to be guided by love." He smiles at Shachi, yet his eyes flicker toward me. He has been silent while Shachi and I have been speaking, but he has been listening, and I understand what he means. He has not made up his mind about Shachi, but he is trying to trust me. He is giving me the lead, agreeing to follow.

"You have told us many things, my queen," I say to Shachi. "Yet you have not said what you want from us."

"Your help if you are willing to give it," Shachi replies, without batting an eyelid. "I make no secret. Indra cannot be on his throne, and he is not the only one who can rule Amaravati. It is true he is the essence of the city, but I have power too. Will you ally with me?"

I blink. Though my disposition toward Shachi has changed, I am shocked that she is asking this so openly. I think of how my devotion has always been in question. I warred against Indra, yet was hailed by him as a hero. I recall Indra's desperation, the weapons spinning around him in the war antechamber. *All I want is the balance of the realms restored*, he says to me in memory.

Yet Shachi's voice whispers on top of it. *We have been angry for a long time.* She has just cause to be furious with Indra. She has a rightful claim to the throne. What will become of Amaravati between them, and whom am I to side with? He is my lord, my king, and I have promised him my loyalty and devotion. But she is the *goddess*, her energy and magic a part of me, binding us together. Shachi's bangle aroused in me a memory of a profound power. Perhaps in rejecting her, I have been blocking myself.

Confronted with such a direct question, I do not know how to answer. I offered Shachi as a compromise to Kaushika, but will Amaravati be safe with the queen? Is it enough that she is tied to Indra? What does she intend to do with the lord on taking the throne, and what am I becoming a part of?

Kaushika comes to my rescue. He squeezes my hand, and leans forward. "We must make up our minds about it, devi," he says smoothly. "This is an audacious request, to help you commit rebellion and treason in your own home. But if you wish us to trust you, you must help us too without conditions."

"What assistance do you require, sage? I would help if it did not earn your ire."

I glance at Kaushika. It is clear that Shachi is thinking, as I am, that her last assistance was reprimanded by Kaushika in the same conversation.

Kaushika smiles, showing his teeth. "Meneka must hone her magic. You have teachers here, and you have said that asura magic is not different from swarga's magic or prana magic. Meneka knows both of those. Teach her this too."

"It will please me greatly to do this," Shachi replies. She gestures to Holika, who steps forward. "Holika is deeply proficient and a wonderful teacher, who trains many royal asura girls. You are acquainted with her already, Meneka. She will fulfill your request."

"As for me," Kaushika continues. "I wish to travel to naraka, to rescue Nanda."

Shachi looks surprised. "Hell is no laughing matter, even for one with your power."

"If you wish our allegiance, then you will grant me this, Queen," Kaushika replies.

Shachi considers this briefly, glancing at me as if to ask my opinion. When I nod, she rises in a fluid motion. "Very well. There are pathways into naraka built from the palace gates. I will accompany you there, and help you prepare for it."

Kaushika and I both rise as well. I look to him, my alarm clear on my face about the prospect of him going to naraka this soon. He leans in to embrace me, kissing me deeply. I hold on to him, the taste of his rosewood, the strength of his grip. I cannot help my despair at being parted from him when we have had so little time.

"Take no risks," Kaushika whispers in my ear. "Be safe; we still don't know everything, and the danger is not past yet. Listen to your own heart, and don't let them influence you unduly about heaven's rule."

I look from him to the asura girls, who have all stopped to watch us, coming to a standstill now that the queen has risen. The lion utters a soft growl in its throat. I shudder, and the peace of the ancient tree is infiltrated with the dark intentions I see around me. Despite Shachi's words of sisterhood, I am no friend to these people, no kin of theirs. I am come here from their enemy's court, a spy within their midst. Shachi has taken me under her wing, but to the others I am still an agent of Indra.

"They don't trust me," I answer in a low voice. "How am I to learn magic from them?"

"If anyone can learn it, you can," Kaushika answers. "But be careful, Meneka. All magic you already know is prana. When you learn from them, you will be attempting to reach the infinite source through many paths instead of just one. There is power in that, but danger too. The more magic you hold, the more you are liable to forget your own mind. Trust me—I've seen its danger."

I nod slowly. Who else would understand this better than Kaushika? He has achieved great feats that hardly anyone is capable of, both mortal and immortal. He has tried to hold on to dispassion, practicing everything he's learned as a sage, but even he has been tempted by the lure of greater magic. It is what urged him into war with Indra once. It is what Rambha showed him in her seduction, nearly destroying him.

I imagine the danger he warns me of coming true—attempting to braid several streams of magic, trying to coax the river to flow through me, only to be washed away. I have warned Kaushika of the perils of trying what Shiva does—now I embark on the same journey, all so I can learn to make a portal to my freedom.

It is a formidable task. I try to wipe my fear from my face and step back from him, knowing we are being watched and that my doubts will only be used by others to weaken me.

He gives me one last look full of meaning, then turns away to Shachi, who leaves with a swirl of attendants. I am left in the grove with the other asuras.

Holika approaches and eyes me, amusement in her eyes. A barbed smile full of secrets flashes on her face. "Well then, apsara," she says softly. "Shall we see what you can do?"

CHAPTER 15

My training with Holika is nothing like that at the hermitage. Nor is it similar to the dance rituals of heaven.

The first day, Holika shows me some basic forms, similar to yogic stances, in the grove where the asura girls practice. After that I do not return to the parijata tree at all. Instead, Holika comes to my chambers every morning with cruel weapons strapped to her back. A sword with serrated edges, a whip that loops around a belt, even a blunt club with a metal head, she lays them out on the grass in the garden outside, and stares at me meaningfully. The weapons, I know, are tools to direct asura magic, much like jewels are for celestials, and amulets for mortals, but I look at them warily. Unlike mortal and celestial instruments, these amulets can hurt me.

Holika gives me a smile like venomous thorns. Every part of her is sharp, from her filed teeth to her enigmatic aura.

"An asura's magic is fueled with rage and hate," she says, grinning. "With all that has been taken from us, and all that has been denied to us. Are you sure you want to learn it?"

I nod tightly, but it is so different from what I know that I fear I will fail even before I try. Holika picks up the sword. I can't help but notice the edges are not blunt. She comes at me, swinging her weapon, and I back away, my blood singing in my ears.

"Resist!" she barks. "Reach inside you for your fury, and connect it to your prana. Think of what Indra has denied you. Think of what he has made you do, driving suspicion between you and Kaushika. You are alone and abandoned, and you will *never* be as powerful as you want unless you embrace your anger. Think of how you have been made to feel, low and unseen and unvalued, and *fight*."

Her words are poison, wrenching my most unacknowledged thoughts about Indra, baring them for display. I spin an illusion to counteract her, forgetting that I am to learn asura magic. Holika cleaves through my mirage easily, slashing with her sword, and I am left breathless, a sharp pain rising from my chest.

She looms over me, sword in hand. "Your devotion to your lord disgusts me."

I want to refute her—tell her that I am no longer the apsara who revered Indra blindly. Yet her revulsion stuns me into speechlessness. Holika has displayed none of this emotion so far, hiding it behind solicitousness and servitude. Now Shachi's permission to train me has given her permission to show her true feelings. I am amazed that she has developed such intense hatred against me, a person she barely knows. At the end of every day, my body is sore, and light gashes score my skin, golden blood dripping. Holika never blunts her blades, despite my many requests.

"Your lord sends you on one mission after another," she says one time. "He presumes to own you. With his every action, he shows his arrogance and hatred of your power. Still you do not wish to depose him?"

I do not believe in Indra's claim to the throne the way I did once, but she wishes me to despise him. Am I wrong to seek mercy for him from Kaushika? Should I have sent Kaushika to Yama, seeking vengeance instead of wisdom?

"Why do you hate Indra so?" I return. "What has the lord done to *you*?"

Holika sneers at me. "Do I need more reason than I have? Look at what he has done to the queen. Look how he wishes to hold a goddess his prisoner. For this alone, he should be overthrown."

She would have me believe her fury is on behalf of Shachi, but I see the same fury in the realm when I walk through the palace. I see it in the guards who watch me, their hands lovingly caressing their weapons; on the murals and tapestries of asura kings and queens burning Amaravati in years past. This hate Holika has for Indra is embedded within all the songs of bloodlust asura maidens sing. Every shard of poison, every maltreatment, each dark emotion is laid at the lord's feet.

I lift my chin up, holding my weapon in front of me. "You are lying to me," I say. "You hate him because he is the king of *heaven*. It is his celestial nature you despise, just as you despise mine. Am I wrong?"

Holika's eyes narrow, and I know I have struck gold. I brace myself for her fury. Sure enough, she utters an incantation, and dark magic rises around me, taking the shape of a giant snake. The snake slithers on the ground coming toward me, and I back away, terror rising in my chest. It circles me, so massive that it blots out Holika behind its body. I spin, trying to watch it in every direction, sweat pouring down my face. I know I should obey her instruction—to learn not just what she is teaching me, but the greater magic of the infinite source—yet every part of me screams that the rage she wants from me will destroy me. I drop the weapon I'm carrying, and let myself be drenched in Amaravati's golden power instead.

I don't expect Holika to answer me, but her voice comes from behind the snake, laden with simmering rage. "*Celestials*," she spits. "You are thieves. The amrit that gives you your immortality and power, the golden nectar that runs through your veins, is rightfully ours too within patala."

"What are you talking about?" I say. The snake hisses, leaping in with its fangs open, but I dart away at the last instant, unleashing an illusion of birds. Momentarily, the snake looks away.

"Indra *lied* to us," Holika snarls, and I hear the swish of her blade as she attacks the air. "A million years ago, when amrit appeared, asuras and devas entered into treaty to churn the waters of the world together to release it. It was agreed that all gifts of the Churning would be shared equally. Yet when the time came to distribute amrit, Indra took it all for himself and his citizens. We were left with none."

I blink and straighten. I know of this version of the story, though it is not sung often in swarga. The Churning of the Oceans is a disputed event. Though Indra relates different versions, I have heard it as a diplomatic event, as a war with the asuras, and as a foretold occurrence, with balance for the universe at the heart of it. Besides, all of it happened millions of years ago. How can the realm carry so much hate for something that ancient?

My distraction exacts a price. The snake leaps, and this time I am unable to stop it. I cry out, lurching, falling to my back, and it rears its head over me, massive maw open, saliva dripping from the fangs. I cower, shielding my face behind an arm, and Holika appears at the snake's head. In the glimmering light of this realm, the story of the Churning spinning in my head, her wrath is incandescent. I know why she has summoned the serpent. It was a snake that the asuras and devas used to churn the oceans.

"The devas meant to weaken us," she scorns, one hand over the snake's head as she looks down on me. "It will take many asuras to stand up to Amaravati's powers, but we have learned to hone our anger. Our immortality comes from our ceaseless rage, wishing to right ancient wrongs. You wish to learn our magic?" She waits until my reluctant nod, then snaps her fingers. The serpent disappears into smoke. "Then submerge yourself in the same fury the asuras do. Learn to hate your lord like we do. Embrace your darkness."

"I am an *apsara*," I snap at her, rising to my feet. "A dancer, a seductress, a lover. In the mortal realm, I learned how to be a yogi, but the rage and hate you speak of are antithetical to my existence."

Holika moves faster than I can blink, and her hand yanks at my neck, baring it to her fangs. I stop speaking, suddenly fearful.

"Excuses," she snarls. "Even if you cannot feel anger for what happened to the asuras, you are a woman, are you not? What has been done to you? What furies are you hiding?" She yanks my hair harder. "*Speak.*"

"Let me go," I wheeze, my fingers trying to free her grasp.

Holika is relentless. "You have buried your wrath so deep that you cannot even feel it. But I have awoken more indoctrinated girls than you." Dark smoke surrounds her, whipping toward me in cords. It ties me in bands, raising me up in the air, and I flail, trying to escape it. This is the same enchantment I saw the young asura girls train with, and I watch in fear as the smoke becomes barbed. Needles flay my skin, and I cry out, writhing. Gold blood gushes from the cuts, and the pain is so extreme I cannot think. My mind blanks, and the runes I attempt diminish, half made, in the air. I can't move. I can't speak. I can only feel pain, pricking every inch of my body.

Holika laughs, and it is a cruel sound. "Soft creature. Your lord has inflicted more pain on you than each barb I conjure. Do you not remember his offenses?"

Behind my eyes, visions erupt. Amaravati decaying while Indra sits on his throne, drunk and engaging in sensual pleasures. Shachi tied to the city, unable to return home, weeping while the lord cavorts with Rambha. Nanda chased by terrible fanged beasts of hell, slipping and sliding on filth, her flesh ripped out, screaming for help. Kaushika becoming a thrall, following Indra mutely, while the lord makes him defile himself.

The images circle me over and over again, a nightmare worse than I endured in naraka. Always a vision of corruption.

Always a vision of imprisonment. And at their heart, Indra. Always Indra.

Tears pour down my face. I see the lord assess me before he sends me to seduce Kaushika, knowing full well he is sending me to my death. I watch him deceive me, disguised as Rambha, extracting secrets from my mouth. Indra cuts me off from Amaravati, he hoards the city's magic, he casts me out from my sisters. I am the lord's plaything. I am his captive. I am his fool.

Red grows in my vision, and I scream, an earth-shattering sound. My rage envelops me, burning my skin with fiery magic. Flames climb all over my body and cut the dark smoke of Holika's enchantment, and I whip it into the shape of a thousand battle-axes, imitating the blades that Holika spins out from behind her back.

I am doing asura magic, but I am too incensed to feel relief and wonder. I turn my magic toward her, fury seething in me, and she is blasted back. Dark smoke explodes around us, raining down like ash. The courtyard we practice in is aflame, the trees scorching, the air thick with stink and fumes.

Holika leaps to her feet immediately, her grip on her axes steady. She watches me, eyes glittering, a thin, satisfied smile on her face.

My body trembles. I am aghast at the transformation of the courtyard. The fury that took me over recedes as quickly as it came, replaced by shame. Something digs deep into my skull, painful, and I wrench it away from my hair.

Kaushika's crescent comb. It shimmers with magic, bringing

me back to myself. I am spasming, unable to catch my breath. My mind reels from the images Holika unleashed within me and how my own rage responded. My skin is in shreds, blood flowing from cuts and gashes. A soft rain begins as Holika utters a chant. The fumes subside, but the burning scent climbs up my nose, choking me.

I sink to my knees, weeping. The anger freed something within me, but I feel sullied by it. The ugliness around me—is this what I hid within all this while? I feel weakened by it, as if it has taken from me that which I was not ready to give. As if this rage was wrenched from me, made to do things I would never countenance if I was in my right mind. I am a creature of love, of beauty. What has Holika planted in me? Do I really blame Indra for everything? My entire life a farce, my every devoted act a lie. Kaushika told me to learn from the asuras, but I hear his warning in my head. *The more magic you hold, the more you are liable to forget your own mind.* This darkness I have unleashed feels wicked. Is my love for Amaravati a falsehood?

Holika stalks forward and looms above me. "Weak girl. Capable of so much power, yet afraid of it. Afraid of herself." She sheathes her blades behind her back and turns to stride away. "We will practice again tomorrow, dancer. Hone your hate tonight before you sleep. I will know it if you don't."

I see her recede in a blur.

Tatters of my rage float around me, unforgiving.

CHAPTER 16

Monsters from naraka hound my dreams.

Holika has commanded me to go to bed nursing old wounds and grudges, seeking my vengeance against Indra, but all I see is my anger taking horrific shapes with asura magic, chasing me through the tunnels of hell.

Amaravati decays in my dreams, and my rage becomes a hundred-faced serpent, wrapping me in its coils and drowning me in the waters of the city. I face Indra, furious that he should control my freedom, and the lord's vajra shatters and Amaravati dies again. Nanda, Rambha, Urvashi, Dhriti, and hundreds of other apsaras dance in the throne room, but my face merges with Shachi's, and we open our mouth and fire pours out, destroying my sisters. I scream then, for though I have had this nightmare before of the city's fall, this time I walk it longer, each image unleashing a fresh version of hell to poison me.

I jerk awake, breathing fast. I can still hear my sisters' shrieks from the dream, but in the gloomy shadows of my room, my fury recedes to the corridors of my mind; now fear coats me in fine beads of sweat. Holika will come again in the morning, wrenching anger and hate out of me. I will destroy the courtyard again, I might even destroy parts of the palace. She will rejoice in my success, but what will I lose of myself the more I give in to the asura way?

I am learning this form of magic faster than I would have believed, but my body trembles in remembrance of how it made me feel. I grow ashamed, knowing that I am dishonoring Shachi with my guilt toward Indra. The lord imprisoned the goddess, he has imprisoned me, and he has always pitted apsara against apsara. Holika is right—how do I call myself a woman at all if I cannot embrace my righteous rage?

Yet I remember Romasha from the hermitage. The two of us were never close, but of all the yogis, she comes to my mind most often—equanimous to the point of dispassionate, wise even in the face of sorrow, detached while still fighting for righteousness. Romasha is Kaushika's second-in-command at the hermitage, a woman and a yogi so powerful, Kaushika often leaves the governance of the hermitage in her hands. I do not claim to be as powerful as she is in tapasvin magic, but I have learned mortal magic too. If I give in to my rage the way Holika wants, then how can I claim this knowledge of the yogis? My task is not just to learn asura magic. It is to learn the magic of infinity—the asura way is simply another path into it. I must hold all forms of magic I know simultaneously in order to reach the infinite. Such a thing . . . even Kaushika was daunted by the thought.

I reach over to the pillow, under which I keep his crescent comb. My fingers caress the wood, and I think of the time he gave it to me, on our horse ride from Shiva's temple, when neither of us trusted the other. I can almost feel his touch from then. The way his breath tickled my skin. His legs moving against mine as we rode back. The image I saw when I looked into his lust and found my own pleasure. Heated kisses, angry eyes, and a slow, torturous lovemaking that created the path to bind us together.

How is he now, and what is he learning from Yama? Naraka terrified me, making me see visions that will haunt me for the rest of my life. Kaushika has already endured such a hell with Rambha. Will he remember he wants to be led by compassion? Or will he descend further into darkness, tempted by Yama's vision to rule Indra? Bile curdles in my stomach as I recall his words. *If destroying your city is truly Yama's counsel, then I will have to decide.*

I want him back with me, safe here in Shachi's palace. I want what we had in the hut only a month ago. I ache so much for him, my heart feeling heavy with loneliness, that a sob wrenches out of me. I wrap my arms around my knees and drop my head down. The action makes me wince, for I am still injured from my training with Holika, and I stifle a whimper.

I look up at the sound of my door creaking open.

Queen Shachi stands at my threshold, watching me with sympathy. She enters, carrying a small basket of thin linens. Wordlessly, she sits next to me and takes my hand, removing the crescent comb from it and setting it aside. The linens are soaked in ointments, scented with herbs. Slowly, Shachi cleans the wounds from my dark fire, wrapping my arms in bandages.

I feel immediate relief, and a sigh escapes me. When she removes a bandage, I see that the deep gashes have reknitted and the skin has already healed.

"Did Holika take it too far?" Shachi asks, her voice low.

"I don't know," I whisper back. "That rage Holika wants me to feel. It is consuming me. I feel it burning a hole through my soul."

Shachi nods in understanding, and continues tending to me. She wraps another bandage, encasing my burned fingers, wrapping it high over my elbow. "Asura magic takes what is within and twists it in unexpected ways. The rage you feel has always been inside you."

"But she warped it," I grit out. "She changed it."

"Yes. That is the way of asura magic. To take an emotion and enflame it beyond the point of endurance. It is not so different from your own magic that plants lusts. What you saw was exaggerated, but it was not a lie."

I try to make sense of it. When Matali and I were traveling through patala, we saw marvelous constructions, resembling those that mortals make. The lamps in the chamber outside my garden trapped dusk, turning it into a different light. All of it made from asura magic, retaining a core of the origin, yet different from it too. Which version was the truth, which the lie? Perhaps like Shachi says, the rage I feel at Indra is true, coexisting with my devotion. Heaven knows I have been angry with the lord, though never in such a furious way. If the queen is right, I am as unclear about choosing between her and Indra as I was before. Pure rage for Indra would shift my devotion completely to Shachi. Seen through the prism of love I have felt . . . I do not know how to illuminate it. I wonder if every daughter feels the same toward her father.

"Do you feel this rage all the time?" I ask.

"All the time," she confirms.

"How does it not destroy you?"

Shachi smiles slightly, patting one bandage, before picking another off the basket. "When you have nursed anger the way I have for so long, you become friends with it. I would not know who I am without it anymore."

I am taken aback to hear this. My body trembles, and I try hard not to snatch my arms away from her, suddenly afraid.

Shachi is not fooled. She looks up sharply, then sighs. "I am not changing your mind about the asuras, am I? You believe us to be a violent, terrible race, just as Indra has branded us in swarga. You still think patala is evil."

"I think patala is beautiful," I say cautiously. "Though I confess I did not expect it after everything we are told in swarga."

"It used to be a thing of great splendor," Shachi replies, and an ache underlies her voice. "Once, our skies were blue and gold, sunlight caught in wind and stream. Our fields were rich and thick, scented with fragrant perfume. In those years, there was little separation between patala and swarga—indeed, any of the three realms. Devas were young, and ancient magics were embraced—magics that were beads of the infinite source. Indra was barely out of his elemental state, and stretching the boundaries of his knowledge, dreaming of the god-king he wanted to be. He had only just finished building Amaravati, tilling its soil, making fruit trees grow. Yet all the devas flocked to patala, wishing to make this their home, wishing to bind their magic to this realm."

Hypnotized by her voice, I stare into the darkness, imagining patala the way she describes it. How many years ago did the underworld resemble this remembered dream? Indra alone is millions of years old. He would have been closer to his elemental form than to his human one, young, handsome, and sharp in an uncontrollable, scattered way. Volatile like the lightning he now controls, and powerful as the storms. Brittle and imprecise, raging for years due to an imagined slight, but heroic and astonishing. Cruel and unpredictable, but spectacular and mighty too.

I shiver. It is hard to think of Indra in such an imprecise state. The lord I know is many things, but more than anything, he is his own person. Time and age have softened his sharp edges, given him his own mind and personality. The Indra of before could not love, but the one now is sustained by it in the form of prayers from his devotees. Somewhere in his ancient life, Indra chose to tie his existence to his believers, and now he's dying—diminishing because of the approaching Vajrayudh and the loss of prayers by the mortals. And with him, so is my city.

"Did Indra ever wish to live here?" I ask.

"Indra?" Shachi's voice is a huff of skeptical laughter. "He loved Amaravati, and he nourished the city with drops of his blood and sweat. It was his tears that created the first pools, the first springs within swarga. He did not wish to stir from his realm. No matter how beautiful patala, no matter how many devas wished to call the underworld their home, Indra made Amaravati for himself—and for those who loved him best."

I glance at her, frowning. "If Indra did not leave the city, then how did your marriage occur?"

Shachi's voice grows reminiscent. "I grew up hearing of this young god," she says softly. "I was born here as the goddess of treasure under an auspicious star. My name was different, and so was my body, my shape. With my birth, patala grew more resplendent. Fruit trees blossomed from seed in a few rapid minutes. Gold and silver sprouted like buds on bushes, free to be plucked by any who wished. Temples were raised in my honor, and asura magic grew tenfold. In those days, our magic did not rely on hate and rage—it relied on any powerful emotion, even happiness and love. I grew up in laughter, among asura sisters, and I heard stories of this deva, who was more beautiful than any other lord. Indra started to carve a place in my heart with every strike of his storm lightning."

I listen to her, spellbound. I think of how beautiful Shachi must have been. Immortals do not age, but in the first flush of womanhood, innocence and hope still trailing her like perfume . . . She would have been irresistible.

Shachi smiles, perhaps knowing what I'm thinking. "When I came of age, my parents left for a pilgrimage of the three realms, seeking wisdom. As is our tradition, they would not return, and so I became queen. The priests we consulted agreed that patala, with its splendor, would forever flourish, and the devas pressed me to allow them to make this their permanent home. I was to live here and rule, as was my birthright. This was supposed to have been what swarga became."

"What changed?" I ask quietly.

Shachi gives me a sad smile. "I fell in love. It was long coming, I suppose. I loved Indra's image from a distance before I knew him. When I became queen, Indra finally arrived in patala and seduced me. He serenaded me, enchanting me with his charm and power, and begged me to marry him. Young as I was, I agreed. I began calling Amaravati my home, and forgot that I must live here in patala. With my absence, patala diminished, for I took my auspicious star with me. I am the goddess of wealth, and Amaravati and swarga glowed with all of my light. Indra coveted me for my beauty and magic, for tales of my majesty were sung all through the three realms—and I, I gave it all to him. Our love for each other was not so different from the love you bear Kaushika."

I flinch to hear her speak of Kaushika. My gaze lands on the crescent comb next to me. A memory lurks within me of what she once said, that she would take Kaushika away to rule by her side. In light of how I have come to understand her, there is no point in raising it. Shachi is atoning already with her care for me.

"I thought you were born of the Churning of the Oceans," I say. It has been the story all the gandharvas sing. Very few remember that Shachi came from the underworld.

Shachi's smile grows bitter. "Twice I have been born, the first in Puloma, and then again during the Churning. But no one in heaven sings of my true origins from patala. They only sing of the time Indra gave me my identity, not of the time I had my own. Why do you think Indra churned the oceans at all?"

"For amrit," I say, frowning. It was this nectar that gave immortals their power, and had the lord not undertaken this sacred task, none of the celestials would have everlasting life. "Indra churned the oceans for his people in Amaravati."

Shachi shakes her head. "The Churning needed to happen because Indra, in his arrogance and ego, disrespected the Goddess Divine. During our wedding, a great sage gave Indra the gift of Shakti in the form of a garland. It was symbolic—he was supposed to protect *me*, the same as he would Shakti. Yet in his drunken state, Indra destroyed the garland, and with its destruction, all the devis that called Amaravati home disappeared, dissolving into the oceans. Everything grew barren and gloomy, and swarga—this realm that had grown to be a jewel—became easy prey to any who coveted it."

"The devis dissolved," I say, slowly, understanding. "Including you."

"Including me," she confirms. "Patala never had forgiven Indra for taking me away from it. When I left my home, I changed its destiny, and the battles between Amaravati and the underworld increased, endangering all the devas, and Indra's beloved city. You know the rest of the story, do you not?"

I nod. The mortals tell their own legends, and even in swarga, the gandharvas sing different songs. Holika told me what they believe here in patala, of the celestials cheating the asuras. Yet all the stories speak of the battles between asuras and devas that brought about the Churning. It was to stop the never-ending wars between the two that the Churning occurred at all. Several treasures flowed from the divine act, amrit, but also halahala, the great poison to destroy the universe, and the kalpavriksh, the wish-fulfilling tree under which I would pray before every mission. Other beings arrived too, Kamadhenu, the divine cow, and enchanting beauties like Rambha—and Queen Shachi.

Yet if Indra's arrogance and ignorance resulted in Shachi's dissolution in the first place . . .

Suddenly I understand the queen better. To fall in love, then be misunderstood—and mistreated—in such a terrible way. Shachi always claimed Indra did not understand her or her power. She is his own half, yet to him, she has merely been a beautiful queen.

"But you are so much more than that," I whisper, tracing my thought out loud. "You and the other devis disappeared after Indra insulted Shakti, because you were a part of Shakti. You still are—but back then, there was no distinction between you and the Divine Goddess."

The queen nods and gazes out toward her kingdom. "Yes. We are manifestations of Shakti, but back then, all power was simpler, merely swirls of prana, droplets of the same source instead of being their own rivers. When the Goddess left, I did too, though during my dissolution, I was still aware of myself. I was frozen for an eternity, but my mind was awake and alive, and I grew to understand my individual power. In some ways, when I was reborn, I became even more powerful than I had been—no longer aware of being a droplet belonging to something else, but a gushing river certain of myself. Indra and I remarried, and he was contrite, but he was scared too. He bound me to heaven like he did other creatures, so I could never dissolve again. I was dependent on being devoted to him, allowed only to leave with his permission. He took the magic that was mine and tied it to Amaravati, trickling it to me as if I were a beggar seeking alms. He told me that was how it was meant to be, for I belonged to his kingdom—and I, I believed it."

A hard look flashes on the queen's beautiful face. "For millennia, I did not challenge Indra," she says, an edge to her voice. "Yet I knew that Indra's fear of me meant something. I was not just Indra's consort. I was what made heaven *heaven*. Without me and the power I represented, swarga became meaningless. It is why it decayed in the first place, why patala lost its grandeur. Indra sought amrit in the oceans, but he sought me too—I, who was the goddess of wealth and splendor, goddess of treasure."

I take Shachi's hand and squeeze it tight. I am swept away by her story, her pain and sadness and fury burrowing into me. The rage I felt at Indra for what he did to Thumri and the mortal realm grows hundredfold. The lord has ever attacked his own devotees, his own lovers. Was I not sent on missions to do the same thing? Was Queen Tara not such a devotee too?

Indra has claimed that he makes the City of Immortals what it is, but he and Shachi are bound deeper than he tells us, unto the existence and glory of Amaravati. Of course, he never thought to let the gandharvas sing her song. Perhaps he even forbade it, wanting her to live in ignorance, dependent on him for her power.

"If you win this war against Indra, what will you do to him?" I ask.

"What should I do?" Shachi returns, and the hard look on her face is replaced by grief and sorrow. "I am married to him. We are a part of each other. I would have him penitent. I would have him change." Her eyes simmer, and she squeezes my hand painfully, perhaps without knowing it. "If he can be neither of those things, then I will have him controlled, so he will stop harming the mortal and immortal realms with his neglect."

I imagine Indra her thrall, made to do her bidding, like an apsara's mark. After everything he has forced her into, does he not deserve such a fate? His own imprisonment would be justice. Still, the prospect chills me, curdling my belly.

"You came to me in the hut," I say, remembering. "You came to the mortal realm to rescue Sundari and Magadhi too, and tripped the ward Kaushika wove around his hermitage. How could you do either of those things if you needed permission to leave swarga?"

"Those were illusions," Shachi says. "A projection of my form. When I finally understood what Indra was doing to me, I learned of my own history, searching in obscure legends, speaking to visiting sages and ambassadors from my own realm, all in secrecy so Indra would not know I was gaining power. With each passing day, I gained more and more control of my magic. I meditated for millennia, trying to understand it, until I could cast my form to another realm briefly. My illusions are not like the ones you create, Meneka, but they are not so different either. Whether to help the other apsaras or to come to you, I could only send a sliver of myself, the tiniest ray of light. Anything more, and the lord would know. Anything more would result in my pain."

Illusions are not only the apsaras' gift; Indra can cast them too, more powerfully than any dancer. I recall the ethereal nature of Shachi's arrival in my hut. In the queen, I see my own reflection, and I know she is telling the truth.

"Then Sundari and Magadhi," I ask. "Were they casting their forms too?"

Shachi nods. "They could not leave swarga without Indra's permission, no more than any other apsara could. I taught them what I could of my magic. I even tried to bring them with me here when Indra finally allowed me leave, but he wished to keep them in Amaravati, as hostages against any of my plans, no doubt. I could not change that. But you—" The queen leans forward. "Holika told me of the magic you did. You accessed asura power. Meneka, you do not know how special you are. All magic flows from the same infinite and endless source. In the very beginning, Indra and I and all the other gods and goddesses were close to the source, channeling its magic directly, before we each formed our own individual tributaries."

"The magic of unbending reality," I say, nodding. "Kaushika told me this. He said it was the same power that Shiva meditates on, that of the universe."

"Yes," Shachi says, eyes gleaming. "That is how he would explain it, for he is a sage—but tell me, Meneka, what *does* Shiva mediate on? What does Shiva *see*?"

My brow crinkles. I try to think. Shiva showed me what he sees. Millions of galaxies. The universe rushing in every direction. Creation, and the birth of a billion Menekas, a billion Indras, countless heavens and total, eternal, absolute cosmic power. From the tiniest dewdrop to the greatest sun, Shiva meditates on infinity in all its forms. He meditates on prana in all its forms. And what was such infinite power if not—

"Shakti," the queen whispers, watching the understanding on my face. "Power incarnate. Shakti is the Goddess Divine, infinite in her form, no different from the universe. Kaushika and the sages will not explain it to you this way, for they have given themselves over to the Lord of Destruction, but they forget that Shiva himself meditates on the eternal power of Shakti, *wanting* to become one with that power. But you—you, my amazing apsara—you have always been a part of Shakti. The Goddess is the source, a pool of water with a hundred tributaries. When you braided your tapasvin magic with your celestial power, you combined two tributaries. By harnessing asura magic, you will combine three—and before long, Shakti's infinite cosmic river will rush through you, each channel opening another, making you unstoppable."

I am awed to hear this. Kaushika told me much the same, but from Shachi's mouth, the words take on another flavor. A great sense of belonging erupts within me, making me breathless. To be a part of something so immense, to permeate it and swim in such waters . . . I have been a rebel apsara, an outcast from my sisters and kingdom, but Shachi offers me a kind of belonging I could never have imagined. A return to my own self. A homecoming unlike any other.

But then I remember. "I cannot harness asura magic the way you can. The rage poisons me. I have no control over it when it takes me."

Shachi only smiles. "You have just begun, Meneka. You have already had success. When you took your power back from Indra, you tapped into this magic, and it showed me that you would be my champion. One who would free not just me but all of us who are a part of the Divine Goddess."

I shake my head. She did not see the way asura magic tainted me. How it overpowered me. Kaushika's warning reverberates in my head. *The more magic you hold, the more you are liable to forget your own mind.*

The queen presses my hand. "Reach into your soul and free all that angers you. Free yourself from Indra. He is a fool. He presents as a man and has taken the worst of what a man can be, wishing to divide us women. But deep down, we all belong to Shakti. To her sisterhood. He cannot change that. Embrace another form of magic, and let Shakti's source flood you."

Her gaze is warm, but a sadness weaves through it. This

woman—this goddess—has seen many millennia of Indra's rule, and lost herself in the process. It has taken her thousands of years simply to remember her own asura magic. How much longer would it take to access Shakti? Of course, she seeks a champion. With me, she has come close to one. I cannot betray her now.

"Mother," I say. "Sister. I will try harder to learn this magic."

This time her smile is pure. "There is nothing that will please me more. You have embraced the grace of swarga, and the equanimity of the sages. But embrace your rage too. Only then will this magic present itself."

"I understand." My heart beats wildly, like a caged bird, at the prospect of feeling so consumed the way I did with Holika. I do not look forward to the training, but if that is what it takes to gain complete power, I would be a coward to deny it.

"Does this mean I have your allegiance in the coming war, Meneka?" Shachi asks, seeing the passage of emotions on my face.

Yes, I think, but Kaushika's parting words stop me, reminding me that we don't know everything yet. I reach for the crescent comb again, my fingers tightening on it. Shachi sees my hesitation, and her face falls for an instant. Behind it is a flash of dark rage, but it disappears so fast I think I have imagined it.

"What can I do to convince you?" she asks.

"It is not you, my lady. Only . . . I must consult Kaushika first. I cannot make this monumental decision without speaking to him. It would be another betrayal."

"I would think you would see the importance of taking a decision without needing a man after everything I told you," Shachi snaps, her voice growing cold. She sees the shock on my face, and her face immediately softens.

The queen sighs, and her hand drifts to her forehead as if it hurts her. "I apologize. Of course, you must speak with him. My harsh words now, and anything I have said or done to create a gulf between you and him are all actions of a desperate woman. Do not judge me harshly for it. Do I have your forgiveness, sister?"

She is speaking of everything she said to me in the hut when she came to me. Strangely, I hear Romasha's voice in my head. *Who among mortals and immortals does not hurt the ones they love? Love is hurt. But it is forgiveness too.*

I find I have no anger toward Queen Shachi. Only empathy.

"There is nothing to forgive," I reassure her.

She gives me a swift smile, then rises, collecting the herbs and ointments she brought with her. I watch her go, but my mind is troubled. Shachi was telling me the truth about everything, I have no doubt. But how desperate is she, and what will she do in her desperation? If she takes the throne, will Indra rule by her side, letting her lead, subservient to her? Or will she need to leash him? I cannot countenance such slavery, such a breaking of consent, not after what Kaushika and I have endured, but knowing what I do about Shachi's suffering, how can I stand in her way? Shachi does not wish to kill Indra. Perhaps I should find comfort in this. As long as Indra is alive,

Amaravati will be safe. Will taking his throne be enough to sate the queen's rage?

I lie back on the bed, staring up at the carved ceiling, thinking for a long time. When I finally fall asleep, my dreams are plagued by visions of Shachi and Indra, intertwined, while Kaushika and I are caught in a web of their making.

CHAPTER 17

My training intensifies. Each morning, Holika attacks me further, pulling fury from inside me in nightmarish visions of all the wrongs that have been done to me. Each afternoon, I find myself on my knees, sobbing. My rage destroys the courtyard over and over again, melting the trees, cracking the rocks, but I am unable to use it to incapacitate Holika. I am poisoned by my emotion, my skin feeling like it might slough off. I know that it is my compassion and consideration for Indra that interferes with my grasp of asura magic. Though Holika taunts and mocks me, and though I am furious with the lord, I cannot get past wondering what will become of him should I align myself totally with Shachi.

Each time I imagine Indra punished, I can only remember the terror on his face. *Do you have any idea what would happen if I did not rule Amaravati? My very essence flows like blood through this realm. If I am not on the throne, the three lokas themselves would suffer beyond reckoning. Mortals would die like insects.*

Shachi claims that she can rule the realm in his stead, and I know she would make a worthy ruler. But would Amaravati survive if Indra were deposed? Would the realm not diminish, tied as it is to him? Who can give me assurance of the city's safety? If only I had confirmation that Indra's defeat would not result in the city's demise, I would choose Shachi in a heartbeat. I would worry less about how my rage destroys.

I wish to speak to Kaushika. To someone wiser, who can tell me how deeply Indra is tied to Amaravati. But weeks pass, and Kaushika does not return. Little over a month remains before the Vajrayudh comes to Amaravati, and I am no closer to controlling asura magic or unleashing the power of Shakti. I grow desperate.

Every night, I sit meditating on the crescent comb Kaushika gave me. The comb is an amplifier. Even if I cannot access asura magic, the comb ought to help me reach what I have before. With it, I accessed mortal magic; I braided tapasvin power with my celestial one. Why should it not help me control asura magic too? I begin taking it to every training, trying to use its focus to control my rage. After a particularly grueling session with Holika, I seek Shachi, to speak with her about my path. I wish to know from her own mouth that Amaravati will be safe with her.

Yet when I arrive at her chambers, her guards tell me that she is preoccupied with other matters. I have little choice in counselors. Though Holika follows me everywhere, she treats me with nothing but contempt. Ever since my arrival, she has been a constant presence at my neck, stringing my emotions with hers, whispering to me about hateful things. She despises Amaravati, but there is another here who loves the city as much as I do. I make my way through the twisting corridors of the palace, seeking Matali.

I have seen him before in some flower garden or the other, surrounded by asura men and maidens, but each time I have attempted to speak with him, he has disdained my presence, telling me to leave him alone. Matali will never see eye to eye with Shachi's rage, but perhaps he will know some obscure lore that will give me answers. That will show me once and for all that Indra is not the only one who can protect the city.

I arrive at his chambers and open the unguarded doors. The suite is as luxurious as mine, but while my rooms are quiet, threaded with meditation and purpose, Matali's are boisterous. Even from the threshold, I can hear the loud music, suggestive laughter, and sounds of pleasure. Holika utters a snort and stops at the entrance, fingering her blade. I walk in alone to see asura maidens and demons in various states of nudity, and the chamber heavy with the smoke of charas and the scent of spilled wine.

I weave my way through it, stepping around two kissing demons touching each other everywhere. It is nothing I haven't seen in swarga before, but that Matali should indulge this way while there is work to be done annoys me. I find him between two stunningly beautiful asura men. He lies reclined on silk cushions, his hand down one of their trousers, while the other asura trails kisses up his chest.

Matali is mid-laughter when his gaze falls on me. Immediately his eyes narrow. "I would ask you to join us," he says complainingly, "but if you're dressed like that, I would only be fooling myself with the invitation."

I frown at him. My wardrobe is filled with clothes from patala, beautiful enough to rival an apsara's attire, and while I have worn those on occasion, today I am in my set from the hermitage. I made the choice to feel closer to Kaushika, but there is no reason for Matali to be rude.

"You're drunk," I say.

"And you're sober," he replies. "Oh, go away, if you're only going to lecture me. What kind of an apsara are you, anyway?"

The question tightens my face, increasing my annoyance. But I have not come through hell for Matali, of all people, to break my equanimity in such a way. I temper my reaction, but my voice is a hiss.

"What are you *doing*?" I ask. "Have you completely forgotten about the mission and why we were sent here?"

"This is what *I* came here for," he says, crossly. The asura man next to him tries to smooth Matali's ringlets, but they bounce back incorrigibly. Matali laughs, looking at the demon, but when he turns back to me, he has no mirth. "I am learning important tales of the realm here," he says, as he continues to stroke the other demon's member. "Did you know they brew an ale here, trapping the first dew of the morning and combining it with—"

"While you *frolic* here," I interrupt, "Indra diminishes in Amaravati. I thought he was your lord. I thought you were devoted to him."

Matali sits up, pushing away his lovers, who retreat with expressions of irritation toward me. Anger flashes across Matali's face, and he looks like he has swallowed something bitter.

"We are trapped here, in case you didn't notice," he barks at me. "Do you think I don't know about the lord? There is nothing I can do about it but try to forget—" His face crumples, and I see beneath his levity, the fear he has been trying to hide. "I saw a vision of this in naraka when Yama showed me my greatest fear—I saw how I would fail Indra, and it is coming true. I am helpless to stop it, too far from him because of my own insistence to come here." He glances at the company next to him, then stops speaking, perhaps knowing that any allegiance to Indra spoken this brazenly would be foolish, even with his lovers.

I don't know what to say. I've asked him before what Yama showed him, but just as the cord of smoke showed me my greatest fear come to fruition—to lose Kaushika, to have him become a thrall—they showed Matali his betrayal of Indra. Nanda is likely reliving her imprisonment by Kaushika, cursed to be inanimate for ten thousand years. How will she take to learning that it is he who arrives to plead with Yama for her release? How is she faring? How is *he*?

Matali's face spasms, and self-loathing, despair, and grief pass over it before he flashes me a brittle smile. "At least I am not deluding myself like you are," he drawls, regaining some of his composure.

"At least be clear if you wish to insult me," I shoot back.

"You are learning their way of magic, are you not?"

"So what if I am?" I cross my arms over my chest.

Matali utters a harsh laugh, shaking his head. He spins a lazy circle with a finger, gold dust trailing from the ends of it. "We are trapped here," he repeats, "and they are keeping us busy. Your lessons, my pleasures . . . Keep doing what you're doing, but don't think for one minute you are better than me. Our movements are watched, and they do not want us to return to Amaravati to aid Indra. Or are they letting you explore this realm without your jailer?"

I stare at him, nonplussed. I have been focusing on learning magic and attempting to find Shakti's power, but even now, Holika waits outside the chamber to accompany me. If I ask her not to, she will simply reply that it is for my own protection. I could go to Shachi and demand I be allowed to explore this realm on my own, even demand that I be returned to Amaravati, but would the queen allow either when she wishes me to fight for her? I have been afforded respect, kindness, even sisterhood, but whether in Amaravati or patala, I am a prisoner of Indra's whims or Shachi's. Kaushika warned me as much before leaving, and I cannot find it in my heart to refute Matali.

I want to ask him more questions. Perhaps the two of us can plan how to leave if we put our minds to it, but he has already turned away, and a maiden has joined the trio, straddling Matali now. He is lost from my view. Shakti's magic still eludes me, my failure at grasping asura ways impedes me, but if the gandharva wanted, I know he would be able to help me. Maybe there is mention of Shakti within one of the legends and songs he knows. Maybe he knows of a way I can access my rage without destroying myself with it.

Yet I have indulged with Kaushika, and the sweet release of our lovemaking cleared my mind, helping me see things better. I cannot deny Matali whatever comfort he gains trying to take his mind away from the horrors he experienced in naraka.

I walk away. Sure enough, Holika follows me wordlessly as I wander through the palace.

Perhaps it is the excess of pleasure I have just witnessed or the furious lurking danger of this realm. Perhaps it is my failure and the panic that threads through me when I remember how close the Vajrayudh is. I miss my friends from the hermitage, they who first taught me about a different magic. If they were here now, Anirudh would remember a prayer to a deity to help unlock my power, and Romasha would quote something from scriptures. Kalyani would help guide me while I struggled with my prana, and Eka and Parasara would teach me about chakras to feel the flow of my life force just so.

What must these yogis make of Rambha, who is even now among them? She fought on our side in the battle, using her apsara magic with the yogis' mortal magic, but I cannot imagine them being friendly. I search for the seed of affection that had once turned into infatuation for her, but I cannot find it inside me. Still, I cannot wish hardship upon her. She was once my sister.

My feet track me out of the palace, and I wander the streets, visiting the market. Holika keeps close to me, and though I do not ask her to leave, her presence itches at my back. Matali's words have burrowed within me. I went to him, hoping to rouse him, but it was my mind that was asleep. Perhaps Holika has not been helping me with my magic, after all. Perhaps I have been seduced by this realm. The last time I struggled with my magic, Anirudh advised me to go meditate at Shiva's temple. There are temples here in patala too, but I have not visited one yet. They are abandoned, the devas now the realm's enemies. I am a celestial, and it would rouse no suspicion if I desired to pray at a temple, but it would earn more scorn from Holika, and I would pay for it at tomorrow's training. I move from stall to stall, trying to think of a way to lose her.

When I come upon the next row, inspiration strikes me.

On the pretext of examining small bottles of perfume at a stall, I sketch out a rune of chaos with a discreet hand. The rune takes form, and I unleash it toward the next stall piled high with spices. Colors burst in the air, the stall toppling into the one with perfumes. Shouts of anger rise from the asura vendors. They begin withdrawing their weapons, and soon several have joined the fight, coming to blows. Spices and perfume spill everywhere, and Holika rises on her toes to look at the commotion.

I spin a mudra, the Dye Shifts. A thin veiling of light covers me, and I am immediately camouflaged. I do not wait anymore.

Pushing past Holika, I rush into the crowd. Holika blinks, and I see her search for me. She calls out my name and casts out a hand, weaving through the shouting and rioting asuras, but the illusion works, and she cannot see me. I slip between the townsfolk, and my illusion shifts like that of a chameleon, taking on the hues of objects around me, the weave of asura clothes, the wood of the stalls, the glimmer of the streets. This is no true illusion of invisibility like Rambha used on Kaushika, but it is enough. I twist away, and no one accosts me, and soon I cannot hear the cries from the market. I leave behind the palace grounds and town, and make my way to the surrounding hills. There is no sense of direction here, no east or west without Surya, but I go where I know there are fewer asuras.

Massive granite boulders dot the landscape, and temples rise and fall, all of them abandoned, following the curve of a river hidden within the rocks. I climb higher on the hills and see carvings of Surya and Agni, even those of Indra, though they have fallen into ruin. I recall Shachi's story of a time when Indra was young and beloved even in patala. When songs of his greatness were sung here, seducing her, making her love him from a distance. Indra's actions resulted in these structures being abandoned. I begin to slow down, captivated by the splendor, and stare for long minutes at the intricately carved arches, the domed chambers, and the wild lotus ponds, with overgrown grass and weeds on their banks.

There is one temple that calls out to me, full of long pathways terraced under stone arches and ceilings. As soon as I cross its threshold, I know that no one has been here in years. The air is too quiet, and though I can hear the buzz of the market in the distance, it is a muted sound, as if a blanket of magic protects and keeps the temple. A nervous flicker grazes through my body. I am entering the presence of a powerful divinity, yet one that slumbers. I wander through the lonesome temple slowly, taking care to remove my slippers. The red sandstone feels cool under my bare feet.

Past a central courtyard, I find myself in a large pillared chamber with a pool of water in the middle instead of a floor. Tiny silver fish swim in it, and smooth, polished stones glitter in the depths, winking silver and gold. I know the pool is sacred, for beyond the water a large sculpture rises on the wall, ten times my size.

It is Shakti, the Divine Goddess, seated in the lotus position, her sari spread around her like petals. Her sculpture is made of stone, but so intricate, I can feel the breeze that lifts her hair on my skin. Full breasted and with lush curves, she reminds me of the many apsaras I know, yet her features blur as I try to capture them with my eyes. Infinity cannot be captured in form, and even the sculpture is magical, representing her in her many states. A dozen arms emerge from her shoulders, each hand holding a different instrument, a conch, a trident, a book, a brass pot. Her many manifestations surround her. Parvati, who is Shiva's consort at Mount Kailash, her wisdom and intelligence shining on her face. Kali, the blue-skinned goddess of fury, her tongue out, eyes furious, and her fangs dripping blood. Durga, with fire racing across her skin, a crown on her head as she steps upon the demon of ignorance. I try to count how many devis Shakti manifests, how many arms she has, how much she is holding, yet there are too many, shifting one within the other on the stone.

I give up the endeavor, and stare into her eyes instead. Though it is only a statue, I find her peace resonating in me like the echo of a hymn. "Devi," I say, bowing my head. "Mother. Won't you help me now in my time of need? I am your daughter. I submit to you. Show me the path. Who must I serve? What must I learn? Will you not allow me into your embrace?"

"A yogi here?" a man's voice says ironically. "Or do I see a celestial being? Or mayhap the woman is of asura origin. I have been deceived before by her, after all."

I jump, startling. I look wildly around me, until I see him seated by one of the pillars, just a silhouette, though the color and power of his aura shine brightly now that I have noticed him. "I beg your forgiveness," I say cautiously. "I did not mean to interrupt your prayer."

"You did not," the man replies. He stands up, coming forward, and I smother my gasp of surprise. Tall and imposing, his aura shines in a thousand different colors, rising behind him like a halo. His white hair is tied in a topknot, with a tuft escaping it, and three lines of the sacred ash vibhuti adorn his crinkled forehead. His gray beard reaches low on his chest, and around his neck are several rudraksha seed necklaces, their brown carved beads chinking against his kurta.

Sage Vashishta looks much the same as he did when I last saw him in the mortal realm during the Mahasabha. I pretended to be a yogi from Kaushika's hermitage then. Vashishta is known to take offense with the smallest deception, and his words now indicate he has not forgotten my small subterfuge.

Alarm races through me. What will he do to me? Will he curse me like Kaushika once cursed Nanda? Sages are not to be trifled with—even Indra knows this. I watch in apprehension as Vashishta strides through the temple toward me. I stand up slowly, a deep sense of danger prickling my skin, my magic coursing through me in defense.

CHAPTER 18

Sage Vashishta stops in front of me. He stares down his long nose, and does not speak, his expression inscrutable.

I bow cautiously to him. Should I prostrate myself the way that my hermitage friends and I did the last time we saw this man? I do not know if it will only anger him further, rubbing in the fact that I lied to him. I thought that he knew my celestial nature; everything he said to me in the Mahasabha indicated it. Yet the words he chose to greet me with frighten me. Do I apologize to him? Tell him why I lied to him then? How much does he know? I do not know the appropriate protocol. The only sage I am familiar with is Kaushika, and that is no help here.

Vashishta watches me for a long second, then his face breaks into amusement. "Be at ease, daughter," he says dryly. "No need for appearances here in Shakti's temple, especially from you. Sit, sit. We do not need such ceremony."

I do not know if the words are said in hidden anger. I am too nervous to ask. I obey slowly, and wait until he has seated himself next to me. I still grip my magic, but I don't know what I am to do with it—Vashishta is far more powerful than I am. Still, it is comforting to know that I am not entirely helpless.

"What are you doing here, guruji?" I venture at last.

"A pilgrimage," he answers. "To all the corners of the three realms. I compose a great hymn to encapsulate the divinity I see everywhere, from the mortal realm to the immortal ones."

"Even here in patala? This is the realm of demons, is it not?"

The sage gives me an amused glance. "Do you test me, girl? You are here yourself."

Caught by him, I blush and glance down. I asked him the question to judge whether he would grow angry with me or with Kaushika for supporting Shachi, should we choose to do so. But he merely hums under this breath.

"Patala has many wonders," he says, "but none more so than the knowledge that is forgotten. This land is as sacred as any other realm, for once upon a time gods and divinities did not distinguish where they lived. I have traveled from kingdom to kingdom, realm to realm, hoping to find the right notes for my hymn, but perhaps those will present themselves only when I finish the pilgrimage. Even sages must sit with their thoughts sometimes for clarity to occur."

"Is that why you are here in this temple?" I ask. "For clarity?"

It is a personal question, verging on the offensive, but Vashishta simply nods instead of reprimanding me. "Indeed. Do you know that every spiritual power can be reduced to a common core? It exists like a creature, the skin and bones over it ever-changing, yet the soul remaining the same, harmonious and everlasting. Still, I am unable to decide. Is it the unshakable soul that gives meaning to the skin and bones? Or does the shifting appearance of the exterior define who a creature must be?"

My brows draw together. "I don't understand."

"Let me put it in a way that might be familiar to you," Vashishta muses. "How many goddesses exist in swarga?"

"Hundreds," I say. There is Shachi, of course, the queen of the devis, but there are others too, Prithvi, who commands earth, and Aditi, who promotes order. There is Aranyani, the queen of forests, and Ratri, who descends only in the night. There are Raka and Mahi and Parendi, goddesses of small and great magics, given a place of honor in Indra's court, their homes spread over Amaravati and heaven, and there are those who were born male but embraced the feminine form, Eravani and Ila and a hundred others, all of them goddesses of change and transformation.

"I cannot count them all," I say. "I only know they are divine beings of great power, greater than normal celestials."

"Indeed," he agreed. "But are there other devis too? Those who do not live in heaven?"

"Of course," I say, nodding.

There are goddesses everywhere. Every mortal kingdom has its own patron deity. Goddesses of luck and fortune, those that protect a family and home, those that nourish and help women in their fertility. Big and small, these goddesses exist in tribal temples, part of the wind and the elements, often unseen and preferring to keep their own hearth. Yet in times of trouble, I have seen them arrive at a mortal farmer's doorstep, delivering the strongest seeds. I have seen them lurking in a queen's stables, bringing food to the horses, disappearing when observed. Even patala has its own devis. In the market, I have encountered several small figurines of asura deities. I have inquired about them in the palace, but no one has told me anything. Perhaps such knowledge is meant for asuras alone.

"Across the mortal and immortal realms, a hundred million devis exist," Vashishta says. "They are all a part of Divine Shakti. But are they Shakti too? Are they, in fact, all the same?"

His gaze takes in the statue in front of us. For a time, we observe the many arms of the sculpture. We see frightening Kali and pious Parvati. We look at wise Saraswati and golden Lakshmi.

"They *are* all the same," I say, after a moment. "Each devi imbibes Shakti's power, able to access it in her time of need. Yet each devi is different too. In heaven, Prithvi is the goddess of earth, and Ratri is a devi of night, but though they belong to the Divine Goddess, each can only control her own realm of magic. Prithvi can no more change the darkness each night than Ratri can control the texture of the soil. Each is valid, each powerful, and none may replace the other." I study him, and he smiles at me. "Shakti's power," I say daringly. "That is the hymn you wish to compose, sage? The reason behind your pilgrimage?"

"Skin and bones ever-changing, yet the soul harmonious everlasting." He tilts his head. "If you see this about the goddesses, then tell me. Does the appearance matter? Or is it the constancy of the soul?"

"They both matter," I say. "A goddess must remain true to herself in order to access her individual power, that which makes her a goddess. Without her skin and bones, Prithvi will not be Prithvi. She will forget herself and the earth she must protect.

But she must belong to Shakti too, otherwise she will become alienated from the source that gives her power meaning. She will be an outcast, her power small and insignificant and selfish. Without Shakti's power anchoring her, she will be fraught with change and inconstancy, one day sure to diminish."

Vashishta smiles at me, and I see pride on his face. My heart feels buoyant, as though I have passed a test. I think of how he once told me I was unique—that he wished for me to train in his hermitage instead of Kaushika's—and how he questioned me about Indra, telling me I was discovering secrets to magic that no one else was. I never told him the truth about myself, but he guessed at my celestial nature. He has pulled these words from me in an attempt to teach me. Pilgrimage or not, it is no coincidence that he is here now, in the same temple within patala where I am.

The sage smiles as if he has heard this, and I draw away. This is not the first time he has given me the impression that he can read minds. I have already encountered magic that I never knew existed, both in naraka and patala. Who is to say what the rishi is capable of?

"Queen Shachi told me that an evolution of her own power separated her from Shakti's," I say. I explain to him what she taught me about magical tributaries, and the cosmic river of Shakti.

Vashishta nods. "Once prana was only prana, every evolution close to the source of all magic. But like all elemental gods, magic evolved too. The primordial form of the universe changed to allow for differentiation and distance—the universe expanding from a congealed, lumpy mess into something with more form and matter. The queen is not wrong when she says that learning more and more magics will take you to the truest source of prana."

"But in order to do that, I must remain true to who I am. Is that not what I must conclude from our discussion?"

"It is. If you understand all this, how are you faring this time? Are the realms to expect another battle?"

I am anticipating such a question, but a flash of fire races within me in annoyance. "I am here at the temple, am I not? You are not the only one seeking clarity."

I am immediately mortified to speak to him so, expecting him to punish me, but Vashishta only laughs. "So you *do* have teeth. You will need them, apsara."

He utters a chant, and his fingers move in yogic gestures that resemble the mudras of apsaras. The air in front of us solidifies like a mirror, similar to the one Indra created in swarga. I am amazed to see him perform the same magic that my king does, when I notice what he is showing me. The very same image that Indra did, of a golden orb rising through the skies, ascending within dark clouds and past burning stars. The corpse belonging to King Satyavrat.

"It is a dangerous thing the boy attempts," Vashishta murmurs. "Once again, he defies the wisdom of the sages and the boundaries of prakriti."

"It is not Kaushika alone who does this. Shachi aids this too, hoping to oust Indra. She has asked me to join her."

"And have you made up your mind?"

I shake my head. I escaped Holika and the palace in order to find an answer to that question, but I am still no closer to a decision.

"If I were you," Vashishta says, "I would not tarry."

His chant changes, and so does the image in the air. Instead of the corpse, we now see Amaravati.

I stifle a gasp, my hand covering my mouth. When I last saw the city, magic was leaching from it in patches of black. Shadows fleetingly infiltrated the light, but the gold still righted itself.

Now I see the city decay. Buildings crumble rapidly, dust flaking off them in darkness. The roads become ash, and gardens wither, their leaves drying like a perpetual drought has come to the realm. Above, the skies crack, the stars splinter, and the constellations make no sense. Acrid smoke curls through the city, and I know it is the smoke of a slow poison seeping from the asura incursions, making its way through the city now that Indra is weakened and cannot hold it back.

"If Lord Indra dies, Amaravati does too," Vashishta says quietly. "The two are bound like body and mind, like matter and spirit. Should the corpse touch the city, Indra will turn to ash, becoming a mindless being again. Amaravati will perish, in minutes or hours or years, no one knows, but the city's death is certain. Everything will change, and heaven will grow pale, immortal no more but ashing into ruin."

I stare at the vision, aghast. "Shachi will not let it come to this," I whisper. "She does not wish to kill Indra. She raises the corpse to frighten him. She will not let the city burn."

"And you are certain of this? Certain that the queen will be merciful to Indra when he has done so much evil to her?"

"I—I have to believe it—" I stutter, but I remember only too vividly the hot anger in Shachi. How she snapped at me just last night, and made rash pronouncements in my hut about stealing Kaushika. How she nearly killed me and my friends at the hermitage, driven by desperation and fury. She does not have the might to challenge Indra directly, but should Kaushika and I join her, one stray arrow during a battle, unleashed in incandescent rage, could ruin everything. It could ruin my city.

"Shachi wants Indra regretful," I say. "If he does not agree, she will settle for controlling him."

"And what will happen to Amaravati, if Indra is under her thrall? I have shown you what will occur if he becomes a mindless creature. You were charged with a mission once, to save your city. Are you gambling its fate now, choosing between ash and ruin?"

I turn away from him. My hurt turns heavy in despair, and I control the soft sob building in my chest.

"No," I say, my voice breaking. "No—I cannot let anything happen to my city, but you are suggesting I must not defy Indra. What of all the wrong he has done?"

"You once told me that Indra should be understood, not taught a lesson. You even tried to teach Kaushika the path of the Goddess."

I utter a soft sound of disbelief. "You think this is my purpose, then? To change these men, and guide them, as if they are little children in need of taming?"

"I think you must decide your own purpose," Vashishta replies dryly, but I am too distressed to be mollified.

"Once everyone questioned me on my devotion, wanting me to be purer than I am. Now they question me on the same devotion, wanting me to betray him. They say I am disloyal to my kind if I do not allow myself to be consumed by rage. They say I am betraying the Goddess if I follow Indra. What am I to do? Who am I to defend? All I know is that I cannot let Amaravati come to any harm."

"Then *save* Amaravati," Vashishta says bluntly, unmoved by my emotion. "Do the one thing that does make sense to you."

"It is why I am here," I protest. The mirage Vashishta has created disappears, misting into nothing, but the horror of it is sharp behind my throat. "I know I must learn the magic of the asuras to understand the power of Shakti, but my trainer tells me I am afraid of my rage, and until I embrace it, I will not learn. Which is the truth?"

"Are you?" Vashishta challenges. "Afraid of your rage?"

"No. I understand it. Just because my trainers don't see me act out of it does not mean I do not feel it, rishi. If I give in to it, I will lose who I am, and I have come through hell retaining my hold on myself."

"A wise answer," Vashishta says, smiling slightly. "Then what is stopping you from accessing Shakti?"

"The balance between different paths," I say. "To be equanimous like a yogi, or to be rageful like an asura, or to be loving like an apsara—I must learn to control them together, but each path fights the other." My body shakes, and I wrench the crescent comb from my hair, my fingers trembling as I caress it. "This amulet contains secrets that would help me. In the past, it has helped me braid two magics, and rightfully, it should help me now too. Yet it refuses to submit them to me—if I could only understand it—"

Vashishta reaches forward and takes the comb from my hand. He snaps it between his fingers.

I am stunned into silence. The rishi drops the pieces of the comb into my hand, and I close my fingers around them, cradling them like a child.

"What did you do?" I whisper, tears in my eyes.

"This is a trinket," the sage says remorselessly. "If he has convinced you that you need an instrument of his invention to understand your power, then he is fooling you."

"Kaushika has said no such thing," I mumble.

My fingers tighten on the pieces of the crescent comb. This was the first thing Kaushika gave to me. Within it lies the memory of our conversation in Shiva's temple. I can almost feel the whisper of his hand in my hair, settling the comb against my tresses. I know the comb is a mere amplifier. But it has given me access into myself, a map. This is more than a mortal amulet. This has been a friend, an ally. With it gone, I feel a part of my own heart break. Vashishta thinks he is helping me, but all he has done is leave me weaker than ever before.

I cannot speak anymore. My shoulders shake in unrepressed emotion. I continue to stare at the comb, tears trickling down my face.

Vashishta's voice gentles. "You do not need it," he says again. "You are becoming dependent on it, and a yogi must know when to discard a tool that is creating obstacles instead of pathways. Listen for the echoes of your heart, girl. The universe rings it back to you, and all you need is allow it to reflect it. Who are you, and what do you seek? Answer those questions, and the magic you desire will have no choice but to submit to you." Vashishta rises and looks at me past his long nose. His gaze is soft, and he gestures with a hand at the statue of the Goddess. "Even Shiva will not be able to deny your power, once you gain this knowledge. Remember that Shiva could never deny Shakti. Only balance her."

I make no reply, for what can I say? This is a sage's advice, cryptic yet full of platitudes, wrapped in useless philosophy. It cannot help me, and all I have done is lose the one thing I held close. Vashishta never liked Kaushika. He always opposed him, even when it was not justified. He is no friend of mine, and I should never have engaged the sage in conversation. I should have offered obeisance and left, knowing him to be a threat.

For a long time, I sit there with the pieces of the comb in my hand. I do not hear the rishi leave. I do not notice evenfall. Night birds chirp and shadows lengthen, the Goddess enclosing me, spreading her arms to embrace me. I look up when a hand falls on my shoulder.

Holika has found me. I sigh, part exasperated, part angry, bracing for more bitterness and fury from her, when I catch the alarmed look on her face.

"Lady," she says, eyes wide. I am surprised to hear respect return to her words, but the points of her ears tremble, and her mouth around her fangs is curved by worry. It is clear from her panting and her relief that she has been searching for me for some time.

"Sage Kaushika is back from naraka, and he wishes to see you urgently. He has news of your sister. You must come at once."

CHAPTER 19

The temple grounds, the stone sculptures, the market, all flash past me in a blur. Hope and fear tumble within me, each taking precedence for a time before giving way to the other.

Kaushika is back, and I feel the rush of relief. Did he fare well at naraka, or did Yama hurt him? What choice did he make in the precedence of his vows? Will he stop the corpse now, or convince Shachi to? He brings news of my sister, but does that mean he failed in retrieving Nanda? If she is safe and here in patala with him, why not simply say so? I have missed him terribly, and there is much to share with him, not least this unexpected visit with Sage Vashishta. I wonder how he will react when I tell him Vashishta broke his amulet.

Holika keeps up with me for a time, leading, following, urging me on, but somewhere along the way—perhaps in the boisterous candlelit market, I lose her. At first, I do not mind: I know the way to palace, and Shachi's bracelet protects me.

Yet on arriving there, I realize I do not know where Kaushika's chambers are. I ask another asura guard and am directed to the part of the palace where I was first taken to Queen Shachi. He must be in conference with the queen. It worries me that he would not wait for me to do so, and my steps grow quicker.

I wind my way past the groves where the asura maidens play, and am about to enter Shachi's visiting chamber when I stop in my tracks.

I can hear a male voice within, but it is not Kaushika. Instead, I picture a great lord, his skin leathery and his countenance fierce, tusks at the corner of his mouth and a garland of blue embers wrapped around his thick neck.

Yama.

My heart judders. Instantly, I am plagued with ruins of my nightmares. The snarling beasts. The terrible judgment in Yama's eyes. The vision of Kaushika enthralled by Rambha. How has Yama come to be here when he would not bestir himself out of naraka for anyone? Is he here to threaten Shachi? Did Nanda break under her torture and tell him the bangle that infuriated him so belonged to the queen? I am awash with terror for my missing sister and my queen, but Shachi's voice is cool and collected. I can hear the two speaking inside, but the words are unintelligible. If Shachi is fearful, then she is not showing it. It would be prudent for me to remain unseen too, in case she needs my assistance. I arm my magic, then glance around me, though I see no guards. Has Yama already done away with them?

I curl my wrists in complex mudras, similar to the one Rambha used on Kaushika. Light ripples and distorts, inverting around me. Though I appear the same to myself, I know that to others I will be invisible.

Heart pounding, I enter the chamber, holding my breath. The illusion can fool mortals and common asuras, but I am attempting to use it on the lord of death. What if it does not work?

I take no chances. I creep behind the chairs, noting that the asura servants are missing too. Shachi is not without defense, however. Her massive lion paces up and down only a few feet from me. Its lethal claws tap-tap on the floor, and its eyes glow green in the flickering light of the lamps. It swings its head in my direction and stares into my eyes, but looks away again, continuing to pace.

The illusion is working, but if there was a way to show Shachi that she is not alone, I would tell her. I wonder if I should cast an illusion just for her, to inform her of my presence, but when I see her, I still.

Shachi in swarga was beautiful but diminished, letting Indra reflect his glory on her, claiming none of her power. She was demure and quiet, speaking only when spoken to, yet subtly reminding everyone who watched that she belonged on the throne, and on Indra's lap. Later, when I saw her in this very chamber in her diaphanous robes, sitting on the same dais, Shachi looked young and feminine. She seemed powerful in a content manner, and I was wary of her, wondering about her agenda.

Now, all thought of rescuing her recedes from my mind.

Shachi is no helpless damsel.

She is an asura queen.

No longer the devi of swarga, Shachi looks several feet taller. Her skin is darker now, and though her aura is just as strong as before, with golden rays spiraling, a sharp darkness blends with the glow of Amaravati, twining through it in infinite chakras, making my vision blur. The air around her throbs with danger and rebellion, and I know that if I were to breathe too deeply, her emotion and rage would find its way into me.

Shachi's face has changed. She is recognizable as the queen, but no longer does she look celestial; she has embraced her form in this realm. Her earlobes are pointed, and gold and silver beads glint through her body, hanging from her nails in sharpened points, looping through her skin like whips, sharpening on her neck like arrows. Her teeth are fangs, pinpointed and gleaming with venom. Even her lashes are rimmed with bejeweled stars, minuscule and shining. I know they contain a mesmerizing magic, making it difficult to hold her gaze for too long.

A massive crown rises over her head, tall enough as to be three times the size of her head, its arch joining over her in a point. I have only ever seen such a kiritamukuta crown in paintings and murals, and I marvel at the inlaid etchings of gold and silver. Each banded layer of the crown is different. One of them depicts the story of the Churning of the Oceans, this time portrayed from the asuras' perspective. Another shows the wedding of Indra and Shachi, the both of them blessed by rishis and devas while they exchange garlands. Yet another shows a war between the devas and asuras, weapons hurled at one another. I know the choice of these images is telling. They move, as though to indicate what the goddess is thinking.

I try to slow my breathing. From her clothes, a regal sari worn in the warrior's way, to her immortal visage, Shachi is a weapon.

I transfer my gaze to Yama. The lord of death stands with his back to me, looking over the balcony, but the line of his shoulders is tense, angry. "Impressive," Yama says. "But I do not like being summoned like a common mortal, devi. You do not have the right to call upon me."

Shachi shrugs and scratches her pet lion behind the ears. It yawns, its giant maw large enough to swallow my head. "Do you deny my charge?" she answers coolly. "You were shirking your duties. You should have heeded my message when I sent it. Do what I ask, and absolve yourself of your shame."

"Your message?" The lord of death holds up the bangle that was once on my wrist. He strokes the simple metal, and the same chant that I heard in naraka emerges again. This time I understand the strange tongue, the language of patala. *Lord of death*, the message sings. *Come and answer for your crimes. You judge all creatures. But who judges you?*

My hand flies to my mouth in shock. I cannot believe it. The queen was behind our arrival at naraka? Why would she send me and Nanda to such danger deliberately? If I had not found the way back, Nanda, Matali, and I would have been trapped. We would have been worse than dead. I want to think of a good reason she would do this—I want to be led by compassion and understanding—but anger so great flares within me that I see red.

"Coded to my touch," Yama sneers. "I thought one of the apsaras that arrived in naraka meant it for me, but only a devi of great power could do this. Only you would have the audacity to speak such words to me, just as you had the audacity to send a *sage* to my home." His eyes flash enough for me to notice the spark in their depths. "You twisted my arm, knowing I could not refuse his logic."

"The sage *agrees* with me," Shachi says, without even looking up. "He sought you, and I facilitated it. I knew that even you would not ignore Shiva's devotee."

A pang of bitterness slices through me. For Shachi to claim this, Kaushika must have spoken to the queen already. After all, the guards directed me here—perhaps he left this chamber minutes before I arrived. Where is he now? Why would he not wait for me? Anger is consuming me too fast, and I know it is because of Shachi's nearness, the force of her magic pulling and twisting this emotion from me. I try to tamp it down, and reach for my yogic control. Now is not the time to give in to this emotion. I must remain clearheaded.

"Shiva's devotee or not, he ought to understand why I cannot participate in this plot," Yama says. "I cannot attack Indra, devi. If he is not on the throne, Amaravati will fall."

"It is not Indra alone who gives Amaravati her splendor."

"Indeed, it is not. Yet Indra is weak with the Vajrayudh approaching. If he is defeated, he will return to the void." Yama studies Shachi carefully. "Do you wish that upon him?"

"I survived it, did I not?" she returns coldly. "We are gods. Can we ever die? I am the embodiment, the proof, of that impossibility."

Yama does not respond to this, but his countenance draws into a thoughtful frown.

My body trembles in fright, my mind growing dizzy. After what Vashishta told me, I hoped to convince the queen to find a different way to reconcile with Indra, in a parley for both their powers to be equal within Amaravati. Yet she has never wanted to control Indra. She has wanted him *gone*. It is true that she did not die after her dissolution, but it took the Churning of the Oceans to return her to her form. What miracle would the three realms have to perform to return Indra from the void? How many lives would be sacrificed to it? How many millennia would it take, how many deaths? I can see the same questions on Yama's face, and he is as frozen as I am. Yet the lord of death does not seem horrified. He seems intrigued, for he would be the one to judge all these souls.

Shachi rises into his silence, radiant and powerful. She glides up to him, staring at him, challengingly. "Do you not *want* to do this? Would it not be righteous? To finally make Indra pay for all that he has done? Do not forget the crimes he committed that have gone unpunished. The deaths of mortals, the desecration of yogis, the arrogance of his will. Is there no part of you that is repulsed by how much power he holds, and how he does not submit to any judgment? You would be freeing him, and unburdening his karma if you did this. You know it to be true."

Fear surges in my body, making my limbs twitch. In her voice, I discern the same seductive cadence she used on me, when convincing me to join her—and as I did, Yama is listening. *Reveal your lust*, I command, directing Amaravati's magic toward Yama, and again I see the image of him, his foot over Indra's chest, while balancing scales weigh the lord's karma. Indra screams in agony, burning, and Amaravati turns into gold dust, disappearing. I gasp quietly and release my magic, remembering the grotesque nature of his yamadut. Those creatures would sack my city.

Shachi stirs, and for a moment I fear she has heard me, but she only looks up at Yama, waiting for his answer.

"Will you submit to the same judgment, Queen?" Yama asks. "Indra has manipulated prana in many ways, making it impossible for me to judge the celestials. Will you allow your citizens to be judged?"

Shachi does not flinch. "A lot can change, lord, when I am on the throne."

"An easy answer, but remember your bond with Indra. You are tied to him more deeply than you know. If I judge him, you may find yourself judged too."

"I will take that chance. Am I to understand you will ally with me?"

Yama holds the question for a moment, examining it. Then he nods curtly.

Shachi smiles, a tilted smile free from humor. "Gather your yamadut, lord of death. We must make haste."

Yama nods again, and leaves in a swish of robes. The chamber door shuts behind him. I stare at it, wondering how I am to make my exit. I need to go to Kaushika, tell him of this; we must make plans to flee, and save Amaravati and the three realms. I might be invisible, but even Shachi would notice a door open and close on its own. I cannot be caught by her, not now when I have learned something so dangerous.

I do not have to make a decision.

"A worthy trick," Shachi says dryly. "But who do you think taught the elite apsaras the mudra of invisibility." The queen utters a strange mantra, and I feel the illusion dissolve like a shimmer of water cascading down me. Terror seizes me and I freeze.

"Rise, Meneka," Queen Shachi says. "You cannot hide from me."

CHAPTER 20

I don't even think to disobey. My knees shaking, I rise and approach her.

I expect the queen to look angry, even cold, but she only watches me, her face unreadable. There is something in the way she stands, beautiful and still, that puts me in mind of a deep untouched lake. If I didn't know better, I would think the queen sad, but she radiates power that is mysterious and familiar all at once.

Caught so easily by her, I am too afraid to speak. My mind is a hornet's nest, buzzing with everything I've heard, each thought stinging me. I have judged her before, but I have forgiven her too. In the past, she has kept secrets to protect herself. Do I know the entire truth now, or is there another secret lurking, sure to shift my allegiance again? I shake my head. She has turned me around. Whatever she did, she lied to me, and I cannot forget that. I let my fury spike in me, clutch its thorns and pierce into my skin, as if it is the only thing keeping me moored. I keep my eyes on the lion. I have no doubt that should Shachi desire it, the creature will attack me swiftly. Discreetly, I draw the rune of cowardliness, ready to unleash it toward the beast.

Shachi does not react to me. Her aura is quiet and contained, yet it thrums like lava within a vessel. Incense, sandalwood, and the heat of spice swirl in my mind, shaping the scent of her majesty. She moves to the balcony, and the lion pads next to her. I follow slowly, looking to where she is gazing, but below us is utter darkness. We are high in the palace, and the golden mountains spread underneath us, yet except for a quiet tinkling of light every now and then, all is silent and still. I wonder what Yama found so impressive here.

She glances at me. "So you heard it all, did you?"

I gather my courage. I keep my voice free of emotion, aware that I am in danger, but still it thrums with heat. "You lied to me. With every breath, with all your intentions, you lied."

"No. Not everything was a lie. All that I told you about my past, my imprisonment, my dissolution, was true."

"You deceived me from the very start. You sent my friends and me to naraka. We endured horrors. You connived with Lord Yama, wishing to destroy Indra."

Shachi does not deny my accusation. "It was my only choice. Do you think I wanted to endanger Nanda? I have come to love her."

"But not me?" I try to ask this as coolly as I can, but I am stung. "You lied about that too?"

"I told you everything," she snaps. "I *taught* you everything. I kept this one secret, and you are judging me on this alone. It tells me I was right to separate you from Indra, just as I separated Rambha—" She cuts herself off and turns away to the darkness to regain her composure, but it is too late. I have already heard.

My heart sinks. My words grow choked. "*You* sent Rambha?"

Shachi does not answer for a long time. I watch her chest rise and fall as she tries to think of a way out of her mistake, but she must know as well as I do that it is a lost cause. She nods curtly. "Rambha loves Indra like no other," she says, and there is a trace of bitterness in her voice. "She would never work against him, not even on knowing all his many offenses. Even when she fought against Indra in the battle, she did it only because she knew Kaushika could destroy him. Indra was displeased with her, and she has been searching for a way to return to the lord's good graces, to prove her allegiance to *him* instead of Kaushika. It was no difficult task to encourage her. She volunteered all on her own to destroy Kaushika for Indra's sake. Just as Matali did. All I had to do was whisper about the many legends yet to discover in the underworld. He persuaded the lord to make him your guide. When I changed the path to patala within the city's walls, I knew Indra would allow me to investigate—not for you, but for Matali."

The scale of her lie is so monstrous, my vision blanks, the blood roaring in my ears. In trying to control my anger, I feel consumed by it. She tells me all this now because I have forced her hand by overhearing her, and perhaps the only reason she has not finished me is because even now Kaushika is back in the palace, awaiting me. Yet had I not freed myself from naraka, Kaushika would have become Rambha's thrall. Maybe he would have broken out of Rambha's spell, but then Shachi would have continued with her plan to seduce him to overthrow Indra. Or he would have forgotten his vow to me and burned Amaravati in his vengeance. My arrival only forced her to pivot.

"So many deceptions," I seethe. "You speak of dissolution, and of loving Nanda, of loving all the apsaras. Yet all you have done is use us." Even as I say it, I realize I still don't know if Nanda is safe, but I hold on to my own rage, focusing it on Shachi.

"There were dangers," Shachi says, shrugging one lovely shoulder. "I hoped the sage would be sufficiently benevolent if he ever learned of Rambha's deception, now that he knew the path of devotion from you. I did not think she would succeed in seducing him—no other apsara has so far, and her charms only showed him you had been abducted. He came seeking you, did he not? As for my encoded message, I hoped it would take you to Yama's palace directly. I embedded it with enough magic for his followers to find you. I always had faith you would survive. You are apsaras and a gandharva. You are not easy prey, whether with a sage or the monsters of hell."

"We suffered," I snap. "Matali, Nanda, I—even Rambha, all so you could have your vengeance."

"You suffered, so we could all have *justice*," Shachi says, and this time her eyes gleam in anger. I take a step back, for fire races over her body, scorching me. "Indra wastes his magic. He deludes us about his magnificence, all the while keeping us in chains. He brought you to swarga and very nearly killed you. Are you not angry—you who took your magic from him, despite his power?"

"Of course I am angry," I retort. "Yet these games you have played, devi. Sending us to Yamalok, raising the corpse to heaven, even the halahala, you do all this to create chaos for

Indra so you can take the throne. It is not merely for justice, is it? If justice was your aim, why did you not tell me the truth from the beginning? You knew all along that defeating Indra during the Vajrayudh will kill him. You never wished to control him, you wished to *destroy* him, even if it resulted in Amaravati's decay. You lied to my face."

Shachi simply studies me. "Would you have agreed? This was the only way I could have you by my side."

"It was my choice to make," I retort. "You say that I am a part of the Goddess Divine. You could have treated me so. Instead, you have been no better than Indra. You have not proven yourself to be my ally. You have simply taken advantage of me. I am an instrument to use, nothing more. Don't pretend as if you care for me."

"I have lived a long life, child," Shachi replies dryly. "I have had to be careful of whom to trust, even those who embrace the power of Shakti. After all, Rambha is as much a part of Shakti as you or I. Yet you have wanted to be like her, haven't you? I have seen the way you struggle with yourself. I have told you everything, but despite it all, are you not still devoted to Indra?"

I have no answer for her.

I think of what Indra did to me, in sending me on the mission to Kaushika, knowing I would fail. I have struggled for so long, trying to figure out the shape of my devotion to the lord. Am I simply condemned to care for him, simply because he is embedded into the fabric of my home?

I am sickened with the thought. To have no choice in my love, my devotion, makes me no better than a thrall.

The queen's face softens. "Do not be too hard on yourself," she says, and looks away back into the dim lights visible from the balcony. "I have struggled with these questions too. I still do, and how can I not—Indra and I are married, and though my actions might not reflect it, we are deeply in love too. A bond like the one he and I have shared through millennia, you cannot understand it, child. Indra has his pleasures and his concubines, as I do mine. But when this universe dissolves into another, he will still be Shachindra, *Shachi's* Indra, and I will be Indrani, Indra's wife. These are not simply names. These are our identities. We have bound ourselves to each other in endless threads of karma, and not even birth and rebirth can separate us. This is why it has been no easy task to try to usurp him. Yet now my plans come to fruition."

Waves of dark magic radiate out of Shachi as she utters a soft chant. Below us, the darkness lifts in a veil, and we look upon a massive courtyard, extending and rippling into the hills as far as I can see. Armored asuras stand still, their gazes silver, the whites of their eyes shining with deep magic. They are immobile, but only because they are in meditation. With the lifting of the veil, their power slams into me, making me stagger. It is a terrible force, pushing me like a great wind. If it were not for the queen's presence, I would be swept away. As it is, a gale rushes through the chamber, howling and keen, whipping my hair around me. I stare at rows upon rows of asura soldiers, each of them more powerful than any deva, now that the Vajrayudh is nearly upon us. The horde extends far over the hills, disappearing into the mountains.

Shachi has amassed an army.

And she is coming for swarga.

"Yama thinks this is impressive," Shachi says. "That I can win this fight alone with my army. But Amaravati is Indra's realm, and the city will try to defend itself. I need the lord of death to aid my victory, and he has agreed."

Horror clasps me in its talons. I have been mesmerized—*seduced*—by Shachi, but she has had millennia to hone her rage. To sharpen it into clarity and serrate the knife with sweet poison, and charm, and smiles that bleed.

Reveal your lust, I think, and I see her on Indra's throne, the grand chamber on fire. Flames lick and burn everything, the beautiful sculptures melting, the tapestries turning into ash, the gold and silver and pearl becoming meaningless sludge. In my vision, Amaravati is sacked, overrun by Shachi's asura army, and pieces of heavenly luster drip away into molten fire, a river of ruin rushing through the city. Shachi's rage takes over *everything*, all the worse for being cold. The justice of her anger leaves a trail of bodies that dissipate into death. Only great magic and furious hate can kill immortals, and her wrath, with all its magnificence and history and justification, promises to burn heaven until it is mere flame and shadow. It delivers devastation to the citizens of Amaravati and all of Indra's devotees, for forgetting her, for making her forget *herself*.

I step back from the queen, horrified. My fingers cover my open mouth, and my body trembles in fear. Suddenly, I can see why she has been kind to me, why she has coveted apsaras. She has wanted our allegiance, and she has wanted to stoke my rage too. To join her as a sister and a friend, and unleash the glorious power of Shakti onto Amaravati to ruin the city. Joining her will erase all I have ever loved—but surely, she does not expect me to do so now when I have seen her true intent. No, my capacity for magic was a threat to her once if I used it to help Indra. It was an opportunity to help her win the war. But now when I have failed to find my power . . .

"You have no use for me anymore, do you?" I whisper. "That is why you are telling me all this now. Why you feel brave enough to be truthful."

Shachi casts me an appraising glance. "Have you found the magic of Shakti?" she challenges. When I don't reply, her mouth curls into a cruel smile. "Dear child, if you had not denied yourself, you could have been my greatest commander. But I cannot wait for you any longer. You've outlasted your use—you brought me Kaushika, a powerful sage whom Indra fears, and he will be my greatest weapon in the looming war. It is the least of what you could achieve, but I am not ungrateful." Shachi pats my cheek, and I flinch, but it only makes her laugh, the sound like rich rain laced with poison.

It should not prick me the way it does, but I diminish with her words. This is why she interfered with Kaushika's vow. Not merely to convince Yama, or to threaten Indra, but to win him over as an ally. She admitted as much to us under the parijata tree, but I finally understand the true scale of her schemes. How many times she changed her strategy, how much she lied and deceived, playing a keen political game just to maneuver us.

"What do you seek from him?" I ask. "Do you still want him by your side to rule, to replace Indra next to you?"

The queen utters a soft huff. Her fingers glisten with a strange golden light. "The sage will join my war. But he merely seeks to fulfill his vow, and I will help him with it. We are allies, nothing more." Her eyes study me, and I sense another judgment. "Don't think I wouldn't have tried to seduce him," she says, smiling a twisted smile. "But even I know which battles are worth my time, and he loves you too much to fall for my charms. This is a fight you have won. Take heart from that, Meneka."

I should feel relief at her answer, but all I feel is a dull despair. The Shachi who came to my hut is one I thought I understood, lethal and seductive. This one, cold and purposeful in her anger, is an enigma. What will she do to Kaushika if he refuses her? Has he really made his mind up about his vows—choosing to destroy Amaravati all to save King Satyavrat's soul? What about the compromise he sought? He cannot mean to abandon me. She must have forced him, somehow.

The queen turns away. "Go. Do what you must. Convince your lover if you can to side with you, but know that it is futile. He has already promised me his allegiance."

I take a few steps back, preparing to hurry, but I cannot help but ask one last question. "You would really destroy Indra, knowing it would destroy Amaravati?"

Shachi stares at her army. "You who kept denying yourself—you showed me I was doing the same, in thinking to offer Indra any kind of mercy. My rage is all I have. If the city must burn for it, then so be it. I don't need you to teach me Shakti's power anymore, Meneka. Soon the Goddess will bless me because I have embraced *my* rage."

Shakti's power became accessible to me on braiding tapasvin and celestial magic together. Yet I am not the only creature with the knowledge of two paths—Shachi can do both celestial and asura magic. If she unlocks Shakti's source, the queen will become unstoppable. Already I can see the golden swirls of prana around her. This war will change everything, for millennia to come.

I leave the chamber, my mind whirling.

CHAPTER 21

Holika waits outside the chambers for me, her brows drawn into a frown. "Where is he?" I demand. "Where is Kaushika?"

"This way," she says. She hurries along a corridor, and I keep up with her, dizzy with all the things I've learned. More than ever, I want to fling myself into Kaushika's arms. I want him to reassure me that he will stand by me. That he will fight with me against Shachi's devious plans, and we will save my city together.

Holika stops at a doorway along one of the corridors and leaves me there. She gives me a searching glance but does not make to follow as I enter.

Kaushika looks up as I walk in. He appears unmarred by his visit to naraka, and though his apartments are as luxurious as mine, it is clear he is not seduced by Shachi's offer of comfort as I have been. I see the holy thread around his muscled chest, slashed like a warning. In naraka, he used every tool at his disposal, and that is the purpose of the thread too, to remind Yama that he is Shiva's devotee. Yet I cannot help but wonder if the wisdom of the sages will direct him now, or his own unrequited thirst for vengeance against Indra. He stands up as I approach, and his eyes widen for an instant before I careen into him, holding him tightly.

Kaushika's arms wrap around me protectively as he returns my embrace. His camphor and rosewood scent nearly undoes me, making me weep, and I shudder against him, letting my body soften.

"She's safe," he murmurs against my hair at once. "Your sister—Nanda—I sent her to the hermitage. I thought it would be better for her to keep away from these intrigues. She is with Rambha and the others." He pulls me closer. "She is unharmed, Meneka, though shaken—as is only to be expected."

I nod gratefully, but it is not the thought of Nanda that troubles me. I can feel the moment approaching like a storm, the conversation Kaushika and I have been avoiding since the end of the last battle. The one we should have had when we'd had the opportunity before Indra whisked me away back to Amaravati. I can still remember it, the heat of our lovemaking, the innocence of our games, both of us pretending as if we had all the time in the world.

He senses my mood. Kaushika pulls back and searches my face. "What is it? What are you thinking?"

I'm thinking of who I am supposed to be. I was supposed to have gained knowledge of myself at the hermitage. I thought I had—in stopping the battle, in standing up to Indra and even to Kaushika, when the time came. Yet have I embraced my power at all? I have been devoted to so many deities all my life: Indra, Shiva, even the Goddess Divine. If there is anything that should return my devotion, it is Shakti—she whose power flows within me as much as it does in Shachi. Yet she has abandoned me. Is it in punishment to my abandonment of Shachi?

Kaushika understands without my speaking. He meets my gaze without any hint of subterfuge or shame. "You've spoken to the queen. She told you."

I nod. "I know everything. I overheard her with Yama. How could you decide to side with her, Kaushika? Without speaking to me first? She—she sent the halahala to the hermitage, nearly killing Kalyani, nearly killing *you*. Have you forgotten that?"

"I have not," he answers. "But, Meneka . . . you told me to treat her with kindness. To speak to her without judgment, and to forgive her for her previous errors." His eyes are quizzical, curious. "Did she tell you everything? About her past, her dissolution?"

"Oh, she made her arguments well," I say bitterly.

"Then are you not convinced?"

I move away from him, touching the objects on his bed in fitful bursts. "She sent Rambha to seduce you. Did you know that too?"

Kaushika's voice grows guarded. "I learned it on my return. The queen admitted it to me."

"And that does not bother you?"

"After hearing her story, her reasons?" Kaushika shakes his head. "I have judged celestials before, Meneka, but I meant what I told you that day in the hut. You have made me better. You have instilled in me a purpose to do good by all creatures and be guided by love. Besides, it is not my judgment Shachi will face. It is Yama's—all tallying against her offenses and benevolences for the day she dissolves again."

"You forgive too easily," I say, but even I can hear the foolishness of my reply. I am too agitated to speak clearly, and Kaushika does not interrupt as I try to master my emotion, pacing up and down the chamber. He sits down on the bed, waiting.

Finally, I turn to look at him. I see the openness on his face. It bolsters me.

"Shachi has wanted me to side with her," I say. "And Indra has sent me here to find his foe. In their own way, both have held blades to my throat in order to force a decision, but I am finally free, and I can choose what I want to do."

"And what is that?" Kaushika asks, though he must know already.

"Indra wants reconciliation with you. He said he wanted you as an ally, and I believe him. He wants peace in the three realms, now especially with the Vajrayudh." I come closer to him, sitting beside him, and my eyes are beseeching. I cannot help the tremor in my voice. "Kaushika, Sage Vashishta came to patala during your absence. He showed me what is happening in swarga. Everything decays, and it will only fall to ashes, the weaker Indra becomes. I understand everything Shachi has said, and all that she has suffered. But fighting Indra now will result in the lord's total annihilation. He will return to the void. That is what Shachi *wants*. When she returned to her elemental state, Amaravati lost all its splendor. What do you think will happen if Indra is dissolved?"

Kaushika frowns. "Death must come to everyone, Meneka. Mortals and immortals, we are bound by the cycle of karma, to be born and reborn again and again. One day, you too will return to nothing when Anantashesha closes his eyes and this universe dissolves to become another."

"A sage's answer, to be so cavalier about *dissolution*. But what does the truth in your heart show?" My words are similar to what Kaushika once hurled at me, and I press my advantage. I tip his chin, forcing him to meet my gaze. "One of the reasons Indra fears the Vajrayudh is because if he dies at this time, he will be trapped as lightning and storm, no longer the lord that he is, capable of conscious thought. You endured such a thing from Rambha. You meted this out to Nanda. You would have Indra suffer too?" When he remains silent, disturbed, my heart leaps in hope. I know I am swaying him. "I saw the lust in Shachi's mind," I say. "She is consumed by rage and hate and what she thinks is justice. She will burn Amaravati down all to spite Indra—because she knows how deeply the lord cares for the city. Because she sees that the city is an extension of the lord, made by his own hands. She will destroy my home."

Kaushika's frown deepens. "You saw her lust. But your vision is not a prophecy, is it? It is only a reflection of her desire."

"A desire that she will fulfill if given half a chance. You did not see what I saw. It is bad enough that Yama has agreed to fight for Shachi, but if you ally with her too—"

Kaushika looks up, interest sparking. "The lord of death agreed?"

I curse myself for a fool, for letting this slip, but it is only for an instant. If I am to convince Kaushika, I cannot be secretive about what I know. I will not lie to him by omission again.

"He did," I say reluctantly, "but not without doubt. Yama

agreed that this close to the Vajrayudh, fighting with Indra was dangerous for the three realms. He only agreed because Shachi promised to allow him to judge immortals too, something Indra has protected the citizens of Amaravati against."

"And is that not fair, my love?" Kaushika says mildly. "The immortals have always been beyond judgment. That is why apsaras seduce their marks so callously, returning to a life unblemished with guilt while their mortal marks suffer. That is why Indra is able to deny rain and fertility to the earth, forgetting his duty—because he has no fear of judgment. Mortals have endured terrible things because of the capricious nature of immortals, ever since the dawn of creation. If Shachi changes that, is that not good?"

"Fear of judgment should never be the incentive to do the right thing," I return. "Have you not told me yourself that one must listen to one's heart? If Yama gets his hands on Indra, and deems Indra worthy of naraka, then Indra's soul will have to serve a sentence for the duration of the Vajrayudh. In his absence, the three realms would get no rain and more people would die, mortals included, leaving more souls for Yama to judge. This is what Yama wants. Why don't you see?"

Kaushika raises his brows. For a long second, he is silent. Then he takes my hand, pulling me closer to him, smoothing back my hair from my forehead.

"You have me there," he says, smiling. "You truly are a sage at heart, my love." A fierce heated look of pride flashes in his eyes, but then he shakes his head. "Your reasoning is sound, Meneka, but I cannot agree with you. Yama alone knows right from wrong, more deeply than any other creature in all the realms. For Shiva, right and wrong are equal, but Yama knows the measure of these things, beyond the shifting tides of time, keeping to ancient precepts that look into each soul to find the imprint of an action. Ethics and morals change with time and place, but Yama's dharma bypasses those to see it all. If the lord of death says Indra deserves to serve a term in naraka, then I cannot stand in his way. Perhaps when Indra dies at the hands of Yama and his soul wanders naraka, punished for his evil, the next time he is born, he will be a reformed deva."

"Or perhaps he will never be born the same way," I say, making a frustrated sound in my throat. I surge away from him, whipping out of his embrace, and stand, startling him.

I had almost convinced Kaushika, but still his stubbornness won't let him see. He has always been a man of rigid convictions. He has tried to follow Shiva, in holding two ideas at once, but he has also been unbending. In Shachi's antechamber, Yama told her that the sage trapped him with his logic, but Kaushika is deterred from his path of love too. Lord Yama has influenced Kaushika with his own lust for Indra's downfall. My fears are come true.

My voice shakes, and I turn to Kaushika from the other end of the chamber. "You promised me you would not hurt my city. You promised you would not hurt my kin, my sisters, the citizens of Amaravati."

"I made another vow too, before that," he says. "The devi brings splendor and magic. She believes she will be able to counter any ill effect of Indra's death." Kaushika's face is unyielding.

"I vowed to help Satyavrat's soul ascend into swarga. For it to find peace. Indra has not allowed this so far, but if Shachi sits on the throne, she will see fair judgment."

"Indra will, too," I insist. "The lord has been prideful, but he sent me on this mission because he sought peace. He wants to make an ally of you, Kaushika. He told me as much. If you are willing to give Shachi a chance, why will you deny it to him?"

"He has already had his chance," Kaushika says. "I do not trust him to keep his word. For years, he has made an enemy of sages, wanting only to thwart us, mocking us by sending apsaras to seduce us, desecrating our meditation, *violating* us. I made a vow not to attack your city or harm your kin. I did not make a vow to leave your lord unharmed."

"Then you are obeying the letter of the vow, not the spirit," I seethe. "You will not attack my city or my kin directly, but you will stand by and watch Shachi do the same. You claim to be guided by love—to be the sage who is a friend to all creatures— yet you have no love for the lord. You say that I am your moral anchor, yet you oppose me."

"And therein lies the truth of it," Kaushika says softly.

He stands up, and there is something deeply weary and sad in his gesture. I come toward him, but Kaushika begins to pace, turning away from me, and in his posture, there is a haunted memory of something he has not spoken of until now.

"You want me to be guided by love, but you do not see that this rivalry I sustain with Indra is guided by love, too. I can forgive the storm lord for myself, but what of all the others who have suffered due to his negligence? Sages more powerful than

I am have tried to teach Indra a lesson. Gautama cut off Indra's manhood for deceiving and seducing his wife, but Indra simply regrew it in time and was never adequately punished for his violation of her. You saw the fall and decay of Thumri, generations of lives lost, with the lord answering to no one for his negligence. Sages have come and gone, yet Indra has not learned his lesson, no matter what we've done." Kaushika's eyes flash, and his mouth is a hard line. "My lesson to him *must* be stronger. It must be decisive. I will side with Yama and with Shachi, not because of their reasons, but because of my own. Perhaps if Indra returns to the void, he will finally learn the lesson he must—and justice will be delivered."

A justice that will destroy my city, I think, but I know that anything I say will be futile.

Justice, he calls it, but what is justice without compassion? Without love? Merely a balancing of scales. Merely a weightage, sterile and heartless and cold. No wonder it is Yama who is charged with overseeing such a thing; the justice Kaushika desires is not one meant for the living, it belongs to the dead.

My body trembles in despair. I stare at Kaushika from where I stand, wondering if I have known him at all. He has always been a gyani, a yogi of rationality and logic, whereas I am a being of water. Of memory and loyalty. He has always been comfortable with the idea of Indra being a thrall, no matter that he despised the idea of becoming one himself. I recall the way he used the lord's elemental power to stop the rain from pouring outside Shiva's temple, twisting the lord's free will for a few minutes, all so he could intimidate a mortal queen. Indra must have raged in his court, unable to understand what was happening to him. An eye for an eye, Kaushika would have it be. Not realizing it is himself that he is blinding.

Kaushika sees the expression on my face, and his own gentles. He comes closer to me, and wraps me in his arms, and despite my despair, I melt against him—because I know that what we had was real. That for a time, we had escaped this conflict. We had felt love.

Kaushika sighs. His breath ruffles my hair.

"When I wanted to consult with Yama before, I did not realize we would end up discussing the depths of dharma. Yama did not give me an answer to my dilemma, but he did show me how to think. He asked me if my actions were led by reasons of pride or those of righteousness." Kaushika nuzzles my neck with his nose, then pulls me back so I can see the sadness in his eyes. "For days, I was confused," he murmurs. "And in that confusion, I thought of you, the one thing I know to be true. The one thing that does not make sense, that *should* not make sense, but is tied to me like the cords of my own karma. I know you do not see it that way, but I did not lie to you, Meneka. I *do* want to be guided by love. You showed me the path once. But you cannot be that guide for me any longer. You cannot hold my hand, leading me down it." He steps away from me, though his fingers still hold mine tightly.

"Why not?" I ask in a small voice. His words are a rejection, yet the way he holds me speaks of love. "If you trust me, then why can't you be guided by me?"

"Because it is *my* path, even if you showed me the way. When

Rambha seduced me, I saw that I would do anything to make you feel happy. I would destroy the three worlds for you. I would burn myself, and everything I hold sacred, all for you. Is that what you want?"

A thrall, I think. I have heard those promises—indeed, I have made my marks do awful things because of their love for me, many times before. Yet that has never been love. If Kaushika burns everything because of me, even his own ideals . . .

I shake my head. "No. Never that. Never from you."

"My heart is set," he says quietly. "This is the decision for me."

"If you do this, we will be on separate sides of the war," I tell him. "I will fight for Indra. I will fight you."

"I know," he says evenly, then tucks a stray strand of my hair behind my ear. "I love you without reserve, Meneka. And I am keeping my promises. I said I would find a compromise between my vows, and I will raise not one weapon against Amaravati or any of its citizens, but I must defeat Indra, for that is the only way forward. I am sorry I did not consult you before agreeing to fight for Shachi. But I could not. I had to come to this myself."

My body wants to stiffen against his embrace, but I breathe in and out, trying to find the grace of a yogi. Because I understand that though the pleasure we receive together is better than the one we claim alone, we need to come to it, complete in ourselves. We are two ends of a duality, a mirror reflecting colors within each other that we cannot see in ourselves. Yet that image is a picture of codependency. He seeks his own enlightenment. I must seek my own purpose.

I nudge his cheek with my nose, and Kaushika turns his

head, capturing my lips in a kiss. His mouth is soft and pliable, and he holds me tight. I clutch his shoulders, my nails digging into the fabric of his kurta. Our kiss is desperate, full of promise, and his tongue slides into my mouth, chasing each kiss with another one, as though not wishing to stop, and I understand what he has not said. That this is difficult. That it could be our last kiss. That love takes time, and if it *is* love between us, then maybe we will learn the depths of it once we have conquered ourselves.

It is strange, to kiss him in this way when it seems that we're doubting everything we have gone through already, doubting what we've had so far. It is strange to think that he is defying me, but calling it an act of love, of trust. He is telling me that he is not my thrall, not my prey. He chooses this path because it is *his*, and I allow him to because we have both seen what can come of obeying the other blindly, a version of me lurking within Rambha's illusion. I do not want him to fight me, but I do not want him controlled by me, either. Is this trust, then? Why does it feel like heartbreak?

A sob wrenches through me. I push back from him, because if I don't let him go now, I will never stop. I will join him, when I know I must not. He steps back too, and there is a wild, undone look in his eyes, like he is thinking the same thing.

"Meneka," he says, and my name on his lips sounds like a plea. "This war will be too dangerous. Hounds of hell, asura demons, Shachi herself. I do not want you harmed."

"You cannot stop me from fighting for my city," I say, my voice shaking.

"No," he replies, and there is fear in his face finally. A seductive thought flashes in me, that neither of us needs to choose this. That we can forget about this and return to our hut. But it lasts only for an instant. Even if Kaushika does not ally with Shachi, I must still defend Amaravati.

He sees this too, and the both of us understand the gravity of our decisions. My fingers sketch a fleeting illusion—the two of us free and in love, our limbs wrapped together, while we watch the dawn from our bed. We came so close to such a destiny. Kaushika utters a heartrending sound on beholding the illusion, and tears fill my eyes. I let the illusion die.

"Meneka, please don't fight," he whispers. "Please."

I make no reply this time. I turn and flee while I can.

The next time we see each other, it will be on the field of battle.

I seek Matali immediately.

I rush through the palace, past asura guards and maidens, through warrens and gardens, going to the only other person I know who loves Amaravati as much as I do. No one tries to stop me. No one follows me, perhaps knowing that my escape is futile. I see glimpses of preparation for war, rageful magic, livery and uniforms, the sound of drums. I rush past a courtyard and see asuras marching toward the palace walls from where they will arrive at heaven's gates.

The gandharva is in his chambers, alone for once. I enter to the strains of music, a melody that tugs at my heart, raises a lump in my throat. The chamber is covered in fumes of heat and wine, countless used goblets strewn all over the bed and floor. I narrow my eyes, trying to see through the smoke of hashish and follow the sound of Matali's beautiful voice, which sings a soft lament. I find him within his deep gold basin, strumming at his sarangi again. Matali looks up as he sees me, and his voice falters to a stop.

I do not have the heart to reprimand him. Tears run down his face. "He is dying," Matali chokes, and my heart catches at the grief in his voice. "The lord is dying, and there is nothing I can do about it."

The sarangi disappears from his hands, and he tips his head back, closing his eyes in pain, his chest heaving up and down in silent tears.

"You *can* do something about it," I say. "Matali, I can portal us out of here back to Amaravati—but I need your help. There must be something in the ancient legends, something in the stories that you can tell me, of Shakti's source magic and how to access it." My voice grows frustrated. "No one will tell me anything except that I must learn about myself to unlock this magic."

Matali jerks his head, and looks at me. He offers me a watery smile. "Obviously you must commune with the divine part of yourself, Meneka. You're a celestial creature. Surely it cannot be that hard?"

I read my own skepticism of this teaching in his voice. "There must be *some* method you know, some story?"

"Oh, I know many stories, but none of them will help you. This seems to be uniquely crafted to—"

His eyes widen. The both of us hear it in the same instant. Voices raised outside in aggression and annoyance. Matali stands up in his bath, dispelling water everywhere. He is naked, but unabashed. Instruments appear around him, the dhol, the flute, the mridangam.

I react in the same movement, turning toward the door, mudras already forming on my fingers. We stand ready to unleash our magic, for both of us have had the same thought: Shachi knows we have decided against her. She has sent her asuras to kill us.

Sure enough, the door opens and Holika marches in, blade drawn. "Well, well," she says, her gaze running down Matali's naked body contemptuously. "Caught you at a vulnerable time, have I?"

CHAPTER 22

Neither Matali nor I have a chance to respond.

The chamber doors widen, and Holika steps aside. Others pour into the room behind her, but they are not enemies. Familiar and welcome, they are celestials. Rambha is haggard, her cheeks tear-stained. She hangs back, but Nanda utters a joyful cry and leaps toward me, crushing me to her.

"How—When—What are you doing here?" I stutter.

Nanda draws away, smiling a little. "He sent us here. He opened a portal to the mortal realm to bring us."

Kaushika, I think. A rush of feelings consumes me, gratitude and pride and love. He did not want me to fight, but he has helped me survive the oncoming battle. I gaze into Nanda's face, searching for signs of despair. She is dressed in hermitage clothes, a simple kurta and pajamas, but of course that cannot detract from her loveliness. Guilt threads through me for abandoning her in naraka. "I'm so sorry, sister," I say, dropping my gaze in shame. "I tried to return, I did. Will you forgive me?"

Nanda tips my chin up. "There is nothing to forgive. I prayed every day for relief, but I was not without hope. I knew you would not rest until you brought me home. I knew you would find a way to save Amaravati."

I nod, but I am still uneasy. I have not yet gained mastery over the power that can save us. "Did the lord of death mistreat you?"

Nanda shakes her head. "After you and Matali left, Yama imprisoned me. I think he was hoping you would return at once or send someone in your stead, another agent of heaven." A soft huff of laughter escapes her. "He was not pleased it was Kaushika who came. He did not mistreat me, Meneka. I was a guest, though it is not a pleasant place to guest in." Nanda shudders, and a spasm passes through her. "I have endured worse."

Her answer is brave, as is only to be expected, but I know she will not heal so easily from her sojourn in naraka. The very place is dark and insidious, worming into one's soul, planting its nightmares like seeds. Though my own stay there was short, I have woken up at nights in a cold sweat, magic flickering on my fingertips ready to unleash in defense, only to realize I have been dreaming.

I have more questions for her, but I hold them back. I turn to Holika, who watches my reunion with a sardonic smile. "You helped me," I say.

"You are a soft creature," she says shrugging. "You could use the assistance."

"Does this mean you will fight for us in the war?"

Holika grins, her sharp teeth glinting. She points her blade at me, then slices through the bangle Shachi gave me, taking away my protection in this realm. "I will kill you, sister," she says softly, "for betraying Shachi. But I will not do it in your weakness. Come in strength, and meet me on the field of battle."

I say nothing, but I understand what she means. Without her, the others would not have found me in Matali's chamber; she protected them in the palace, leading them here—it is the reason her blade was unsheathed. But that is all I will receive from her. Holika has been exacting in her training of me, and I have disappointed her with my failure to be consumed by rage. Yet this is a sign of respect, of sisterhood. I do not attempt to persuade her as she walks out of the chamber.

I turn my attention to Rambha. She is already ensconced in Matali's arms. Music spins around the both of them, inviting, *seducing*, and Rambha and Matali are both teary-eyed, touching each other, kissing and fondling, murmuring words of comfort and praise for Indra.

Unlike Nanda, who looks healthy, though shaken, Rambha appears as though she has aged. It is startling to see her this way; celestials do not show age on their bodies and faces. Yet her eyes are exhausted and red, as if she has been crying, and I know her imprisonment in the mortal realm has not been easy. The yogis must have put her to work like any other disciple, but Rambha is heavenly royalty, Indra's most favored concubine, used to a life of wine and jewels and songs sung of her beauty. She would not have found life in the hermitage easy. Even from this distance, I can smell her aura, once fresh star-anise now turned into burned spice.

I know that her actions in the mortal realm are not her fault, and she presents a sorry figure, but I cannot feel pity for her. She has betrayed me at every turn. Shachi might have manipulated her into it, but Rambha still volunteered to seduce Kaushika, despite knowing what he means to me. If I had not intervened, she would have him for her thrall. She would have killed him too, a step beyond what Shachi asked of her. I think of how tolerant Kaushika has become, to look past her grievances and allow her forgiveness. He is on the path to embracing his love for all creatures, but I never claimed that was my path. My anger toward Rambha pulses in my veins, and she must see it in my eyes, for she looks away from me, tears still glistening on her cheeks. She busies herself with Matali, helping him dress back in his clothes from heaven.

"Kaushika sent you here," I say to the two apsaras. "Did he tell you what is occurring?"

"He told us everything," Nanda replies. She gazes up at the ceiling as if she can see through the roof, past the realm we are in, to perceive the skies. "Shachi's betrayal . . . I cannot believe it. Once I was seduced by Indra, and then by Shachi. I feel like a fool. Because of my blindness, you and Kaushika were in danger too."

"Do not blame yourself," I say. "Shachi fooled me too. She has been playing this game with the lord far longer than any of us. The Vajrayudh is nearly at heaven's door, and war is coming to Amaravati. I intend to protect Indra, despite what he has done. As for Kaushika . . . He has chosen a side, and it is not this one."

The three of them pause, staring at me in disbelief. Are they so surprised that I would wish to protect the city even against Kaushika? I feel my temper rise, but then Nanda squeezes my hand, and I understand that they pity me. I have been separated from Kaushika again, despite the life I wished to carve with him. My throat feels tight.

"You have my loyalty, sister," Nanda says. "But Rambha and I have been trying to call the lord from the hermitage. He cannot hear us."

"There must be a way," I insist. "When we were summoned by Indra, his call to us was his alone, not of Amaravati. Is there no song, no illusion we can cast to him? I remember the scent on the wind when the lord called to us. It smelled of you." I say this last phrase to Rambha, and her eyes widen. Matali pauses in adjusting the cuffs of his sleeves, looking wildly up at her.

The both of them speak at the same time.

"You don't think—" Rambha breathes.

"Would he remember?" Matali asks. "It was centuries ago, was it not?"

I cannot make sense of it, but I am not expected to. Indra, Matali, and Rambha have always been more than lord and devotees. They are lovers, and Matali wept openly for the deva. I realize the grief etched on Rambha's face has less to do with her time in the hermitage, and more to do with being away from the lord. Rambha must feel the lord's demise in her heart too. Some of my anger toward her vanishes.

Rambha shivers. "He will not want me to do this. He allowed me to go to the mortal realm to seduce Kaushika because he did not want me in heaven, when he knew Shachi was plotting."

"It is the reason he allowed me on this journey to patala too," Matali says. "He feared Amaravati would not survive what was coming, and wished me away. Shachi thinks she manipulated us into leaving, but in truth we obeyed the lord's command."

I raise an eyebrow. "If your love for him is based on obedience, is it truly love?"

Something in Rambha's eyes shifts at those words, an awakening. She straightens and nods. Matali takes his cue. The both of them come to stand next to me and Nanda, and a drum appears out of thin air in front of Matali. He begins a beat, slow at first, then much faster. We watch as Rambha's eyes close, and her body begins to sway. Though she is not wearing her clothes from heaven anymore or her jewels, a strain of power surrounds her, visible to my eyes like a chain link made of gold. It loops from her to Matali, disappearing into the wind.

Rambha begins to dance. Mudras erupt from her fingertips. The Lover's Wait. Song of the Deprived. The Wheatstalks Hum. These are mudras as old as the most ancient apsaras, basic forms that young apsaras are taught in heaven. I do not expect them to do much, but Rambha's magic is languid and graceful, lending a beauty to the simple sigils I have not seen before. Matali's drumbeats echo in my heart, and he begins to sing in his high, clear voice, a song of sweet love.

I feel a strange pressure in the air. It is tinged with sadness and yearning, and Matali's call becomes more woeful. The breeze that rustles within the room becomes a whooshing wind. Nanda and I move closer to Matali, watching as air envelops Rambha. Her illusion is silvery and translucent, and the breeze pricks my eyes. I have to squint to make out what she is crafting, but all I see is Indra surrounded by a hundred versions of her, in his bed, in his arms, in his council. I see Matali too, guiding Indra's chariot to war, tending the lord's wounds, putting the lord to sleep.

This is simple magic but powerful. There is a message here to the lord, a memory, an innocence, an incompletion. It is as if the song and dance are of a time when neither Matali nor Rambha were as practiced in their arts as they are now. When perhaps Indra himself was not as ancient as he has become.

Wind churns, and tears prick my eyes. My heart soars with Matali's melody, and I think of Kaushika and our first kiss. I think of him in my arms, telling me he loves me. This is a true song of devotion, and it leaps within me, twining my love for Kaushika with my love for the city. Nanda utters a soft sob, and she must feel the same devotion to home, because in the next instant, the wind wraps around the four of us. Though we are still in patala, the crescent gates of Amaravati shimmer in my eyes, overtaking the chamber. The gates creak open, winking in gold and black, as though forced to appear. I see Indra—not the lord I know him to be, but a young man remembered, rising tall and handsome, an image from Matali and Rambha's memories. Scent threads through me, star-anise and cardamom, limned with lightning.

Under us, the chamber floor begins to shake.

The music reaches a crescendo, and Rambha's feet are just a blur.

Patala blinks away from us, the crescent gates of Amaravati arching thousands of feet high.

We stumble through, all of us falling against one another, coming to our knees. Matali's instruments disappear, and Rambha stills, her breath coming out in pants. Silence overtakes us, shrill and ominous.

We are in Amaravati again.

CHAPTER 23

Nanda and I are the first to rise. We are not so affected by the sickening magic of the city, our devotion to Indra shaky as it is. I assist Rambha, and Nanda slowly revives Matali, who whimpers on the ground as if in pain. When the gandharva comes to, he sways where he stands, staring up at the skies, his mouth dropping open.

We all gaze up. The skies are a riot of storm clouds, grays merging with blues, indigo slashing through thick heavy white. The effect is beautiful, for this is Amaravati still, but a queasiness spreads in my stomach like wine gone rancid. The city is ailing, and my tether to its magic lies limp, no longer a glittering gold but a yellow pale enough to be almost colorless.

This is the effect of the Vajrayudh, made worse by the disharmony within swarga. I inhale, and all I smell is ash. I am reminded of the illusion Rambha carved for me months ago, when she forced me to seduce Kaushika. This is what she feared, and it has come to pass. Even now, he prepares with Shachi, planning for Indra's downfall and with it the end of Amaravati as I have known it.

I tilt my eyes to the distance where clouds surround the orb that carries King Satyavrat's corpse to the city. So unnatural is this magic that the skies look corrupted in that direction, endlessly roiling and churning with hues of darkness. No longer is the orb a thing resembling a golden sun. Shachi's asura magic aids it openly, and the orb is a massive black moon, as large as a mountain, approaching Amaravati like a comet. It screeches with a terrible sound, cleaving through any defense Indra may have spun. I feel the cuts it makes to the air like a keening in my ears, arrhythmic and piercing.

We are all stunned into silence at beholding it. I cannot imagine the scale of destruction it will unleash, and my thoughts turn to water. I begin walking toward the palace, and the others tear their gaze from the skies, hurrying beside me. Mansions, gardens, and temples pass by us, gold and shadows turning into ash. The hum of song permeating the city is replaced by a deathly silence, echoing with regrets. Song, prayer, and devotion have abandoned Amaravati. We walk through a wraith town, death at its doorstep.

"Where is everyone?" I ask. "The citizens, the guards?"

"Sent away," Rambha says, and her voice shakes, full of tears. Her face has drained of all color, and she cannot speak anymore, so overwrought is she. I look to Matali to answer as all of us hasten our footsteps.

Matali looks uncharacteristically grim. "This evacuation has happened in times of great war, but never like this. Indra has sent them all to the mortal realm, to disguise themselves and hide their celestial natures. It is for their own safety, should asuras attempt to hunt them down for their lineage and devotion to the lord. Shachi has promised retribution to his devotees.

He must know that she will punish them for forgetting her and for loving him."

"He will not be happy to see us," Rambha whimpers, though her pace becomes faster. "We more than most were instructed to keep away in case the city falls."

The road under us cracks, and she leaps away just in time. Before, Amaravati righted itself, but now the cracks simply spread farther, opening into yawning darkness.

Nanda sidesteps another large crack too. "You have come to help him, haven't you? He cannot be so angry."

"The lord lives in us," Matali answers. "When you are loved the way we are, you own a piece of Indra. That is what devotion means. If he dies, we will still carry pieces of him, in song and legend and prayer, and deep within our hearts. Those pieces will never die, not as long as we remember. And if we remember who he is, we can remind him too. That is our role—mine and Rambha's."

"He has accepted defeat," Rambha says, choking. In her voice, I hear all the love and grief she has for Indra. I can see suddenly why the lord made an exception for her, to free her from her missions. "He would not send everyone away if he thought he had a chance of winning. He has taken the magic he ordinarily allows them into himself, to preserve the walls of the city from falling too soon, leaving naught but a kindling for them, but he feels his demise. This is an attempt to do his duty—and they—they have abandoned him in obeying him."

I am surprised to hear Rambha speak of obedience, when

she raised it as an objection to come here, but then I remember how once she came to fight by my side to stop the war between Indra and Kaushika. How she kissed me and transferred some of her own aura to save me, even though she knew the act would anger Indra. Rambha is devoted to the lord, and I do not claim to understand the shape of her love for Indra, but it is not mere obedience that motivates her. Her love for Indra is as complex as mine for Kaushika.

"The Vajrayudh is days away yet," I say. "The city is in disharmony, but no legend has said the deterioration would be this fast."

"The Vajrayudh advances because of *that*." Rambha points to the orb, pulsing toward Amaravati, leaving a streak of darkness through the clouds. "We would have had more time to broker peace, but such an unnatural event, this crime against nature, has displaced the cosmic energy of the planets. The Vajrayudh is accelerated, racing towards heaven, attracted by the energy of the corpse."

"Where are the other devas?" Nanda asks. She stumbles, and I draw a rune of stability, unleashing it under her feet, as the ground shakes. "They are charged to defend Amaravati, are they not?"

Matali glances at her and shakes his head. "They are charged to preserve themselves. They have no true allegiance to Indra, only to the throne. They will not stir out of their deep sleep until after the Vajrayudh has passed, and then they will renew their vows of faith to whoever rules Amaravati. It could well be Shachi. This is why the devis do not join the battle either." He shudders. "It is a sign. They wish for Indra and Shachi to find their harmony first and decide the victor between them, before they choose a side."

Rambha merely whimpers again. Fresh tears rush from her eyes, and it is a wonder she can see where she is going. Mudras form from her fingers, but the golden dust swirling around her is weak, barely giving her any power. I feel for my own tether inside me, and it quivers like a dying animal, as though I am in naraka instead of the City of Immortals.

We arrive at the palace, entering through the crescent-shaped gates. Made of pearl and diamond, the gates have always been strong, yet now they chip away into dust. Nanda and I follow Rambha and Matali to the throne room. I exchange a despairing look with Nanda. I can see my fear on her face. Magic usually lies heavy in the palace, so close to the lord, but now it is a thin breeze, stale with ruin and decay. Matali and Rambha love the lord like no other, but Nanda and I have loved the city too; we are here to protect it. An ache grips my heart, and I try not to give in to my fear. I hurry along, squeezing Nanda's hand, feeling her squeeze mine in return.

We enter the throne room, and my footsteps slow down. Murals, paintings, and artifacts all are smashed, trailing away into ash. One sculpture of an apsara is missing a torso, and a tapestry leaches color, staining the walls. The ceiling is a broken mess, gold streaming through it, ash falling in dark flakes. Ahead of us, Indra sits alone on his throne, his eyes closed in obvious pain. His skin is gray, and his body is bent. He supports himself on his massive vajra, the lightning bolt the only true sign of radiance here in this crumbling throne room, and dust withers off his body too. My heart skips a beat in terror. I am watching him diminish before my eyes. Unlike the amazing lord I have known him to be, he appears weak, old. Scared.

The lord's eyes drift open as we approach. He blinks at Rambha and Matali.

"No," Indra whispers. "No, get away. Leave. You should not be here."

His voice breaks, and in that moment, I cannot help but think that he appears more human than celestial.

"She promised me," Indra whimpers. "She promised me you would be unharmed. Rambha, I sent you to the mortal realm so you would never have to see me this way. And you, Matali, I told you to keep away should I be in danger. You have betrayed me with your arrival here. You have *betrayed* me." His last words are a wheeze, and Rambha and Matali exchange a startled look and rush to him, even as he collapses farther, bending over.

I keep back, startled as well.

Shachi admitted she sent Rambha away, twisting Indra's arm. She was the one who manipulated Matali's absence from the lord too. Perhaps Indra relented, knowing he was enmeshed in a losing battle. I remember his desperation and anger when he charged me with finding the conspirators in patala. I recall the turmoil he was unable to contain in his own court even when I arrived, others whispering of his powerlessness, his impotence. Shachi might not have gained the alliance of the celestials in this war, but she did not need to. It was enough that she created doubt in them for *Indra*. He weakened because of it.

I step forward, and Indra looks up at me. Whatever Matali and Rambha have been saying to him seems to have bolstered him. They stand back, one on either side, as he eyes me. A hint of grandeur and appraisal enters his voice.

"Apsara," Indra intones. "You did not fulfill your mission."

I meet his gaze unflinchingly. "You always knew it was Shachi. You knew it was she who released the halahala, that it was her magic raising the corpse."

Indra flashes me a weak smile, full of lightning shards. "Did you think me unaware of what occurs in my own home? Shachi is cunning, but she is half of my soul. She cannot keep secrets from me, not for long. I suspected her, but the others needed to see her for who she is."

"And you sent me to collect the evidence, a rebel apsara. You could have sent any minor deva, a gandharva, any other creature of the realm, but you insisted it must be me. I would know the true reason why, lord."

"Why?" Indra laughs, but it is a brittle sound. "I was told you were an apsara like no other. Rambha said once that you would become heaven's greatest weapon. You have demonstrated great power. I wanted you as an ally. Is that not what you promised me?"

The words I spoke to Indra at the end of the battle in the mortal realm return to me. *Amaravati is my home. You are still my king. I intend to return there.* My message was clear, that he could either have me as an ally or as an enemy, but I am amazed he remembered it. That he thought to act on it. Yet I am not appeased.

"If you wanted me as an ally, you could have told me your mind from the start," I say coldly. "Instead of threatening me with being parted from Kaushika, you could have come to me as a friend, as the god you are, responding to my fidelity. Yet you wanted me obedient, wishing for me to turn Kaushika in your favor, wishing for me not to love you but to fear you. You never understood that my devotion has more to do with me than to do with you. For years, you failed me. You failed your mortal believers. You failed Shachi, she who you claim is part of your own soul. Now you reap the fruit of what you have sowed."

The lord's eyes narrow, but he does not interrupt me, and when Rambha tries to protest, he silences her with a hand to the knee.

"You are the lord of heaven," I continue, my voice still hard. "You are the deva who brings rain and fertility, who promises change, yet instead of looking to your own heart for what *you* must evolve into, whom you must become, you have sought to control and intimidate, forgetting the role you play in the balance of the cosmos. Now Yama comes to judge you, riding the winds with Shachi, and your devas have abandoned you." I take a deep breath and meet his sunken eyes, which watch me unblinkingly. "I will fight for you, lord, but I will not stop Yama if he finds it in himself to weigh your crimes against your benevolences. I am here for my home, for this city, for Amaravati. That you benefit from it is your fortune, but do not think my allyship with you means my forgiveness."

"I do not need your forgiveness," the lord says, scoffing. "I need your loyalty." Indra's face is hard as lightning, and he squeezes Rambha's hand with his, while Matali croons in his ear. "Many words you have spoken, all of them in criticism. Yet you have always said you are devoted to me in your own way."

"I am," I reply. "You have never seen this."

"Then show me," Indra snaps. "Be devoted and advise me. Or do you only have castigations for your lord?"

It is ironic he says this. Indra told me not to presume to advise him before I left for this mission. A part of me is amazed I am speaking to him so, for despite his decay, he is still divine, one of the most ancient beings in the universe.

I think of Kaushika, the mortal who completes me, whose love taught me to look inside myself for my strength. I look at my friends who returned to me to help me. I feel the decay of Amaravati, like a burning of my own flesh, and the lord who is broken, yet sent his devotees to safety, finally the king I have known him to be. In peacetime, Indra has been a drunken lord. But now he asserts his nature. He remembers his duty—both to the celestials and to the human world.

I know I have made the right decision to stay and fight.

I finally say to him the one thing I have been itching to all this time. "Amaravati's magic is not yours. You cut me off from the city, and from my wild prana, once, but I snatched it back from you. You have been hoarding power from the celestials, giving it to us drip by drip. Release the power back to us. Return it to me, to Matali and Rambha now, and to whoever remains here. We will use it to keep the city safe."

Indra's face changes. Of all the words I have said, it is these ones that shock him.

"I—I cannot," he whispers. "Doing such a thing would give greater power to Shachi too, for she can access celestial power as well. But even if it did not, I—I don't remember how to." I stare at him, and Indra shakes his head. "There is a memory of an intention . . ." he whispers. "Of a reason I hoarded this magic . . . a million, million years ago . . ." His voice grows quieter, eyes looking inward, and he shakes his head again.

"Then you will give me nothing?" I ask, in disbelief. "Nothing to help me fight for you? To save you?"

"Your freedom," Indra offers, looking up at me. "Freedom from your missions forevermore, not just for you, but your sisters too, those who still remain within their grove and those elsewhere in the three realms, fleeing from Shachi's war. Within the grove in my temple, you will find my armor. Take it for your own for the war. Rambha will show you. And should I remember how to return the dancers their power, I will do so—though do not count on that, apsara. I am older than you can know, and there is much I have forgotten."

I watch him for signs of subterfuge, but Indra merely looks tired. It is the best I will get from the king of heaven. I nod curtly.

Indra nudges Rambha, and she reluctantly leaves his side to come stand next to me. The lord turns to Nanda. She blushes, looking taken aback under his attention, but holds her ground, lifting her chin up. "Daughter," he says. "I remember you fought against me in the last war, but you fought against Kaushika too. What side do you choose now?"

Nanda shoots me an alarmed glance. "I fight on the side Meneka does," she says.

"Do you, now?" Indra asks with a glinting smile. "You are an elite apsara. Devise a strategy of battle with Rambha and Meneka. Earn my favor again. That is what you seek in your heart, don't you?"

Nanda looks confused for a second, perhaps wondering how the lord knows how hurt she has been with his negligence. She is thinking what I am. Indra has not been as oblivious to her as he has pretended. She is an elite apsara, one of his most dangerous weapons. Of course he has been watching her. She nods.

I beckon to Rambha and Nanda, intending to make my way to the apsara groves to corral the other dancers who have stayed behind, but the lord arrests me with a look. "Apsara, you should know that I did want peace with him," he says, and I know that he means Kaushika. "You reprimanded me for my neglect, but I was not always this way. Neither were things so broken between Shachi and me. There will come a time again when she and I will be closer to each other than our own breath." His smile is small and wistful. "She and I are a planet and its moon, circling each other, sometimes destined to be far, sometimes near enough to pull the other into ourselves. It is a wisdom I have not forgotten. Our duality, I have not forgotten."

I don't know what to make of it. Indra's optimism regarding his wife seems naïve. He has not seen the rage in her, the one she learned so well to obscure, but that burns her and will soon burn my city. Yet he has known her longer; he has loved her in many forms. Who am I to dictate their knowledge of each other?

"You have an opportunity here," I say. "Consider this a second chance, my lord."

Indra nods wearily. I watch him go into the antechamber, accompanied by Matali, where the two will dress for war. They disappear from my sight, and I turn away, to my own task within the apsara groves.

CHAPTER 24

Rambha, Nanda, and I are silent as we make our way to the apsara groves. Perhaps, like me, my sisters are thinking of what Indra said. We are readying for battle, and though we do not make a wish under the kalpavriksh for our success, we do not need to. Indra will make a prayer, and the tree will respond to his divinity more than it does to us. We pass the bathing pools, and Shachi's residence, and all along the way I notice the architecture flaking. Gold rushes in a river of radiance above us to the walls of the city. It is Indra doing this. Our presence has given him courage, and though the city is damaged, perhaps we have a fighting chance.

We arrive at the grove, and it is only then that I hesitate.

Nanda stops next to me, studying me quizzically. "What is it?"

I think of my sisters waiting in there for me. Sarala, Dhriti, Urvashi, and Titollama, the ones who greeted Nanda and me when we were summoned by Indra. I am certain they have remained, choosing their home over any safety fleeing could have offered. Their anger to me was a silent thing, but Matali told me they thought me selfish. I did not just fight against Indra in the last battle. I fought them too. Now I stand ready to defend the lord, but can I ask them to do the same thing, knowing everything I know about what he has done? How he has hoarded their power? How he has treated Shachi? The thought of lying for him makes me sick.

I stare at Rambha, trying to understand her devotion to Indra. She is an elite apsara. She was my handler and has lived longer. What would she do?

Rambha seems to read my mind. She cannot meet my gaze, but her voice is steady all the same. "We should go there to remind them of their duty," she says softly.

"Their duty," I repeat. "Yes, you would say that. Yet I must know their minds if I must remind them of their duty. You have always watched your sisters for your lord. Tell me now, what do they seek? What do they fear?"

Nanda looks curious, and the both of us study Rambha, who hesitates. Her eyes drift to the grove, and it takes her a moment to gather herself.

"We heard rumors of the strange magic you can wield," she says at last. "You knew the secret of wrenching back your magic from Indra, but you did not see fit to give it to them—your kin, your sisters. Instead, you chose to abandon them and live in the mortal realm with your lover, content with your freedom but uncaring of their imprisonment. They are angry because you did not share your power."

I close my eyes briefly in pain. I do not know how to refute her. I want to tell her that I do not know the secret, not enough to give it. That Shachi herself thinks me incapable and incompetent, my burst of Shakti's magic but a stroke of luck.

I lived in the mortal realm with Kaushika, but I did not

wish to neglect my sisters, yet all of Indra's flowery words in the throne room while publicly showing me forgiveness return to me. It was to remind the apsaras of their duty, but it was a warning too. *Do not rebel against me*, Indra said in his speech. *I will take you away from everything you love. Your sister is* my *agent,* my *champion. She will not betray me.* With his noose around my neck, sending Rambha to seduce Kaushika, reminding me that he could separate me forever from my love, Indra ensured my compliance. Matali tried to convince me that I was bound to my sisters because of Indra—all of us united by our devotion to him, weapons of his army. Will I give in to this explanation? Ask the apsaras to join this fight, all of us still led by the lord? Will I let him dictate my sisterhood, even now?

I open my eyes and straighten my spine.

No.

Indra is not the only power uniting the dancers. We have been bred as his weapons, my desire for freedom mirrors theirs. None dared to make an audacious request from Indra the way I did, but they must have felt the same chains tying them to him like shackles. I may not be able to touch Shakti's source power at will, but I have tasted that water. I have felt its caress. I will let the Goddess be my guide, instead of Lord Indra. I enter the grove, and Nanda and Rambha follow me silently.

It is heady to be back here in these gardens where I grew up. Illusory magic beads the air, hanging on trees like luscious fruit. I see mirages of dancers at every turn. A twirl there as the elite ones teach the younger girls how to execute a perfect mudra. A sashay here where a young apsara spins her wrists, throwing her head back in gaiety and abandon.

The mirages blink behind every tree, and I take a sharp breath, for I see these are images of my past. Rambha is in them, whispering in my ear, exciting and unnerving me with her closeness, as she corrects my stance. Nanda is there too, sitting on a rock, clapping her hands to a singer's rhythm, telling me to move my feet faster. I know the two of them can see the same images, for when I glance at them, their eyes are wide. We follow the hum of voices to the center of the grove and come upon our sisters, a hundred of them, milling together, speaking in hushed voices. All of them are dressed in their apsara raiment, a glittering collection of jewels and saris, arched eyebrows and heavy braids.

Emotion locks my throat to see so many of them all at once. Apsaras are sisters, but Indra has always pitted us against one another, asking us to prove our devotion to him to judge who is the best apsara. In every mission, in every training, we have tried to outdo one another. I have not seen all of us collected this way, save for brief instances in my childhood. I stare as Urvashi, Dhriti, and Titollama, clearly the leaders here, step forward from the mass, the others arrayed behind them.

"Meneka," Urvashi says. "You are back from your mission, with Nanda and Rambha no less. Then you have found a way to weave your future between Indra's and Shachi's desires?"

I am amazed that Urvashi speaks to me, instead of the two

apsaras who are of her own cohort and more senior to me. Yet Indra declared me his hero. Nanda was already in ill grace, and Rambha walks half a step behind me in clear deference. I do not have to declare myself as the one in charge here. Urvashi understands. I grow humbled with this honor. Urvashi always was astute, deeply entrenched in court politics. She must have suffered after my rebellion in the last battle. All of them did.

"Do we trust the girl at all?" Titollama asks, swinging her braid behind her and staring at me. "She has picked Indra if she comes here with his lover, but perhaps we should be fighting for Shachi. She is the goddess of this realm. Nanda herself has sung her praises. Have you changed your mind about the devi, Nanda? Why are you here, wanting to fight for the lord?"

Nanda looks to me. I take a deep breath, and she squeezes my hand in quiet encouragement.

"Nanda knows of Shachi's design on the city," I say. "She knows that Shachi wishes to burn the city and sack it. The queen claims to love Amaravati, but her love is overpowered by her rage for Indra. She will return to patala, letting Amaravati lie in ruin for a thousand years and longer. She will lay claim to the throne when her vengeance is sated and Indra has dissolved."

"Lies," a new voice says as the apsaras start to mutter. There is disturbance among the women gathered, then Sundari marches forward, Magadhi trailing her. The two are apsaras who have been loyal to Shachi since she rescued them from their missions to seduce Kaushika, and now both of them stand in front of me, arms crossed.

"She tried to protect you," Sundari says accusingly. "She told you everything about her. Still, you fight for *him*? How dare you?"

Magadhi strokes Sundari's arms, trying to calm her, but there is accusation in her eyes too. Urvashi and the others still, waiting for me to speak. I realize that both Sundari and Magadhi have shared all of Shachi's grievances with the other apsaras. This is the reason the apsaras still remain here in Amaravati, despite Indra's command to flee. Because they have not decided who they will lend their power to, who they will fight for. I cannot make them fight for the lord against their will. *I* chose this path, but I chose it myself. Kaushika chose his own, and I would be no better than Indra or Shachi if I forced my sisters to do a bidding they do not come to.

"I am not lying," I say. Though my voice is loud enough to be pitched to the entire gathering, it is without force. I do not want to manipulate them. "Lord Indra is weakening, and with him, Amaravati, this beloved city of mine. You see this—even our grove diminishes, mirages of our past blooming without our control. Shachi brings her asura army to our doorstep, and Yama, lord of death, rides with her to leash Indra. Sage Kaushika rides with them too, bringing his army. Mortal and immortal forces array around us, to burn Amaravati down. I have seen these armies."

The apsaras glance at one another. Urvashi's face pales, and Titollama and Dhriti reach for each other's hands. Next to me, Nanda and Rambha do not speak, but I hear Rambha's panicked breathing. I know what she's thinking. *We must hurry.*

They could be here already. Perhaps she can feel the lord's deterioration in her heart.

I don't flinch. I meet the eyes of my sisters, as many as I can. Urvashi stares back, watchful, and Titollama is wary, but I see the fear in Dhriti, and in the younger ones too, Sadhya and Ramani and Yodhita, who are only girls. Sundari and Magadhi both frown at me, but they are listening too.

"I will not force you," I say quietly. "Fight now for your city, or leave for the mortal realm, escape to safety while you can like the other devotees. Or choose to side with Shachi and fight those of us here who would protect Amaravati. Whatever you choose is your decision alone. None may judge you for it." I take a deep breath and measure my next words, knowing them to be blasphemous. "Indra has failed you at several turns," I say, and feel Rambha stiffen next to me. "Yet I ask you to fight on his side, a king who does not deserve his throne. But know this—he has already promised to grant freedom from your missions. The lord knows he cannot win against Shachi without us, and he is bound by his karma to me to fulfill this oath. I ask you now to fight not for a flawed king, a weak king, but for the sake of your city and the people here. What comes after we cannot know. But Amaravati does not deserve to burn."

My speech is met with silence. My heart beats rapidly against my rib cage. If they leave, Indra has no chance. Amaravati *will* burn.

Yet to my relief, one by one, the apsaras nod. Some of the older ones take the others by the hand, and then the younger girls are running, to gather this jewel or that, preparing to arm themselves. Nanda gives my hand another squeeze and joins Urvashi and the other elite apsaras. Magadhi and Sundari confer with each other for a long minute, then join them too. Between the elites, they will design a great illusion. They are all dancers, warriors, weapons. I watch them disperse, and then Rambha and I are standing alone together, for the first time since our last conversation. Since the last battle.

So much has occurred since then. Her seduction of Kaushika and her betrayal of my love. Her entrapment by Shachi, and her internment in the mortal realm. I see the fear in her eyes, the hesitation, and my own anger resurfaces. I asked Kaushika to forgive her, but I do not know how well *I* have succeeded. I understand her circumstance, of being forced into her mission, as subtly as I was—our love kept hostage to Shachi's plans. But I cannot rid myself of the image of her body sashaying around Kaushika. Her illusions luring him, making him descend into darkness. I am furious, and I do not know how to speak to her as if I am not.

"Indra told me to wear his armor," I say shortly. "What did he mean?"

Rambha nods, and the relief in her eyes that I am not about to censure her is almost pitiful. "Come with me," she says, and hurries through the grove until we are at the lord's shrine.

Like all of Indra's temples, this one is magnificent, though much smaller than the ones I have come to expect. Built out of diamond dust, glittering with edges as lethal as lightning, this temple is large enough only for a few people to visit at a time. It is meant for apsaras alone; here, a young apsara communes with the lord, in an imitation of what she must expect when she grows up and is sent to the kalpavriksh. The temple is designed to be sharp, to remind a dancer that she is the lord's weapon, that she is his servant. I myself have come here on occasion, searching for peace between missions.

I enter ahead of Rambha, and a wave of nostalgia, remorse, and homecoming sweeps through me, staggering me. It is ingrained in us so deeply, this devotion to the lord, and here in his temple it grows tenfold. Hundreds of apsaras have visited here, day after day, honing their love for their lord. Promising to seduce mortals and immortals in his name. Risking their lives, their safety, their morals, all to serve him.

I should feel repulsed with this now that I know what I do, about the lord hoarding our magic for his own purpose. Yet all I feel is a deep sadness that pricks my eyes.

There is beauty in the kind of devotion apsaras showed to Indra. There is purity and sacredness. Fearful of us—remembering how Shachi's absence lost Amaravati her splendor—Indra chose to imprison us and *command* our devotion to him. What if he had asked us to give it freely? What if he had seen Shachi from the very beginning for who she is? It would never have come to this. She would never have thought to burn the city down. I would not have to fight her, giving my allyship to Indra. I think of Kaushika, whose love showed me my astonishing power once. He claimed none of the credit for it. Would that the immortal lord of devas had the wisdom of a mortal sage.

Rambha turns to the statue at the center of the temple. It is a small one, no bigger than half my body. A heavily jeweled

Indra made out of gold stands upon a stone serpent, one foot on the serpent's head, his vajra impaling the creature. This is Indra of ancient legend, protecting the earth's waters from the dragon-demon Vritra. He wears an iridescent blue dhoti of the softest silk.

Clouds, lightning, and fog swirl upon the cloth, mesmerizing me, creating illusions around the statue. Indra larger than life, his glory blinking in flashes of storm. There he is, facing a thousand asura armies, at the height of his power. Here in this vision, reigning over Agni and Surya and Samudra, lords of fire, sun, and ocean. Always the first of devas, atop his great elephant, Airavat, Indra shines from within illusory clouds, yoking stormlight in crackles of lightning, which spear around him like a crown.

I stare, for though I have seen these visions before on the statue, they remind me now of the lord he once was. Perhaps with the turning of time and ages, he can become like that once again. It is his only hope. Even should we win this war, Indra will have me to answer to. I will not allow my imprisonment, nor that of Shachi or my sisters anymore.

With trembling hands, Rambha begins to remove the dhoti from around the statue. Her fingers are intimate, and a strange expression comes into her face; she is thinking of taking the clothes off the lord's own person, as she has done many times. Sorrow, hunger, and grief flash in her eyes, and her aura is a brittle star-anise. I look away, for though this is not the lord, there is something too profound in this action. I do not need to intrude, or to steal this illusion of privacy.

The cloth comes free in her hands, and I turn back to her. My mouth drops open in astonishment.

On the deity, the cloth was simply a dhoti, magnificent and magical, but made for the statue.

In Rambha's hands now, the dhoti ripples, becoming a sari.

Embroidery races across it in knitting threads—and this time it is not Indra's story. It is the story of Amaravati, of gold-threaded spires and silver crescent gates. Of lush forests and woods, and glinting blue bathing pools. A hum emanates from the silk like war drums and sweet sitar, and it is reminiscent of the gandharvas. The tether behind my navel sharpens, flooding with power.

At Rambha's gesture, I begin to disrobe. My body trembles in the slight breeze as I stand in Indra's temple, naked. Rambha is silent as she approaches me, but there is music in the air, reverberating from the sari. She begins to wrap the cloth around me. Her fingers are soft and delicate, creating a dance on my skin, and her head is tipped down so I can see the shape of her ear, hear the melody of her breath as she moves around me, instructing me to lift my leg while she wraps the garment around my thigh, pleating.

The song rises as she continues, and I think, *This should move me to lust*. Yet somehow lust is the farthest thing from my mind. There is something too weighty about this moment. I cannot believe it—that it is Rambha here, the apsara I have always wanted to be, cradling me in the lord's clothes. Rambha, who is the epitome of devotion, giving me, a rebel apsara, so much power taken from her king. We are here for the same reason, to protect that which we love, the city and the lord, even if those have meant different things to us. Memories sink into me, of all that Rambha and I have been, friends, near lovers, adversaries. No matter who we were in the past, here we are now together, sisters at last.

One by one, Rambha takes the jewelry off the deity. The ruby and sapphire rings and armbands. The necklaces, long and silvery, studded with intricate beadwork. The heavy rings, filled with gemstones, circling each finger. Like the silk, the jewels resize on their own to fit me. They have been consecrated with years and years of untainted devotion. Their power washes over me, making me breathless. I sway where I stand, and Amaravati's tether is a roaring golden flood inside me. I feel capable of the greatest illusions, the most arcane of magics. My ears ring as the music becomes a symphony. Rambha places the crown marked with gold lightning and pearl clouds over my head, and tears leak out of my eyes at how much power I contain.

She steps back, and there is a hushed silence.

"You are beautiful," she says at last, and her voice is choked.

She has tears in her eyes. I wear her lord's clothes, drenched in his power, and illusions surround me, created by this attire. I wonder what she is thinking. I wonder what she is seeing.

I flex my fingers, and the rings chink against one another like warning bells.

Heaven's greatest weapon, she once called me, and I see in her eyes how she remembers it too.

It is time to find out if her assessment is true.

"Come," I say, and my voice sounds deeper, more sonorous.

I march out of the temple, Rambha on my heels. The sky is a bruise, lit by the unnatural light of the approaching corpse.

In a testing, I draw a rune of wind, and it flares in the air, charging me. It is a greater rune than any I have created before, responding not merely to my tapasvin power but to my celestial one. I understand now how this is possible, when it wasn't at the hermitage a few months ago. Power is power; prana is prana. All of these different magics come from the same source. I am silent as the wind carries Rambha and me above the city. We say nothing, but Rambha points to where a small army stands just beyond the massive crescent gates.

I allow the wind to lower us. The apsaras are a fierce party, forming a defensive line outside the gates. All are resplendent in their saris and jewels, and gold dust dances around them, ready to be unleashed. Urvashi and Nanda stand in the front, their smiles sharp, their faces lethal, each curve of their body ready to set free dangerous charm.

Indra's massive armored elephant trumpets loudly. Matali is perched by the elephant's neck, fulfilling his role as the lord's charioteer—but Rambha and I come to stand next to Lord Indra, who waits on the ground, one hand on the elephant's great foreleg. The lord glances at us, and in his eyes I see fear and determination. He is dressed in blue too, like I am, though gold armor covers him. His breastplate, armbands, and thigh bracers are engraved, and gold swirls around his person like a whip. The lightning-bolt vajra shines in his hand, its edges blurring, and the lord spins it once. I feel my tether sharpen behind my navel in anticipation.

Indra looks away to the sky in the west, where the comet rushes toward us, encasing King Satyavrat's corpse. Shadow and smoke surge. Stars disappear.

Rambha and I exchange a glance. My heart beats in nervous terror.

"She comes," Indra says.

CHAPTER 25

Drumbeats thunder, quaking the skies.

Matali begins chanting a war song. Behind my navel, my tether to the city bursts, flaming into magic, soaking me in amber. My vision grows golden, and Indra leaps onto his elephant, light as air.

The orb is upon us, shining not a few leagues away, hurtling ever closer. Rakshasas and asura armies appear in a blink, the skies filling with hordes upon hordes of the gigantic creatures. Shachi is a glowing force so powerful it hurts me to behold her. She is twice the size she has been in swarga, her limbs muscled under her black asura armor, her hair braided and jeweled, hanging over her shoulder. The kiritamukuta crown on her sends out beams of light, a rainbow radiance on her asura army. My heart thunders, and I shield my eyes. The halo behind her is a silver moon. She is commanding, she is powerful, she is terrifying.

Shachi's gaze sweeps over our small force outside Amaravati's walls. Even from this far, I see her rage at her husband, at the apsaras, and most of all at me. Her eyes lock on mine, and I hear her voice in my head. *I gave you a choice, sister. You betrayed me.* A bloodcurdling cry of wrath erupts from her, for she sees me in Indra's clothes and jewels. She knows I have promised my devotion to him despite my reservations. My knees shake, and doubt takes me over.

"Steady," Indra calls out. "Steady!"

We watch her army approach, riding the clouds. Shachi sits atop her lion, the beast grown several times its size. I see now that it was kept diminished in the palace of patala. It has reached its true proportions now in wartime, and it *roars*, the terrifying sound reverberating through our ranks. Terror streaks through me, but I stand my ground. Indra's clothes give me power and strength, and Matali's song becomes feral in response to the hordes.

Shachi waves her hand in a forward motion. More creatures appear, and Airavat trumpets in fear. Lord Indra must surely see the same thing I see. Waves upon waves of yamadut, their terrible twisted forms filling the skies like an ocean full of debris. Lord Yama rides on a fanged ox, almost as massive as Airavat. I search for Kaushika among them, and sure enough he comes, riding on Shachi's other side, atop a black steed. His mortal army is smaller than both Shachi's and Yama's but every single one of his soldiers glows with prana magic, incandescent with light. I try to search his face, see what he's thinking, but he is hidden behind a translucent shield. I only know it is him because of the brilliance of his aura, one that rivals Shachi's.

My heart sinks. He has replenished himself with tapasvin fire. He has returned with his mortal allies. Is Queen Tara among them? Will all of them hunt Indra? I know how much power Kaushika contains, how quickly he can defeat the lord, now when the lord is weakened. Shachi has wanted him on her side because, alone, she cannot defeat Indra—she and the lord are matched evenly. Yama is here with her to take the city. The lord of death wants every celestial bent to his justice, answering for their crimes, no immortal to be above his law of righteousness. Shachi wishes the throne. But Kaushika . . . He claims no enmity with the celestials of Amaravati, and I see his head pointed toward the lord like an arrow. The others will turn ruin upon the city, but Kaushika will destroy Indra, or leash him. The lord will receive no quarter from the sage.

Indra seems to know this. He did not blink on beholding Shachi, but seeing Kaushika frightens him. I glance up at him atop Airavat, and the lightning shard in his hand trembles.

"Do you know how to accomplish your task, my lord?" I call out.

"Yes," Indra replies tightly. "I must stop the corpse from reaching the city. I have kept it from hurtling forward, slowing it down as much as I can, but I will need time, all that you can spare, and as much devotion and love for me as you can muster."

The apsaras are already lending all their power to the elite among us, in order to conjure a great illusion to confuse the enemy army. We will not attack, but merely defend the city. It is as much time as we can give the lord. As for love and devotion—those will sustain and power Indra, but there is little of that to go around, thanks to Indra's own actions. He will have to make do with what we have.

"Prepare yourself," I reply, in answer to him.

The enemy army advances, and Urvashi calls out a command. I feel my golden tether drenched with light. Gold streams rise from each apsara, spinning around the elites. Urvashi nods at

Rambha, who directs a stream of fog around Indra's chariot. He grows obscured to the enemy, though visible to my apsara eyes. The illusion will not stop Shachi, Kaushika, or Yama, but should their soldiers attempt to strike Indra, they will have trouble.

Shachi understands. Her voice rings out, shaking the air.

"Lord of the skies! Submit to me, and relinquish the throne. Present yourself to the preservers of dharma to account for your infinite crimes. Do so, and I promise to be lenient to your devotees who have forgotten their queen. I promise to spare these mistaken fools who would protect you instead of worshipping me."

Indra shudders but ignores her. With one last look at the apsaras, his mouth moving in Rambha's name, he streaks across the sky in a sudden force of thunder and lightning, making for the orb in the west.

A war bugle blows from the enemy army, furious and vehement.

Shachi roars, taken aback by Indra's speed—but Kaushika has anticipated this. He races across the sky, a blur of color. I can hear Matali's music from afar, a war song that charges my illusion.

I wish to follow him, both to keep Indra from hurting Kaushika and to stop Kaushika from killing Indra. Instead, I stand my ground, and curl my wrists into mudras. My power merges with that of my sisters, and a forest sparks from Urvashi, bursting in front of us in the clouds. It is not any forest I know, yet my own remembered terror from the time in Kaushika's forest infuses the illusion, curling my emotion into it.

Beasts erupt out of thin air, and rampage the forest. Massive tigers, trumpeting elephants, wolves that hunt in packs, all are unleashed by the apsaras' power, some of them stalking asuras who scream, others headed toward the yamadut. Combined with one anothers' powers, our illusion is a hundred times more potent than any single dancer's. We infuse each creature with life. Each howl sends my own body trembling. Each fang is sharpened, each footprint real, each bloodied maw terrifying. Small details bring alive the imagery, and we unleash this horror toward the enemy, forcing the beasts to hunt them through the forest.

Every dancer is a shining force lit up by golden light—and Matali's song and drumbeats rise in a crescendo. I see Urvashi unleash an illusion of despair, mudras flung from her like arrows. The mirage bursts, and a great serpent appears within the army, lashing through the yamadut and the asuras, flinging them away from the wall. If the enemy had been trained to see that the serpent was not real, it would not affect them, but their bodies react on their own, cringing, scattering. She breaks a wave on the oncoming horde, dispersing it, before turning to another company.

Elsewhere, Shachi has advanced upon Rambha and Nanda together. The goddess is atop her lion, and both Nanda and Rambha spin around her. Shachi lashes out with a whip; it curls around Rambha's neck, and she chokes. Before Shachi can pull her closer, Nanda attacks, blinding Shachi with a burst of light. Shachi cries out, and I feel a thrill of victory rise in me. We are holding our own. Here in Amaravati, with desperation marking our footsteps, we are unleashing all the power we have. Shachi will not find this an easy victory, and—

The scent of camphor comes to me.

I spin on the spot to see Kaushika above me in the skies, chasing the lord. The smoke of battle has left streaks on his cheeks, and righteous tapasvin fire burns inside him, sparking all his chakras. Indra has almost reached the corpse in his chariot, but the lord has not begun his incantation yet, and he needs more time.

Horror takes me.

I break formation. I float up, coming to a stop between Indra and Kaushika, who pauses too, surprised. For once, he does not look either like a prince or like a sage. This is Kaushika, the kshatriya, the warrior. Hair undone, eyes gleaming in bloodlust and wrath, his muscles rippling underneath his armor, Kaushika advances toward me, knowing me to be the enemy. It is intoxicating to see him like this, and my breath hitches. We have come to this while in love. Would this have happened if we had never cared for each other? I know it with certainty. This moment was inevitable.

Kaushika smiles, and there is amusement in his eyes, laced behind his grimness. "You would not hurt me, would you, my love?"

In response, I spin on my toes, thrusting my arms out and over me, fingers curling from one mudra to another. This is Kaushika. I know his lust. I know his weakness. I have never used it against him.

But we are at war.

Streams of gold flood through me in a cosmic radiance, and suddenly we are surrounded by a hundred Menekas, a hundred Kaushikas. There we are at the banks of an unnamed river, his hand in mine, his head nestling my own. Here in this illusion, I ride him, naked, my head thrown back, a vision of ecstasy on both our faces. He crooks his fingers into me in one. I weep on his shoulder in another. I dance, and he watches me, both in an illusion I create and in the skies. Kaushika blinks, his mouth falling open—and I surround him everywhere, using every memory in my arsenal. He has broken through the illusions Urvashi carved. Can he break through those of *me*?

He slumps on his horse, eyes wide, as more and more versions of me surround him—reminding him of his choices. Of what he could have had with me, if he had not chosen to fight me.

A part of me wants to go to him, to stop this haunting assault. But I glance below and see that in the long minutes it has taken me to carve these illusions, Amaravati is already on fire. Shachi and Yama have breached the slim defense of the apsaras. An arrow whips from the archers, and lodges into Dhriti's arm. She cries out, her skin flaming into golden dust. Shachi's lion pounces on Revathi, a young apsara girl. I hear her painful shriek, before she vanishes into ash.

We are dying. We cannot contain them. We were never going to hold them back for too long, and behind me in the skies, I see Indra flagging too.

His chariot is now at the corpse, and he is attempting to undo Kaushika and Shachi's magic. Should the corpse reach Amaravati, all will be undone, but in Indra's movements I see his weakness. Airavat stomps in the sky, chasing the orb, even as the corpse rushes toward the city. Lightning bolts barrage the orb, and Indra flies around it, twisting and turning, slamming his vajra at it, trying to break the enchantment.

I feel my power lessening. Indra is taking all the energy of Amaravati, all the prana that he normally relinquishes to us. Amaravati *shivers* as if the city is a mirage too. Cries echo up to me, and I stare in horror as apsaras fall. They will no longer feel as much power in their tether. Even my own, despite my clothes and jewelry, diminishes with everything Indra takes. My illusion falters—

And disappears.

Kaushika blinks, then his eyes clear, a sinister expression gathering in them. It is the same expression I saw when he broke out of Rambha's enchantment, when he whipped a cord of fire around her neck. He straightens and dismounts. His movements are slow, deliberate. A small smile forms on his lips, and I see admiration and threat on his face.

"I always knew your power," he says quietly. "I never knew your danger."

He faces me, and I stare back at him, hovering only a few feet from him. I don't know what to say. My illusions were a base attack, to use his love for me as a weapon, but the burning city reminds me of my desperation. I stare at him, the hair hanging around his face, the glint in his eyes, the beads of sweat over his dark skin. I don't know how he will react, what he will do. I have crossed a line, and his words return to me. *You violate.*

"Kaushika—" I begin, my heart wrenching.

He doesn't let me finish. Kaushika surges forward, and captures my mouth in a kiss. He tastes of sweat and heat and violence, and I cling to him like he is the safest shore here in this mindless arena of war and death. His mouth metes out punishment, each stroke harsh and brutal. Kaushika's hands grip my bottom, his fingers tightening over my braid and pulling. He boxes me in with the cage of his body, and pleasure streaks through me, desire hurtling in my body. This is insanity. We should stop. But his touch is everywhere, and his kisses move from my mouth to my neck, biting the skin there, taking the pearl necklaces in his mouth and tearing them, until beads tumble into the open sky. He is a savage animal, and I am enthralled, too aroused, and the song of fire around us threatens to take me under within my lust—

Too late, I realize what he is doing.

I see a flash of cold smile on his face, and jerk back.

This is part of the same game we've played. I punished him with my illusions, and he has brought his weapon to me. Kaushika ravages my mouth in a kiss too swift to make sense of and steps back from me. His head inclines in a bow, and the next thing I know, he has mounted his horse again and shot past me into the sky toward Indra. I utter a cry of frustration, wanting to chase him, but my feet are caught in a shield of air made solid. He was manipulating the elements as he kissed me. He was relieving me of my jewelry that gave me power. It was never that easy with him. He has never been that naïve, that simple to seduce.

I pull against my prison, crafting runes that do not take. Kaushika is at the lord, and Indra is weakening. I watch him circle Indra, a blazing sun of chakras unleashing from him in a whip, tying around Indra's neck, pulling him from the chariot. Matali's song is a sob. Kaushika is one mortal alone against the lord of heaven—and yet, Kaushika is winning, and my city blazes, unprotected.

Below I see apsaras drop amidst rakshasas and asuras, exhausted from their dance. Shachi screams in righteous fury atop her lion, bloodlust in her eyes. There is no sign of Nanda, none of Rambha. Holika and other asura warriors battle through Urvashi's illusion. Sister against sister, woman against woman. All of us dying. Is this what it has come to? I stare around me in horror. *I never wanted this*, I think. *I never wanted to choose between them all. I never wanted war.*

They are all a part of Shakti, Vashishta whispers in my mind. *Are they Shakti too?*

I shake my head. I don't know.

Are they all the same?

I inhale the smoke. I hear the cries. I am paralyzed.

Decide, the great sage whispers to me, in the shadow of the Goddess. *Decide your own purpose.*

My head falls back, and I stare at the skies, at the stars. This battle will destroy Amaravati. Worse, it will burn away all bonds of sisterhood. How can any of us live with what we have done? Shachi is consumed by her rage, but she has loved us too. She is simply too blinded by anger to see it. I know I can stop her—stop this madness—if I can only find Shakti's power within me. Straining, I reach for the source, searching. I see glimpses of my past. The queen who brought me sweetmeats when I was a child.

Rambha who befriended me, trained me, betrayed me. Nanda who loved me, suffered for me. Holika who disdained me, helped me. Each a part of Shakti. Each a part of their own mind too. What is the lesson here? What knowledge am I missing?

I utter a cry, and it is song overtaking every other sound I hear. I think of them all, and who I am. My fury the same as Shachi's. My mudras those taught by the apsaras. The rage awakened in me through Holika's instruction. My tapasvin magic, taught by Romasha. Each of these women using prana in some form, accepting the power of Shakti.

Who are you? Kaushika once asked me.

I am Meneka, I think. A dancer, a lover, a seductress. A woman, fearful and strong and passionate and pure. Rageful and wrong, immortal yet weak. Who can answer who they really are? I can never know, not in completion, for I transform, I evolve, I become. *Skin and bones ever-changing, yet the heart harmonious and everlasting.* Tears leak from my eyes, the smoke of battle making my skin singe. *Listen for the echoes of your own heart, girl*, I hear Vashishta say. *The universe rings it back to you.*

I have taken things from each of these women. But are they me? Am I just a tapestry with threads stolen from their bodies and minds? A mosaic of shards acquired?

I open my eyes and see myself from a distance. My body up in the air, frozen in stillness. I see my sisters. I see my friends, my teachers, and I see the menfolk too, those who have parts of the Female Divine embedded in them. Power is power, prana is prana. Shiva entwines with Shakti; he cannot separate from her if he is to have any meaning. I see him, and it is an image of

Indra and Rambha, of Indra and *Shachi*, and Kaushika and me. With Kaushika I have never needed to be anyone else but who I am. Then why do I pretend to be someone strange to myself?

My body begins to glow.

A fiery radiance erupts from me, filling up the skies. I see myself from a distance, and my body sways in a strange dance. Not the form of the apsaras but that forgotten rhythm of the Goddess. Lasya, it is called, a gentle form of Shakti's dance, a nurturing of movement. This dance takes no mudras, it uses life as its sigils. The burning city, the screams, the orb and its enchantment, all become like mudras to me. I pull their energy, and my prana swirls around them, powering with every tilt of my head, every curl of my fingers.

Skin and bones ever-changing, I think. *The heart harmonious.*

I have judged myself. I have been ashamed. Of betraying Shachi, Indra, Kaushika, Nanda, and my sisters whom I abandoned. I, who asked for forgiveness and gave it to others, have never forgiven myself—for everything I endured, everything I unleashed.

I open my heart, and I stand aside, out of my way.

I forgive.

I accept.

That I never need to be like Rambha or Shachi or Nanda. That I never need to prove myself. That whoever I am, with all my doubts, all my inconsistencies, all my faults, all my purity, I am enough. That I have always been enough—and I have never been alone. I have sought to balance myself, thinking each part of me must remain equal to the other. I have thought to tame my magics, thinking one should be even with the other, an act of sterile justice.

But it is not balance that rules the universe.

It is harmony, embedded within chaos.

I reach for my celestial power, and I exhale in the way of the yogis. I embrace the asura magic I learned from Holika, and an enormous power braids around me, all three forms I know, mortal, celestial, demonic. Coils of fire, gold, and smoke rise in massive towers of water. The dispassion of tapasvin magic tempers the dark emotion of asura smoke. The divinity of celestial magic coats the mortal prana in immortality. Asura fumes leap to give Amaravati's power meaning. Each of them fills the other's empty spaces. Each of them completes the other's lack.

Radiance bursts through the skies, centering around me.

A power that has been haunting me for so long rushes through me, mirrored in all those who can see me. The source I have been seeking floods into me, silvery waters of Shakti rising all around me as if I am in a deep basin. Shachi stops, staring at me across the distance. Indra and Kaushika pause, their battle forgotten.

I am a tiny figure, holding on to myself, caught by this ancient, terrifying power. I am a globe of light, the sun incandescent, and I grow drenched in its enormous magnificence. The cacophony of war silences. Galaxies rise and fall in my vision. The silvery waters shimmer.

Who are you? I think.

Daughter, the power answers me. And the endless echo of it—*daughter, daughter, daughter.*

Spoken not from one goddess, but from many. From an infinity of them.

In my mind, I see the great statue of the Divine Goddess I found in patala, her many arms, her many faces. Full breasted, lushly curved, her features blurring, and her hands holding different instruments, a trident, a conch, a book, a pot.

I grow terrified. I watch as the silvery waters crash down on me. I swirl in the storm of the power, unable to tread water, sinking. I cannot breathe. I cannot move. What have I done? I have unleashed something greater than myself, more potent than I can know.

I feel all the devis of heaven crowd within me, Prithvi, Parendi, Aditi, and all the others besides. Behind me, one by one, other goddesses appear.

Lakshmi, the goddess made of gold, her eyes glinting, arrives out of a massive lotus, carrying flowers in her hand. The devi of knowledge and liberation and prosperity.

Sarasvati appears with the rush of water, to stand beside Lakshmi, strumming her veena. The goddess of wisdom, her song an echo, a dirge, a demand for the ignorance displayed in war, for the desecrations she has felt.

Kali is next, fierce and frightening, her skin a shiny black, giant arms protruding from her shoulders, her teeth bloodied and fanged, her hair a wild thing. She is the goddess of rage and destruction, and serpents hiss around her. She stands next to me, and I feel her fury, her threat and vengeance.

Durga appears on her lion, a creature even larger than

Shachi's, or perhaps the same, for who are all of us if not containers of the same power?

On and on they come. The goddesses fill my mind, they fill up the skies, more than I can count blinking next to me and behind me, infinite in their forms. Each of them different. Each unique. All in competition with one another. All coexisting together.

I am all of them.

I am their essence.

Shakti.

The armies diminish. Shachi trembles and falls to her feet, clambering down from her lion, bending to her own cosmic power. Yama's mouth hangs open, and he utters a chant. In a blink, the yamadut are all gone, though along with some of his generals, the lord of death remains, falling to his knees. I search for Indra and Kaushika. They are overtaken by my power too. I find them by the crescent gates of Amaravati, kneeling alongside Shachi and Yama, their duel abandoned.

All of them know our anger.

All of them can see our love.

"Yield," we say, and my voice echoes in the universe, uttered from the mouths of every devi who stands next to me. "Yield," I repeat. "Or you will be made to."

CHAPTER 26

The skies grow hushed.

I float where I am, and everywhere I see only me. The power of the goddesses fills me, taking over my heart and mind. The fighting mortals and immortals tremble before my might, for they can see the infinite goddesses arrayed behind me too. Their awe and fear radiate to me, and all of them shake where they kneel, their eyes downcast in horror and humility.

Only one person looks up at us, bold enough to meet my gaze. Kaushika's eyes are hooded and wary. With all my power bursting in me, I can see his intention writ clear over his aura. He is concerned, deeply so, and his gaze sweeps over me, calling me softly in homecoming.

I ignore it. The goddesses rage, their voices chaotic yet unified in purpose, directing me, speaking through me to all who have dared this. I am invincible, and none of them can defy me, not even this sage who attempts to follow the path of purity and grace yet comes here to war on my land, on my watch.

I descend to them, floating a few feet above them yet close enough that I may hear them speak. My brilliance is sharp, and all of them cower, mortal, demon, and divine alike, for though I stand now in front of them, the skies reflect my power. The universe throbs in time to my heart, telling them that a slip here would be their ultimate end.

Shachi is the first to speak. There is wariness in the queen's eyes, but it is only correct that she speaks first. She has the right, for she is a part of me too.

The queen prostrates herself. I gaze at her, and her body trembles. "Mother," she breathes to Shakti burning within me. "Sister," she says, to each of the other goddesses, who hum in my mind. "Daughter," she whispers, and this time it is for the apsara girl whose body I occupy. I feel this apsara inside me— Meneka is her name, and she watches, quiet and awed, her throat and heart filling with power that leaves her speechless. She is me, but she is not-me too. I hold her close, but I do not let her take me over.

"I won this battle fairly," Shachi says. "By right of conquest. By the divine right of my being. By all the precepts, I have won here fairly."

I look at her, and she flinches.

"What is it you want, Shachi?" My voice is a quiet rumble, a thunderstorm, a quaking of heaven and earth. I speak with the speech of all the goddesses.

"Justice," Shachi says, her mouth hardening. "Only justice." She gestures to Indra, who is still kneeling a few feet away from her. "The throne, this realm, they will never be mine with Indra presenting as a man." Shachi glances at Yama. "It is why I asked Dharmaraj to join me. The lord of dharma sides with me, for he sees the righteousness of my cause. Only he can mete out justice."

"Then let Dharmaraj decide." Parvati speaks with my tongue. Dressed in a blooming red sari, she is light-skinned and beautiful. Her hips are rounded in childbirth, and she sounds curious, her voice like honeyed soma. Obeying her instruction, I look to Yama.

The lord of death comes forward, bending on one knee and dropping his head in a bow. Indra shivers where he kneels. He must know his position now.

"Devi," Yama rumbles. "I am afraid it isn't that easy. I am the lord of death, besides being that of dharma. I cannot judge Indra until he is dead."

I lean forward, and it is as if the whole universe is rebuking him. Yama's eyes widen, and he shakes where he kneels.

"Birth and death are illusions," Kali hisses, and her anger makes the skies darken, poisonous clouds collecting over us all, brimming with hellfire. She carries a bloodied axe in one hand and a decapitated head in another, and it is a reminder to Yama, that while he might be the god of death, she is the devi of destruction. "You are the only one who can weigh his good against his crimes," she snarls, using my mouth. "Decide what Indra's fate should be. He has forgotten for a long time who he is, but is he worthy of the throne? If you cannot judge this, no one can."

My words are greeted with silence. Yama frowns, thinking, and Indra's eyes dart everywhere, searching for an escape. Shachi has a small smile on her lips. It is Kaushika who stares at me unblinkingly. His lips move soundlessly, and I recognize the word they form. *Meneka.*

I jerk within my body. Amaravati smolders with war fires, and the city's future hangs in the balance. I called upon the devis to help me, and they have, but I am unprepared for this. What if they allow Indra's destruction? This is not my thought; it is Meneka's, but she is me too. I look away from Kaushika. He is dangerous. Like Shiva, he will try to balance me now, but my own harmony is enough. It is what is needed here. Not Shiva's power, but mine. Shakti's.

Yama is quiet for a long time. I can tell that he struggles with his desire for Indra's defeat and my command to act as arbitrator. He turns his head to the best of his lieutenants, and a familiar figure rides up on a hound to join him. Chitragupt alights from his hound, prostrating himself before me, then rising swiftly to join Yama where he stands. The two of them confer, and Chitragupt sketches a rune in the air.

It is due to the divine sight given to me by the devis that I can see what occurs next.

Chitragupt's rune unleashes a massive scale, made out of stars glittering in a tremendous constellation. Indra's image flickers on both sides of the scales, all that he has done through his millennia-long lifespan. The images cascade one to another, too fast for me to catch, though I am made of infinity. I see glimpses. Indra tilling lands. Indra defeating Vritra and saving the mortals. Indra starving his devotees. Indra betraying Shachi. On and on they come, the lord of storm, both in war and at peace, seducing sages through his apsaras and saving sages too, through his righteous defense of them against asura hordes. The evil and the good, all is weighed flashing in this cosmic balance.

I look to Indra, kneeling by Amaravati's gates, and his teeth are gritted in a grimace, eyes shut in pain. He can feel this judgment, though he cannot see the scales.

The constellation blinks one last time, a silent firework crackling in the sky, before disappearing. Yama looks up at me. "I have come to a conclusion," he says.

"Speak," I reply, and clouds cascade with my voice.

Yama bows to me, but his eyes draw in Shachi. "For devas, whose essences are an integral part of their being, judgment cannot be simple. Lord of storm and water, lord of fertility and harvest, Indra bears the weight of each drought, each flood, each bounty, each crop. As the lord of heaven, there is ongoing action of good and evil occurring with his every breath. It will continue even should he return to the void, for such is his nature. The scales will never show us what we wish to see in certainty."

"He *must* be punished," Shachi snaps. Her power mirrors in mine, sister to sister, goddess to goddess. Shachi senses this, and turns to me, her eyes searing. "Mother," she says. "Durga devi, Ma Kali, Shakti. Hear me now. I see your anger and fury, and it is mine. I am a part of you, I am your mirror. You cannot deny me this."

Within my mind, I despair. I hear the devis clamoring, each responding to Shachi's words. I asked for this power, but it is too much. I try to speak, but my words lock up. Again, a sense of Meneka thinking this. I look away from her.

Lord Indra turns to Shachi, and his face is horrified, like he is seeing her for the first time. "You would truly have me become nothing," he says wonderingly. "We have lived and grown together, found each other and ourselves. Yet you would have me *gone*?"

"I would have you be worthy of the throne," Shachi snaps. "I would have you worthy of *me*, and all that I can be—"

"Silence!" I command, and all fall silent before me again.

I listen to the goddesses confer. *Death*, Kali growls, and Durga agrees, sharpening her blade. They have ever been devis of anger and vengeance, righteous in their paths, cutting off evil at every turn, protecting. Parvati grimaces however, politic and rational. Gauri hums too, both of them nurturing in their hearts, wishing to forgive, wishing for evolution.

What say you, apsara? the devis ask me.

I blink. I turn to Meneka within me, but she is me, and I am unsure, even now. I glance at Kaushika, and he understands.

"Exile," Kaushika says, head inclined but his eyes capturing mine. "Exile Indra during this time of the Vajrayudh to the mortal realm and to patala and naraka—not as punishment but to learn. Learn about himself and his role in the future, and return only when he has gained wisdom. The lord of death can judge it, and the sages of the Mahasabha will arbitrate it. I speak on their behalf."

The devis turns to me again. It is Kaushika's counsel, but it is my decision.

Yes, I whisper. *Yes*.

The skies glow with my approval, and Yama leans in, nodding, now that I have decided. "An appropriate punishment," he says, his brows no longer creased. He turns to Shachi. "Devi, will you agree?"

Before Shachi can speak, Indra rises, hastening closer to me and falling to his feet. "Mother," he says urgently. "The corpse—my city—please, I beg you. Please—without me—it cannot—"

He does not have to be coherent. The consequences are clear for all of us to know and see. The corpse approaches us, bringing with it a terrible stench, and the outskirts of the city begin to flake.

I only have to look at Yama. He understands. He and Chitragupt consult again, and I see the weighing of scales once more. This time it is but a blink, a judgment of a mortal's life instead of that of divinity. The good King Satyavrat has done weighs the scale in one direction before blinking away, and now that Yama has decided to judge the king's soul, Shachi's asura magic is unable to defy his natural law.

The orb trembles and shakes, and explodes. Something golden escapes out of it, while the encasing orb crumbles into dust. King Satyavrat's soul blinks for an instant before arcing into a ray of light, heading into Amaravati, where it rightfully belongs. After so long, the king has finally been judged, and Kaushika's chest rises and falls in a deep breath of relief. He is freed of his vow.

He hangs his head, trembling, before steadying himself.

So does Indra. The lord knows how he has escaped the utter destruction of his city by a fingernail. "I accept my exile," he says.

"But Amaravati . . . in my absence . . ." His eyes dart between me and Shachi. "Devi, which goddess is to rule heaven while I am gone?"

His question is clear. Within me flows the rush of a hundred oceans, one tidal wave lashing after another. I see Indra's nervousness at the thought of me on the throne, and it is tempting. The power is magnificent, and if I wanted, I could be queen. I could be a devi in every sense of the word, something promised to me when I set out on my mission to seduce—

Kaushika.

I glance to him again, and I see horror on his face.

He shakes his head. *Meneka.*

Once again, a whispered thought calls me back. It brushes the surface of my mind, as if I am submerged within a deep pool. I tremble, and he blinks, nearly standing.

"You cannot deny me this," Shachi says, eyes wide as the realization comes to her as well that I can simply take the throne from her. "The throne is mine by rights."

"You have received your justice," I say coolly. "Indra will be exiled, no longer your master or that of your home. You have patala to return to."

"Amaravati is mine!" Shachi says, and there is a sob in her voice. "Mother, the city—I have loved it too. And my vengeance, my rage is not satisfied."

"You *will* be satisfied," I thunder, and with the power of all the devis within me, I draw Shachi in.

Cascades of my light lift her up toward me, encircling us in a brilliance that no one else can breach. I show her all that I'm seeing, the grace of Parvati within me, and the fury of Kali. The knowledge of Saraswati, and the nurture of Gauri.

You have wished for home, Shakti says. I see myself reflected in Shachi, and I know, the Goddess Divine speaks not just to the queen but to me too.

You have wished to be seen, the Goddess says.

I have, Shachi replies.

I have, I murmur.

You do not need them to see yourself, daughter, Shakti hums. Shachi and I weep within our own bodies. *Open your eyes*, the Goddess says, and this time I hear all my sisters listening. Rambha, Nanda, Holika, and every other creature who ever claimed to be devoted to Shakti. Whoever wished to be a part of her. *Accept your freedom*, I say, and this time I hear my own voice within the Goddess. *Become whole in yourself.*

I let the queen go, and she falls on the ground, her hair tumbling all over her. She is undone, in a way the war could not do, and before me I see a flourishing, a repair. Shachi did not want this war either. It was forced on her, by millennia of humiliation. Of injustice and neglect.

"I have been lost," she sobs bitterly, and there is healing in her cries. "I have been lost."

"Never lost," I say gently, and it is a memory that speaks from my mouth. "Never lost as long as you have yourself."

The queen rises, stepping back. Gone are the clothes of the military from her body. She is once again dressed for peacetime, a white sari bordered with gold streaming from her body, a vision of light and complexity. It is more than simply her clothes that have changed. Shachi's asura fangs retract, but her teeth remain sharp, as if she has found a reconciliation between her heavenly form and that of the underworld. Her unbound hair swirls into a braid, changing with her acceptance of herself. Bangles and necklaces glint over her arms and neck, jewels of heaven summoned to her, but she wears amulets of patala too. Shachi is once again the goddess of heaven, more so than ever before, with Indra's relinquishing of power. Yet she is the asura queen too, finally recognized within her own soul.

She walks over to Indra, and he looks up at her, unflinchingly.

Then, aware that all eyes are on her, Indra prostrates himself in front of her.

Shachi studies him silently for a long moment. Skies crack, pouring rain as the clouds are finally unable to keep the cascade away. The rain weeps down Indra's face, and there is something in its taste—sorrow, remorse, fragility. Shachi relents, her face growing soft again. With a sob, she pulls Indra upright, pulling him to her, capturing his mouth in a brutal kiss. I glance at Rambha to see what she makes of it, but Rambha is openly crying, and I know those are tears of healing. Heaven has suffered with the war of Indra and Shachi, and these divine forces have endured too much together for their faith in each other to be shaken. I find my throat choking with emotion, but there is still something that remains.

I gesture to Shachi, and she steps away. Indra gazes up at me, the tilt of his head anxious.

"Lord of the skies," I rumble, and he flinches at the power of my magic. "Long have you hoarded magic that belongs to all living creatures. The amrit you denied the asuras during the Churning of the Oceans cannot be returned to them, but the power of prana belongs to all, mortals and immortals."

"I—I never took it from the mortals," Indra stutters. "The sages use the same magic—I have not kept it from them."

"Only because you were unable to," I reply, eyes flashing. "Would that you had been unable with the celestials and asuras too, but it is time this deed is undone."

I raise my arms, and Indra and Shachi stumble back.

A roar fills my ears, as the power of the universe surges within my body. The devis within me scream in victory and joy, and rejoice in how I am every one of them, Kali's vengeance and Durga's rage. Parvati's reason and Lakshmi's prosperity. I am Shachi and Rambha and Holika and Nanda, though I am not them at all. The magic burns my skin, flesh sloughing off, and I scream as the power of a million suns bursts in my heart. I am in agony, but there is ecstasy too, and my head falls back as I rise higher and higher. Power scorches me, the pure cosmic prana of the universe, and I bend my arms, releasing it to my sisters. They are suspended in stillness, their eyes glowing bright, their auras sparkling as I give them that which always belonged to them. The light takes them all over, and everyone else backs away, shielding their eyes, crying out loud.

Only one shape runs toward me, heedless of the burning

light. I see his mere silhouette, but I know who he is. I know who would dare to be incinerated by my power, to come to me despite it. I float higher, but he is there, tugging at my hand, looking up at me with fear and love in his eyes.

I hear his alarmed voice through a dark echo. *Come back to me. Meneka, come back to me.*

I remember his warning from a lifetime ago. *The more magic you hold, the more you are liable to forget your own mind.* I remember the knowledge I gained at the hermitage. That pure prana can destroy a practitioner of tapasya. There are dangers to uncontrolled power, as there are to healing. What I do now will burn me. In returning power to all those to whom it belongs, I am conducting a healing of unseen proportions.

This will kill you, Kaushika says. Tears fill his eyes, and fire races up his body. He is destroying himself, burning because of my uncontained power just as I am. His fingers clasp mine, and he pulls again. His mouth moves in a chant, and I expect a mantra of great power to come from it, to break this enchantment, yet it is only a repetition of my name. *Meneka*, he says, not Shakti. But in his mouth the word "Meneka" is a prayer too.

Images blink behind my eyes. The first time we kissed in the hermitage. The first time he unclothed me by the pond. His smile, and our laughter, the sweetness of summer within our hut, and the scent of camphor and rosewood.

Come back, he says, and the same memories I used to trap him turn on me, yet this time they are pure. I turn to the devis within me, pleading. They nod at me, understanding. One by one, the devis retreat, though Kali is the last to go—she who is Shiva's raging consort. Parvati tugs at her, and Kali utters an amused huff. I can see in her mind how she sees Shiva in Kaushika, how she is unwilling to leave him.

Meneka, he says again, pleading. Begging.

Shakti's power leaches out of me abruptly.

I fall from the skies. My last sight is Kaushika as he rushes toward me, his arms open, calling out my name.

CHAPTER 27

I awake in strange chambers.

My eyes take in a high domed ceiling, carved with clouds and inlaid with mother-of-pearl. The clouds seem to move, swimming from light into darkness. Lightning shines in them, in slivers of diamond. That is how I know I am in Indra's palace.

Memory returns to me abruptly. The war. The devis. Kaushika and me. Burning.

I rise slowly. The chambers I am in are luxuriously appointed, yet there is something temple-like in their structure. Incense burns in an altar to Shiva in a corner, and flowers are placed in offering at the threshold and by my feet. I have only ever been in apsara quarters in the city when not on a mission, or within the halls of gandharvas for a dalliance or two. That they have placed me here in the palace is telling of the respect I suddenly command. I climb out of the bed slowly and approach the closest window.

Beyond the courtyard and the spread of trees, I see Amaravati reknitting, gold dust swirling around buildings, gleams of radiance bursting in pinpricks as the mending occurs. It is as if I am submerged within a gem-encrusted star. Geodes open and close like flowers on the buildings; light repairs the structures. I breathe in, and the air smells fresh like morning dew.

Citizens mill, watching the repairs, and it takes me a moment to understand why that is surprising. The people are back. The war is over.

I stretch my neck side to side, and an ache spreads through me. Now that I have woken, I feel my body's soreness. I have only inklings of memory, of what happened to end the war, but the ache within me is peaceful as if I have been practicing my dance relentlessly for days. I feel quiet, and satisfied—and *myself*. The devis have left me, and I am grateful. Their presence was a blessing, but my body, though celestial and immortal, was never meant to hold so much power all at once. I feel the residual pain of holding their minds, in attempting to heal a wound of millennia that Indra inflicted upon Shachi and all the apsaras. Healing exacts a cost. I feel it in every movement my body makes.

"Lady," a voice says nervously. "You're awake. The queen will wish to see you."

I turn to see a palace maid. No longer in the blue livery of Indra, the woman wears a yellow slashed sari. She carries a bundle of clothes, saris layered with pleats, blouses in glistening silk, and among them simpler cottons too, in gray and white and cream. I become aware that I am dressed only in my shift, yet my body is clean and perfumed. Someone has been bathing me and taking care of me through my recovery.

I greet the maid with a smile, and beckon to her to bring me the clothes. Each sari is more glorious than the next, and I pick out a green one with embroidery that reminds me of the mortal realm, the gold in the weaving like a burnished sun. There is a touch of the hermitage in these clothes, luxurious though they are. It is in the simple stitches on the embroidery, intricate yet soft. I nod to the maid, and she helps me wrap the clothes around me like a dhoti. I pick a soft indigo blue kurta to go with it, and though there is a vast selection of jewelry set aside for whoever must occupy this chamber, I pick only the ones that belong to me, earned through my missions. The gold necklaces. The sparkling diamond nose stud. A slim crown that sits on my head like a band.

The maid is silent as she dresses me, and I want to speak to her, ask her for her name, ask her what is happening with Amaravati's citizens, but there is a peace in our silence. Perhaps, like me, she feels the wonder of Amaravati within her again. A repair, and a closure, for my adventures and whatever she— another woman—has undergone in the mortal realm.

I make my way to the throne room, following the direction the maid gives me. I have been in Indra's throne room many times now, each to a different effect, yet for the first time the radiance that emanates from it sweeps over me, taking me within it. Citizens and courtiers mill about the room again, chatting with one another, their voices soft but free of despair. Several notice me and bow, and though they resume their conversation as I wander past them, their eyes follow me. They have been in the mortal realm and were summoned back to the city now that the war is over. Rumor must have spread of what I did.

I weave past them all until I see Shachi on the throne. The queen appears tired but at peace, her aura no longer spiraling with gold in rage, but settled into a harmonious hum. The magic of this realm has worked on her; already she looks more celestial than asura, though her features from patala remain. Her ears are still sharp, and she is grand in her height, yet the benevolent look on her face is the same one I remember from my childhood. Another citizen sits next to her on a chair, speaking about repairs, and I realize she is in open attendance today. Any may come up to speak with her about any grievance. It is an ancient ritual, one Indra used to perform, according to the stories, before he became embroiled in wanting only to be worshipped. I am assured in the result of the war, seeing her take up this mantle again.

Shachi notices me, and so does her visitor. They both rise at the same time, the citizen giving her a quick bow, followed by a wary look toward me. I come forward, climbing up the dais, though I have not been invited to do so, and the queen fidgets, her gaze growing uncertain. She joins her palms to me, bending her head, then steps away from the throne almost in deference. Her movements are inelegant, and her eyes dart between the throne and the smaller seat before landing back on me.

She is nervous. She does not know which seat I wish to take.

Deliberately, I move toward the smaller one, settling myself on it. I hear Shachi's soft sigh of relief as she takes the throne. Around us, the hum of conversation returns. We have been watched, the rule of the throne still unclear, though with my gesture and my permission, I have already returned a measure of peace to the realm. It is amazing to think that.

Shachi and I are silent as an attendant brings a selection of drinks for us, offering it first to me, then to the queen, another sign of respect toward me. I sip the golden nectar of heaven from a small crystal cup, and Shachi takes a similar concoction too. In her every movement, I see a mirror. Whether practiced or natural, I am comforted by that. Shachi has not forgotten what has happened, even if I remember it only in shards. She will answer my questions when I ask them, but for a while I simply sip the nectar, tasting its honey and bite, relishing in the soft spice of it.

"The city is safe," I say finally, looking out to the throne room where courtiers and attendants chat to one another, studying the new artifacts.

My words break the unease between us. Shachi breathes a heavy sigh, and nods. "Repairs are underway. There is damage from the war, and the Vajrayudh is coming. With King Satyavrat's corpse dismantled, the cosmic event no longer hurries with the breath of fire, but it still comes to Amaravati steadily. We have a few days to shore up the damage, and now we can attempt to have harmony."

"Then the king's soul . . ." I say, trying to remember. "It resides in heaven?"

"It does," the queen confirms. "The body has returned to the mortal realm to become dust again, as per the laws of prakriti. The sage's vow has been fulfilled."

I recall the radiance from the soul entering the city, but much of it lies in haze, like trying to capture memories dispersing into vapor. I study Shachi, and this is the perfect moment to ask about Kaushika, but I do not trust myself to speak of him. Not with her. Not without understanding the rest of it.

"What has become of Lord Indra, then?" I ask.

Shachi looks up at the ceiling, which retains the shape and scent of the sky outside, purple and blue and the burst of daylight fast approaching. Yet Shachi's eyes see far beyond it into something else. Though my memory is misty, I remember all too clearly the kiss she and Indra exchanged, and with it the promise and hope of peace between them. I wonder what she is seeing.

"Indra prepares for exile," she says. "This is not the first time he has been exiled from swarga to learn a lesson. Sages in the past have counseled this, and sages in the future will too. Kaushika has fulfilled his role, as have you."

"And the throne?" I ask, frowning. "Without him, will Amaravati survive? He is the architect of the city."

"And I am its breath," Shachi says. "As are we all. Without us, the city is merely stone and dust. You showed us this." She shrugs, and several pearls chink together around her neck with the gesture. "If we suffer during the Vajrayudh, we will only be fulfilling our karma. This has ever been the purpose of the Vajrayudh. It has been a curse that swarga and Indra had to endure, one that Shiva set upon Indra millennia ago for ignoring his duties. Indra was meant to meditate on his role and divinity, understanding his role in the universe, but of course, true to himself, he simply commanded all of us to shut ourselves up in the city along with him, obeying the letter of Shiva's law, not the spirit. By sending him into exile, you may have broken this ancient curse. Perhaps there might never again be another Vajrayudh, and Indra will finally fulfill what he was meant to do from the very start. One day Indra will return to heaven to rule. He will have me by his side, but the next time, I will have him by my side too."

I say nothing to this. I am immortal, but I cannot imagine easily how much time will pass before Shachi forgives Indra in her heart. Before she believes justice is served and invites him to rule next to her again. Kaushika said Yama would magistrate the length of the exile, and the sages of the Mahasabha would arbitrate it. How many centuries will that take? Still, the cycle of life keeps turning. I can only hope Indra learns wisdom. I look away to the chatting people and remain still.

This time it is Shachi who breaks the silence. "You should know," she begins hesitantly. "I have commanded all the apsaras back from their missions. All your sisters who were still in the mortal realm seducing one imagined enemy or another. They are here now in Amaravati, resting, and I have vowed not to force them to another mission. It will be their choice if they are to go."

Shachi's words inspire no confidence. Indra, too, made it appear like it would be an apsara's choice. I remember all too well how he wished for me to *volunteer* for my mission to Kaushika, how careful and adamant he was that I made my intention clear. I never had any choice, not with my home and magic held hostage to his whim.

"It is not merely their choice you must return to them, Queen," I say icily. "It is the promise to never hoard their magic.

I gave it to them, but you could take it away like Indra, couldn't you? You have always been powerful."

Shachi's face grows nervous. Perhaps in my voice, she hears the fury of Kali, the skepticism of Parvati. The lord of heaven kept apsaras to himself, but Shachi always wished for the dancers to be her charge, calling it her right. *You belong to me*, she told me once, her fingernails cutting into my cheeks.

"The apsaras' magic is their own," she says hurriedly. "No one can take it from them—they can access pure prana. But the knowledge of how to use it cannot be *given*, sister. Apsaras will have to learn to wield it—like you have. They will have to recognize it and embrace it."

I recognize the truth in her words, for such is the nature of magic. I have had to learn magic in its various forms, to look past the duality of the universe into the wholeness of prana. Still, I am not satisfied.

Shachi has not said it, but I know that she will contain the flow of magic into Amaravati now that Indra has gone. The throne grants her that right and duty. It is the only way for the city to survive and for magic to flow through it to the celestials, even though now they can access cosmic prana.

Yet I have seen the lure and temptation of power. Will Shachi be a better ruler than Indra? The both of them are creatures of the same divinity, the same politics. Unless celestials learn to break past their own ignorance, any magic they have will only be given to them through divinity. Of the celestials, only divine beings like Shachi and Indra, those born at the dawn of creation, know how to manipulate prana in its pure form. That

I discovered my role in it is my fortune. It could not have happened without Kaushika, had I not been sent for his mission.

"Ever it has been the celestial dancers at the heart of your battle," I say quietly.

"It was freedom at the heart of our battle," Shachi replies. "The dancers have personified it like no other, for it is your closeness with illusion that allows you to see reality. Mistresses of illusion, you have always contained the power to *break* illusion, even at the cosmic stage. It is no coincidence that it was an apsara who discovered the magic of prana, who performed mortal tapasvin magic, once thought to be impossible by a celestial." The queen's mouth trembles, and she inhales a shaky breath. "You freed me," she says. "When you finally embraced the power of Shakti, you freed me because you freed yourself."

I want to take her hand in mine, but I resist the urge. Memories wash over me, of the war again and all the devis. Shachi and I learned our lesson together, and I see her as a sister, as a woman. But she sits on the throne too, queen of my realm. I look away, giving her a moment to compose herself, unsure of whether my affection now will only be misconstrued as another political gesture.

"Where are the others?" I ask. "My friends and allies?"

"All of them are helping to repair the city," Shachi says, and her voice is under control again. "Nanda did not wish to leave your side, but we needed to shore up the city before the Vajrayudh arrives in earnest. She is with the other dancers, praying and performing at the areas which need it most. The apsaras are instrumental in Amaravati's repair, and they are weaving magic back into the city. Their magic is connected to the potency of the city—it always has been. With your presence alone, the city strengthens."

Shachi hesitates, and her next words are slow, careful.

"The sage did not leave your side either. Only a few hours ago did he return to the mortal realm to prepare his home, but he has permission to come here again should he wish it. It will not work during the Vajrayudh when the city must be sealed to be protected, but at peacetime, it is his right. As it is yours."

I nod. I did not expect anything different, but finally speaking of Kaushika is cue enough. I rise from my chair and make to descend down the dais.

Shachi arrests me with a touch on my hand. "Where will you go now? What will you do?"

I glance at her. "I have freedom to come and go as I please, yes?"

"Yes. All apsaras do, and I will not chain them, but—"

"Then let me go," I say softly.

Her hand drops, but she hesitates as if wanting to say more. I look away from her. My power is unleashed, and no doubt Shachi will want me to ally with her fully, both to promote peace in heaven and to consolidate her rule now that Indra is unseated. There will be games in heaven, and politics to be maneuvered. Shachi wishes to know my mind; it is why she asks me what I will do now. But I do not owe her an answer.

I climb down the dais wordlessly, making my way out of the throne room.

CHAPTER 28

For a time, I wander aimlessly. There is something peaceful in being part of the palace, moving without intention. Didn't I want this right from the start? When I arrived in swarga after my mission with Tara, oblivious to all that life would take from me and teach me, I hoped to be a part of Indra's court. To live here and perform my dance, and never have to return to the mortal realm to seduce a mark. I am no longer the same apsara, but as I watch the city's repairs from a stray balcony, as I run my hands down the intricately carved murals, I can't help but feel a small nostalgia for the woman before. How far she has come. How deeply she has loved, and how much she has gained. I am stunned at my transformation, and my own power throbs inside me, pure and transcendental.

I continue walking, touching a statue here, stopping to look at a painting there. I pause when I hear a soft melody, twining its rhythm inside my heart.

I recognize the song, and a smile alights on my lips. I follow the music until I come upon a small garden, heavy with the scent of roses. Three people wait there, anticipating me. Matali grins, his curly head looking up from his lute. Nanda utters a raucous laugh, embracing me and nearly bowling me over. Rambha offers me a small, watery smile, still pale, the star-anise of her scent burned but not bitter. She and I have had a reckoning, and too much has transpired between us for matters to return to the way they were once. Still, I find no hostility in my heart for her anymore, and when she comes forward to embrace me, her movements hesitant, I return her hug with warmth and affection.

"You came," Matali says, smiling, pinching my cheek in affection.

I swat his hand away, rolling my eyes. "Your song was persuasive. It is nice to know your magic has not been hurt after the war. The city will need your strength now."

He shakes his head, and so does Rambha.

"We are not staying," she says. She lifts her head, gazing to the sky. Though it is a clear day, I see lightning in one part, silvery and gold. "The lord will need us now," Rambha continues. "Though the city is safe, Indra's power is sorely depleted. When he is in exile, away from his beloved Amaravati, he will only deplete further. It will be up to us," she says, gesturing between herself and Matali, "to remind him of who he is. To lend him our power from the city, directed to us through Shachi, to give to him."

The lightning flashes once again, as if to corroborate this. It is only fitting that I do not see Indra again, reduced to whatever state he is in. He saw me last when I was the confluence of all the devis, but once he was my lord, my king, to whom I owed allegiance. It would be too intimate to see him in his fragility, a vision meant only for those dearest to him. I know

now I am not one of them. The thought does not bother me like it once did.

"There is a sage conducting a pilgrimage to all corners of the three realms," Matali says. "We will accompany him. I have already made the arrangements." The singer's eyes gleam in excitement. "There are chants I will learn, Meneka, much like the one your own sage taught you."

Vashishta, I think. Yes, it is wise that the three of them learn from him. Vashishta has always been fair, though far more exacting than Kaushika. If it is wisdom the lord needs to learn during the Vajrayudh, there is no one better to teach him reflection and contemplation.

Lightning flashes soundlessly, and Matali smiles again. "He calls now," the gandharva says. He moves forward, his lips brushing across mine, and places a chaste kiss on my cheek. "Do you know why I came on your mission with you?" he whispers.

I am taken aback at the question. "Indra desired you to watch over me, did he not?"

"Yes. But I desired it too. We were bound to each other after you softened Sage Kaushika, a task at which I failed when I was sent to treat with him. I was compelled by our bond, needing to watch over you for your own welfare. But you have given me many songs to compose, and I will compose one to the rise of the celestials for you. Farewell, sweet Meneka." Without another word, he closes his eyes. His form becomes glittery, a kaleidoscope of stars. Matali becomes a ray of light, arcing across the garden up to the sky, joining his lover and lord.

Rambha lingers for an instant longer. Though we have made our peace, she looks like she wishes to say something else. In the end, she merely shakes her head. Nanda and I watch together as she becomes a beam of light and joins Matali and Indra. The lightning flashes once more, then it is gone.

Nanda turns to me, with a question in her eyes. *What now?*

I utter a chant. It is the same chant I have tried so many times before, but this time it works without the need for Kaushika's comb. I have accepted the power is my own, and it braids without difficulty within me, sparking with fire, layered with dew, touching the source of Shakti. I feel the Goddess within me—I nod to her, to all of them, and I sense them smile.

A portal opens, and beyond it, woods sigh in a small breeze. I inhale deeply, and I can smell it, the hint of camphor lingering in the air. Nanda's brows rise. She knows this is the path to my home, to the hut where I once lived with Kaushika.

"Did you see how I did this?" I ask her. "Can you learn it?"

Nanda frowns. "I think so. With practice, yes, I can learn it."

"Then practice. And teach it to the others during the quiet of the Vajrayudh."

The apsaras have their freedom, but once the gates of Amaravati are open, no doubt they will be sent on missions again, even if it is by their choice. What else would an apsara do? We were designed for one purpose, trained into it for millennia. Not all my sisters think like me. To them, serving the city and their lord is to seduce the lord's enemies. That is the form of devotion they know, and no single war or wish can change that.

Yet I will not have them trapped again. With this magic,

with this incantation and spell, they will be able to extract themselves. I have not forgotten that Nanda once suffered at the hands of a great sage. That I myself was ensnared.

She seems to understand this. Nanda nods, then embraces me. "Thank you," she whispers, tears in her eyes.

"Don't wait for me," I answer, and she laughs, brushing away her tears.

"Show him the meaning of pleasure, sister," she says, winking.

I cannot help but grin. Waving farewell, I pass through the portal and let it close behind me.

THE HUT IS EMPTY AND QUIET WHEN I ENTER.

I glance around, and I can almost fool myself that no time has passed since I was summoned by Indra. The bed is made, and the window filters in sunlight. In a corner, the candle stub is untouched, and all my possessions are the way I left them, despite Rambha rummaging through them. Kaushika has tidied up, in anticipation of me; this is why he left for the mortal realm, perhaps intending to return to Amaravati in time for my waking. The scent of camphor lingers in the air, and fresh flowers are strewn around the floor as though in welcome. Wherever Kaushika is, he has not wandered far. I do not close the door. I simply make my way to the bed, and sit down.

Slowly, I start to disrobe myself. I take everything off save the jewels from heaven. The pearl necklaces roll softly on my skin, their touch like smooth fingers. The gold bangles trap sunlight, sending cascades of glitter dancing about the walls. My anklets chime, and I lie back, taking one hand and running it feather-light over my stomach, and my waist, then my breasts, back down to my bent knees and over my thighs.

I think of Kaushika and the games we played on this bed. My touch begins to grow more passionate, in this loving of my body. I stroke my fingers at the sensitive skin on my inner thighs, then pause at my entrance, my body rising slightly as wetness gathers between my legs.

My pleasure builds, and at the sound of the door, my eyes snap open.

Kaushika stands by the entrance, his gaze full of heat and longing, his arms filled with wildflowers. Moringa, primrose, honeyleaf, their scent sweeps over me, but it is threaded with spicy camphor and musky rosewood. We lock eyes, and I do not stop. I continue to stroke myself, my breasts rising and falling.

Kaushika drops the flowers, but instead of floating to the ground, they swirl toward me, bathing me in petals. I shiver at the coolness of their touch, the softness of their feel. My eyes flutter; I am reaching the first of my climaxes swiftly, but I force myself to watch him, still standing there, mesmerized and handsome and mine—fully mine, because I am now my own.

His lips lift in a small smile. He approaches me, his footsteps silent and unhurried.

"Do you know why I love you?" he asks, as if we have been in the middle of a conversation.

I smile, for we have—our conversation started the first time we saw each other. It will continue for lifetimes still.

"Why?" I ask. I insert one finger within me, pushing and stroking gently at my nub. Startling, familiar shock courses through me, and I tremble.

"I love you because you are never anyone but yourself," he says. "Oh, it's not that you don't change—you do, evolving like few people can. But you do it on your terms. Unapologetic, fierce, wise, and always wholly yourself. Who else but you could touch the source of all power and return from it unscathed? This is something even sages cannot do, despite years of meditation."

I shiver, as a wave of pleasure washes over me. His words are a balm I've been needing to hear, and they succor me, but the both of us know that I have not always been this way. Our journey together taught me how to be who I am, to have the courage to accept it. I came to him in subterfuge once. Now I lie in his bed—in *my* bed—claiming ownership over myself.

"You saw the Goddess in me," I say, as my body bucks. I ride my fingers, and my voice is breathless.

Kaushika's voice is gruff, nearly a growl. I can hear his arousal in it. "I always saw the Goddess in you. But all I ever wanted was for you to see who you are."

He does not have to explain. It is clear. My magic during the war was amazing, but it was *I* who needed to see Shakti and all her forms within me, showing me all the possibilities of who I could be. Kaushika needed nothing, no evidence.

"I learned what I needed to," I say. "Did you? You wished to be guided by love, did you not? You coveted this power once."

He steps closer to me, and though he is looking down at me,

sprawled as I am on the cot, I am too powerful and contained for it to appear as if he is looming. Still, he drops to his knees, his head close to mine. He inhales deeply, and a groan escapes him in his exhale.

"Tell me, Kaushika," I ask, "are you content?"

"Teach me," Kaushika whispers in response, his breath warm in my ear. "Teach me about love. So I can be worthy of you."

"Then watch," I whisper, my voice shuddering. "Watch and learn."

My climax rushes me, and I take his hand, replacing my fingers with his, directing him with my gasps. His other hand interlaces with mine, fingers tight within my own, raised over my head. As pleasure washes over me, magic drenches the air, colored with the dyes of our love. I, Meneka, give myself to me, and to him, without restraint.

EPILOGUE: COUNTLESS YEARS LATER

Kaushika runs his eyes over the gathering. His chant still reverberates through the air, though it has been some time since the song ended. A silence thrums around the assembled people, disciples and royalty, sages and soldiers, farmers and nobles, all seated in front of the pavilion, their eyes slowly opening in wonder.

The hermitage has never been as crowded, and all of these people arrived here over the last few days in answer to his summons. It took weeks of negotiations, but he has finally concluded it as mediator, and today he performed the last of the ceremonies, in an ode to peace.

He sees his name on their lips as they rise from their seats. *Kaushika*, most of them call him, but another name too, *Vishwamitra*, friend to all creatures.

He smiles. He has not taken on that name himself; it has been gifted to him. A rich gift, one he continues to strive to be worthy of each day.

He stands up, nodding to Romasha and Anirudh. The two of them will lead these people from here on, helping them with the peace treaty that was forged today. He watches as each of them approaches the warring parties, King Jayai and Queen Yati, bringing them into conversation.

An itch builds under his skin, and he looks away in the direction of the forest beyond. He cannot see it, but he can sense the ripple in the air. *She* has returned. Just in time.

Kaushika descends the short stairs of the pavilion, nodding to one devotee here, another noble there. He wishes to leave instantly, create a portal right here to his hut, but that would be too rude a gesture. He is a sage, a rishi, but only first among equals, even if his power exceeds all of theirs. Once, innumerable years ago, to take advantage of such power would have been second nature. He has learned to be more careful. More sensitive. He is almost through the gathering, when a man steps in front of him.

Kaushika stops. His brows rise. "Guruji," he says carefully.

Vashishta's lips lift in a mocking smile, but Kaushika does not let himself react. It is just what Vashishta wants.

"I've heard the name you are being called," Vashishta says.

The silence continues to build. Kaushika grows annoyed. This is a test, a poor one, but that is Vashishta's way, to never relent. Surely the older man can sense Kaushika's hurry. She *waits* for him, and the news she brings—*he* has been waiting for this moment. He almost breaks the silence, damn whatever the consequences, but then notices the twinkle in the other sage's eyes. "You did well today," Vashishta says. "I will send you the scrolls on my return."

Elation lifts Kaushika's heart. He bows over folded hands,

watches Vashishta drift away to speak to someone else—then he begins running through the forest to the path to his hut. His excitement gives him speed, long legs carrying him. He bursts into the house, to see her at the window, lost in thought.

Meneka turns to him and smiles, and he takes her in his arms, kissing her until she is breathless. "Well?" he asks, his eyes shining. She is so beautiful, he can hardly believe she is his.

Meneka shakes her head in amusement. "You first."

He shrugs, but he cannot hide his pride from her. "It couldn't have been better. Vashishta will send me the last syllables of the mantra. He discovered it during his pilgrimage."

Her wonder and pride at him make her face glow. It humbles him, for the pride should be rightfully hers. This was all because of her; he could not have done it alone. Once he had used the same mantra to design a meadow of abomination. Now, working with her and the celestial knowledge she brought, he has been turning it into a gift for humankind—a mantra to the Goddess, to the Mother of Vedas. A song that can be used by anyone to illuminate the sacred within themselves, regardless of whether they are celestial, mortal, or asura, regardless of whether they contain magic or not. The Gayatri Mantra is nearly finished. With it, peace can reign in one's heart. His greatest composition, all because of her.

"Your turn," he says, nudging her nose with his. His arms circle her waist, and he brings one hand to rest on her stomach. He can feel the life within, but it is only celestials who can confirm the knowledge. Meneka's sojourn in Amaravati was precisely for this reason.

Her eyes glitter in happiness. "A daughter," she says, laughing. "*Our* daughter, Kaushika."

His laughter shakes the rafters, and birds squawk, disturbed by the noise. He swings Meneka around, and above, the birds flit too, their squawks turning into sweet song. He understands it is significant, that the song is an offering. The birds are a symbol of wisdom. Their daughter will be born with their grace.

"Indra and Shachi wish to visit, to bless her, when she comes," Meneka says.

He nods. It has been years since Indra returned to swarga to rule by Shachi's side. There can be no better blessing than that of the lord and lady of heaven, reconciled.

"What do we name her?" Meneka asks.

He embraces her to him. He glances up at the birds—shakun, they are called—and happiness makes his heart swell in emotion. He whispers in her ear, and Meneka laughs, nodding. And though he has found the wisdom of the sages, Kaushika knows that it is only now his heart is fully complete.

AUTHOR'S NOTE

I never knew how special Meneka was going to become to me when I first started writing the Divine Dancers duology.

Like any author who undertakes a retelling, I had a hundred decisions to make—which characters to give prominence to, which stories to highlight, which gods to acknowledge, and which philosophies to ignore. How to center my decisions around Meneka, this woman who was undertaking a journey of self-realization without even knowing she was on such a path. And ultimately, how to tell a good story—a story, which by its nature as a *re*telling, was meant to expand a mythos while staying true to its source.

In essence, the writing of this duology was a balance—between the past and the future, the other and the self, the personal and the shared. I borrowed from the culture I belong to, and I invented where I needed to.

Readers who are familiar with Hinduism will see many unrelated legends intersecting within *The Rise of the Celestials*—including Shachi's birth during the Churning of the Oceans, Rambha's seduction of Sage Vishwamitra, and philosophies of Yama and dharma, the last of which have no direct relationship to the Kaushika–Meneka lore, but which I felt were fitting for this story. The Vajrayudh is also an invention, and I chose to give importance to certain aspects that are bypassed in religion—for instance, the threat to heaven, something Hinduism does not concern itself with.

In Hinduism, the focus is on what a life chooses to do when it lives. While the cycle of birth and rebirth is a cornerstone in the religion, the interim period of heaven or hell is so unimportant that those are barely mentioned in scripture. In slightly reductive terms, a good life must be lived for a future possibility of another good life—however, even such a rebirth is hardly the point. The point is to *break* the cycle of birth and rebirth, to gain moksha and freedom from it. To be enlightened with the knowledge of the universe.

I sought to maintain this balance while telling this story, and in order to do so, I returned to the roots of the religion.

Hinduism started as hymns called the Vedas, composed by the banks of the river Saraswati more than four thousand years ago. The Vedas dealt with extolling the elements. In the Rigveda, elemental deities such as Indra, Agni, and Surya are all mentioned and worshipped—Indra prominently being featured as the first of all lords.

Eventually, though, the Vedas gave way to the Upanishads. The Upanishads were arcane texts that focused on esoteric concepts such as consciousness, meditation, and the oneness of the soul with the universe. The Upanishads provided a treatise on how to get to that oneness. Elemental spirituality folded itself within universal spirituality, indicating the change that Indra saw in his own status. Hinduism evolved into a religion where neither heaven nor hell became places to aspire to or fear.

Heaven began to lose its importance, and as lord of heaven, so did Indra. In the Vedas, Indra was a prominent hero, virile and life-giving as the lord of rain and storm, without whom lands would be arid and life impossible. After the Upanishads, he became a drunk debaucher, fighting incessant battles with asuras, and sending apsaras to deter sages who would become more powerful than him because of their meditation.

This crossroads in the religion is where the Divine Dancers duology is situated. Meneka's faith is one of the primary drivers of the books, and I asked myself—how would a god who has been worshipped for so long as the primary deity take to being downgraded to an afterthought? What would that do to his power, his devotees, his own existence? The hoarding of Meneka's power by Indra was another creative choice, as he dealt with the consequences of his own insignificance in a world that was evolving beyond his understanding. Reflecting the evolution of Hinduism, Indra in this retelling conspired and rebelled against, then sought to imprison, then finally bowed down to the deities of oneness—personified in this book as Shakti.

Shakti—depending on which part of the four-thousand-year-old history you're looking at—is alternately interpreted as Brahman, the unchanging reality of the universe, existing beyond all limitation; as the phenomenological creative energy of the universe, different from Brahman, yet complementing it; and as a personal power in the form of personified goddesses.

Within the duology, she is all of these.

I did not feel the need to limit the Goddess to one interpretation or the other; Hinduism is ultimately a religion that allows for multiple perspectives to exist at the same time, and the Divine Dancers duology, first and foremost, is a feminist retelling of a myth.

Meneka—as the heroine of this story—becomes everything Shakti can be, beyond what her male deity has let her believe—and even beyond what Shachi, part of the feminine, wishes from her.

Meneka achieves harmony.

Between elemental and cosmic, between redundancy and evolution, Meneka embraces her own identity and power.

For me, the journey of writing this story dovetailed with the mythos I was retelling. There are few experiences more rewarding than that for an artist.

GLOSSARY

Amaravati: The City of Immortals, and the capital of swarga, heaven.

Amrit: The golden nectar that appeared during the Churning of the Oceans, which gives celestials their immortality.

Apsara: A celestial dancer of Lord Indra's court and heaven.

Asura: A creature of the hellish realm, akin to a demon.

Churning of the Oceans: An ancient event where the oceans were churned by creatures of both heaven and hell, in order to release amrit. Other substances emerged from this churning too.

Deva: A male deity, though collectively this often is gender neutral.

Devi: A female deity.

Dharma: The study and path of righteousness, encompassing all concepts of law, custom, rights, virtues, morals, and ethics.

Gandharva: A celestial musician.

Goddess vs goddess: *Goddess* (capitalized) usually refers to the one power of the feminine energy, Shakti, as she is known; *goddess* (lowercase) is an individual representation of that power.

Halahala: The most dangerous poison that exists, which appeared during the Churning of the Oceans.

Kalpavriksh: A wish-fulfilling tree that grows in Lord Indra's garden.

Lingam: A representation of Lord Shiva, which is similar to a cylindrical shaft sitting inside an oval-shaped basin.

Mahasabha: A sage's gathering, where decisions about yogis and hermitages are made.

Mantra: Chants of great power, consecrated through meditation.

Mudra: A dance sigil that mimics different shapes and unleashes an apsara's magic.

Naraka: The hellish realm. Also known as Yamalok.

Patala: The underworld.

Prakriti: Nature in its most fundamental essence.

Prana: Magic of the universe. All magic can be traced to prana, and mortal yogis yoke this directly through a process called tapasya. Immortals only have access to it through elemental deities such as Lord Indra, who harnesses it to provide it to the rest of the citizens of Amaravati.

Rakshasa: A creature of the hellish realm, akin to a monster.

Rishi: A yogi of great power, a sage. This is a self-proclaimed title, though assessed by other sages.

Soma: A celestial alcohol.

Swarga: Indra's heaven. Also known as Indralok.

Tapasvin: One who does tapasya. Also refers to the kind of magic that tapasya unleashes.

Tapasya: Arduous meditation that yogis undertake, which allows them to access the power of the universal prana.

Thumri: A village in the mortal realm.

Vajra: Lord Indra's lightning bolt, a weapon of great power.

Vajrayudh: A cosmic event that occurs every thousand years or so, when the beings of heaven grow weaker.

Vedas: Ancient texts that discuss rituals, philosophy, and a variety of spiritual knowledge.

Yogi: A practitioner of yoga, one who often undertakes arduous meditation in order to gain enlightenment.

ACKNOWLEDGMENTS

Thanks to my publishing team, first and foremost: editors Julia Elliott, Natasha Bardon, Chloe Gough, Mikaela Pedlow, Ana Deboo, and all of the many others who have worked so hard on this project; thanks to my agent and agency, Lucienne Diver and the Knight Agency, for all management behind the scenes; thanks to cover artists Galen Dara and Hoan Phan for their incredible work and amazing talent; thanks to audiobook narrator Sharmila Devar for her gorgeous voice; thanks to the wider marketing, publicity, and sales teams—the MVPs of the process; thanks to the booksellers and readers who love and promote my work.

To my family, Tate, Rohan, and Ishmish, please tidy up the kitchen. Also, we need bananas and blueberries, and no, boys, you are still not allowed into my office, maybe in a few years. And to the usual suspects, you know who you are: At book six of my career, this is just getting embarrassing, love you, kthanksbye.